Botolph
the
Travelling Saint

This is the First Edition of "Botolph the Travelling Saint."
It was first published in Great Britain in February 2019
by Earlsgate Publishing
PO Box 721
FOLKESTONE
CT20 9EY

ISBN 978-0-9567508-2-2

Copyright © D.S. Pepper 2019
D.S. Pepper has asserted his right to be identified as the author of this work in accordance with the Copyright, Design and Patents Act, 1988.

All rights reserved. No part of this publication may be reproduced, stored in or introduced into a retrieval system, or transmitted in any form, or by any means (electronic, mechanical, photocopying, recording or otherwise) without the prior written permission of the publisher. Any person who does any unauthorised act in relation to this publication may be liable to criminal prosecution and civil claims for damages.

A CIP catalogue reference for this book is available from the British Library.

This book is sold subject to the condition that it shall not by way of trade or otherwise, be lent, re-sold, hired out, or otherwise circulated without the publisher's prior consent in any form of binding or cover other than that in which it is published and without a similar condition including this condition being imposed on the subsequent purchaser.

Typeset in Book Antiqua / Papyrus.

The picture on the front cover showing the icon of Saint Botolph is Copyright © Holy Transfiguration Monastery, Brookline, MA, used by permission. All rights reserved.

To all my friends
who are or have been members of the
Rotary Club of The Channel, Folkestone.

If you require a further copy of this book,

or any other books by the same author

please email your order to

botolph@virginmedia.com

or visit the website at www.botolph.info, or write to:-
Earlsgate Publishing,
PO Box 721,
Folkestone,
CT20 9EY.

Other books in the Botolph Trilogy

Volume I (Dec. 2010) **'BOTOLPH'** (from his birth to 18 years of age)

Volume II (Aug. 2014) **'BROTHER BOTOLPH AND THE ABBESS'**
(from 18 to 27 years of age).

Provisional titles of 'books in the pipeline'

Voyages around Saint Botolph Churches.

Daniel Papebroch and the Saint Botolph Manuscripts.

Acknowledgements

My wife Zina has, once again, been most supportive and helped me greatly by reading the draughts chapter by chapter as I wrote this book. I took on board most of her adverse comments and did my best to turn water into wine. If you find the book at all readable then much of that is down to her; if you find it unsatisfactory then it is my fault.

I am also most grateful to the proof readers who have helped with this volume: Helen Barker, Patricia Taylor, Duncan Hopkin, Peter Van Demark, Ray Beaglehole and John Krawczyk.   These kind people have spent a great deal of their valuable time subjecting my writing to intense scrutiny and then doing their best to point out my inadequacies without upsetting me. I herewith formally absolve them from all responsibility regarding page layout and punctuation about which I have strong idiosyncratic views. I deplore for example the modern habit (evolved since the 1950s) of using only *one* space after a full stop. In my young day *three* spaces were commonly inserted thus clearly separating each sentence and I have persisted with this technique which I consider a fundamental part of my artistic style.

Foreword

Over the years there have been many different patron saints of travellers but Saint Botolph reigned pre-eminently until the high middle ages when, probably due to the preferences of England's new Norman masters, he was replaced by Saint Christopher. Signs of St Botolph's tenure persists however in the archaeological evidence provided by such items as the foundations of the churches dedicated to his name which lie at four main gates of the city of London. Here travellers would seek his intercession for guardianship as they departed - and give thanks for their safe arrival when they returned.   Along many of the roads that they travelled they would find similar Saint Botolph churches ready to cater for their spiritual and physical needs.   It is a matter of ongoing research which of these seventy or so foundations were a product of the saint's own travels and which arose subsequently as a result of the Saint Botolph Tradition but the clear evidence of their positioning serves to underline his importance in the field.

In writing this trilogy I have followed the historical pointers that show us the path he trod and from this we can deduce his life story.   Although Luka and his family constitute fictional garnish there is no doubt that Botolph would have had similar friends who would have brought enrichment to his life.

Saint Botolph was an enigma in his lifetime as we can see from the visit to his monastery of Ceolfrid, mentor of the Venerable Bede, who *'left for Kent to study more fully the rules both of a monk's life and that of a priest . . .   He also came to East Anglia to see the monastic observance of Abbot Botulf, known everywhere as a man of outstanding life and teaching and one filled by the grace of the Holy Spirit.'*

I hope that you enjoy reading this trilogy because it is more than just a story.   Its importance lies in the fact that it is one of the few works that trace the life of one of several thousand saints, by taking historically documented facts from a *'Vita'* and then 'joining the dots' to string all the facts together in a credible way to give us something which cannot be far from a true biography.   In the process, it puts into perspective the major Celtic, British and French players of the seventh century at the time of the foundation of British culture.

I once saw a sign which read: 'OPEN for compliments but CLOSED for complaints.'   I do not subscribe to this and I am always pleased to hear from my readers so please do not hesitate to contact me.

Denis Pepper, Folkestone.   February 2019.

Index to Illustrations

Page	Fig.	Description
xxviii	1	Outline of Botolph's principal journeys
3	2	The Voyage from Gaul to Britain
34	3	Bradbryc
67	4	Escape from Bradbryc
79	5	Haninge to Lewys
123	6	Gwentchesil to Folcanstane
132	7	Folcanstane in Eanswythe's time
157	8	The Marsh after the storm
177	9	Norflot monastery
206	10	Norflot to Rookslea
220	11	Voyage from Norflot to Lundwic
225	12	Lundwic
254	13	The River Tamesis and its tributaries
264	14	Engla
279	15	Rendelsham and Dommoc
295	16	Route followed by the Icknield Way
308	17	Engla, the Fens and Lindum
316	18	Eoforwic and northwards
332	19	Skirbeck, Elig and Lindum
339	20	Northern Engla
350	21	Ycan Ho
364	22	Icanho Abbey buildings
390	23	Eastrige & the sub-kingdoms of Cantium
398	24	Domne Eafe's family tree
405	25	The Journey to Wininicas
414	26	Viraconium, Wininicas & the Sabbina
434	27	Lugdunum in the Frisian Islands

Chapter and Page Index

Chapter	Page	Title
	v	Acknowledgements and Foreword
	vii	INDEX TO ILLUSTRATIONS
	viii	CHAPTER AND PAGE INDEX
	ix	LIST OF MAIN CHARACTERS
	xiii	GLOSSARY
	xiv	THE STORY SO FAR
1	1	Return to Britain
2	9	Bradbryc
3	36	The Church
4	60	Escape
5	66	Circles
6	73	Haninge
7	82	Pursuit
8	122	Cantium
9	132	Folcanstane re-visited
10	142	The Storm
11	156	Return to the Marsh
12	169	Norflot
13	194	Visit of the King and Queen
14	205	An Expedition
15	218	Voyage of *The Ganot*
16	253	The River Lea
17	263	Engla
18	275	Flight
19	293	Journey to the southwest
20	305	Enemy territory
21	313	An Alternative Plan
22	331	The Fens
23	341	Dommoc
24	348	Botolph's Challenge
25	358	Another Miracle
26	366	Disaster
27	374	Family Ash
28	383	The Synod of Streoneshalh
29	396	A.D. 670 Wininicas
30	411	Field Chapels
31	431	A.D.672 Adulph
32	442	The Final Chapter
	448	The South English Legendary

Main characters in Volume III of the Trilogy.
Those in bold type are real historical characters. All dates are A.D.

Adulph	**Botolph's elder brother.**
Aethelheah	**Prior of Icanho who became abbot after Botolph's death.**
Aethelwald	**Sub-king Ruler of West Kent, c.616-c.657.**
Aethelwold	**Brother of King Anna. King of Engla c.654-c.664**
Aethelwealh	**King of Sussex c.660-c.685.**
Aldor	Fictional generic name for the chief elder of a village.
Alfred	Headman at Bren Sete
Algar	Boy at Norflot
Anna	**King of East Anglia 636-654.**
Ash	Luka's son - wife: Lislia; sons: Eldred, Bron and Gar.
Bernard	"The Pot-Stirrer," friend of Botolph at Evoriacum.
Botolph	**Central character of this book. During the latter years of his life, reputed to be the wisest and holiest man in England.**
Bron	Son of Ash - wife: Nelda
BurgundoFara	**Abbess of Faremoutiers 620-655.**
Ceolfrid	**Also written as Ceolfrith. After his historically-recorded (in *The Anonymous Life of Abbot Ceolfrid*) meeting with Botolph he was in 674 'headhunted' by Benedict Biscop and, with Bishop Wilfrid's permission, became prior of Biscop's new abbey of Monkwearmouth (in Northumbria). In 679 he joined Biscop on a journey to Rome and they returned with a vast collection of books. In the next year he became tutor to a 7-year-old boy called Bede and in 682 at Biscop's**

behest, he, Bede and 22 monks (ten of whom were tonsured) left Monkwearmouth to found a new monastery 6 miles to the northwest. Jarrow Abbey opened in 684 but two years after its foundation the community was hit by a terrible plague from which the only useful survivors were Ceolfrid and Bede (then aged 13). Ceolfrid remained Bede's mentor for the remaining 30 years of his life. Ceolfrid became the very successful abbot of the combined monasteries of Monkwearmouth St Peters and Jarrow St Pauls. He died at Langres in Burgundy in 716 whilst on what he knew was his final journey towards Rome.

Clarisse	Archdeacon Gaubert's stepdaughter. Wife of Luka.
Constantia	Abbess of Folcanstane in 648.
Dagobert I	**(c.603-639) King of the Franks.**
Durwin	Boy at Norflot
Eadbald	**King of Cantium 616-640. Eanswythe's father.**
Eanfled	**Daughter of Aunt Ethelburga. Married King Oswiu.**
Eanswythe	**618-640. Abbess of Folcanstane. Daughter of King Eadbald.**
Ecgberht	**King of Kent 664-673. Murderer of the princes at Eastry.**
Edwin	**King of Northumbria 616-633. Married to Ethelburga of Lyminge.**
Eldred	Luka's son - wife: Maria - son: Lufan
Elegius	**Later known as St Eloi. A wise and talented goldsmith who became chief councillor to King Dagobert.**
Eormenred	**The elder of Eanswythe's two brothers.**

Eorcenberht	**Younger brother of Eanswythe. Succeeded Eadbald as King of Kent.**
Erchinoald	**Very powerful French nobleman. Mayor of Neustria and Burgundia 641-658. Now thought to have been either the father or the brother of Queen Ymme of Kent.**
Eric	Old Folcanstane ex-fisherman and lately caretaker of the nunnery church.
Ethelbert	**560-616. First Bretwalda-king of all England south of the River Humber. Eanswythe's grandfather.**
Ethelburga	**Abbess of Liminge. Eanswythe's Aunt.**
Ethelburg	**Daughter of King Anna of East Anglia.**
Fara	**Abbess of Evoriacum. Also known as BurgundoFara.**
Germanus	**Adulph's alternative name.**
Godric	Boy at Norflot.
Hereswith	**Sister of Hilda of Whitby. Nun at Chelles.**
Honorius	**Archbishop of Canterbury 630-653.**
Idan	Monk in Cantwarebury Scriptorium.
Leudesius	**Erchinoald and Leutsinde's son. Eventual mayor of the Neustrian palace.**
Leutsinde	**Erchinoald's wife.**
Lislia	Ash's wife
Lufan	Luka's great-grandson fathered by Eldred.
Luka	Central but fictional character. Botolph's friend.
Liobsyne	**Nun at Chelles in France. Aunt of Domne Eafe.**
Magburga	One of the twin nuns from West Kent.
Margaret	Disgraced nun at Faremoutiers.
Maria	Wife of Luka's elder son.
Martin	**Saint who gave half his cloak to a beggar at Samarobriva.**
Mervic	Thane subject to King Aethelwealh. Headman at Bradbryc

Mosel	Farmer from Apuldre.
Nelburga	One of the twin nuns from West Kent.
Nelda	Wife of Luka's younger son.
Olred	King Aethelwald of West Kent's right hand man.
Oswald	**King of Northumbria 634-642.**
Oswin	**Oswin, King of Deira c.644-c.654.**
Oswine	**Oswine of Kent, youngest son of Sub-king Eormenred of Kent.**
Oswiu	**King of Northumbria 642-670. Married to Eanfled of Kent.**
Penda	**King of Mercia 626-655.**
Putnam	One of Mervic's seven farmers.
Saethryth	**King Anna's foster daughter.**
Seaxburh	**Daughter of King Anna of East Anglia; wife of King Eorcenberht of Kent; mother and regent of King Ecgberht of Kent.**
Selwyn	Prior at Norflot
Sigeberht	**King of East Anglia who became a monk.**
Torrel	Sailing master at Cnobersburg.
Wybert	Manager of Mervic's farms.
Ymme	**Eanswythe's mother. Now thought to be daughter or sister of Erchinoald.**

Glossary

Abaft	Behind - e.g. 'abaft the thwart' means 'behind the seat' (when looking forwards). The opposite of *abaft* is *forward* (or *for'd*).
Abbey	A building inhabited by a religious institution of monks or nuns governed by an Abbot or Abbess.
Aethelwealh	King of Sussex (c.645-685).
Aldor	Fictional generic name for the chief elder of a village.
Alspath	Meriden, Warwickshire.
Apuldre	Appledore near Tenterden, Kent.
Arnulf of Mettis	Saint Arnulf of Metz (c.582-c.640), bishop and priest.
Aspergorum	Bowl containing holy water
Atrebatum	Arras, France.
Austrasia	Ancient part of Northwest France including today's Boulogne.
Beodricsworth	Bury St Edmunds, Suffolk.
Beormingan	Birmingham.
Berecingum	Barking, London - (from 'dwellers among the birch trees').
Besom	A broom made from twigs.
Bilges	The lower part of the inside of the boat where any inboard water will collect.
Bourn	A stream.
Bradbryc	Fictional name for Bosham before Botolph's arrival.
Burel	Natural undyed wool. Varies in colour between white and brown.
Burh	Town (i.e. larger than a village).
Caleton	Sands off that part of the coast of Gaul which eventually became Calais.
Calleva	Silchester, Hampshire.

Cantium	Kent. A province in England.
Cantwarebury	Canterbury. Known in Roman times as Durovernum Cantiacorum and later as Burh. Although the latter would have been the correct choice of name for Botolph's time, I have chosen not to use this in order to avoid confusion between Burh and Burgh in East Anglia. Occupied by Roman forces until c.400 AD when they were recalled, after which little is heard of the town until c.590 AD when Ethelbert became king. By the time Augustine arrived in AD 597 via Ebbsfleet on the island of Tanatus, Cantwarebury had become well-established again.
Capellanu	Chaplain - here the carrier of part of the revered cloak (capella) of St Martin.
Caricatonum	Le Havre
Ceodham	Chidham, West Sussex.
Cnobersburg	A monastery near Great Yarmouth, under the control of Abbot Fursey and, in this book, Prior Matthew.
Cofatre	Coventry.
Colneceaster	Colchester, Essex – the original Roman capital of Britain.
Combretovium	Settlement in the area of Baylham House, Suffolk.
Contubernium	The 'tent party' - an essential element in a large entourage.
Cubit	An ancient measure from the tip of an adult's middle finger to the elbow. 18 inches (45.72 cms).
Dalriada	Area in Argyllshire which was one of the seats of the early Scottish kings.

Deira	An area covering west Yorkshire between the Rivers Tees and Humber.
Dofras	Dover (also at other times called Dubris).
Dommoc	The original seat of the Anglo-Saxon bishops of East Anglia. Also referred to as Dummoc. Thought to have been located near Dunwich but some believe it was at Walton Castle.
Dorceaster	Dorchester-on-Thames, Oxfordshire.
Dorter	Dormitory
Dubris	Dover (also at other times called Dofras).
Dudelei	Dudley, West Midlands.
Ealdenburh	Oldbury.
Eastrige	Eastry, Kent.
Egensford	Eynsford, near Lullingstone, Kent.
Elig	Isle of Ely.
Engla	The area now known as East Anglia.
Evoriacum	The name of Faremoutiers until Fara's death.
Eoforwic	York.
Exning	10 miles south-south-east of Ely.
Fairlight	A prominent hill to the west of Gwentchesil (Winchelsea) in Kent.
Faremoutiers	A village in France about 30 miles east of Paris. The site of BurgundoFara's monastery.
Fillercha	Pagham.
Folcanstane	A town in Kent, now known as Folkestone, at the narrowest part of the '*South Sea*' (the English Channel). Site of the first nunnery in England founded in 630 by Princess Eanswythe, daughter of King Eadbald.
For'd	Forward (see *abaft* above). e.g. in the for'd part of the boat.

Francia	That part of Gaul populated by the Franks (following the collapse of the Western Roman Empire).
Furlong	From *furh* furrow and *lang* (long), a furlong (220 yards) was the length of a furrow that a team of oxen could plough before needing to rest. An acre in Anglo-Saxon terms was one furlong by one tenth of a furlong (known as a *chain*) and this was traditionally the area of land that could be ploughed by one man with one ox in one day. Turning a team of oxen was not easy so the number of turns was kept to a minimum by cultivating the fields in long thin strips.
Fyrd	A militia band called to fight in times of danger
Gallia	Gaul. A large area comprising the southern part of the Netherlands, Belgium, part of Germany, France and northern Italy subject to constant alteration of sovereignty.
Gasket	To gasket the sail is to put ties on it to stop it opening to the wind.
Gat	An opening in the land - cf. Ramsgate, Margate, Sandgate.
German Ocean	North Sea
Gesoriacum	Boulogne. Also known as Bononia and Itius Portus.
Gewisse	A tribe based around Dorchester-on-Thames but stretching to Winchester.
Gig	A large boat with several sets of oars.
Gippeswic	Ipswich.
Glanford	Brigg, Lincolnshire.
Grantabryc	Cambridge
Greynose	Cap Gris Nez, France
Guella	Wells-next-the-sea, Norfolk.

Gullney	Village near Icanho
Gunnel	The top edge of the side of a boat.
Gwentchesil	Literally 'west beach' - Old Winchelsea (now washed away) in Kent.
Hand the sail	Lower the sail
Hanfelde	Henfield, West Sussex.
Haninge	Annington, West Sussex.
Harringdun	Harrington, Northants.
Helm down	An age-old sailing term that dates from the time of the steering oar and continues to be used today even when a vessel is steered the use of a wheel rather than a tiller. (The tiller is the stick-like thing that, on a small boat, is attached to the rudder). The dinghy sailor habitually sits on the windward side of the vessel so that he can lean out and balance it if the wind gets stronger. When the boat starts to be pushed over by the wind it starts to heel away from him and when he pushes the tiller away the helmsman is pushing it down ... and this alters the boat's course so that it comes up into the wind.
Helm up	If, on the other hand, he chooses to pull the tiller towards him, he is pulling the helm *up* and the vessel responds by turning *away* from the wind.
Hethburh	North Cove, Suffolk. (See Fig. 19, p.304).
Hide	Originally a parcel of land of a size suitable for supporting a family and its dependents. Later a specific size of 60 to 120 acres - used for assessing taxes.
Hnaefsburh	Naseby, Northants.

Hoe or Ho	Anglo-Saxon word referring to a sloping ridge of land shaped like an inverted foot and heel where the upper part is often used as a look-out point. (cf. Plymouth Hoe, Samphire Hoe, Land Ho, Ahoy etc.).
Hrofsceaster	Rochester, Kent. Also known as Durobrivae.
Icknield Way	An ancient trackway running southwest from East Anglia. (See Fig. 15, p.265).
Ingetlingham	Gilling, Yorkshire.
Inhrypum	Ripon, North Yorkshire.
Kyteringan	Kettering, Northants.
Lastingham	Village in the North York Moors, 25 miles NNE of York.
Laver	A washroom with running water.
League	Three miles (the distance a man or a horse could walk in an hour).
Liman	A bay or harbour (the Turkish language still uses the same word). In the 4th century, the Celts used this word for an "elm-wood" or "marshy" river. Before that time, the word may have been used to describe the whole Romney Marsh area when it was a lagoon.
Liminge	Lyminge. A village in Kent which took its name from the tribe who lived by the Liman (see above). The site of England's first mixed-gender Monastery (under the control of Abbess Ethelburga).
Lindesege	Isle of Lindsey, Lincolnshire.
Lindesfarena	Lindesfarne - Holy Isle.
Lindum	Lincoln.
Longseax	A large Saxon fighting knife.
Lotha's Croft	Lowestoft

Luddam	Ludham, Norfolk.
Lugdunum	Lugdunum Batavorum - Katwijk (in the Netherlands).
Lundwic	London. When the City became large and divided into two, Lundwic became "Ealdwic" (or "old"city) which eventually became the more familiar "Aldwych". During Roman times, the capital was called "Londinium" and this name was used for many centuries after the Romans left, but "Lundwic" was in common use in Botolph's time.
Lutetia	Paris. Originally the home of the Parisii tribe.
Maenwud	The Manhood Peninsula in Sussex.
Manigfual	Cnobersburg sailing vessel. (Name "borrowed" from Frisian legend).
Mile	A Roman mile was 1,000 paces, i.e. 1,000 "yards".
Minster	Any large church originally connected to a monastery.
Misericord	As well as meaning a seat, this word is also used in Benedictine Monasteries to indicate a 'room of relaxation' where the rules of the monastery are not so strictly observed.
Mithras	God popular with Roman military between 1st and 4th centuries A.D.
Monastery	From Greek "Monos" meaning "Alone"; a religious institution living in seclusion from secular society and bound by religious vows. Usually (but not necessarily) consisting of monks.
Neustria	Ancient area of Western France including today's Paris.

Niowebot	Newbold-on-Avon.
Niwendenne	Newenden, Kent.
Novitiate	A person who has entered a religious order but has not yet taken their final vows.
Nyn	River Nene
Nunnery	A religious institution consisting of a community of nuns.
Osterbryc	Literally 'east bridge' - also the fictional name for Bosham.
Ox Island	Isle of Oxney, Kent.
Painter	Rope tied to the front of the boat for mooring it with.
Pax in terra	Peace on earth.
Pax vobiscum	Peace be with you.
Petuaria	Brough, Yorkshire.
Plainchant	Unaccompanied church music sung in unison in free rhythm.
Plesingho	Taken to be Beauchamp Roding in Essex.
Portus Limanis	A Roman port near Lympne, Kent. Functional c.130-350AD. Site of Studfall Castle.
Pottam	Potters Heigham, Norfolk.
Prow	Alternative name for the bow of a boat - i.e. the front (sharp end).
Priory	A religious institution governed by a Prior. Sometimes subordinate to an abbey.
Prior	The deputy head of a monastery or abbey, ranking directly below the Abbot. In certain religious orders the Prior is the actual and only head of the community.
Rendelsham	The modern Rendlesham in Suffolk. Seat of the East Anglian kings.
Rhee Wall	Raised land-wall on Romney Marsh, running from Appledore to New Romney. Origin controversial but possibly Roman.

River Limen	A stream, running along the northern edge of Romney Marsh, consisting of a tidal saltwater creek at its eastern end and a narrow freshwater tributary from the River Rother at its western end.
River Rhenus	River Rhein.
River Rother	A river running from the Weald to the Marshes of Rumniae. The river's name was not in fact acquired until the later middle ages.
River Sequana	River Seine.
Rumniae	Romney Marsh in Kent.
Rutupiae	Richborough in Kent just north of Dover. Early Roman harbour.
Sabbina Crossing	A crossing of the River Severn near Bridgnorth.
Scir	Administrative region similar to a 'shire.'
Scrip	A leather pouch typically carried by a pilgrim.
Seax	A Saxon fighting knife.
Selwaraden	Now Saltwood in Kent
Shallow deep	*The deep* is commonly applied to the ocean. In the context used in this book *shallow deep* refers to water which is of sufficient enough depth to accommodate sirens.
Shingles	Wooden tiles.
Sithiu	Saint Omer, France.
Sixmile	Hamlet on Stone Street, Kent, six miles from Canterbury, and also six miles from Portus Lemanis, Folkestone and Ashford.
Skirbeck	The area which eventually became known as Botolph's Town or Boston.
Snape	A small settlement near Icanho (on the opposite side of the River Alde).
South Sea	English Channel

Springhead	See *Vagniacis*.
Springs	'On top of the springs' - Spring Tide - maximum depth of water and strongest currents.
Stade	A name of ancient derivation used in southern England for "quay" or "strand".
Steort Ford	Stortford - now Bishop's Stortford.
Stone Street	Roman Road between Canterbury and Portus Lemanis, Kent
Stow	Stow Longa, Cambridgeshire.
Streoneshalh	Whitby, Yorkshire.
Subben	Village near Icanho
Sudtun	Sutton. Now Sutton-on-the-forest, Yorkshire.
Tanatus	Isle of Thanet, Kent.
Tenetwaraden	Tenterden, Kent. (Thanet-men's forest den).
Theydon	Theydon Bois in Essex.
Thole Pins	Twin pegs on the edge of a small craft used to locate the oars like rowlocks.
Thwart	A structural crosspiece in an open boat. Used as a seat.
Tonsure	The partial shaving of the head to indicate membership of a monastic order.
Topsides	The outside part of an open boat above water level.
Totehalh	Tettenhall, Wolverhampton.
Traiectum	Utrecht in Holland.
Uxacona	Roman site near Telford, Shropshire.
Vagniacis	(Springhead) Ancient site of worship near Dartford in Kent.
Venta Icanorum	(Also, later, Norwic) Norwich.
Veteri Ponte	Literally the 'old bridge' historically recorded over the River Adur in Sussex.
Viroconium	Wroxeter, Shropshire.
Vittles	Victuals, i.e. Food and drink.

Waceling Street	Watling Street.
Wad	The Waddensee - area of shallow water lying between the Frisian Islands and the Dutch coast.
Waddenboat	A shallow-draught flat-bottomed boat designed for use in the Waddensee.
Warp	A hemp line used to tie a boat to a mooring.
Way	The motion of a boat forwards or backwards. If a boat loses way it is slowing down.
Wealdham	The town at Waltham Abbey.
Whitenose	Cap Blanc Nez, France.
Whin	Furze or gorse. A word that is nowadays more traditionally used in Scotland.
Wic	Suffix meaning "Trading Station."
Wilfrid	Controversial Bishop of Ripon (c.633-c.709).
Wininicas	Much Wenlock, Shropshire.
Winteringe	Winteringham, Lincolnshire.
Wintanceastre	(Pronounced *Wintanchaster*) Winchester.
Witham	River that passes through Lincoln.
Yeavering	Northumberland site of seventh century Anglo-Saxon kings.
Yelver	Yelvertoft, Northants.
Ycan	Iken in Suffolk.
Yrtlingaburh	Irthlingborough, Northants.

The Story so far.

Volume I (620-638)

In A.D. 620 Botolph's parents and their two children, Adulph and Matild, flee from persecution in the north and settle in a community in East Sussex where Botolph is born shortly afterwards. An itinerant monk inspires the family with the good news of Christianity and once they are of age the two boys go with him to join the abbey at Cantwarebury which had been founded by Saint Augustine only three decades previously.

After a short while they are moved to a new monastery at Cnobersburg near Great Yarmouth where Botolph meets Luka. The monastery is sacked by the warlord Penda not long afterwards and the monks (including Botolph's brother Adulph) escape using the monastery boat. Botolph and Luka are left behind. Using a smaller craft they make their way towards Francia but are blown ahore and shipwrecked at Folcanstane where they meet Princess Eanswythe, daughter of the king of Cantium and abbess of a newly founded nunnery. In one of several adventures they are involved in the dramatic rescue of a farmer drowning in the muddy waters of Romney Marsh.

The church at Cantwarebury grants them permission to travel to Francia to join the highly-reputed monastery at Evoriacum. They take passage on a cargo boat and travel to the new monastery of Sithiu where they join the passing retinue of King Dagobert I. During their journey they stop at Amiens. Here the toddler Prince Clovis goes missing and is fortuitously discovered by Luka. This brings both Botolph and Luka close to the royal family and to the king's councillor Eligius. After their arrival at Lutetia (Paris) they are invited to stay for a few days before continuing their journey to the monastery at Evoriacum. Just as they are about to leave the king bows to his queen's request to build a monastery close to the city. As they have by this time lived and worked in a variety of such foundations the king demands that, before moving on, Botolph and Luka help with planning the new minster.

Volume II (638-647)

Work on the monastery proves to be exciting and enjoyable but when Botolph and Luka are at last free to start on the next stage of their journey to Evoriacum their efforts are further frustrated by their becoming separated due to an unfortunate series of events during which Luka ends up in a tricky situation which results in his his capture by slave-traders. After a long and complicated search Botolph locates Luka and a group of slave-children he has managed to save. Botolph masterminds a rescue but this involves the cooperation of a gang of outlaws led by the stern but good-hearted ruffian Bonitius whose terms involve a ransom for the children and a stipulation that Luka joins his band. Since Luka now has a price on his head there is no alternative but to agree although, with the connivance of Eligius, the children are taken into the care of the royal palace. Botolph presses on to the mixed monastery at Evoriacum run by the redoubtable Abbess Fara. Here he is first professed as a monk, then ordained as a priest and subsequently becomes chaplain.

Botolph maintains his contact with the Neustrian royal family and becomes well-acquainted with personages at the royal court including a young British slave-girl Balthild who has been donated to the king by a powerful nobleman called Erchinoald.

As a result of false intelligence covertly supplied by hostile rebels Bonitius is encouraged to lead his group in an attack on a royal gold-coach. As a result many are killed and Bonitius' son Helgot is captured and imprisoned in the dungeons at Meaux. Luka and a rescue party dress as monks so that they can mingle with people attending the local synod at which Botolph is a delegate. The two friends are surprised to meet and Botolph is able to help with Helgot's rescue but they all become trapped in vaults under the cathedral. Much of their survival is due to Clarisse - the vivacious red-haired stepdaughter of the corrupt Archdeacon of Meaux. When they at last escape from the dungeons they flee to the rebels' lair at Bonoriacum and Luka and Clarisse marry shortly afterwards.

Some years later King Dagobert dies and Queen Nanthild takes over as regent for her son Clovis. After many refusals Botolph is given permission to attend the palace to plead for a royal pardon for Luka. On his return journey he visits Luka and is delighted to find that he is now married and has a son called Ash. Clarisse falls pregnant again but dies tragically in childbirth. Luka is distraught but puts his grief behind him so that he can concentrate on bringing up his son.

At the palace Queen Nanthild dies soon after appointing Erchinoald as mayor of both the Neustrian and the Burgundian courts. The new young king Clovis becomes a ward of court under the gardianship of Erchinoald thus making the mayor the most powerful man in the country.

At Evoriacum the princesses Saethryth and Ethelburg from King Anna's court in Engla become nuns and Abbot Fursey of Cnobersburg pays the monastery a visit. Botolph receives an invitation to build an abbey in Cantium and then shortly afterwards receives a similar offer to build another in Engla. The time had come for him to return to Britain and he makes contact with Luka to tell him of his plans. Luka asks if he and Ash can join him. Botolph is delighted and makes arrangements for their accommodation on a vessel bound for Britain. As they are about to leave Luka and Ash are captured by agents of the corrupt archdeacon of Meaux. His plan, as part of his revenge on Luka, is to offer blood from Ash's body as a sacrifice to the heathen gods. An unlikely saviour in the form of a reprobate cart-driver upsets the archdeacon's plans and Luka and Ash make their escape on horseback closely pursued by their captors. They drive their horses into the fast ebbing tide of the Sequana River where Botolph in a boat speeding under full sail effects a timely rescue and the trio head for Britain.

Volume III of The Botolph Trilogy

Botolph
the
Travelling Saint

Fig. 1. Outline of Botolph's principal journeys.

CHAPTER 1
A.D. 647
Return to Britain

Bang! The two ships collided with a sickening crunch.

The man in the black hat had judged his attack well, hitting the front of the other vessel just abaft the prow. It spun round tossing Botolph and Luka into the bilges.

The skipper let out a bellyful of oaths as his craft scraped down the side of the marauder scoring a long gash in its evil paintwork. Expecting to be boarded he grabbed the boathook and leapt across Luka's prostrate body ready to do battle, but the momentum of the other ship took it on its way, the man in the black hat turning only briefly to leer at the mayhem he had caused.

"Get that sail up again," roared the skipper putting the boathook aside and returning to the steering oar. "C'mon - smartly now," he called impatiently as his crew untangled themselves and leapt towards the mast.

The sail was soon up and drawing. The black boat continued towards the northwest her crew jeering and making insulting gestures and catcalls. The skipper ignored them and, with what he hoped would be seen as a sign of contempt, turned his craft back to the northeast.

"Hold onto this oar Ash," he said, "while I go up

for'rd and look at the damage."

He was back shortly cussing and swearing.

"I don't know what they had to do that for," he fumed. "There's not much harm done though - she's a strong boat and won a point gouging that score in their topsides."

He shook his head in disbelief.

"Steer down that channel Ash," he said, pointing. "We'll soon be there now. We'll need to hand half the sail as soon as the quay comes into sight."

Until then they had had a good crossing of what the Gauls call the Gallic Sea. On their arrival off the British coast on 13th March 647 the curtain of dawn had just been raised to reveal fluffy clouds floating across a shimmering coastline as their home country hovered magically over a misty horizon.

Following their life-or-death departure from Lutetia it had taken every part of five days before they had even seen the open sea. For four of those days they had battled with the perverse currents of the Sequana River which at some points seemed determined to push them back the way they had come. The wide and powerful waterway twisted and turned in dramatic loops carved over millions of years through the Frankish foothills during which time it had brought many ships to grief, but *their* skipper was equal to his task having sailed this way many times before.

The currents were powerful and the eddies were strong. Some progress could have been made against an adverse tide but the skipper saw no virtue in profitless struggle, so each time the tide turned he had them pull to the bank and tie to a friendly tree. As they restored themselves with simple food the tranquillity was frequently interrupted by shouts from the skipper as he greeted others of his ilk who passed close by as *they* worked the flood tide up to Lutetia.

As soon as there was a sign of the current slackening they wasted no time in freeing the painter and setting off again.

Fig. 2. The voyage from Gaul to Britain

Even the seven-year-old Ash was expected to take his turn at the helm, but the skill came naturally and offered him great pleasure as he worked the ship round the bends and past the whizzing rushes. With the wind behind them and the tide in their favour they tossed along at the speed of a trotting horse, though the perfidious shallows were a constant threat. Hitting one of those would spell disaster but the skipper was alert to every hazard and he piloted them skilfully ensuring that each steersman kept to the deepest water. For this to be successful they needed good visibility so each night they laid up ashore rather than tempting the sirens of the shallow deep.

As they approached the estuary a ballet unfolded of craft tacking backwards and forwards - each grasping what advantage the wind afforded while the tide raced in. As the great sea filled and the estuary widened, the meanderings of the serpentine river-bed became lost to view and more than one vessel was brought up short as it strayed out of the now-hidden channel and ploughed wildly into an underwater bank.

When at last they reached the open sea the motion changed as the estuarine cross tides fought with each other, making the vessel buck and creak as she was tossed from side to side by the turbulent water.

"Bring yer helm up a bit now," the skipper had called. "We need to come off the wind a touch more or this see-sawing'll strain 'er timbers. Take 'er across the waves at an angle Luka. The swell'll get longer once we're further out an' then ye'll be able to come back on course again."

Luka had pulled the steering oar towards him and it made the motion a little easier although they were by no means steady. Ash was asleep under the cuddy and he stirred as he was found by some mischievous spray.

"He's a good lad," said Botolph.

"Aye," replied Luka with more than a hint of pride, "he's one of the best and deserves more'n I've been able to give him over these past years."

"You've done amazingly well on your own," said Botolph. "You've taught him to swim and ride and hunt and shoot and above all you've taught him to be honest . . . like his father," he added thoughtfully.

"Ah well, I've done my best but we've been so confined. The only people he knows are robbers and villains . . . and you!"

"Well there's virtue in variety," laughed the monk.

"The camp was good for him in many ways though. Bonitius was a hard task-master and everybody, young and old alike had to pull their weight. They might've been a bit of a rabble but they were a *disciplined* rabble. When Bonitius said 'Jump' we all jumped together and fought like fury until he told us to pull back."

"Hmm," said Botolph non-committally. He did not want to ponder too closely on the style and reasons for their fighting. They remained quiet - each with his own thoughts until Luka said:

"I know what you're thinking but ours was a community. We had a sort of code between us and we had to live by that. It wasn't always easy and some could do it better than others, but Ash did alright. An' now he'll have a *different* community with a *different* code and he'll do alright with that too - you see."

"I'm sure he will Luka. I've no doubts about either of you. I love you both dearly and hope that you'll stay with me in Britain and help to build my monastery."

"Lord luvyer Botolph, we're not going anywhere else *now*. I'll certainly *stay* with you. Now I've got you back I'm not going to let you go again in a hurry."

They laughed and fell into a companionable silence. The swell lengthened as predicted. The skipper was pottering around preparing for the night passage and, as the motion eased, he barked at Luka to put the helm down a nudge. The boat came up into the wind and the little ship stopped rolling. Glancing over his shoulder, Botolph looked back at the receding land that had been their home for the past nine years. Looking forwards again he contemplated the fact that they were apparently heading towards nothing but sea and more sea . . . and the unknown.

--o--

The water had calmed as they entered a wide bay.

"That's better," Luka grinned at the skipper, who had taken the helm himself. "Where to next then?"

"There's a great river at the top of this island," - he waved abstractedly towards the west - "but once we're deep enough into the channel we'll fall off the wind towards the nor'east. As we get closer you'll see three gats open up. We'll go through the most easterly one 'n' then take the river up to Bradbryc."

"You been here often then?"

"Aw bless you yes. I trade 'ere regularly. Mind you they're funny people 'n' I wouldn't trust any of 'em further than I could see 'em."

"Funny? How do you mean?"

"Gruff, unfriendly, spiteful and generally unhelpful - but they pay well enough. The headman here's called Mervic and he's as awkward a beggar as I've ever met."

"Oh great," said Luka - "I see we're going to have a wonderful welcome back to Britain."

"The best thing you can do is to make your peace with 'im and then move off quickly - he don't like foreigners at the best of times."

"We're not foreigners . . ."

"Anyone's foreign to Mervic if they don't come from 'is own family - take my advice - get away as soon as you can."

Botolph and Ash had been listening quietly to this interchange and neither of them made any comments but foreboding began to fill the minds of all three of them. Had they leapt out of the cooking pot only to land in another fire?

"Time for prayers I think," said Botolph to nobody's surprise.

They bowed their heads and Botolph petitioned for their safe arrival and a plea that the hearts of Mervic and his family would soften towards them.

Luka re-discovered the last of some now-hardened bread and they shared that and some cheese and mead with the skipper as he pulled the helm up and bore off towards the shore.

The gat was wide with trees sparsely bordering the low-lying banks.

"Hah," laughed the skipper but said no more.

"What?" queried Luka.

"Water's just right," he said triumphantly "t' current will take us all the way up."

It was then that Botolph noticed a small boat with a black sail running close inshore.

"We've got company," he said.

The skipper turned to his right, following Botolph's gaze.

"Ahrr," he said, "looks as if he's heading for the same entrance as us."

They watched silently as the boats' courses converged. The skipper was heading for the centre of the gat leaving plenty of room for the black boat to pass inside him. Sure enough as soon as he passed the point the black-hatted helmsman turned northwards so that the boats were now running parallel. The two skippers watched each other intently.

"Is that Mervic?" whispered Ash.

"Nah - but I think it might be his head man."

Minutes passed in silence but 'Blackhat' must have nudged his helm down because the boats' courses began to converge again. There were two others in his boat and all three suddenly seemed to lose interest in the visitors and turned their gaze away ... but the boat kept coming on. It was clear that, unless one of the helmsmen changed course the boats were going to collide.

"Hey," shouted the skipper but the occupants of the other boat showed no sign of hearing.

"Luka - drop that sail," he said with a sigh, "smartly now."

Luka sprang to the sail and with Botolph and the boatboy's help spar and sail came tumbling down. The craft immediately slowed and in normal circumstances the other vessel would have passed clear ahead but, without any apparent reaction from its occupants, it instead turned sharply upwind and aimed straight at their bow. Having lost way, the skipper's steering oar was ineffective and their boat was at the mercy of the current. A collision was inevitable.

The skipper, boatboy, Luka, Botolph and Ash all shouted at once but the crew of the black boat looked stubbornly the other way pretending they had not seen them.

Bang! The two ships collided with a sickening crunch.

CHAPTER 2
Bradbryc

As they approached Bradbryc they passed several other craft heading in the opposite direction on their way towards the open sea.   The skipper waved at each in turn but no pleasantries were exchanged.   The boatboy coiled the warps ready for their arrival.

Being mid afternoon the place was a hive of activity. In the distance trees on the shoreline fluttered in the light wind and wisps of thready smoke rose from the roofs of the huts lining the water's edge.   In front of them, alongside the quay, was a boat from which timber was being unloaded and above on the quayside stood two rows of logs.   A rich smell of smoky fish wafted past and Ash raised his nose to it, sniffing appreciatively.   To their right some boats had been pulled up on the beach and others were anchored in the fairway.

"Where're we going to lay?" asked Luka.

"It's past high water now and we're on top of the springs so I'd rather stay afloat than risk being grounded for a week. I'll come alongside that centre boat on the quay and once you're all safely ashore I'll drop back into the fairway and moor there."

"D'you want the sail down?" asked Botolph.

"No, I've changed my mind about that.   There's not much wind and we can feather that quite comfortably until we're alongside and drop it then ... here we are ... "

The skipper closed the quay and at the last minute

pushed down the helm so that the boat came up into the wind and stopped neatly alongside the outermost vessel. The boy in the bows looped a rope through a gunnel hole and Luka did the same at the stern.

Since the first time he had sailed at Cnobersburg Botolph had never been simply a passenger in a boat. In each vessel since then, whether or not he himself was in charge, he was customarily aware of the boat's every movement – every yield to the wind – every lurch to the waves – every creak – in short he was aware of the vessel's every need and became part of it.

So too, as they came up to the quayside at Bradbryc, Botolph was alert to the skipper's actions. At the precise moment the time came for the steering oar to be pushed down, Botolph found himself willing the skipper to do just that. He was only dimly aware of the satisfaction it gave him when it happened exactly as he had foreseen.

Thus it was not until the boat was moored and the sail safely gasketted that he became free to take stock of his new surroundings.

The quayside was constructed from great wooden pilings that offered grudging accommodation for the ships that used them. The vessels lay against the structure - wood on wood causing minimal damage to either party as the craft rose and fell with the fluctuating tide. Some piles, longer than others, served as bollards around which rough spiky hemp mooring lines were secured.

Above, dark and untidy hovels littered the harbour area, wisps of smoke rising from each like flags warning of the presence of a hidden army. Large gaps had been left between the huts to prevent the easy spread of fire, and this had resulted in a network of alleyways part-blocked by the clutter of fishing life: wicker eel traps; old sails and spars; coils of rope.

A fish-wife with long greasy hair came down the track carrying a heavy basket on her shoulder. She cast them a curious glance before making her way into one of the huts. The smell of fish and smoke was all-pervading.

Botolph fumbled in the depths of his scrip and extracted a little bundle wrapped in a cloth before walking to the stern.

"Here we are then Skipper," he said, "You've earned this and we're grateful to you for bringing us back safely."

He unwrapped the cloth and handed the golden bird with the garnet eyes to the skipper.

"Thank you Father," he said, re-wrapping the ornament and pushing it deeply into one of his pockets. "It's been a good trip, all things considered."

"That's true," said Luka joining them. "Well - we wish you good health and good luck. What's your plan now?"

"It doesn't look as if this next door vessel's going t' move t'night so I'll come ashore w' you and get some vittals 'n' fresh water and then the lad 'n' I'll moor her in mid-stream 'n' get a good night's sleep. There's no hurry though - yon bird's more 'n' enough to cover the cost of a meal 'n' mead for all of us at Mistress Meg's so shall us go round 'n' see her?"

Luka and Ash greeted this prospect enthusiastically and Botolph could see that it made sense. He also thought that with the skipper's knowledge of the place, he might be able to find them lodging for the night. They collected their possessions together, made their way across the neighbouring boat and clambered up on to the jetty leaving the boatboy on his own. Sitting on the quayside, their legs dangling over the edge, were two young lads who sullenly watched every move the newcomers made.

The skipper led them along the stade and round a corner to the head of the small bay. "This is Meg's Tavern," he said pulling open a large, low, wooden door. "In you go."

The hubbub that was in progress suddenly ceased and they were greeted by hostile stares.

"Wassail," called the skipper cheerily. There was no answer and the silence was palpable as they made their way across the straw-lined floor to a table in the corner where they arranged themselves on a couple of benches.

"Right," said the skipper, drawing their attention to him. "Now what are ye going to take? Meg does some very tasty mutton pies and both the mead and beer are very good here."

The swell of new hubbub was starting again, enabling the skipper to say in a quieter tone: "Try not to catch anyone's eye or move about too much and keep yer voices down. They're not keen on strangers here - even though they get a lot of them with the sea traffic and so on. Ye'll be alright once they've got used to you. Jest keep yourselves to yourselves until they make the effort to talk to you ... ah - here's Mistress Meg ... what're you going to have?"

"How're we going to pay?" asked Luka.

"Don't worry about that - the refreshments are on me - consider them all part of the services of your trip."

"That's good of you," said Botolph.

"C'mon now boys," she said "I 'aven't got all day. What can I get you?"

"On your recommendation skipper I'll have pie and beer," said Botolph - and they all agreed to have the same.

"Four pies and four beers it will be then."

"No make it five," said the skipper "I'll take one for the boy.

"You spoil 'im," sniffed Meg, shooting him a glance of disapproval, before she headed back to the kitchen.

They looked around them. The low-ceilinged hall was rustically furnished with tables and benches. A good thickness of dirty straw covered the floor excepting the central hearth where glowing charcoal embers kept hot the contents of a suspended iron cauldron. Around the fire had been placed a square of stones that held back the straw. Four benches of varying sizes offered seating accommodation for those who wished to sit and warm their hands on cold days. Six sets of tables and benches were dotted around the hall.

Three men were sitting at a table to the right of the doorway and there were another two on the opposite side, with a further group of three at a table adjacent to the outside wall. They were all busily talking amongst themselves and seemed to have forgotten the skipper and his passengers.

The pies and beers arrived. The skipper had the pie between his teeth and was about to crunch into it when Botolph stood and bowed his head. The skipper's jaws froze in mid-crunch and he put the pie back on the table. They all stood, pushing the benches backwards with the inside of their knees, and Botolph pronounced a short grace giving thanks for the food and their safe arrival. They sat again and joined the skipper in continuing where he had left off.

A shadow appeared by Luka's side.

"You're not *Christians* are you?" said a deep gravelly voice.

They looked up.

At that point it crossed Luka's mind that he was not really sure whether he was a Christian these days or not but, always ready for a fight, the fellow's tone forced his resolve and his lips hardened as he replied: "Yes we are - what of it?"

"We don't like Christians here," came a swift retort as the unsavoury customer moved round to Luka's right and stared down at Botolph.

"Are you a monk?"

"I certainly am," said Botolph, putting the remains of his pie on the table again and standing. "Peace be with you my son."

"Oi b'aint your son, 'n' oi don't want no peace nor any blessing from the loikes o' you," came the answer.

"I'm sorry about that," said Botolph, *warming* to the theme just as quickly as Luka was *cooling* towards the new company. "Perhaps we could talk about it. Do your friends feel the same way as you?"

This was not the direction the ruffian had expected the conversation to take and the last thing he wanted was what Botolph was offering.

"I'll tell you one thing," he said, pointing his finger at Botolph, "and that is that Mervic certainly feels the same way as me so you'd better watch your step," and he brushed roughly past Botolph as he returned to his corner. Luka made to get up but as Botolph sat he placed his hand firmly on Luka's forearm while looking him straight in the eye. Luka took the hint and settled back on the bench. There was a roar of laughter from the other table at a comment from the interlocutor as he too regained his seat.

"Best we move on as fast as we can then," mumbled Luka between mouthfuls. "Looks if we're not welcome here nor ever will be."

"Oh I don't think so," replied Botolph. "God must have brought us here for a reason."

Luka stopped chewing and, with his mouth open wide revealing pieces of half-chewed pie and mutton on his tongue, looked at Botolph in astonishment. "You're pleased about this aren't you?"

"Well of course," replied the priest "this is just what I need for my first mission. So many places have already converted to Christianity and here we are - instantly placed in what seems to be a totally pagan community - absolutely ripe for me to bring them the good news of Jesus Christ."

Luka's mouth closed - and clumsily swallowed the piece of half-consumed pie - but his eyes stayed wide open and riveted upon Botolph. His features showed disbelief in what he was hearing. After his and Ash's dangerous and uncertain days in Francia, he had been looking forward to spending time with his dear friend Botolph, working to build a new monastery under the benevolent gaze of a local king, a bit like they did with Clovis's monastery in Lutetia - days that he had really enjoyed. But he did not have a good feeling about this place and some of his dreams were beginning to look a bit far-fetched in the light of Botolph's latest revelations. Luka knew the fragility of life only too well. He had lost Clarisse and the baby but, by the skin of his teeth and good fortune, had managed to save Ash. He could not bear to lose him now, but what Botolph was proposing would put them all in danger again.

Botolph's eyes were also wide open - but they were *shining*. Luka could see that now was not a good time to argue the point. He would have to 'go with it' for the moment and pray his own prayers that something would crop up to change Botolph's mind. He suddenly realised what turn his thoughts had taken: *'to pray . . .'* - it had been quite a while since he had done that. Perhaps this was the way forward. He chose to remain silent.

It was the skipper's turn to speak.

"Dear Father Botolph," he said, rather condescendingly, "it would not be the first time that the word of Christ has been brought to Mervic-land and the result was a less than happy one for the person who brought it. His head ended up on top of a stake on the road that leads north from here so that, as Mervic said, if God chose to work a miracle on his behalf, he could proclaim the word of Christ for as long as he liked. There's another pole on the opposite side of the road and I am afraid that I can see your head ending up on it."

Botolph laughed. "Well I'm sorry to hear about my predecessor but, never fear skipper, I'm sure that God will defend me."

Like Luka, the skipper decided it was best to labour the point no further so he changed the subject: "What are your plans then Father? I presume you're going to want lodging for the night?"

"Yes, certainly. Do you know of any?"

"Mistress Meg's the one to ask . . . Meg!"

She reappeared, wiping her hands on her pinafore and raised her eyebrows questioningly.

"My passengers need a bed for the night Meg, - what've yer got?"

She looked at Luka.

"Well we're a bit short of room 'ere but there's plenty in the village who'll put ye up. What d'ye want - just one night?"

"Yes," said Luka . . .

"No," said Botolph.

All eyes spun towards him.

"We'll need somewhere for a few weeks," he said.

There was silence for some seconds as Mistress Meg recovered from her surprise.

"Oh, so ye're moving into the village then?"

"Just for a while," said Botolph "until we've answered our calling."

"Answered yer calling? What's all that about then?" she retorted.

"What indeed?" mumbled Luka under his breath.

"Right," said the skipper thinking that it was time to break the link with his passengers. "Now I can't hang about all day. I've got to get the boat into midstream afore the tide grounds 'er. Where shall I take 'em Mistress Meg?"

--o--

An hour later they were settled into a thatched hut further round the bay. It was the usual pattern with a central hearth and a hidden chimney somewhere in the middle of the roof but it smelt of dank stale wood-smoke together with an overpowering stench of fish. Luka went round the building poking in all the corners looking for the source of the smell, but without success.

"I suppose we'll just have to put up with it," he grumbled. "Let's get the fire going - that might clear it."

Outside were some chopped logs and he brought those in and laid them by the hearth. In his search of the hut he had found a stack of kindling in one corner and, after clearing the hearth and placing it there, he used his strike-a-light to get it smouldering and then blew the embers into a flame. The logs were soon ablaze and the three of them sat around it gazing into the flickering orange lights, each with his own thoughts. The skipper had long-since returned to the boat, taking his pie back to the boatboy. By now they would have slipped their moorings and be lying to a line in the middle of the river.

Luka's eyes were beginning to droop - partly due to the smoke from the fire and partly due to natural tiredness as a result of the journey and the beer.

"I don't know about you two," he said, "but I'm

going to get my head down. I'll take the top bunk by the window light if that's alright with you Father?"

"Fine," said Botolph. "I'm going to stretch my legs and say my devotions while I walk along the beach. What about you Ash? Are you coming with me or staying here?"

"If it's all the same to you I'll stay here Father. I have two fathers now," he giggled.

Luka laughed, "So ye have me boy. Well you'll have to behave yourself twice as much now."

Botolph smiled and headed towards the door. As he opened it the smoke billowed out of the hearth and set Luka and Ash coughing. He closed the door softly behind him forcing the smoke to billow in the opposite direction.

"We'll have to do something about that if we're going to stay longer," said Luka. "And longer it looks as if we're going to stay."

"You're not happy about that are you Pa?"

"No I'm not, and I'll tell you for why - I don't like the smell or the feel of this place. There's something creepy and unfriendly about it. I don't like it at all. Still, - that's what the Father wants - and we've placed ourselves in his hands so I reckon we're stuck with it."

"So are we staying with him forever now then?"

They were sitting side by side on a bench overlooking the hearth. Luka placed an arm around Ash's shoulder.

"I'm sure we don't have to," he said slowly. "We could go and set up our own lives whenever we wanted to - the Father wouldn't try and stop us but . . . ." He paused, trying to find the words.

"What?"

"Well, you see son, Botolph's more like family to me than anyone I've ever had. There's you of course and there was your Ma but I'm talking about *senior* figures. Botolph's like a brother to me and alwez has been since the day we met."

He chuckled. "I used to hate him at first. But then in those days I hated everyone." He laughed again. "I gave him a really tough time but it all went over his head. He stayed just the same. It was like punching him with punches that just kept bouncing off. Then suddenly I knew there was no point in punching him any more and . . . we just sort of melded. A link formed between our spirits. We've done a lot together - we've survived some dangerous times - but we've also been apart a lot - but it didn't seem to matter. Although for a long time I was with Bonitius and Botolph was in the monastery, the link between us was alwez there - and that were a comfort to me when things started going wrong. I knew he'd be there for me when I needed him . . . and here we are!"

"So *forever* then?"

"We'll see how it goes son. I'm going to be with him while he builds his monastery and I'll expect you to help too. He'll be like a second Pa to you - you see. He's very fond of you. But, like me, he knows you're growin' up . . . and one day you'll find a pretty wench and set up home on your own. You might choose to stay with us or move on elsewhere. We both understand that. But for the moment - where Botolph goes I go and where I go you go. In your young mind, 'forever' means anything more than a year - so the answer as far as you are concerned is 'Yes it's forever'."

"Alright Pa - if that's what you want, it's fine with me."

"Good lad. Now c'mon - off to bed with you. Let's see what these smelly pallets are like."

By the time Botolph returned both were sleeping

peacefully. He sat by the fire for a while, watching the dying embers and wondering what God had in store for them. He had enjoyed his walk around the water's edge and had found a secluded corner by an old tree stump where he had knelt to pray. He had asked for God's guidance on his mission to bring Christianity to Bradbryc and wondered how he was going to go about it.

The fire was nearly spent.

He went over to his pallet, ducked under the beam of the upper bunk and settled himself down to sleep.

Thorunsday 14 March 647

Ash woke first and stretched silently. Once his eyes were fully open he turned and slipped off the bunk and headed for the door the hinges of which groaned protestingly as he opened it.

He glanced across at the bunks. Both figures were still sleeping. Leaving the door open he went round the corner to collect more logs for the fire, which was now cold. As he had been trained he pushed the ash to one side of the hearth and set some fresh kindling in the centre, building a few more logs around it. He did not light it since he guessed they would be elsewhere during the day, but at least it was ready for the evening.

Luka stirred and his face appeared over the edge of the bunk. Ash grinned at him.

"Mornin' son, - I see you're busy already."

At the sound of his voice Botolph woke too and, after a few moments, swung his legs out. He stood and stretched. "Good morning to you Ash – and God's blessing for the day."

"Thank you and good morning Father. I hope you slept well."

"I certainly did, thank you. And now I feel revived and ready for whatever today might bring."

Luka joined them.

"Well I don't know about you two, but I've got a parched throat and an empty belly so I reckon Mistress Meg is our next stop."

There was no arguing about the state of Luka's hunger so a short while later found them in the tavern. The door had been wedged open and a cacophony of noise was coming from inside. The only empty bench was on one side of a table by the north wall. Opposite sat two characters who Luka guessed might be farm workers. They looked up and grunted as the trio squeezed onto the bench. They were too busy munching the bread that they had used to wipe the broth out of their earthenware bowls to be able to say anything coherent.

Meg appeared at Botolph's shoulder.

"What can I get for you this mornin' Father?"

"I think three bowls of broth like that," he said, pointing to the now empty vessels, "if there's any left?"

Botolph looked questioningly at Luka and Ash. They both nodded enthusiastically.

"'N' three loaves I guess?" she said. "Beer?"

"Please," said Botolph, "- A small one watered down for the lad."

"Peace be with you brothers," said Botolph to their fellow customers, "do you live locally or are you visitors like us?"

They said nothing but looked the priest straight in the eye. One turned to his companion and then back to Botolph again.

"What's it to you?" he said. "We come 'ere to eat, not to bother people so I suggest you keep y'r questions to y'rself. C'mon, let's go," whereupon the two of them threw their legs over the bench and left.

"Nice," said Luka.

Botolph shook his head sorrowfully.

Luka mumbled, "I knew this place was no good."

The gloom left by the harsh words was rapidly lifted as the broth and three small loaves were placed in front of them. Botolph moved to the recently-vacated bench to give the others more room. Ash picked up a loaf, tore it in half and took a bite. He screwed up his nose and grunted.

"What's up lad?" said Luka.

"It's not a patch on the bread that you make Pa," he said.

Luka took a bite out of his own loaf and looked up into the air as he savoured it.

"No, - I see what you mean lad," he said ponderously. "It's flat isn't it? I don't know what she's done – not enough salt perhaps?"

"Do you remember when you upset Prior Peter by making the bread so tasty at Cantwarebury?" said Botolph.

"I do," said Luka "Do you reckon Prior Peter and Brother Idan are still there?"

"Don't know," said Botolph, "There's only one way to find out and that's to go and see."

"Can we do that then?" said Luka.

"I don't see why not . . . ."

Now it was Luka's eyes which were shining.

". . . but not yet," Botolph continued. "We've work to do here first. Once we have a monastery up and running I'm sure we'll be able to find time to visit everyone at our Blessed Father Augustine's Abbey."

"Aah . . . oh," said Luka disappointed. "Not until then?"

"Not until then."

There was a time when Luka would have argued the toss at this point - even *strongly* argued - but he had learned a lot since those days. There might be different paths that he *wished* to take but he was content to let Botolph decide the paths they *needed* to take. At least that was the way he felt at the moment but little at that stage did he realise what events were approaching.

The tavern had emptied and now only Meg remained. She was leaning on a counter and watching the friends with just the suggestion of a smile on her lips.

Botolph became aware of her gaze.

"Mistress Meg," he said, "we're taking unfair advantage of your hospitality. How are we going to pay for this and for our accommodation? We've no money nor anything to barter. Is there work we can do?"

"Oh now. So ye've no money 'ave ye? Well if I'd a-known that I'd ne'er ha' let ye eat my food and burn my logs."

Both Ash and Luka had turned to look at her and Ash's countenance was full of despair.

Her face had turned stony and her lips were short and thin. She stared hard at them and they stared back with open mouths trying to find something to say. Luka squirmed in his discomfort and performed a little mannerism that he often did when embarrassed. He wriggled his bum to the left at the same time raising his left shoulder, turning his head to the left and lifting his chin so that he looked down his nose at her. His mouth opened further and a little croak came out. Meg could keep a straight face no longer. She suddenly crumpled, let out a great hoop of laughter and then bent double as, like a toddler in its first fit of rage, she emitted one long silent exhalation that totally exhausted the air in her lungs. As she reached the bottom of the cycle she struggled to raise herself - fighting for air. Her face went bright pink and the great noise of a dozen donkey-brays filled the hut as her lungs refilled.

This startled Luka, whose face was already a picture of incomprehension. A glimpse of this started her off again and she bent her head to the floor once more and the braying was repeated.

Botolph worried that she might be having a fit and he rose and went to her side: "Mistress Meg, are you alright . . . ?"

She slapped him on the shoulder and pointed at Luka gasping "It's 'im, - it's 'is fault - 'e do so make me laugh. I was chuckling away all last night after you left but I managed to keep it to meself . . . but just then . . . "

She let out another peal of laughter.

Botolph was really concerned as her colour was bright scarlet by now "Luka - go away."

"What?"

"Out! - go outside - take him outside Ash."

Ash chuckled "C'mon Pa - you've done it again," and grabbing a handful of his father's tunic he hauled him off the bench and bundled him out through the doorway.

The woman's mirth gradually subsided in spite of a few relapses as she relived the event.

"I'm sorry," she said "but he's so funny," and she treated herself to a final burst of giggles.

"Now," she said, pulling herself together, "payment. I knew you didn't have anything to pay with. Nobody does 'ere - this isn't yer Francia ye know. The boys who were in 'ere earlier work at the farm yonder. I feed 'em free but 'tis the farmer who provides the corn, the miller 'oo grinds it 'n' me what bakes it. The miller gets extra corn for doing the work. The boys get well-fed so they're 'appy, the farmer gets good 'ard work so 'e's 'appy, 'n' I get the pleasure of feeding Luka Funny-Face so I'm 'appy."

Botolph could see she was about to start again so he hastily said: "Yes, well you may be happy today but we need to come to a proper arrangement. Is there work to be had here?"

"Aw bless ye yes. There's alwez folk looking for good strong men. There's the farm of course - then there's the farrier, the miller, and the blacksmith - they're alwez looking for casual labour. The saltpans!"

"What?"

"The saltpans. I 'eard only yesterday that men are needed there. The old boy that used to run them died last month and even I only have one bag left now. Something'll have to be done soon or the salt'll sour in t' pans. 'Is widow 'as been doin' the best she can but she really can't cope. Why don' ye go and see 'er - it's only round the corner from y'r 'ut."

"Thanks, I will but there's something else I want to ask you."

"What's that?"

"A chapel, - I want to build a chapel here."

She flinched as if she'd been stung by a bee.

"A what!"

She didn't wait for an answer; the colour was once again filling her cheeks.

"Ye can't be serious. Didn't ye get the message from those layabouts last ni'? Look Father, - I'll do my best to feed and care for ye while ye're 'ere but this shire don' like Christians. We get enough trouble from those Francias 'oo come over but the wisest ones 'r' careful to fit in wi' our customs and keep their Christianity to themselves. Ye'll be tolerated f'r a while but t' best thing ye can do is to f'rget y'r Christianity while ye're 'ere. Take off them monks' clothes and put on or'nary garb 'n' then once ye've got yer breath back press on to a Christian-land where ye'll be comfortable - 'cos ye'r' certainly out of yer depth 'ere. Cantium's yer best bet."

Botolph persisted with a different approach. "I'd like to talk to the headman," he said, "I gather his name's Mervic."

She flinched again at the sound of the name and her voice was icy as she said: "I'll take yer bowls." She collected them from the table piling each so forcefully into the other that Botolph expected them to break ...

"But I ..."

She spun round and glared vehemently at him: "I'm sorry but I've told ye 'n' I don' want t' 'ave t' tell ye again. There's an end to it. Good day to ye."

Botolph noticed the lack of 'Father.' She turned her back on him and strode purposefully into the kitchen.

--o--

Once outside, Ash pushed the door behind them.

"C'mon Pa," he said "Let's go back to the hut."

They had only been there for a few moments when Botolph strode in looking uncharacteristically flustered.

"Whatever's the matter Father?" said Luka.

"I've been talking to Mistress Meg."

"What's she done now?"

"It's not what she's done but what she won't do. I tried to get her advice about getting a chapel built but the only advice she wanted to give me was that she thought it would be best if we were to move on."

"She might have a point," said Luka – but then, seeing Botolph's hurt look, he added more gently:

"One thing at a time Father. If you really have a wish to bide here for a while then the first thing we've got to do is get work. That way, don't you see, we begin to fit into the community rather than sticking out like sore thumbs. Once they get a bit used to us, then maybe you'll get a bit more help from them."

Botolph looked with surprise and affection into his old friend's eyes and marvelled at how wise he had become. He smiled.

"You're right of course, Luka and I thank God for your wisdom."

And then, his spirits soaring again, he led away with "What sort of work are we going to take then?"

"Well - looks like farming or saltpans I suppose. I know which I'd prefer."

"Farming?" said Botolph.

"Aye, - I get wet feet often enough in everyday life without paddling about in saltpans."

"Talking of salt," said Ash.

"Yes son?"

"You could offer your services to Mistress Meg as a baker of better bread?"

"Now there's a thought," said Luka. "I'd enjoy getting back to that – but I couldn't spend all day in a hot kitchen – I need to be out in the open air. Farming sounds better to me."

--o--

And so it came to pass. Botolph was persuaded that he should drop all talk of building chapels and settle down to work as a humble farmhand. Luka followed Mistress Meg's line and suggested that he should dispose of his monk's habit and stop shaving his tonsure on the basis that they needed to blend in with the community, but Botolph drew the line at this. Nevertheless he joined in fully and when they were doing the wet and dirty work of digging ditches, he simply pulled up the bottom of his habit and secured it with his girdle.

Their boss was Farmer Putnam who lived in a neatly thatched croft close to the Saltpans. Their first day found them waiting outside his door at daybreak. They were early and stood outside feeling apprehensive and looking to the East. As soon as the sun poked the top of its head over the salt flats Luka rat-a-tat-tatted on the wooden door. Before the final 'tat' it was flung open making Luka jump back in alarm. Before them stood a man as tall as Botolph. He had a ruddy complexion surrounded by a white beard and was topped by a shiny bald head.

"Yes?" he growled, taking a step forwards.

"We've been sent by Mistress Meg," said Luka, backing away. "She said you might have some work for us."

The ruddy complexion said nothing but looked at each of them in turn, scrutinising them from head to toe in a way which said that he had done this many times before and was an expert judge of character.

Botolph was the last to receive this quizzical examination. The farmer looked straight into Botolph's eyes which were level with his. Botolph looked back steadily – unabashed.

"You're a monk?" said the white beard.

"I am . . . well actually I'm a priest now."

"Why would you be looking for farm work?"

"We've travelled from Francia – and I see here a place where I can spread the word of God."

Luka groaned inwardly. This was not part of the plan. They were supposed to be merging into the community and earning some money for their keep before they pressed onwards. He made as if to interrupt in the hope of pouring some oil on what were likely to become troubled waters but the big man anticipated him and held up his hand, never taking his eyes from Botolph's.

"Do you now?" he said in a voice that Luka took to be aggressive. "Do you indeed?"

"Indeed I do," said Botolph. "I am a monk. I have committed my life to God and I see here a spiritual desert. I see aggression and confusion. I see pain and grief. I see fear and discomfiture. I see very little love for one's neighbour or one's fellow man. I see a place to which I think God must have sent me to spread the good news about Jesus Christ. I am here to follow His calling."

Luka cringed and waited for the explosion that would surely come. He studied the farmer's face to see if it was turning apoplectic but his skin was already so red that he could not come to any firm conclusion.

The big man and Botolph continued to look straight into each other's eyes. Botolph did not waver. There was a long silence and then, without averting his gaze the farmer simply said in a low voice "Go and wait for me by the cart" and turned back into the croft, pushing the door, which closed with a gentle click.

Luka and Ash gazed up at Botolph.

"What?" he said.

"I don't believe you sometimes," said Luka.

"Huh?"

"Never mind – where's this cart?"

"Over there by the barn," said Ash and they stumbled over towards it, Luka leading the way shaking his head slowly from side to side.

"What?" said Botolph again.

"Nothing Father," said Luka, brightening up as he put the recent prospect of disaster behind him. "I suppose we've got the job then," he said.

"Looks like it," said Botolph as their eyes met.

"Hahaha," chuckled Luka.

"What?" said Botolph for the third time.

"Looks like it's going to be a nice day," said Luka gesturing to the sight of the sun rising into a cloudless sky.

--o--

The farmer worked them hard each day from daybreak to sunset. They never knew in advance which fields they would be labouring in or what sort of work they would be doing. They always met at Farmer Putnam's house. At first, after loading the cart with the tools that they would need, he would drive them to the field and set them to work before driving away to supervise his other workers. When the sun was at its highest he would reappear to see what progress they were making with the tasks he had given them. They then received not only lunch of bread, cheese and fruit wrapped up in a cloth – and a flagon of mead - but also further directions regarding the afternoon's work. He never showed any signs of being particularly pleased with them – but there again he never complained about their work. After he had gone they would find themselves a comfortable place to sit where they would pass around the flagon of mead, each one quaffing his fill, and divide the vittles equally between them.

Within a few weeks they had became completely familiar with the area and Putnam would direct them to his chosen location and allow them to take the cart themselves. The food and mead was always tucked away under the seat and at different times during the day Putnam would appear on horseback in the same way that he visited each of his working gangs. He was a cautious man who gave the impression of trusting nobody – but he was fair.

He was one of seven farmers who rented land from the thane Mervic who in turn was subject to King

Aethelwealh. Mervic's manager was Wybert and it was he who was responsible for the management of all the farms.

Putnam's holdings comprised the Bradbryc peninsula and the area surrounding Cissa's Caster – once the Roman town of Noviomagus Reginorum but now subject to King Aethelwealh.

The land was fertile and the crops comprised wheat, barley and rye. Smaller areas were devoted to root vegetables such as parsnips and carrots; cabbages and peas were also grown. Sheep, goats, cattle and pigs were pastured on the hillsides to the north.

Wybert was Mervic's right-hand man but he had a brother who farmed the land and the hills west of Bradbryc and there was a certain amount of jealousy about this farm which, through Mervic's attention, often received favours that the other farms would have liked for themselves.

After several weeks of working for Putnam they had come to know the countryside, having travelled extensively around the area during both work and play.

One day as Luka was driving the plough through some heavy soil with Botolph and Ash guiding the pair of oxen, their progress was curtailed by a small copse of handsome oak trees. They turned the oxen, headed back to the borders of the field and then turned again to make another run. As they approached the copse for the second time, Botolph studied the trees ahead and thought pragmatically that the ploughing of this field would be much easier if those trees were not there.

Later that day, after they had put the oxen in the byre, Botolph said to Luka,

"I have an idea. I'd like to go and talk to Farmer Putnam – we'll be passing his hut on the way back."

As they tramped home along the muddy path Luka kept pestering Botolph to reveal his idea, but Botolph could not be persuaded.   By the time they reached the hut Luka was as relieved about the fact that his acute curiosity would soon be satisfied, as Botolph was that he would soon be afforded some peace from his inquisitive friend.

The more they had come to know Farmer Putnam the more affable he had become and, after opening his door to them, he ushered them inside the smoky hall.

"Sit ye down," he said – "Wife – bring some mead . . . now then – what sort of day have ye had boys?"

The horns of mead arrived and they raised them in the air as a toast to their master.

"We've been ploughing the Lower Field," said Botolph.

Farmer Putnam nodded.

"There's a copse right in the middle of it which, because of the extra turns, makes ploughing twice as difficult as it would if the copse were taken out."

The farmer, ever a good judge of character and a man who always saw more than he would let on, looked Botolph straight in the eye . . .

"And?" he said.

"And?" said Botolph innocently.

"And . . ." repeated Putnam "there's more to it than that isn't there?"

Botolph lowered his eyes, cleared this throat and fired off a quick prayer for assistance before answering,

"Yes Master.   I wondered if we cut those oaks down and cleared the ground in our free time, whether you might let us have the wood to build a chapel in the village."

Luka's horn was halfway to his lips when Botolph made this pronouncement but a butterfly suddenly flew straight into his stomach and the horn hovered in mid-air. His eyes opened wide as he stared at the farmer who had also become immobile.   Quickly through Luka's mind there ran the scenario of the 'affable old man' turning into a fire and brimstone demon and throwing them and Botolph's ideas out of the hut.

There was a deathly prolonged silence.

Putnam turned slowly back to Botolph and held him with his eyes. He was not smiling.

"I'll think about it," he said at last. Now it's time you got back to your billets," and he rose and held the door open for them.

They left silently. Once they were out of earshot Luka said
"Oh dear, Father I think you've done it now. We'll either be dead in our beds tonight or run out of the village tomorrow."

But nothing of the sort happened. It was as if the words had not been spoken. They went to work as usual in the morning and were greeted by Putnam quite normally.

Botolph continued to include the project in his prayers but even *he* was beginning to think that this was not the work that God had in mind for them.

Whenever they met other village people they were invariably treated with contempt and surliness but not more and no less than had always been the case. Botolph felt that he had done all he could and, for the moment, contented himself with trying to spread the Word whenever and wherever he could, but there seemed to be little chance of Christianity gaining many converts in this ungracious place - but Botolph was not one to give up easily.

"Surly as they may be, they're all God's people," he reasoned. "I will keep praying. I will keep looking. If it takes to the end of my life I will bring these people to God."

And then, several weeks later, when they arrived at

Farmer Putnam's door for their orders, he simply said, "Come with me," and strode off towards the village trailing the trio behind him.   He turned along a track which took them behind the houses and then, on reaching the river bank he spun round to face them.

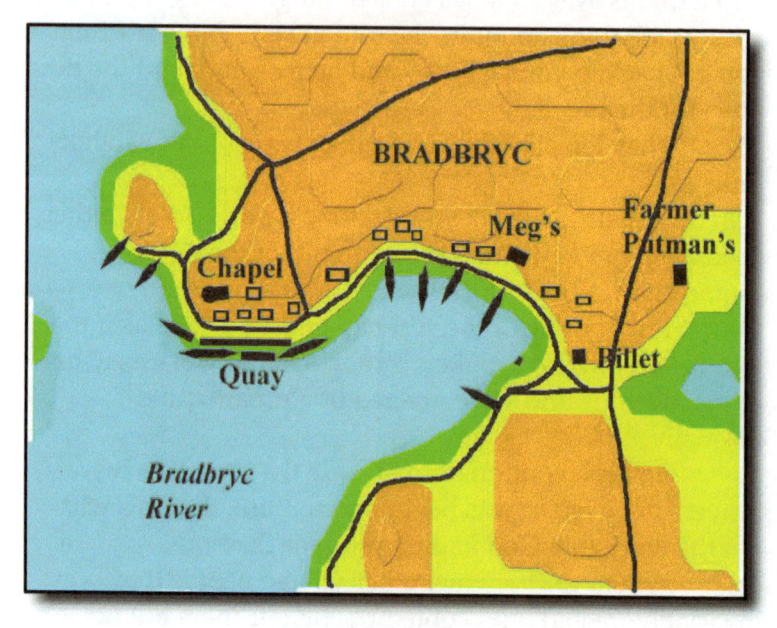

Fig. 3.   Bradbryc.

"Now then," he said to Botolph pointing to a scrub-covered area - "*that's* where your church will be."

Botolph could hardly believe his ears. His heart leapt into his mouth, upon which a grin appeared which was wider than Luka had ever seen.

"Here?" said Botolph.   "How wonderful – right in the village and close by the quay to welcome travellers."

Putnam gave a brief smile.

"I'm taking you at your word though.   It's down to

you to clear the scrub, cut down the coppice, plough out the roots and transport the timber.   There's a lot of work there. You can use the cart and the oxen but it'll have to be in your own time."

"How did you do it?" asked Botolph.

"Never you mind – Mervic's agreed and that's all there is to it - but you'll have to keep your eye on Wybert because he's less than happy."

Botolph, on the other hand, was overjoyed and he kept up a constant excited chatter for the rest of the morning until Luka said: "Father - I know you're pleased about the church – and I'm pleased for you too.   I don't want to dampen your spirits but we've an awful lot of work ahead of us, putting up a building that nobody else wants."

"Ah, but don't you see Luka?   Once we get going people *will* want it."

Luka looked glumly at his old friend and noted the sparkling eyes flanked by crows-feet wrinkles.   He glanced across at Ash who shrugged his shoulders.   Luka sighed . . . and then laughed as he lurched forward and embraced this happy priest whose deep and irrepressible faith would lead them God knows where.

CHAPTER 3
The Church

They started by cutting down the trees but, bearing in mind the limited time they had available, it was not until a month later that they were able to arrange for the old pair of oxen to trundle the flatbed oxcart round to the site for them to unload the last of the wood. A couple of weeks later, back at the copse, they had ploughed the roots out of the rough ground and as the sun went down the three stood back tired and happy as they looked at the neat continuous furrows and reflected that Lower Field would be much easier to plough in the future.

In spite of Luka's forebodings to the contrary, the tree trunks were left undisturbed. The three spent all their spare time at the church site, hacking away at the undergrowth until a flat area had been cleared. Luka made some wooden pegs and, as the sun tipped the horizon, Botolph lined the pegs up to the west. The following morning before dawn, Botolph returned to check their alignment in an easterly direction.

The size of the church was determined by the length of the timbers. Luka and Ash assumed that the building would be more or less square but Botolph insisted that it be (as he put it) a 'double square'. Accordingly their next job was to start the work of trimming the tree trunks into the sizes they required. It was here that Luka came into his own, since he had done similar work many times for Bonitius. First they dug the postholes using the wooden pegs as a guide.   Then a timber was placed vertically in each hole and fixed with bracing ties.   Botolph stood by each timber in turn and gazed skywards.   At last his dream was being fulfilled.

Frustratingly the weather then deteriorated and they had a long period of heavy rain, during which Farmer Putnam prevailed upon their spare time for the emergency work of clearing ditches.   At one time when they were working on a field that overlooked the lower reaches of the river, Luka noticed, during a period when the rain had eased a little, that Ash was studying the river in great detail.

"What's up?" he called as he went over to him.

"Why've they planted those trees in the water banks?"

"Where?"

"There . . . and there and there."

"They're not trees, - they're withies."

"What're withies?"

"They're usually willow stems.   They've no roots. People just stick 'em in the shallower bits of water so that at half tide you don't run aground.   See it's low water now so the river's only half its usual width.   If you look you'll see that none of those withies is in the water now.   With the tide in this state you could row a boat down the river now with no problem 'cos you can see the edges.   At high tide it'd be the same 'cos you'd 'ave plenty or water right up to the proper river edges. But at half tide, although the water would take up the full width of the river, there'd only be an ankle's depth of water over some o' those banks - so they stick a branch where it gets shallow so that you know not to sail over it.   D'y' see?"

Ash nodded - "Why are they called withies Pa?"

"I . . . I've no idea – that's just what they're called –

now come and get on with clearing these ditches."

When at last they managed to get back to the building site they found a nasty surprise waiting. All the posts had been pulled out and an unsuccessful attempt had been made to burn some of them. Ash burst into tears while Botolph and Luka stared at the chaos in disbelief.

Luka was the first to recover. "Here we go again then Father," he said determinedly. He strode forward and picked up one of the posts - making it clear that he intended to waste no time in recovering the lost ground.

"There's no point in just looking at it and there's no time to be lost. Come on Ash - dig those post holes out again - the soil is only soft there. Father - give me a hand with these timbers and let's get them back to their proper positions."

Botolph shook himself back to the present and they started to bring some order out of the chaos.

"'Tis'nt a bad thing really," said Luka.

"How do you make that out?" replied Botolph.

"Well," said Luka "Once we had the verticals up it occurred to me that, while they were still flat, we should have notched them out ready to take the cross pieces. I wasn't relishing the idea of taking them down again so perhaps God had the same idea."

As Botolph bent to lift his end of the beam he smiled and shook his head, marvelling again at how good Luka was in a time of crisis. His smile was short-lived because the timber was heavy. He needed all his strength and concentration to lift his end and carry it to its rightful position. True to his plan, Luka cut notches in each of the posts before they were slotted back into their holes and, by the end of the day, they had regained half the ground they had lost. Reluctant as they were to leave the site unguarded, they were tired and hungry so decided that it was a risk they would have to take. The following day when food and a good night's sleep had cleared their heads they discussed what security arrangements they could make for the future.

"It's going to be a continuing problem," said Luka. "Even when the church is built we're going to have to keep a constant eye on it or Wybert's going to torch it."

"Yes I know," mumbled Botolph ruefully. "We seem to have no alternative but for one or all of us to sleep there."

"I was thinking the same thing. We'll have to get some thatch and create some sort of shelter and then build new pallets inside it."

When they arrived at Farmer Putnam's hut he was standing outside.

"I hear you had some problems yesterday," he said.

Botolph nodded and said cheerfully "Yes but we've already repaired a lot of the damage."

"So I've heard," said Putnam "but how're you going to prevent it happening again and again."

"We've thought of that," said Luka. "We're going to move our billet and sleep on the site."

"You'll be a bit cold," said the farmer "and, until you get the roof on you're going to get soaked by the rain and the dew."

"We're going to get some thatch and build ourselves a kennel within the walls – just enough to keep us dry," said Luka.

"I've a better idea," said Putnam. "Once the locals have got used to it I reckon they'll see your church as an asset. You'll not Christianise many of the villagers 'cos they're a stubborn lot but they'll soon realise that having a church here will raise the place's status. I was talking to some of the shipmasters and traders yesterday. They'd seen yer posts had been pulled out 'n' said what a shame it was."

"Huh – so Wybert's not done himself any favours then?" chortled Luka.

"We don't *know* it was Wybert," said Botolph.

"Course it was," retorted Luka.

"You're probably right Luka," sighed Putnam "but whoever it was we've just got to make sure it doesn't happen again. It seems to me that, now you've started, the most important thing is to get the church up and running as soon as possible. Once it's established it'll be a lot more difficult for Wybert or anybody else to wreak more havoc. Some of the shipmasters I was talking to were Christians from Gaul and they were saying how they'd appreciate a chapel to pray in. It could even increase our trade here 'n' that would please Mervic *and* his boss King Athelweah even if Wybert was unhappy about it."

Botolph had been studying Putnam's face as he talked. Up until then he had thought that the gift of wood had simply been God's answer to his prayers but as he watched Putnam's face he realised that God had given them an extra gift – Putnam was on their side.

"So what are you saying, Farmer Putnam?"

It was now the farmer's turn to be a little embarrassed. He looked down at his feet before turning his eyes back towards Botolph.

"Well . . . "he said. "Well it seems to me the best thing we can do (Botolph noted the 'we' with delight) is to take all the farm gangs off their work for a couple of days and all pull together to get this building finished."

Botolph wanted to hug him. "That would be wonderful," he said "I don't know how to thank you."

"Well we're not too busy this time of the season," said Putnam by way of an excuse, "so working on your church'll keep the lads out of mischief."

Both Botolph and Luka knew that this was anything but the truth. This was a very *busy* part of the farming calendar and two working days lost now could make all the difference between financial success and catastrophe. But Putnam was prepared to risk it and Botolph prayed that his gamble would pay off. Work on the church would start on the morrow and the trio were despatched to tidy up what they could of loose ends of part-finished farming projects. As they walked across to the byre to get one of the oxen Luka said, "I really don't know about you, Father."

"What?" said Botolph.

"I reckon Father, that if you fell into a cess pit you'd come up with a juicy apple in your mouth."

Ash giggled and Botolph smiled, "It's the power of God Luka – seek and ye shall find – ask and ye shall receive – as long as it is in the name of the Lord."

The following day they were at the site just after dawn when Putnam arrived with a group of ten men and boys. He hesitated for a moment but then left quickly realising that, much as he would like to join in, it would not be right for him to take instructions from one of his workers. Luka and Botolph had already devised a plan of action and they divided the men into two groups, each led by one of them; Ash went with Luka.

The site soon burst into activity with the sound of hammering, sawing and happy men whistling and chattering. The cheerful noise attracted an ever-increasing crowd of onlookers. As the rising tide brought boat after boat up to the quayside to be unloaded, skippers and crew found time to join the throng watching the builders at work.

This was not the sort of thing that was usually seen in Bradbryc. The construction of huts was usually an unhurried process involving three men at the most. Both Wybert and Mervic lived outside the village so they had never seen any need to have a great hall so all this activity created quite a sight and attracted a crowd. This was not all good however because more than a few spectators had evil in their hearts and destruction in their minds.

At one point Luka and his team had just erected an upper cross member when a worker knocked into one of the supporting uprights sending the beam crashing down on his head. This brought joyful jeers and catcalls from the bystanders. The man was unconscious and blood was pouring from a gash in his head. Ash was one of the first to react and quickly leapt to the man's support, resting his head on his knees and using his tunic to stem the flow of blood. The crowd pressed round and a call came from one of them,

"Don't waste yer time wi' him lad – he's already dead," which raised a great guffaw of laughter. A few moments later someone heaved a bucket of cold water over the top of the front line of viewers and on to the casualty's face.

This had three effects. The splashes made the front row of the crowd press back and then someone in the second row lost their footing and fell over and the front row fell backwards over them – including the man with the bucket.

Ash's tunic was soaked and the casualty suddenly regained consciousness and rose from the ground with a roar. He was a big man and was a ferocious sight with blood running down his face. He grabbed a staff and advanced on the crowd who were scrambling over each other in the mud trying to escape. He swung his staff this way and that and the former spectators, many of them on all fours, scattered as best they could. One or two were caught by the staff's working end and they too added crimson to the scene. The attacker seemed to have no idea of where he was or what had happened but he continued to roar and flail with his staff until all the bodies were out of range. He was about to chase them further when he was confronted by Botolph who raised his fingers in a bishop's blessing.

"Peace my son," he said.

The man stopped and stared and dropped his raised arm.

"Christ be with you," said Botolph.

Inexplicably to the onlookers, the man fell to his knees and lowered his head.

Botolph moved forward and placed his hand gently on the matted hair. The man said nothing but Ash appeared at Botolph's side with a piece of clean white linen and a horn of water.

"Come Ash," said Botolph "let's mend our friend.

The man raised his head and saw the boy and docilely let him wash the blood from his face and bind the linen over the wound. The man's senses seemed to gradually return and when Ash had finished, the man looked up at Botolph and said, "What happened?"

"The cross member slipped off the post and knocked you out."

"Ah." He shook his head and stood up.

"Thank'ee lad," he said, putting up his hand to feel the bandage. "Ye've done a good job."

Ash blushed.

"And thank'ee Father."

He knelt again and, taking Botolph's hand pressed the back of it to his forehead. He then stood and said,

"Well I've recovered now – let's get on with it. Let's get that beam back up into place."

After that setback the day went swimmingly. The jeering crowd lost interest and its people went home to lick their own wounds. A new crowd of onlookers drifted in and out from time to time. Many of them were strangers who had arrived by boat and some of them offered to help with the building work.

In the middle of the afternoon Farmer Putnam turned up with a thatcher and a cartful of straw. By this time the roof timbers were already in place and the work of thatching could begin immediately. After unloading his cart the farmer took two men from the site and went off to collect a load of willow stems. He arrived back with these just before the sun touched the horizon. At the same time, Meg and a couple of young girls arrived with loaves of bread and oysters and cheese and mussels and pies and flagons of mead and ale.

They all sat or lay where they could and restored themselves. As Meg passed Luka who had a horn of ale in one hand and half a loaf in the other, he stood and said, "This is right generous of you mistress."

"Huh," she said. "Don't thank me – thank Farmer Putnam, - he's had me baking bread an' pies as if there's no tomorrow."

"And very good they are," said Luka through a mouthful of food.

"Looks like your Botolph got his wish about the church then?"

"Yes it does," replied Luka.

"I wouldn't hold yer breath though. It won't last a moon. Wybert won't have it."

"Wybert'll have to have it if Mervic says so, won't he?"

"Never on yer life. Wybert does what Wybert does."

"Hmm," said Luka. "We're going to have to find a way of stopping him then."

"Well good luck with that," said Meg "but he's not on his own ye know. You won't find any here who'll accept this new religion – 'n' I'm one of them. We don't want it, see. We've got our own gods and we've 'ad them for generations. We know that it's the sun and the wood gods and the river sprites what rules our destinies – not some Jesus Christ. Who was he anyway? He's never been to Bradbryc nor ever likely to now he's dead. What's the use of a dead god when ye've got the fiends and devils of the countryside to contend with? We kill our sacrifices and we cast our tokens and we burn our rituals . . . and it works alright for us, so why should we change?"

Botolph had walked across behind her during this latest tirade.

"Does it always work?" he asked gently.

She spun round.

"You," she said.

"Yes me. I asked if it always worked. Do things always go as you want them to? Do you always have good harvests? Do your magic men always manage to cure your ill children? Does your bread always taste as good as this?"

She blushed and shuffled – half flattered and half annoyed at being called out.

"Well . . . no," she admitted reluctantly "we've actually 'ad a bad time lately. We've 'ad a lot of miscarriages in the village – both of babies and cattle and the last harvest was not good either. But . . . "

After initially looking a little crushed, she spun around - re-invigorated again, "Ye can't expect everything to go right all the time, - these things 'appen."

"What, in spite of your pagan sacrifices, tokens and

rituals?" said Botolph, raising his eyebrows.

She stared at him for a second and then without another word she turned her back on him and walked away.

--o--

By the end of the second day the chapel was built, thatched, wattled and daubed and had, at its eastern end, a simple altar table upon which stood a wooden cross with a tallow candle flickering on either side.

Botolph had hoped that he would be able to inaugurate the building by getting all his workers to join him in a short service of thanksgiving. He gathered them together and broached the subject but it was clear from their downcast eyes that all they wanted to do was to go home. Disappointing as it was, Botolph read their mood and capitulated by once again raising his fingers in a blessing from the God they had barely heard of and wished them good fortune and his thanks as they all melted away into the darkness.

All, that is, except one – and that was the big man with the bandage around his head.

"Will you join us?" asked Botolph.

"Aye, Father, - that I will."

"Good," said Botolph and, looking at Luka and Ash, "shall we then?"

They entered the church. Botolph knelt immediately before the altar and the other three knelt on the straw-strewn floor behind him.

After the service they went through the open doorway and gazed across the river towards Ceodham on the other side. The setting moon glinted on the water, making it sparkle and the houses near the quay were in silhouette. Somewhere to the right a nightjar called and then an owl hooted and then another. Botolph had his hand on Ash's shoulder. To Ash's right stood the big man whose name they had discovered was Tolan and on Botolph's left stood Luka.

"Thank you my friends," said Botolph. "We have done great works today and yesterday. This chapel is a triumph achieved against all odds and I have no doubt that its success is due to the fact that in building it we have carried out God's will."

"What shall we do about guarding it?" asked Luka.

"I shall sleep here each night from now onwards," said Botolph.

"We'll need to build you a thicker pallet then," said Luka "there's not much comfort in the straw floor."

Botolph laughed. "Thank you for your concern my friend but I'll be fine."

Luka was not having that however and the four of them returned to the billet and carried the wood and straw of Botolph's pallet back to the chapel.

"What are you going to do, Tolan?"

"Don't you worry about me Father – I shall be alright. I'll be off now but I'll come back in the morning."

"Oh? Right. Thanks again Tolan. God be wi' ye," and, to a chorus of 'God be wi' yes' from Luka and Ash, the big man headed off towards the river path and was soon lost to the darkness.

--o--

Botolph passed what seemed to him an idyllic night in the new chapel. Here he was – sleeping in the presence of God – what more could he want? He had the feeling that God had folded his loving arms around him and he was at peace. He felt like a parent protecting his child. He was convinced that his mere presence would ensure that the church was not attacked again.

After waking from his slumbers he walked to the door of the church and flung it open – and nearly fell over Tolan who was sitting cross-legged at the entrance.

"Peace be with you brother," said Botolph in surprise, "and what, may I ask, are you doing here so early?"

Tolan looked a little embarrassed.

"Well I wanted to catch ye afore ye headed off to the fields."

"Why's that then?"

"Well it seems to me that, although ye're guarding the church by night – it's left unguarded when ye're out by day."

"That's true," said Botolph "but I was hoping that a daytime attack would be less likely because there will be people about and I guess the attacker would rather not be identified."

"Ye won't be needin' me then?"

"What?"

"Well I thought that I could perhaps guard the church during daytime for ye – but if ye don' think it's necessary . . . " and he turned to go away.

"No . . . wait . . . I think you're quite right. It's just that I couldn't think of anyone to ask so thought it was worth the risk – but it seems that God has sent you to do His work."

Tolan brightened visibly and this was aided further by the sun's rays striking him as it rose from behind the church.

"Well that's dramatic," Botolph thought to himself, "God's in fine form this morning."

Leaving Tolan to settle into his new occupation, Botolph headed back to the billet, stopping by the river's edge to splash his face with cold water.

"Had a good night Father?" Luka called as he entered the hut.

"Great thanks – and we seem to have our first convert."

"How's that then?"

Botolph told them about Tolan.

"I wondered how we were going to solve that problem," said Luka. "Doesn't he have a job then?"

"I must admit I didn't ask, he seemed so eager to help."

"One thing at a time then," said Luka "C'mon Ash, let's get along to the farm."

The next couple of weeks passed peaceably and the little chapel became more business-like as, each day, Tolan worked away at clearing more scrub and creating a path to the church. He also began to build a store of logs.

"What are they for," asked Botolph.

"Well Father, winter's coming and we're all going to freeze if we don't have a fire."

"I hadn't thought of putting in a hearth," said Botolph "and we haven't built a chimney into the thatch."

"Nah – I noticed that," said Tolan "but ye're goin' to need one."

This became Tolan's next daytime project. He seemed to be able to turn his hand to anything – even thatching and it was not long before the four of them were sitting round the new hearth as the first lot of logs were being put to use.

"It certainly makes it more homely," said Botolph.

"Aye," said Tolan "and it'll help to dry out the rest of that daub and stop it smelling."

Luka had not liked to mention the stench for fear of upsetting his friend, but it was true that the smell of rotting daub had not been adding to the attraction of the new chapel. Luka had been wondering if anybody other than themselves would ever be rash enough to venture through the doorway.

From the first, Botolph had been performing his own devotions privately within the church and lately he had been holding a service each early morning and late evening at which the four of them would attend. At the same time he had been hesitantly trying to work out how to try to include the villagers. At the moment he had no idea how this could be done since, after the first wave of partial interest, the locals had returned to their surly ways. Indeed, rather than things getting better, it looked as if they were taking a turn for the worst.

--o--

Wybert decided that enough was enough. He had kept his head down since being over-ruled about the building of the church but now he felt that his authority was beginning to suffer. The time had come for him to make a stand. He gathered his henchmen around him and they rode into the village in full force and headed straight for the chapel. Here they were confronted by Tolan standing resolutely in front of the doorway, his feet placed wide apart and a staff in his right hand.

Wybert was a big man and the horse gave him extra height. Tolan looked into the cruel face, shaded as it was by a black hat. The beaked, pock-marked nose did nothing to help the face's lack of beauty and the left side of the underlying thin lip curled as he sneered down at him with a tirade which berated him for joining the 'Christ-lovers.'

One of the group dismounted and walked right up to Tolan as if he were going to enter the chapel. Tolan blocked his way but said nothing. The man looked up at his adversary and considered whether or not he should try to push past but Tolan was a mountain that would not be moved aside easily and the man thought better of it.

A crowd of traders had heard the hubbub and started to collect on one side to watch what was going on. Wybert could see that this was not the time to cause trouble so, calling his man back, he reined his horse around and led his men down to the quayside, where they sat looking at the ships that had come in and watching the approach of the latest one as it headed up the channel towards them.

Soon bored, they walked their horses along the river's edge until they came to Meg's place where they tied the nags up and went inside - calling for ale and food as they did so.

Meg adopted her servile pose and did their bidding. Wybert, through a mouthful of food, which he spat at her as he talked, said that they wanted a hut.

"Ye comin' t' live 'ere?" she said – unable to conceal her horror.

"'N' what if we are?" said one of the men, "what's it to you?"

"Oh nothing lord nothing," replied Meg "we'll be pleased to 'ave yer – we've got a hut right next door if ye wish."

"Nah," said Wybert "we don' want to live amongst ye smelly snivellin' lot – we need somewhere secluded where we can 'ave a bit of privacy."

"There's the Riverside Hut down on the Ho," said Meg. "That'll be big enough for ye and would have everything ye'd want."

And so, when Farmer Putnam's workers returned from the fields that day, Tolan had a lot to tell them and the rest they were able to discover from Meg.

"I don't like it," said Luka. "They're up to something."

"Well whatever it is, there's not much we can do about it," replied Botolph. "We'll just have to wait and see."

"I'm not so sure," said Luka. "Whatever they're up to they'll be planning it in that hut tonight. We need to find out what it is."

"'N' just how are ye goin' to do that?" said Tolan. "Ye can't just march up the riverside path, knock at the door and tell 'em ye'd like to join their meeting."

Luka looked at Tolan and wondered if he was such an asset after all.

"No," he said "but it's getting dark and the southerly wind's been blowing a sea fog about all day today. It'll likely thicken tonight as the air cools down. I reckon we could creep up that path tonight and there'd be a good chance of our eavesdropping from outside the hut."

"Right," said Tolan "best we get goin' then."

"Not you," replied Luka "you're too big to 'creep' anywhere. No - Ash and I will go. You and the Father stay here at the chapel and make it look as if things are carrying on as normal."

Needless to say, Botolph was not happy about his friends doing this and did all he could to find an alternative solution. In his heart however he knew that Luka was right and that it seemed that trouble was looming on the horizon.

--o--

Luka and Ash walked back along the river's edge as if they were returning to their billet. On their arrival they went past the hut and took the path that followed the river. It soon narrowed leaving a thick border of trees to their left and the river to their right.

It was a pitch black night but Luka's predicted fog

had not materialised. Luka led the way, feeling at the trunks of the trees and they made silent progress as quickly as they could.

Suddenly there came the sound of distant voices and the smell of wood smoke.

"We can't be there already," whispered Ash "the Riverside Hut's a lot further on."

"Stay here," said Luka "I'll be back shortly."

Ash melted into the shadow of the trees and, as Luka crept forward, the voices gradually increased in volume. He cautiously approached a corner. When he peered around it he could see the flicker of a flame illuminating the faces of two men sitting by a makeshift fireside. Two horses were tied up nearby. There was no way around them. Luka crept back to Ash, who was so well-hidden that it made him jump when Ash emerged from the shadows.

"They've set a guard," whispered Luka "so it looks pretty certain that there's something going on up there that they don't want people to know about."

"What're we going to do Pa?"

"Well there's no way round the guards and the path is the only approach so . . . ah – we need a boat – that's the only chance we've got. Come on – we passed a boat which was pulled up on the beach just a little way back."

They retraced their steps and found a small skyff which they slid stern first into the water. Luka sent Ash aboard and then pushed it further and climbed aboard too. There were two oars which they put to good use poling the craft out into deeper water, after which Luka put each of the oars between its thole pins and was able to row out into the middle of the channel.

It was not long before they could see the glow of the guards' riverside fire as, keeping well to the opposite bank,

Luka felt his way downstream. Once past the fire he rowed out of the shadows and crossed to the other side of the river. It was not long before they could hear more voices followed by raucous laughter and loud shouting and the Riverside Hut loomed above them.

The men had tethered their horses immediately outside the building so, for fear of disturbing the animals, Luka let the vessel continue to drift and only gained the river bank when they were well clear.

As he clambered over the gunnels he took the painter and lashed it to a tree. Telling Ash to stay in the boat, he made his way quickly through the thickets in the direction of the hut, hoping against hope that he was not too late, and that they hadn't already made their plans and were now just getting drunk. He calculated that there would be less need for stealth here since there were unlikely to be guards on this side of the hut as there was no proper path.

The 'windows' were wide open - their wooden shutters having been pulled upwards by stout hessian ropes. Keeping his head down below the openings Luka moved to the middle window, which was closest to the most voluble speaker - whom he guessed was Wybert. At the time Luka arrived the group were more interested in eating and drinking than making plans. He crouched just below the cill and then, reasoning that he would be able to hear just as well if he was comfortable, he slid down and made a seat for himself with his back to the wall.

The party went on and on with the conversation revolving around bawdy stories and crude jokes - but at last a voice said:

"Well what's the plan for tonight then Wybert?"
"Tonight ... " came the slightly slurred reply.
"Tonight we're going to have to rid the village of

these so-called Christians for once and all."

"Mervic won't like it," said another voice.

A bellyful of oaths came from Wybert making it clear that he didn't care what Mervic thought. He wasn't going to have Jesus-preachers on *his* patch.

"Drive 'em away 'n' they'll only come back," said another voice.

"Well this lot won't," replied Wybert. "I want the heads of each of them stuck on poles outside that chapel. We'll not take the horses 'cos I don't want us to be seen as being involved. We'll wait until the early hours, then walk back to the village. You four'll go and get the dwarf and his son from their billet. Don't mess about – kill them both and then one of you bring just their heads to the church. The rest of you come back here."

"What, kill the little lad?" said a voice "Couldn't he be more useful to us in other ways?"

"No!" said Wybert. "I want 'em all dead – it's the only way. Now the rest of us'll press on to the church. When we arrive there we'll kill the priest and put his head on a stake near the front door and when the other two heads arrive we'll add one of those on either side. This'll 'ave to be done as *silently* as possible. If you 'ave to talk keep it to a whisper. Folks'll generally be asleep so if we're clever enough we won't be seen. Once done, the rest of us'll get back here as quietly and quickly as we can - just leaving Jake to fire the church once we're well clear. Jake'll then head north rather than coming back to us because once that fire takes hold the whole village will be up and panicking and trying to make sure the fire doesn't catch the other houses. Understand Jake?"

"The heads'll have to be set well back from the church 'cos I don't want them to get trampled on when people are bringing buckets of water. Once the fire's burnt out, the sight of the black hulk with three skulls in front of it should be enough to deter any other would-be Christian preachers."

"What about the big fellow?"

"He doesn't sleep there anyway so we needn't worry about him, and once he sees those skulls he'll find something better to do with his life – you mark my words."

Someone else started to speak but Luka had heard enough and he cautiously lifted himself off his perch and pushed through the tree trunks, making his way along the river's edge. It was pitch black and there was a low haze which was even blotting out the stars. He couldn't see a thing but a low voice called, "Pa."

Ash's voice came from behind him so he retraced his steps and then whispered "Ash?"

"Over here Pa."

He followed the voice and then saw the outline of the boat. He untied the painter and clambered in.

"There's no time to lose boy. We've got to get back as soon as we can," he whispered. "Don't talk. I reckon it's so dark we can go straight up the middle of the river without the guards seeing us – so . . . quiet as you can."

Luka pulled away from the bank and Ash leant forwards and hissed: "I can see the beacon on the end of the quay Pa."

"Good boy," said Luka, who had his back towards it, "guide me to that then."

He wasted no words for fear of being heard but he had been relieved to hear about the beacon since, in this intense darkness, there was no chance of returning the boat to where they had found it.

Ash leant forwards again.

"I can see the guards' fire."

Luka grunted and pulled across to the opposite

bank which, with this new illumination, he could now vaguely see. He was afraid that they would be spotted but they managed to slip past safely and Luka was soon looking back at the smoke from the guards' fire as it swirled upwards and joined the foggy layer above them.

Soon they were at the quayside where, after tying the boat up, they climbed the dew-covered rickety wooden steps and made their way to the chapel, where they found candles burning on the altar and Botolph and Tolan waiting for them. Once inside Luka closed the door firmly behind them. He kept his voice low as he said, "Father, we've gotta go."

"Go?" replied Botolph in a voice that Luka would have wished quieter. "What do you mean 'Go?' Where can we go to?"

"Well, put it this way Father, we can't stay."

He outlined the plans that he had heard Wybert making and told Botolph about the boat.

"Hmm," said Tolan. "If there'd been just one or two of them we might have been able to defend ourselves but there are just too many. Luka's right – ye've got to go."

"But ... but we've just managed to build the church and we're gradually getting through to the local people and ... "

"We're *not*, Father," said Luka.

"What?"

"We're *not* getting through to the local people. There's as much chance of a dozen being baptised as there is of the old king coming back to life. Accept it Father, - they're not ready for Christianity yet. Ye've done a great job building this chapel and that's made a start but if we stay here we're going to be dead by morning and we'll be no earthly use to God no more."

He took one of Botolph's hands and stared into his

face and said gently, "Father, there are many more communities where you can spread the Word of God, but surely this is a sign that God doesn't want you to stay here but to move on?"

Botolph looked down at him and was silent for a while and then said, "I must pray."

He went and knelt down at the foot of the altar. Luka jerked his head towards the door and the three of them crept out into the misty air and silently closed the door behind them.

"What will *you* do Tolan," asked Luka.

"Well, I dunno really. I think I'd be too much baggage if I came with you so I reckon I'll stay here."

"Do you think that's wise?" said Luka. "If they can't put our heads on poles they might think that your head was the next best thing."

"True. Well perhaps I'll head north for a while and then maybe come back in a few moons when things have settled down and they've forgotten me."

"Why come back?" asked Ash.

"Well . . . I like it here and this church has somehow become special to me. I know it's destined for the bone-fire but . . . I just have the feeling that I should come back. Tha's all I can say."

The church door opened and Botolph came out looking only a little happier.

"It seems that you're right Luka. It's time to go," he said. "But I'm so sad to be leaving God's work half done."

"Tolan's going to stay," said Luka. "He'll keep an eye on it for you."

"Tolan – that's so kind but I wouldn't want you to be in danger."

"I'm not staying immediately Father. I shall head north for a few moons and then return after the . . ." - he paused - "the . . . ashes have settled," and he looked at Botolph apologetically.

"Bless you, my son. Perhaps you will be able to get word to us . . . "

"Father we have to go," interrupted Luka. "There's no time to be lost. We need to get our sacks from the billet."

"Wait," said Botolph "I must go and get the cross – but . . . " he faltered "the cross is a sign that this is still God's house – no – I shall leave it there. Let the heathens do what they dare and on their own heads be it."

"Father – come," insisted Luka.

"No," said Botolph "I need to talk to Tolan – you get the sacks and I'll meet you at the quayside."

The two left and he turned to Tolan.

"Tolan – there are two other things you can do for me."

"Whatever I can Father."

"We're about to leave in a stolen boat and desert Farmer Putnam who has been kind to us – both these things lie uneasily on my conscience. I'd be grateful if you'd go and explain to the farmer why we've had to leave at such short notice - and thank him for all he's done for us. Tell him about the boat – he might know the owner - if so then beg him to make our peace with him. Will you do that for me Tolan?"

"Aye I will Father and willingly."

"Thank you Tolan, you're a good man and I wish you God's peace and happiness for the future."

CHAPTER 4
Escape

An hour later they were in the boat with Ash in the bows surrounded by their three sacks, Luka rowing and Botolph in the stern. Once again they approached the guards' fire, which flared up brighter than previously as fresh logs caught flame. The tide, though not strong, had turned and this, together with Botolph's extra weight, created more pressure on the oars and they began to creak as they rubbed against the thole pins. Getting past the guards was not going to be so easy this time.

Luka stopped rowing and said, "Ash – get a couple of woollens out of my sack and use them to muffle these oars. Quick as you can – we're drifting backwards."

The boy instinctively knew what his father meant and, as Luka lifted each oar, Ash wound the woollen between the gunnel and the pins.

"Good lad."

He started rowing again. They were making silent headway this time and the guard's fire had reduced to a simple glow. Luka hoped it was going to stay that way. He kept well to the opposite bank and again they slipped past unseen. Then came the Riverside Hut but the river was wider at this point and Luka had no difficulty passing that too. As the current grew a little stronger he had to work a little harder - although he was pleased to note that they were still making good headway past the river bank which they were now skirting closely.

Then the fog came down in all its murky thickness and Ash could hardly see Botolph, let alone the river bank.

The only way Luka knew which way he was going was the fact that if he inadvertently turned the boat so that it began to *cross* the incoming flow there came the sound of water gently rippling against one side of the hull. To correct this he pulled harder on the opposite oar whereupon the rippling sound stopped. He could see absolutely nothing but by using his ears in this way he kept the boat in the middle of the stream. He reasoned that, if he just kept rowing, so long as the tide remained in flood, they would eventually find the sea. Botolph offered to take over but Luka was strong and fit and he wanted to do it his way.

Then the fog started to play its tricks with noises that should have been far away but seemed to come from right by the side of them. A cow mooed and Ash nearly jumped out of his skin. A short while later Luka thought he heard the sound of voices behind them.

"You hear that?" puffed Luka.

"What?" said Botolph.

"I heard it Pa," said Ash, whose ears were pointing in the same direction as his father's. "Some voices - but they've gone again now."

"Keep yourselves quiet," said Luka.

They pressed on for a long time. Occasionally, as the fog swirled, they seemed to hear the noise of people as if they were so close as to almost be on top of them but then the sounds receded into the distance again.

Suddenly, as Luka pulled, he felt his right hand oar hit something. He lifted both oars out of the water to take another sweep but when he did so the same thing happened.

"What . . . ?" said Luka.

The fog lifted a little.

"It's one of those withies you were telling me about," said Ash leaning forwards and grabbing it so that they became temporarily moored.

Luka stopped rowing and turned to look. "I thought we were further than this. We're still a long way from the sea. We're only at the junction of the two rivers. Just look at that tide ripping past.

I'll never be able to row against that. I thought that we were making good speed but, in spite of all my efforts, we must've been hardly moving across the ground at all."

Voices swirled again through the fog behind them, together with the noise of what sounded like several sets of oars. Luka made a decision. He was about to tell Ash to let the withie go when the decision was made for him as the strain of the current on the boat pulled the withie clean out of the mud and they took off backwards.

Ash's eyes opened wide in alarm as the boat hurtled out of control and he could foresee them being swept back into their pursuers' arms.

"It's alright Ash - just drop it in the water," hissed Luka, pulling gently on one oar. "If we keep to the south side this flood'll push us up the channel towards Ciss's Ceaster."

He was about to say something else when suddenly from right next to them there came the sounds of voices, the splash of oars and the grunts and curses of those still plying them against the current.

Luka deftly lifted his oars out of the water and brought them into the boat for fear that the passing craft would run into them. Each person froze rigid - wide-eyed and alert - anticipating discovery. There was nothing to do but hold their breaths and, in Botolph's case, pray for deliverance. His prayers seemed to have been answered when the fog suddenly became so thick that they could not even see each other. They were blind. Their clothes were wet. They breathed in moisture. Each was in his own world which was of necessity silent . . . waiting . . . waiting. Each heard the beating drum of his own heart. Ash wanted to sneeze and he grabbed at his nose in an effort to prevent it. Suddenly his Pa came into view again but the sounds of splashes, grunts and curses also returned, although they seemed much further away.

They remained silent, still hardly daring to breathe. They were totally disoriented. Luka softly plied his oars again although he could see neither them nor the water. He listened while he pulled. No sound of ripples came from behind him so he reasoned that he must be going *with* the current rather than against it. He pulled harder on the right hand oar hoping to crab the boat across the stream to the river bank.

"Pa," whispered Ash.

"Yes son."

"The voices have stopped."

"So they have. Stay quiet though. We're not safe yet."

Then came a gentle bump whilst, at the same time, Luka's left oar hit mud. They had stopped. Luka felt the stern of the boat start to swing round as she was caught by the tide.

"Quick Ash, get into the stern," called Luka as he heaved strongly again on the oars.

The bow, relieved of its weight, floated again and with Ash's extra weight in the stern, Luka heaved as hard as he could on the oars and was able to plough a furrow up into the muddy bank. Once they were well and truly wedged Luka let go the oars and, grabbing the painter, rashly leapt over the side.

"Ugh!" he said as he sank up to his knees in thick cold ooze. "C'mon you two – quick as you can. Pass me those sacks."

Ash passed them over and then he and Botolph followed Luka into the mud. Luka dropped the painter and did his best to run – as much as anyone *could* run in those foul conditions. Ash kept up with him and Botolph brought up the rear. It was exhausting work and after several minutes without reaching drier ground Luka stopped.

"I didn't expect the bank to be as wide as this," he puffed.

"I think perhaps we're going *along* the river Pa," said Ash. "I reckon the shore's over there."

"Hmm you could be right. C'mon then, let's try that."

A few more steps and the mud was only ankle deep and then they were on dry land.

"Good lad," said Luka. "Well done son."

"Where now?" said Botolph.

"Well, if we're where I think we are, this will be Maenwud and if we're going to put some distance between ourselves and Wybert we need to move south."

"So which way is that?" said Botolph.

"I've no idea," replied Luka.

They walked . . . and walked. Stumbling over tree stumps and falling into ditches. At one point Luka tripped headlong over a mound, which rose up and went 'Baa' and joined other suddenly 'Baa-ing' mounds which ran off to another part of whichever field they were in.

The others were still laughing as Luka regained his feet.

"I thought it was a Bog Demon," he said.

They laughed again.

"You shouldn't laugh," said Luka earnestly, "they're serious things out here. I've heard tell that each one likes to eat a man and a child every night."

Ash was not sure if he was joking or not but was then suddenly overcome by fatigue.

"You alright son?" he said.

The boy yawned before answering "Yes but is it much further?"

"You're tired," said Luka. "What sort of father am I, leading a youngster such a dance in the middle of the night?"

"I'll be alright pa," the lad said.

"Course you will. C'mon, we'll find somewhere to lay up. We must have got well away from them by now."

It was not long before they came across a big shed. Visibility was improving a bit and Botolph managed to find the doors and lift the latch. They couldn't make out much in the darkness but it was dry and seemed to be full of hay so they felt around for places to lie down and before long they were each dead to the world.

CHAPTER 5
Circles

Luka was woken by sunlight glinting through the planks in the walls.

Ash and Botolph were still sound asleep.

He slid off his pallet of hay and, as he opened the barn door, light flooded in, making the other two stir. He went out, closing the door behind him, and stretched up his arms as he gazed around.

He then stopped, dropped his arms to his side and stared.

"I don't believe it," he said to himself.

He looked at the sun – there it was to the east, just as he would have expected at this time of morning, but there to the north was . . . a river.

"How can that be?" he asked out loud.

"What's that Luka?" said Botolph as he joined him with Ash close by his side.

"The river."

"Well?"

"The river," he repeated. "We came up that river last night and then we walked for hours and hours and yet there the river is again now."

He clasped his hands to his head. "Circles," he said. "We must have walked in a circle last night and then ended up almost where we started."

"Oh," they said, not being able to think of a more appropriate comment.

"I'm so so sorry Father."

"It's not your fault Luka – it was the fog and anyway you had no landmarks to follow and you don't know this countryside."

"Even so Father, I should have done better than that," said Luka who prided himself on his tracking ability.

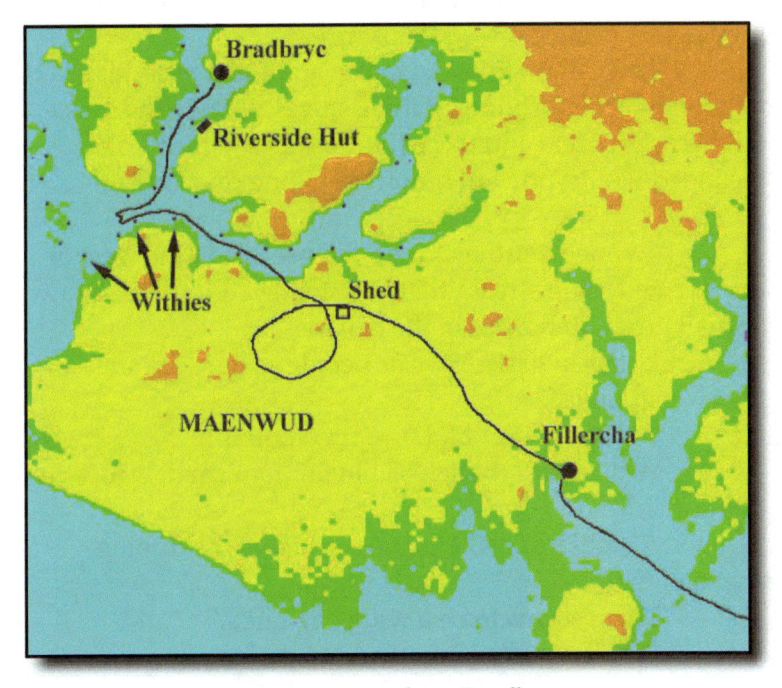

Fig. 4. Escape from Bradbryc.

"I feel deeply ashamed of myself."

"Well never mind that," said Botolph, "shame yourself into finding us some food so that we can break our fast and prepare for the new day which, God willing, will be bereft of fog."

"Aye it looks that way," said Luka, relenting a little

and sniffing the air. "Wind's gone around to the west, so I doubt we'll get more fog today."

They set off, keeping the morning sun to their left. The ground was quite flat but very wet with numerous drainage ditches.

"We were digging these not so long ago," said Luka to Botolph, as they waded across another one," and now they're just being a blessed nuisance."

They came across a coppice and Luka used his seax to good effect in producing three staves to carry the sacks on their shoulders and three thumb sticks, which Luka reckoned would prevent him from falling over any more sheep.

A while later they found themselves to the west of an ever-widening stream that they followed until they saw a small group of houses in the distance.

"Looks like there's *some* people as live 'ere after all then," said Luka.

"Is that good or bad?" replied Botolph.

"Well good I think 'cos I'm fair famished. How ye doing Ash?"

"Alright Pa," said the young stalwart skipping ahead of them.

"There seems to be a wide bay Luka."

"Where there's a bay there might be some boats and where there are boats that might signify the next part of our journey."

"Wise words my friend for so early in the day without any food inside you."

Luka grinned.

"Perhaps I'm better when starved?"

They laughed and plodded on through the sticky soil.

As they came closer Luka said, "There – what did I

tell you? A mast."

Closer still and they could make out a low quay against which a small sailing vessel lay aground on the mud. The vessel was not dissimilar to the one in which they had crossed from Gallia. Grazing nearby was a herd of goats, one of which had just been picked up by a stocky bearded man in a leather apron. He carried it to the edge of the quay on which he sat before half-slithering down to the boat, into which he deposited the goat amongst three or four of its companions. He was just turning to clamber out of the boat again when the three travellers arrived.

"Can we lend you a hand?" asked Luka.

"A hand? It looks if you've got six of 'em there," came the reply. "Can ye lend me six hands?"

"Certainly can," said Luka. "How many of these beasts do you want?"

"All of 'em."

"All? Ye'll never get them all in there?"

"Ha-ha, won't I just? I've done it many times before and, the devil willing, I'll do it many times more."

They dumped their sacks and sticks on one side and all three of them set about catching the animals. Luka and Ash were quite adept at this, having done the same thing previously for Bonitius, but Botolph was completely at a loss. The goats seemed to sense this and taunted him. While he was bending trying to pick one up, another of the goats butted him from behind and sent him sprawling. Luka and Ash had already served up half a dozen to the goatman, who was very happy to stay in his boat and await each delivery, but Botolph had not yet managed to capture one.

"Best you get down and pray for success, monk," laughed the farmer.

Luka took pity on his friend and thwarted the

attempt of Botolph's intended victim to escape his clutches for the tenth time. Botolph managed to grab it and clasp it to his chest, whereupon it became quite docile. Triumphantly he passed it down to the farmer.

"There now – I knew you could do it monk."

"He's not a monk," piped up Ash, "he's a priest and should be addressed as 'Father'"

"Oh, should he now? Well then *Father* – off you go and see how long it takes you to get another one."

Botolph felt that he was not representing Christianity too well and so, having tasted success, he watched Luka and Ash's techniques for a while before copying them himself. Sure enough this brought more triumphs and it was not long before all forty of the beasts were standing docilely on the sole of the boat.

"Where are you bound for?" asked Botolph, trying to dust the mud off his habit.

"Haninge on the River Adur," came the reply.

"How far's that?"

"Just a few hours," he said. "The tide's just beginning to make and as soon as we're afloat I'll be off."

Indeed the water was now lapping at the boat's planking and every so often, as some swell came in from the sea, the boat would rise and then bang down on to the mud again, making a hundred and sixty hooves stagger.

"Can you take three more goats?" asked Botolph.

"Three more? I thought we had them all."

"No, I mean us – can we come with you?"

"Well," he paused "I don't see why not – ye could make yerselves useful helping me to unload when we get there."

"Great," said Botolph looking at Ash, "the only problem is we've not yet broken our fast and our little champion goat-catcher is dying of hunger."

"Oh, that's no problem," laughed the farmer "I've food 'ere – but not enough for all of us. Ye just come down into the boat now and make yerselves comfortable while I go and get some more vittals from me house."

Botolph and Luka offered the farmer their hands to help him regain the quayside and then, after grabbing their sacks, they cautiously slid down to join the goats which reluctantly gave them space. The farmer soon returned with the happy sight of a loaf, cheese, fruit and milk.

Slipping the line holding the boat to the quay he fixed his scarred leather boots firmly against the bank, lent his hands to the gunnel of the bow and applied all his weight. Nothing happened. Ship, goats and passengers remained resolutely still - but the master was in no hurry.

Muscles rippling in compression *he* was more obstinate than *she* and gradually, like an arm-wrestler tiring at a contest, she was overcome. Little by little he saw daylight dawn between her wood and the shore. Not ready yet, he waited with a soldier's rigidity until the white of her eye brought a ripple from the sea and, like a pigeon in its mating dance, the old boat gave in, bowed once to the sea and bent to the inevitable. Standing now with pretended impartiality he sauntered back towards the stern as a zephyr pushed her forwards. Nimbly then he joined the goats and, standing on the stern sculled her ahead with the steering oar.

In view of their recent experience Botolph asked him: "Why are you leaving now just as the tide's making. Won't the current build up against you? Wouldn't it be better to leave on the ebb?"

"Ha. Ye'd think so wouldn't ye? But the current's only slight here and once we leave Fillercha we'll soon pick up the wind in our sail and that'll take us out of the bay. By the time we reach the sea the current'll be flooding to the east 'n' will push us on handsomely so that we reach the Adur while *it's* still flooding and that will drive us up river. Now ye can stop yer questions and leave me to worry about my job and ye worry about feeding that young lad."

In spite of the goats, which actually provided good low ballast and kept the boat very stable, they had an idyllic sail. Much to Botolph's amazement the goats just stood stock still as if they feared that any movement might cause catastrophe. They made little noise except for the sound of an occasional dropping. He stroked the back of one of them and it seemed to appreciate it, for it turned its head sideways in acknowledgement but soon turned forwards again.

Ash guzzled the milk as if there was no tomorrow and they all tucked into the bread and cheese. The farmer had brought some extra horns along and he filled two of these with mead and passed them over. Our three heroes were soon slumbering contentedly while their boat was swept on by a fine southwesterly wind.

They awoke when the motion changed as the farmer hardened the sail when he brought the boat up into the wind as they entered a wide river estuary. As he had predicted, the current was still with them but reduced when they entered the narrow river.

"How far now?" asked Ash.

"Not far," said the farmer. "Just round this bend the river's blocked by the Veteri Ponte bridge 'n' just afore it ye'll see the quayside of Haninge where we'll tie up and unload the cargo."

CHAPTER 6
Haninge

Unloading their cargo was made easier due to the fact that the depth of water allowed the boat right up to the quay - but it was still heavy work as each of the goats had to be lifted ashore. Various spectators came and went and they had all but finished when another grizzled goatherd, accompanied by a grizzled wife crossed the old wooden bridge and joined them.

"What's this then, you got yer own fyrd now?"

"Wassail you two. Where d'ye want these beasts put then?"

"Ah that's alright - we'll drive 'em down the path."

"I'll be off then. The ebb's started and I can't afford to leave it any longer."

"What about yer army - aren't you takin' them with ye?"

"Na - they're all yours - along with the goats," he said, pushing his boat away from the wall. "Thanks for yer 'elp you three. Good luck to 'ee."

"Thanks to you too," they chorused and Botolph added.

"God bless and keep you safe farmer," and raised his hand in blessing.

"Now then," said Farmer Grizzle, as Ash came to call him. "What are you three going to do? Where are you bound for?"

"We're heading east towards Cantium," said

Botolph "but we need board and lodging for the night."

"Well," said Grizzle "you come 'n' help me pen the goats while Mistress prepares some food for us all, 'n' then we've an outhouse where ye can spend the night."

Penning the goats was not as simple as it sounded. The farmer wanted them split up into eight different fields and the animals had their own ideas. By the time the goatherds came back they were hot, sweaty and covered in mud. Mistress Grizzle's hot broth followed by a good meal soon put them to rights, however and they spent a blissful night in the next-door building.

The following day the weather had changed dramatically. The southwesterly wind had veered to a strong northerly which brought rain with it.

"Well ye b'aint goin' nowhere t'day me dearies," said Mistress Grizzle, who had taken a liking to Ash and was reluctant to lose him too soon. "Why don't ye bide a while? The farmer could do wi' some more 'ands."

And so they did 'bide a while' continuing to sleep in the outhouse and turning their hands to farming once more. Haninge was a thriving community with two or three small farms and four times as many smallholders. The locals were used to travellers, since the Veteri Ponte had carried folks east and west over the River Adur for hundreds of years.

Botolph tried his best to convert the farmer and his wife to Christianity but, although they maintained that they had no argument with the new religion, they left him in no doubt that they were quite content with their own. The old pair had an altar to the sun and the moon and another to the river and the sky and that is where they prayed at the beginning and end of each day.

"Someone's looking fer ye," said Grizzle to Luka a couple of evenings later.

"What do you mean?"

"Down at the estuary. A boat came in late this a'ternoon with half a dozen men in it but it couldn't get up the river with the northerly wind. They'll come up first thing tomorrow on the flood I reckon."

"How d'ye know they're looking for us?" said Luka feeling uneasy.

"Ah – well, they asked one of the shepherds if he'd seen a priest, a dwarf and a boy 'n' so there's little doubt that he'd be talking 'bout you three."

"Where's the shepherd now?"

"Well he must be in his hut at the foot of the 'ills. I met him down by the brook while he was walking 'is sheep back to the upper pasture and 'e told me about it as we walked back together."

"We'll have to go," said Luka "and it'll have to be now. There's not a moment to lose."

"What? Now?" cried Mistress Grizzle. "Ye can't go now in the dark with this driving north wind. Stay until mornin'."

"Don't think we can do that," said Luka. "I must find the other two."

So saying, he went out quickly and ran round to the outhouse where he flung the door open to find Ash lying on his pallet, about to go to sleep, and Botolph on his own pallet with his hands behind his head, looking up into the rafters to where the bats flitted to and fro, half illuminated by the light of the flickering candle.

"Wake up Ash, we've got to go," said Luka. "C'mon Father – we've no time to lose."

"What's up Pa?" asked Ash sleepily.

"Wybert – that's what's up. He arrived at the estuary late this afternoon but couldn't get up 'cos of the wind but he'll be up as soon as the flood starts and we must be long gone by then."

"How many of them?" asked Botolph sitting up.

"Half a dozen apparently. Too many for us anyway. We'll have to leave now. C'mon Ash, get yer things together."

They put the candle out and closed the door behind them.

"We must go and thank the Grizzles," said Botolph.

They burst in to find Mistress Grizzle cutting some food for them to take.

"Ye must have this," she said, continuing with her cutting.

"Mistress that's kind of you," said Luka, "and we're very grateful - but we have no time to spare so, not wishing to be rude, just forget the cutting and put it in a cloth – we can do the cutting later."

"Of course," she said and did his bidding, throwing it all in a cloth which she tied by the four corners.

"'Ere," said the farmer – "a couple of bladders of mead 'n' three leathers to put on yer shoulders to keep the wind out."

They were lost for words by the kindness of this old couple and Ash ran to Mistress Grizzle who cuddled him as if he were her own grandchild. Botolph and Luka in turn embraced both the elderly couple and Luka said, "Now we really must go."

And Botolph said "Thanks for everything and may our God bless you both."

And Ash said politely, "Thank you mistress," and they ran out of the doorway and were gone.

It was just at the end of twilight as they made their way to the Veteri Ponte and felt their way across. The road on the other side was straight.

"I reckon they'll be up here before first light," said

Luka, "which means that if we keep moving fast we'll get about eight leagues ahead of them. There shouldn't be anyone about this time of night but, as soon as daylight comes, we'll have to get off the main road and hide up."

Ash was wide awake now and keen to scamper on ahead, but Luka called him back since it was difficult to see where they were putting their feet and he was afraid he might fall and get injured. They had to content themselves with just hurrying along as fast as they dared.

"We'll be alright soon," said Luka. "It must be top of the full moon now so that big bit o' cheese will soon be there to help us on our way. See – the sky's lightening already."

"Is it really cheese Pa?" asked Ash

"'Course it is. That's why it shines so brightly in the winter. It's all been freshly made then. It's getting more yellow now it's older – just you watch."

As the moon took mastery of the sky, the roads and trees began to take shape and Ash was allowed to skip on ahead. They made good progress, keeping to the base of the hills. At one point Ash was a good twenty paces in front and running along the side of a hedge when the noise disturbed a cow in the adjacent field and she let out a loud 'Moo' that startled the wits out of Ash who raced back to Luka's side.

"That'll teach you," said Luka. "I've told you to watch out for Bog Devils."

"But there're no bogs here," protested the child.

"Ah maybe not – but there'll still be plenty of devils about. Now you stay here by me side and stop running back'ards and for'ards. Save yer energy cos yer going to need it soon."

"I'm getting hungry Pa."

"Yes, I expect you are but if we sit down and eat

now, we'll all start to feel tired and we'll want to lie down and sleep rather than pressing on, which is what we need to do. Do you think ye can last a bit longer?"

Ash nodded.

"Good lad. You watch that moon. You remember it was right ahead of us when it rose?"

The boy nodded again.

"Well when it gets high in the sky on our right side and just starts to fall it'll be around midnight and then we'll find somewhere to sit down and have our midnight feast. Alright?"

"Alright Pa. I'll watch it for you and tell you when it's time to eat."

"Good lad."

Ash scampered off again – as much now to take his mind off his hunger and tiredness rather than, as was first the case, because he was excited and wanted to expend some pent up energy.

Botolph, of course, was striding purposely forwards with his eyes on the horizon, concentrating on the job in hand.

"I'm worried about the Grizzles," he said."

"Yeah, I know what you mean," said Luka. "They'll probably be alright.

"I'm not so sure. We should've told them to go to their neighbours for safety."

"Well, they knew we were worried so perhaps they'll work that out for themselves."

"I'll pray for them," said Botolph fixing his eyes on a bright star in the sky ahead. Luka went quiet to give him praying-space.

Ash started to slow down and reached the point where he was more often behind them than ahead, so that they frequently had to stop and call him onwards.

"Where's the moon Pa?"

"Alright my boy, it's a little earlier than I intended but you've done very well.   Let's find somewhere to rest up for a bit."

They had just passed through a wooded area where the wind had been eerily rustling the leaves.

"I don't want to stop here," said Ash.   "I reckon there'll be Bog Devils in those trees."

"Oh I wouldn't know about that," said Luka but let's go up this side lane – it looks as if there's a barn at the top there 'n' we can sit with our backs to that 'n' keep the wind off.

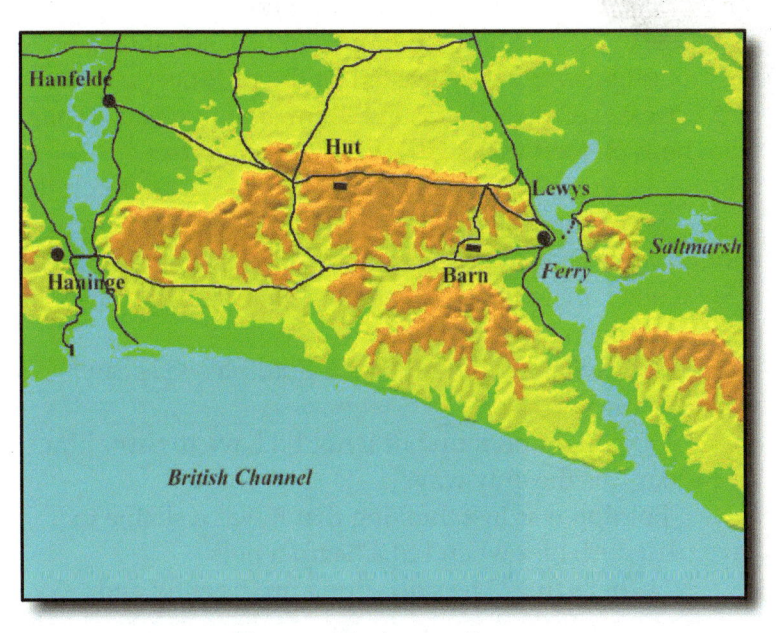

Fig. 5.   Haninge to Lewys.

The lane was uphill and this was almost the final straw for poor Ash whose little legs were aching badly.

Botolph scooped him up onto his shoulders for the last part but, by the time they reached the barn, Ash was leaning fast asleep on Botolph's head. The two of them waited outside while Luka struggled to see if he could open the door. It suddenly gave way and, leaving it wide open to let in the moonlight, he explored the barn's interior. He found some bundles of straw, which he spread out as a nest for Ash.

"There, Father, lie him down there," he said.

The boy did not stir and Luka fondly covered him with one of the leathers given to them by the Grizzles.

"His hunger'll have to wait 'til the morning," he said. "Sleep's more important to him now."

They left the barn door open to take advantage of the moonlight while they feasted on the produce supplied by Mistress Grizzle and washed it down with mead. They were both pleased to take the weight off their feet.

"How far do you think we've come?" said Botolph.

"Oh about four leagues I should think. Not far enough. We need to keep going for another four and then find somewhere to hide. As sure as eggs are eggs they'll be chasing us soon after daybreak.

"But what about Ash?" said Botolph. "He can't walk any further."

"He might perk up but if not I'll have to carry him," said Luka "'tis the only way."

Botolph was just thinking that it was a shame to have to disturb him when Luka heard a noise.

"What's that?" he said sitting up urgently and looking towards the edge of the wood where Ash had said there would be Bog Devils. A line of horsemen emerged from the trees. Some of the horses were trotting and some were going faster but a couple were lagging behind. The front runners were shouting at them, urging them onwards.

"How many are there Father," said Luka.

"I can make out seven, I think."

"It's got to be them, hasn't it? They must've rowed up the river in the dark with the first of the tide."

"Yes, your cheese-moon that has been helping us, also seems to have helped them," said Botolph. "But where would they have got the horses from? They wouldn't have brought them with them."

"Don't ask," said Luka with a terrible feeling in his stomach.

"What? You don't think ... ?"

"I don't know Father but I don't feel good about it."

"What're we going to do?"

Luka didn't answer for a while as they both watched the horses disappear into the distance.

"Well they'll be back – that's sure – but *they're* going to be getting tired too. The trouble is we don't know what lies ahead on this road. My bet is they'll ride for another three or four hours by which time it'll be close to daylight. Then they'll turn and work their way back, searching as they go."

"What do you reckon then?" said Botolph.

"I think we should get our heads down and get two hours' sleep 'n' then wake Ash, give him his breakfast and strike out northwards before the sun gets up," said Luka decisively - but secretly hoping that he had made the right decision.

CHAPTER 7
Pursuit

Wybert was not a happy man.

He had lost face badly when he launched his attack at Bradbryc. He couldn't understand what had happened. Nobody could have got to know of his plans so what made them leave? It crossed his mind that it was this God of Botolph's that was giving him protection.

His men had confidently made their way down the path from the Riverside Hut, stopping just short of Botolph's billet, where four of them had dismounted, unsheathed their swords, flung open the door and plunged their blades into the sleeping figures with eager anticipation of the mass of blood and screaming that would ensue. In the event, all they got was an anticlimactic silence. Sending one man off for a light, they cautiously felt their way round the hut expecting, at any moment, a ferocious Luka to attack from a corner or drop down from the roof. When the man returned with a burning brand and they were able to inspect the building, it became clear that they had been fooled.

By this time Wybert was on his horse outside the hut.

"What's going on?" he growled.

"They're not there."

"Damn and Blast their souls," he cursed.

If it had not been so dark his men would have seen the apoplectic bulging redness of his face.

"They've got to be sleeping in the church then. Quickly now - mount up and follow me."

He led the horsemen at speed through the village. At the church they leapt from their mounts and, unsheathing their swords once again, ran to the door and thrust it open. Wybert stood back as the rest of them flooded in. This time they needed no burning brands, for two candles were giving their light serenely from the altar and once again the place was devoid of occupants.

Wybert was furious. He howled with rage and frustration and thrust his sword time and time again into Botolph's pallet as if the priest were still sleeping there.

By this time, alerted by the galloping horses and Wybert's howls, the village was awake and an audience was forming outside the door.

"Burn it," screamed Wybert at his man. "Burn it!"

The man went to fetch a brand from his horse with a view to lighting it from the candle flame but, as he opened the door, was shocked to find a semi-circle of silent watchers.

Wybert came out.

The crowd parted and Putnam came through and faced Wybert.

"What are you doing?" asked Putnam.

"We're going to burn the church," said Wybert.

"I don't think so," said Putnam.

"Why not?"

"Because it's my building and it's on my ground. The priest's gone and it'll make a good barn. Call off your men."

Wybert wrenched a dagger from his belt, advanced towards Putnam and put the point of the dagger under his chin.

"Where's the priest gone?"

"I've no idea."

"Where's he *gone*?"

Putnam didn't answer and Wybert increased the pressure on his dagger. His face was close to Putman's and the peak of his black hat brushed Putman's forehead as the odours of his foul breath flooded up the farmer's nostrils.

"Tell me or by Jupiter I swear this knife will come out of the top of your head."

Putnam was not a man to be easily scared but he never planned on dying to save a Christian priest.

"I believe ... "

"Yes?"

"I believe it will be easier for me to talk if you remove your dagger from beneath my chin. Put it up and I will tell you," he said patronisingly.

Wybert's eyes blazed at the insolence and his rage increased as he was tempted to make one final upward thrust of his knife, but common sense told him that he needed this man alive, so he thrust the blade back into his belt.

"Well?"

Putnam rubbed the underside of his chin where the dagger had cut.

"From what I understand, they took a boat and I imagine they are now escaping towards the open sea," he said.

Wybert screamed with frustration and pushed through the crowd. "Get me a boat," he shouted, and strode towards the jetty urging his men before him.

The horses stood back looking bewildered but, after parting to let Wybert and his men through, the crowd followed and watched, as they clambered in an ungainly fashion over the inner boats before commandeering a largish gig moored outside the others. Once Wybert had joined them and taken charge of the steering oar they cast the vessel off and, after a shaky start with oars clashing and Wybert swearing, they disappeared into the foggy blackness.

At one point Wybert thought he glimpsed a vessel ahead of them and he urged the rowers to greater efforts but then the fog clamped down, making him curse his men for their ineptitude. He knew, however that as long as they kept clear of the river edges, his vessel with its six oars would soon run down anything smaller.

The Riverside Hut appeared through the murk and, remembering that just past it the river turned westwards, he edged the vessel over towards the steerboard side. He groaned as the fog became ridiculously thick. He thought he heard the creak of a thole pin. He cursed the rowers again.

"Pull," he shouted, urging them to put in more effort but, with a crash, they suddenly hit the bank. Wybert fell face forwards into the bottom of the boat while several of the rowers somersaulted backwards and two men had their faces smashed by the oars as the blades were forced into the mud by the forward motion of the boat, which then swung round and swirled away out of control in the grip of the current while its occupants regained their composure as best they could. It took a while for them to regain lost ground but just as they had done so the fog suddenly lifted, allowing Wybert to make out the edges of the river ... but there was no sign of the other boat.

Reasoning that it must have got further ahead during the confrontation with the river bank, he steered seawards again and urged his men ever faster. Tired as they were, they did not dare to show reluctance or weakness and they soon found open water – but they were on their own.

With another scream of frustration Wybert aimed a kick at the leg of the nearest rower. He could not see how they could have got so far ahead. He considered going further out to sea in case they had rounded the headland but he was getting tired too and, seeing no alternative, he turned the boat around and headed back to Bradbryc.

The following day the light southerly wind had veered to the southwest and the fog had vanished. They commandeered the boat again and retraced their passage of the previous night looking for signs of wreckage or of a potential landing place that the fugitives could have used for their escape. There were a couple of creeks where a craft could have been hidden and, while Wybert stayed aboard keeping his feet dry, he had his men searching for places where a skiff could have been pulled up and hidden. They looked all day without success and he reluctantly came to the conclusion that they must have made the open sea after all, so once again he turned back towards Bradbryc.

As he reached the division of the rivers however, something told him to take the right fork this time and they soon came upon the abandoned skiff bumping its way upstream, pushed by the incoming tide. He cursed himself for failing to come this way earlier and the fact that it was now too late to start a search since the sun was getting close to the horizon. They would have to leave it until the morrow. He called on the rowers to turn the gig and they fought the tide back to the river junction before running up to Bradbryc again.

The following morning he and his men were up at first light and were soon riding their horses to Maenwud. He observed silently that he felt more at home on a horse than he did in a boat. He had hardly slept at all that night but when he had managed to drop off, his sleep was broken by dreams of a dwarf mocking him with laughter and a priest raising his hand as if to bless him but, instead of a blessing, a lightning bolt shot from the priest's fingers and seared into the calf of his right leg. He jumped and let out a scream, thrusting his leg forwards but soon realised that his pain was in fact due to cramp. He hated these people and wanted them dead but at the same time he was reluctantly becoming in awe of their God, who seemed to be very effective against *him* whilst being protective towards *them*.

They rode along Maenwud's north coast until they found the place where they'd seen the skiff - although now there was no sign of it.

Wybert sent two of his men towards the southwest and two to the south while he and two others headed southeast - all of them combing through the peninsula checking each farm building and habitation. Although Wybert soon found the barn in which his prey had slept he remained unaware of its significance, since they had left no evidence of their stay. By the time Wybert reached Fillercha they had drawn a complete blank. Nobody seemed to have seen or heard of the escapees.

Wybert opened the door of one of the quayside huts. "Anyone in?"

A middle-aged woman rose from a stool looking frightened.

"I'm looking for three fugitives – a priest, a dwarf and a boy. Have you seen them?"

"No sire."

"Where's yer man?"

"He's at sea sire. He's moving our goats."

Wybert grunted, apparently satisfied and made to leave. In fact he had closed the door behind him when he had second thoughts and opened it again.

"When did he go?"

She had just sat down but jumped back up again.

"Yesterday sire."

"Was he alone?"

"No sire ... "

His eyes opened triumphantly.

" ... he had forty goats with him."

Wybert's nerves were at breaking point. He leapt at her and smashed his arm across her face, knocking her to the floor. She put her arm up protectively and stared into his eyes whimpering.

"Did he have any *other* passengers?" growled Wybert.

"No ... well I ... "

"What?" he said raising his arm again.

She flinched.

"Well, I never saw anyone else but he came back and collected more food so perhaps he did take someone."

"Hah! I knew it. That's where they've gone. When'll he be back?"

"I don't know sire – it depends on the tide and the weather. Maybe a week or so."

"Where's he taken them?"

"He never told me – somewhere to the east."

"Get up."

She struggled up from the floor and smoothed her apron down.

"Well mistress, you're got yourselves some guests for a few days. We'll be staying here until your husband returns," and then, in a sickly-sweet voice, "I *do* hope you won't mind sharing your food with us."

—o—

It was three days later in the early afternoon that the goatman arrived back at Fillercha. He was just climbing onto the quayside when his nose drew level with the boots of Wybert. The boots moved back a pace. Wybert scowled at him but said nothing.

"Sire?" said the goatman.

Wybert grabbed the material of the left shoulder of his tunic and, hauling him upwards, bundled him quickly and roughly towards the hut where he opened the door and threw him onto the floor. As he clambered to his knees he saw the six other men and his wife standing in a semi-circle in front of him. Wybert came round to his side.

"Where've you been?"

"To the east – to Haninge sire."

"You took some passengers with you I believe?"

"Yes sire, two men and a boy."

"One of the men was a priest and the other a dwarf?"

"A monk, yes and the other was short but I wouldn't call him a dwarf."

Wybert aimed a kick at his thigh. It found its mark and he gasped with pain.

"If I call him a dwarf then *you'll* call him a dwarf too. What did you do with them?"

"I left them there. The weather turned bad and I think they decided to stay in the village for a while."

Wybert said nothing but turned his back on him and paced to and fro . . . and to and fro . . . before returning to the recumbent figure who had dared not move.

He kicked him again saying "Right – on yer feet – you're taking us to Haninge."

"What? *Now*?" said the goatman.

"Is that a problem?"

"Err – no sire."

"Well come on then – get on with it" and he grasped the shoulder of his tunic again and thrust him back out of the door.

The men followed silently. They piled into the boat and pushed off. Wybert sat in the bows. The men found resting places where they could as the goatman pushed his craft away from the quayside again. It was near bottom of the tide and his steering oar kept touching the ground. If they had left it a short while longer the boat would have been stuck in the harbour until the new tide, but unknown to him Wybert had luck this time - the water gradually deepened and as they approached the harbour mouth the goatman hoisted the sail to the northerly wind.

They entered the Adur estuary as the sun was going down but, just after they had made their entrance, the northerly wind increased to the point that the goatman had no chance of sculling against it. The boat veered sideways across the bay and they were lucky to be able to pull alongside a small jetty. Wybert was furious but his men tumbled onto the shore, pleased that they could at last stretch their legs and feel firm ground again.

A shepherd passed, using the last of the daylight to drive unwilling sheep into the strong wind towards new pasture.

"Oi!" called one of the men. "You seen any sign of a priest, a dwarf and a boy here?"

The shepherd said something but his words were lost to the wind and he put his head down again and pressed on after his woolly flock.

Wybert's obsession with killing Botolph and Luka gave way to his need for some ale to ease his parched lips. He realised that he was hungry too and that killing Christians would be easier and more enjoyable on a full stomach.

With the wind gusting at their backs they walked down a muddy path grooved by cart tracks filled with sheep's droppings. Before them was a large cluster of huts at the water's edge. In the distance a woman came out of one of the nearest huts, her dress blowing against her legs, making it difficult for her to move without it tripping her. She was carrying a large wooden bucket, which she took to a nearby well and wound the handle, keeping her back to the wind and the approaching men. By the time they reached her she had just wound the full well-bucket to the top and placed the locking line on it. She started to ladle the water out into her own bucket when she was startled by Wybert's, "Ale! Where can we get ale and some food?"

Recovering her senses, she pointed to a hut sporting a leafy branch tied to its roof and lying at a crazy angle. When they arrived Wybert pulled the door open against the wind and strode inside. The last to enter let the door close with a bang.

The place was not dissimilar to Meg's except that it was a dull-looking scraggly-bearded man with a greasy apron who came to serve them.

"Seven ales and some food," said Wybert. "What've yer got?"

"I've got some eels 'n' some bread," said the man.

"What about pies? Ain't yer got no pies?"

"No," he said "I won't be makin' them 'til tomorrow."

"Can't you make 'em now?"

"I've got no mutton – but I can make you some *eel* pies if yer like."

"Curse you and yer miserable fare," said Wybert. "If I'm going to 'ave to eat eels I'd prefer to *see* what I'm eatin' rather than 'aving it bound up in a pie. Bring us what you've got then and be quick about it. We'll have the ale first."

Wybert maintained it was the worst meal he had ever eaten and they left without paying either for it or for the ale – of which they had drunk a fair amount. They left the hut with full bellies though. As they stood outside the gale still raged around them.

"There's no point in going back to that cursed goatboat," said Wybert.

"What?" called one of his men. "I can't hear you in this wind."

Wybert looked up at the sky and watched the clouds scudding past the full moon, which was high in the south.

"Let's go back inside where we can talk," he said.

The Aleman thought they might have come back to pay but his optimism died as it was born. The men gathered in a circle around their leader.

"It's a rotten windy night," said Wybert "but at least it's not raining and we've got a full moon. The idea of rousting them out of their beds and killing them in its light rather appeals to me, so I want to leave *now*. If we can't take a boat we'll have to take some horses."

He looked across at the man in the corner but decided it would be a waste of his breath asking *him* for horses.

"Come on," he said, pushing the door open again.

It took them very little time to find a paddock where a dozen short stocky horses were huddling for protection under some trees. At the edge of the field was a small hut in which they found their harnesses and with a little coaxing seven of the horses were soon mounted and passing through the gate which, true to his nature, Wybert left open.

As fast as they could, they picked their way along

the river bank until they reached Haninge. Here they found plenty of huts, but which was the one that held the priest and his friends? They dismounted and tethered the horses while they walked around the apparently-empty village. One hut was slightly larger than the rest and, as they walked past it, there came the bleat of a tethered goat.

"That'll be it," said Wybert, his evil senses rarely failing him. They tried the door. It was locked. They hammered on it and shouted

"Open up. Come on. We know you've got the priest."

Wybert grinned as he imagined the consternation inside and one of the men continued to hammer at the door with the pommel of his sword while Wybert and the others went round the sides to see if they could raise the shutters and enter that way.

"Alright, alright I'm coming," came a voice from within and noises came of the door being unbarred and opened.

"What're you doing barring your doors?" said Wybert as he walked in. "Is it because you've got guests you don't want others to see?"

"What d'yer mean?" answered Farmer Grizzle.

"You know very well what I mean," said Wybert pacing forwards with a sour look on his face. He stood over the man.

"Where's the priest?"

"There's no priest here." Wybert struck him hard and he fell to the ground.

Wybert drew his sword.

"I'll ask you once more before I kill you," he said. "Now where is he?"

"He's gone," wailed the old man. "He's gone. They've all gone. They left hours ago."

Wybert looked around the hut. It was too small to contain any other people. Mistress Grizzle was sitting up on her pallet in the corner looking anxious and frightened.

"Where did they sleep?" he asked the farmer.

"In the hut next door."

"Show me."

He let the man get up and lead them out. The farmer pulled open the door of an adjacent hut and they went inside. By this time one of the men was carrying a burning brand, which he had taken from the farmer's hut and lit at the hearth. This now illuminated the smaller hut and they could see signs of the trio's former habitation.

Wybert felt the straw. It was cold.

"Where've they gone?"

"I don't know. East I think."

"On foot or on horseback?"

"No. On foot."

"How long ago?"

"Several hours – they left just after sunset."

Wybert was puzzled.

"Why did they leave?"

"We ... we had word that some strangers had arrived at the estuary and they felt they were in danger."

"They were right. Come on men, mount up, they won't have got far. We'll easily catch them."

--o--

They galloped over the bridge and along a country road that at first led to the east but after only a short distance it divided. The leading horseman stopped and circled.

"Which way now?"

Wybert cursed. Had their quarry continued east or had they gone north? He bit on his knuckle in frustration.

Would this confounded wind never drop? It stopped him thinking clearly. He looked up at the moon.

"East," he decided at last. "They'll have gone east. This way," and he took the lead, eager to reach his goal and finish the job.

But there was no sign of them. A couple of hours later, having made no contact with a single human, they trotted through a wood, the other side of which was a large river. By then the moon was low in the sky and it made the riverside dwellings cast eerie shadows. Wybert looked down at two ferryboats straining at their moorings as the wind whipped down the river valley. 'I hate the wind,' he thought. 'Had they already crossed the river? Should we rouse the ferryman from his bed or should we wait for morning?' Never one to show consideration he decided on the former and hammered on the likeliest door. Shouting came immediately from within and the door was opened by a burly giant in a nightshirt.

"What in Woden's name do you want at this time of the morning?" he roared.

Wybert put aside thoughts of intimidation and decided that placation would be a better move.

"I'm sorry to disturb you," he said.

"I should think so too."

"We're looking for a priest, a dwarf and a boy."

"Are you now?" the ferry man glowered down. "'N' what's that got to do with me?"

"Have you seen them?"

"No, in Frige's name, I haven't," with which he stepped back and slammed the door behind him.

Wybert felt that, sparse as it was, this evidence was fairly conclusive. If the three were here, he reasoned, they would also have arrived during darkness and were perhaps waiting for dawn when they would take the first ferry. In which case, his thoughts continued, they would have had to find somewhere to sleep. His encounter with the ferryman had unnerved him slightly and he did not relish working his way around the village waking up the other inhabitants in case they were all as big and bad-tempered as him. He looked towards the huts and saw that behind them the land rose up to the edge of a wood where there was a natural wall that would offer them some protection from the ravages of the wretched wind. It would also give them a clear view of the village.

"Come on." They found a suitable place and tethered the horses. Wybert lay down to sleep, telling his men to keep watch in pairs and wake him as soon they saw the fugitives. He slept soundly, confident that the morrow would bring him satisfaction.

--o—

Luka tried to sleep but could not. He was worried. The enemy were too close. He was pleased to hear Botolph snoring gently and Ash had not stirred since he had lain him down. Luka turned on his side and tried again. He also worried that they might sleep too long. Eventually he fell into a doze but suddenly woke again, in what seemed to him, only a short while later. He rolled into a sitting position and then rose and went over to the door, opened it and went outside. He sniffed the air - as he always did - and once again he wondered why he did so but concluded that the smells might tell him something useful one day - although today was not that day.

He looked along the track towards the wood into which the riders had disappeared but all was quiet and the wind had eased. There was no sign of any dawn-lightening in the eastern sky. He looked to the west where the big moon was close to the horizon and reckoned that dawn was not far away. He went back into the barn and shook Botolph - who woke immediately.

"Time to go, Father."

Botolph rose without a word and then fell back onto his knees to pray. Luka shook Ash gently. He was not so easy to rouse. He shook him again and eventually got a, "Wha'sup Pa?"

"Time to go son. Up you get."

The lad complied without more ado.

"Here boy. Take a little mead to freshen you up. Are ye ready to eat now?"

"No Pa, I'm not awake yet. Can we stop in an hour or so?"

"Course we can lad," he said while secretly thinking to himself 'as long as we're not being run down by seven horsemen at the time.'

They left the barn as they found it, leaving nothing to reveal their presence, and walked up the hill to the north. It was getting darker as the moon set. They went over the hill and on to an ever-rising valley path. They each stumbled from time to time on the uneven ground. Suddenly there was a rustling on their left. Luka unsheathed his seax while Botolph instinctively went back to protect Ash. The rustling stopped. Luka motioned the other two to keep moving forwards while he stood looking in the direction of the last noise. He started to walk backwards following the others. All was quiet except for a nightjar calling in the distance. Luka re-sheathed his seax and ran to catch up.

"Just a hog I guess," he said in an attempt to reassure them . . . and hoping that he was right. At the end of the valley there was a steep climb that they started just as the sky began to lighten in the east.

"I'm ready to eat now Pa," said Ash.

"Yes, so am I," admitted Botolph.

They could see well enough to settle themselves on the grassy slope and, as they tucked into Mistress Grizzle's produce, the sun started to rise.

"Pa – there's a river over there," said Ash excitedly.

"Yes, I was just about to say the same thing myself. It gets wider down that way. It looks like there's some buildings on the other side of that wood but it's too far away to make much out."

"There's probably a ferry where we could cross Pa."

"Yes, there probably is, but that must've been where Wybert was heading. The river'll probably be narrower further up, so we'll cross there."

They finished eating and started their climb again and soon reached the summit, where they had a good clear view all around.

"It's all lakes and marsh," said Botolph feeling some despair.

"There's no way we can cross there," said Luka. "We could keep going north but it'll be difficult to work our way through the bogs, and if Wybert and his horsemen come up on to a hill like this they will be able to see us from miles away and we'd be trapped. I think that even taking into account that Wybert was going that way, our only choice *is* to go down to yonder village and hope we can get across there. What d'ye think Father?"

"It sounds like the best choice," agreed Botolph "but what about Wybert?"

They wandered along the ridge for a while and followed it as it dropped down into a wood. The path led between oak trees and it was clear that once upon a time there had been many more, but a lot had been cut down. This had allowed masses of vegetation to grow on the woodland floor. They were wading through this with Ash in the lead when the boy saw a movement to his left. He immediately dropped to his knees and pointed, putting his other finger to his lips. His father and Botolph followed his cue and both ducked down too and moved slowly forwards until they could see what he was pointing at.

"What do you think?" Botolph asked Luka.

"I don't know," he replied. "It could just be woodmen but I'm not sure it would be safe for us to go any closer to find out. They're sitting just under a ledge. I think if we go back and bear off to the right we might be able to get on top of that ledge and be able to hear what they're saying without them seeing us. That'll tell us whether they're woodmen or our villains."

They crept away retracing their steps and crossed a gully that led them up to the ledge from where they could hear the murmur of voices.

"You two stay here," Luka whispered, "I'll see if I can get closer."

He picked his way carefully through the undergrowth, watching where he put his feet and endeavouring not to step on anything that might create a noise. He sidled slowly onto the ledge until he could hear them quite clearly. He found he was right at the edge of the wood and had a clear and unimpeded view of the village below, which was now slowly coming to life.

"We're wasting our time sire," came a voice. "They must've taken the northern road just after the bridge."

"May the gods damn and curse them," said a voice that was unmistakably Wybert's. "If they were here and going to cross they'd have taken the ferry by now. We'd better get back to the northern road or they'll be halfway to Lundwic by the time we catch up with them. Mount up – quickly now."

Luka stayed stock still at first but then dropped to

the ground as the first of the horses' heads appeared from under the ledge. He stayed flat as he heard them galloping down the hill, whereupon he raised his head cautiously. He saw the seven riders go down into the village and along the quayside and he guessed they would be carefully scrutinising the people. They turned to their right and headed west along the road that would lead them back through the woods and past the barn to Haninge. Luka made his way back to the others.

"It was certainly them," he said, "and they're now heading back to Haninge - so the quicker we can get across the river the better. We'll be a lot safer on the other side."

They went back to the main path and half ran and half walked through the woods onto the lower road. They approached the village from the opposite direction that their pursuers had just taken.

The village, which they discovered was called Lewys, was a kaleidoscope of colour and activity. There were stalls set out on the quayside selling herbs ... and dyes ... and fish ... and meat and ... cheese ... and bread. A couple of half-grown piglets were running around and making a nuisance of themselves, tripping people up and snuffling mischievously into anything that took their fancy. A big man with rough brown hair and a brewer's belly was sitting on a bench by the water's edge talking to a woman who had come over from the other side of the river to buy provisions. On her arm she had an old wicker basket that had seen better days. In it were some oysters and a large loaf.

"When you goin' across then?" she was saying.

"When I've got enough passengers. 'Tain't worth my while jus' for one."

"Well I can't wait all day. It's comin' up to noon now."

"Well that's as mebbe but ... "

Botolph interrupted him.

"We'd like to cross when you're ready to go."

He looked up at the three of them and recognition swept across his face.

"Someone's been 'ere lookin' for ye three. Got me up in the middle of the night 'e did."

"Ah," said Luka non-committally. "Well we're here now and, if it's all the same to you, we'd like to cross."

"I don't know that it *is* all the same to me. 'Ave yer got money?"

Luka dug into his sack and produced a small round piece of copper and offered it to him saying, "That's more'n enough to take us all there and back – including the lady."

"Where d'ye get that then?" said the man. "Oi b'aint seen one of them before."

"Never you mind – I got it and now it's yours so let's get on with it."

"Yeah – that'll do nicely – come on then," and he rose to his feet and clambered down a rickety ladder and dropped into the boat that was floating beneath. The woman went next and then Luka and Ash and finally Botolph. The ferryman untied the lines, leaving them dangling, and applied himself to the oars.

"So what d'ye want me t' say t'yer frien' if he comes lookin' fer you again in t' middle o' t' night? Would ye rather I said I 'adn't seen ye?"

It was only a narrow stretch of water and they were almost there.

Luka looked him in the eye. "You'll say what you've a mind to say anyway I expect ... but yes – if you can forget ye've ever seen us we'd be obliged," and one after the other they climbed the steps onto the dry land.

"Thank'ee fer my passage," said the lady. "I was

expectin' to 'ave to pay 'im an oyster fer that but it's one extra fer me husban' now. Now ye'll come and sup wi' us afore ye journey on."

She was not a lady to be refused even if they had wanted to, and they followed her to a dwelling on the corner where she prepared food and drink.

"I work as a spinster," she said as they tucked into the food. "See 'ere young thane, - this is my spinner. The farmers bring me the wool 'n' I card it t' remove the tangles and then I spin it into balls o' wool."

Ash tried to look interested but the art of spinning was nothing new to him. He humoured her nevertheless and she seemed to have taken to him. Luka was getting edgy. They needed to move on in case Wybert came back. Even if the ferryman did not give them away, there were plenty of others who had seen them, so they needed to press on.

They escaped as soon as they could, having replenished their supplies of food and mead. They followed the river north for a while before striking out eastwards again. Most of it was easy walking although, whereas some grassy parts were so springy that they fairly bounced along, there were others that looked similar but were so boggy that they sucked at their feet and they had to work twice as hard to get through it. Everywhere was lush green and fertile. A skylark, so high above that they had difficulty making him out, kept up his constant song as they marched. Soon they found themselves skirting a vast lake and Luka pointed out some willow traps that had been laid. Ash wanted to go closer but Luka demurred saying that they needed to keep moving fast. They kept a close eye behind them and, although they saw other travellers on the horizon from time to time, nothing caused them to worry until a lone horseman appeared - travelling fast.

There was nowhere for them to hide or run to, so bowing to the inevitable they stood aside and turned to face the oncoming peril. As he approached Luka tensed and put his hand ready on his seax.   They each focussed on the rider's bouncing face, trying to see if there was anything about him they recognised but to their relief there was nothing and he passed them by swiftly with barely a glance.

Others too passed in the opposite direction.   They shared greetings but generally managed to avoid having to stop. The whole area was desolate with only the odd shed here and there and no sign of other habitations.

Ahead of them some wispy smoke plumes were rising. As they came closer they realised that they were at the edge of a saltmarsh. An ox-cart was standing to one side while four men busied themselves in drawing salt-laden, half-evapourated water from the shallow reservoirs. As they approached they saw that the source of the smoke was a series of peat fires atop which wide clay trays containing brine were slowly turning the concentrate into salt cakes.

They made their way up an escarpment and rested on the top where they had good views all around. To their right they could see the path back to Lewys; ahead of them was the sea and to their left was a river valley.

"Why don't we rest a while here and have some food," said Botolph.

"Why – ye getting' tired Father?"

"No, but I was thinking of legs that are shorter than ours."

"Ooh ah," said Luka.

"I'm fine," said Ash, suddenly realising that they were talking about him, "but I'm hungry too."

"Of course you are," said Botolph "you're your

father's son."

They laughed.

"We seem to have given Wybert the slip," he continued, "so let's eat and drink while we can."

Luka screwed his face up but nevertheless set about liberating the food from his sack. He was uneasy about stopping but realised they had to keep their bodies fed, so he supposed that here was as good a place as any. He would not let them tarry long however and they soon resumed their walking, travelling along the ridge and then down into the valley where they forded a stream before rising again onto higher ground.

By this time the sun was low in the sky and finding somewhere to sleep became a priority. Botolph regretted the absence of churches and monasteries which, in Francia, would always provide accommodation for the traveller. He thought back to Haninge. If only he could have built a church there it would have fulfilled that very function. He comforted himself with the thought of their successful foundation at Bradbryc and wondered how Putnam would use the building. It was too much to hope that his church would have seen any sacraments but he hoped that travelling Christians might be worshipping there. Or had Putnam turned it into a byre? Worse could happen – and nearly did . . . and might yet.

"What do you think then Luka?"

"Huh?"

"About laying up for the night. Is it going to be the forest floor or do you think there might be somewhere more comfortable further on?"

"It doesn't look very hopeful, does it Father? We've hardly seen any buildings all day. I don't know how they manage here. There must be a farm nearby, although there've been no signs of one."

"It's not cold," said Botolph. "We have those leathers that Mistress Grizzle gave us."

"True. How do you feel Ash? Forest floor tonight?"

Ash shrugged.

"We'd better move well off the path then," said Luka and he turned off the track and trampled through the ferns and undergrowth as he headed for the edge of the trees; the others followed in his wake.

The going became easier once they were in the forest, despite there being no trackway made by human or beast. They loped from tree to tree searching for a place where they might stretch out in comfort but God's sentinels were packed so tightly together that for acre after acre there was no such possibility. Botolph began to wonder if they would ever find a suitable clearing. Eventually, deep into the canopy, the Good Lord finally provided and it was with relief that they stamped flat the meagre vegetation and retrieved the leathers from their sacks. Botolph wondered if he would be better lying on it or covering himself with it.

"The ground's quite dry," he muttered to nobody in particular.

They collected wood. They built a fire. They lit the tinder. A tired Ash sank to the ground and stared into the flames, watching the miniature Bog Demons in their fiery palaces until his attention was distracted by Luka calling him to food. They ate, drank, talked, prayed, re-stoked the fire and, by consensus of opinion, lay down on their leathers to sleep.

They passed an uneventful night and woke at dawn. After stamping out what was left of the fire's embers and taking swigs from their water bladders they were soon on a grassy track walking southeast on a high ridge that offered beautiful views of the countryside with the sea beyond.

The ridge maintained its height right up to the coast and, as they stood there, high on the cliff and gazed towards the northeast, Botolph pointed to a headland in the distance saying to Ash:

"That's where we're going. That's Folcanstane ... and between there and here do you see? That's the Marsh of Rumniae?"

The boy nodded.

"Below that's the Camber Lake and running round its edge is a land spur and the port of Gwentchesil. That's where we're going next. Look at the boats – what a lot there are. There. And there. And over there. And out at sea those two look as if they're coming from Gallia, and the three down there are coming up the coast – perhaps from Haninge ..."

He stopped and looked back at Luka "... perhaps from Haninge? - You don't think ... ?"

"Nah," said Luka. "He's no idea we're coming here. Anyway he's not a boatman – he's more used to a horse. Nah – if he follows us it will be by land."

They picked their way down an ever-descending path which for them was easy walking. The poor souls travelling in the opposite direction were having a harder time of it and they frequently came upon clusters pausing for breath and rest.

One such group comprised two elderly women with their husbands and a boy of Ash's age who was possibly the grandson of one of them. He was hopelessly overladen with two sacks that were tied together and slung around his neck. As the travellers came puffing and panting to a standstill, the young lad tossed his twin burdens over his head and both they and he sank to the ground simultaneously. By the time Ash passed the boy's eyes were closed and he seemed to be asleep.

"There was nowt of 'im," said Luka once they were out of earshot. "He was all skin and bone - and his grandparents weren't much better."

Ash glanced behind. The old folk were now sitting on the ground too and they looked a sorry sight. He had little time to ponder further before they came across another rather more colourful couple - she sitting sideways on a donkey and he cheerfully padding along beside her, poling his way up the slope with the aid of a long staff.

"Good day to ye Father," he called with a smile when they were within hailing distance.

"Good day friend," they chorused as both groups came to a standstill.

"Where're ye heading?"

"We're bound for Folcanstane - and you?"

"Ah, we're from Lewys. Been down to Gwentchesil to sell a few bits and buy a few bits. Ye know how it is."

They nodded hesitantly, not knowing how it was at all - but it seemed polite to pretend. He did enough talking for all five of them so they listened attentively until he had covered all his topics - she smiling and nodding benignly through all of them. Once his repertoire was exhausted he raised the point of his staff from its grounding place and, with a "Farewell t'ye then," strode forward as if he had suddenly remembered the many miles they had ahead of them.

A short while later Ash, inevitably in front, turned and, after a few seconds of looking up the slope, pointed behind them. Botolph and Luka turned to see what had caught his attention. The sacks belonging to the scrawny grandson were now stretched across the donkey's withers and the sad group and the happy pair had merged into a half-happy party of seven as they tackled the top of the hill together.

Botolph and Luka turned back and continued their descent. As the path flattened out, the ground changed from a grassy track to a shingle bank of large pebbles, which crunched loudly beneath their feet.

It occurred to Ash that the tuneless scrunching of their feet was like the sound of a marching and the noise accompanied them as they entered the vibrant village of Gwentchesil.

Two small boats had just entered the harbour and now they swung round to approach the quay. The fishing port was a busy, colourful, noisy place. The constant whooshing of the breakers on the outside beach was interspersed with the laughing calls of herring gulls that alternately swooped and soared above a cluster of huts, halls and stores while the quaymaster shouted at the two incoming boats. A fishwife's rasping voice pierced the cacophony.

Ash was pleased to see children of his own age – both boys and girls. Some were playing. One was making a downright nuisance of himself. A baby was sitting on the pebbles and bawling. But other children were responsibly engaged in doing jobs that in other circumstances would have been considered the province of adults.

One such was a little lad who was sitting on a bench with an elderly man – perhaps his grandfather – and they were companionably mending nets while, near another hut, a little girl was busily turning a handle for her mother. Ash decided that he really liked this place.

"Can we go on to the beach?"

"Course ye can – c'mon."

Once at the water's edge Ash picked up a pebble and threw it into the sea.

"What d' you call that?" said Luka. "You could

throw further than that when you were a baby."

Ash laughed and chose another pebble, which he hurled with all his might.

"That's better," called Luka as he bent to pick a pebble for himself.

All three of them threw pebbles until the novelty was overtaken by the desire for food and drink. The beach was steep and climbing back up was a totally different prospect to their skidding descent. As each of their feet gained a hold, the pebbles would slip back time and time again, so that they only made half the progress they would have done on firmer ground.

Ash's head was the first to come level with the top of the beach and he instinctively ducked back again. A group of seven riders were coming down the hill.

--o--

Wybert and his men had ridden at full speed along the Haninge road. He was desperate to catch the fugitives before they gained too much of a lead. At the bridge they wheeled to the right and, with Wybert at the head, took the road northwards, following the river. Wybert could smell blood and his excitement mounted as his senses told him that his quarry was not far away. Frenziedly he spurred his horse and lashed at its rump with his whip. In spite of the abuse it had taken during the past five leagues the creature responded and did all that it could to please him, but suddenly stumbled and fell sideways, throwing him into a cowpat at the side of the road. Cursing and swearing Wybert picked himself up, at the same time grabbing a broken branch. He strode across to the beast which was lying on its side, its upper hind leg stretching and contracting in its death throes. To any other man the poor animal's flared nostrils and frothed mouth would have been grim evidence of its failing heart - but not to Wybert. He kicked its sweating rump and screamed, "Get up you stupid animal."

Raising the cruel branch above his head he thrashed it again and again. The merciful end was not long in coming. The creature's steaming body gave a final terrible shudder and the carcass, its eyes wide open, emptied its life.

Wybert screamed and kicked again. His men sat in a small group on their panting horses. They'd seen him many times in such a temper before and they dreaded what might happen next. He wheeled round. His eyes too were wide open. He too was frothing at the mouth. He too was steaming with sweat. Striding over to a luckless man, he pulled him from his saddle, swung himself up onto the horse and spurred it forwards.

It skittered a little sideways but with little forward motion. He screamed at it and spurred it again – hard. Heaving to catch its breath after four hours of abuse it offered all it had left and started to plod slowly along the path - and there was nothing that Wybert could do to make it move any faster. The rest of the riders rode after him silently, followed by the dismounted man who had had ideas of doubling up with one of the other horsemen, but they were all moving so slowly now that walking seemed as good an option. After a short while Wybert's tantrum left him and his brain began to function properly again. He turned and shouted to the walking man, "Go back and get the harness off the dead horse and bring it with you." It was not this man's lucky day.

There was a fair-sized village not far ahead of them and slowly and painfully the horses picked their way towards it. On the outskirts was a swinery, which Wybert cursed for its foul smell and further on they found a few villagers - although most of them must have been out in the fields.   Some children who were sitting outside one of the huts looked up as they passed by. Wybert glowered down at them – he did not like children. The sight of them brought his mind back to the one child he had come to like less than all others, and whom he would find great pleasure in killing.

Further down the road a plume of smoke was rising from a smithy outside which a teenage boy was holding a horse's head while the blacksmith attended to one of its back hooves.

"Hey, smith," Wybert called down from his horse.

The smith ignored him and continued with his work. One of Wybert's men sniggered and then a couple of the others laughed. Wybert turned and gave them a look so foul that they shut up and paled a little. Wybert was not having a good day. He swung off his horse and went over to the smith and said, "Talk to me man or I'll have the hide off you."

The man stopped what he was doing, put the horse's leg back on the ground and straightened up. With his left hand, for the right was holding his hammer, he took half a dozen nails out of his mouth. He was a muscular character, his top half bare except for the black leather apron that he was wearing. He looked Wybert squarely in the eye and said evenly, "Beg pardon sire but 'tis difficult to talk wi' a mouthful o' nails. Now – what d'ye want?"

Wybert looked squarely back at him, searching his face for a sign of insolence but the man returned his gaze steadily, so Wybert gave him the benefit of the doubt. The last thing he wanted was to make a bad day even worse.

"I'm looking for a horse," he said. "Mine just died under me – it's on the road half a league back – you're welcome to the meat if you wish – but I need a replacement and my men need a change of horses."

"Ah," said the man, looking at the riders and the steaming horses. "It looks as if ye've bin riding 'em hard."

"We're in a hurry," said Wybert. "We're looking for a priest, a dwarf and a boy who might have passed this way. Might you have seen them?"

The smith wasn't too sure that he'd tell Wybert even if he had seen them but he was pleased not to have to lie.

"Nope," he said. "There's nobody of that description bin through."

"Are you sure?" said Wybert, feeling intense irritation. "They *must* have come this way."

"Well if they did they must've crept around the back cos they 'ain't passed 'ere and I've bin 'ere all day."

"No," said Wybert, calculating. "'Twouldn't've been daytime – they'd've gone through a while afore midnight last night."

The smith laughed in his face.

"D'ye think I'd've seen them then? I was tucked up in me pallet like all other law abidin' villagers."

"Well," said Wybert impatiently - beginning to tire of this muscular fool, "did ye hear the dogs bark or any other disturbance which might have made ye think a traveller was passing through?"

"I sleep well. I heard nothing. Now if ye want more horses, go down to the tavern. 'E keeps 'is 'orses out the back."

They found the horses easily enough but saw no reason to disturb the taverner. Wybert opened the gate and they went into the field. There was no sign of any watchers - the village seemed quite deserted. They rode their horses across the field and behind some trees where they could'nt be seen from the tavern. The other horses were curious and neighed a greeting and came over, which made it easy to catch them and transfer the tack. They were still calling occasionally and Wybert looked around the edge of the trees wondering if the taverner might have been alerted, but there was no sign of him. He didn't want to have to tempt providence by riding past the tavern again, so they broke down part of the fence and left without re-entering the village.

They continued to head north but Wybert kept the pace at an easy trot to avoid the possibility of any further dead-horse holdups.

A league and a half later they came to some cross roads where there was another village. Wybert spent some considerable time questioning as many villagers as he could find and even some who were reluctant to be found - and they endured a hammering at their doors until they could stand it no longer and came out. He calculated that if the three had taken this route they would have arrived around midnight and they would surely have sought lodging for the night. Nobody had seen anything though. By the time Wybert had finished his inquisition the sun was close to the horizon and he decided, in view of the aches and pains he was still suffering as a result of his previous night in the forest and his tumble from the horse, that it would be good to find a comfortable billet. So, in spite of his frustrations, he decided they would eat and sleep in the village and hope for a better day on the morrow. It did occur to him that the taverner from Hanfelde might wake up to the fact that his horses had gone and come north seeking revenge, so he left orders for his men to 'sleep with one eye open' and keep their swords unsheathed and handy.

The night passed quietly though. Wybert constantly dreamt about the 'dead village of Hanfelde' with only a blacksmith and a boy to its name, but he shook the dream from his mind on waking. It was not his problem and he was glad of the fresh horses.

They left soon after the sun was up and headed east, enquiring briefly of most of the travellers that they met on the way, but Wybert was beginning to lose hope. The trio seemed to have vanished into thin air. He hated them more with every day. His stomach was acid with the acrimony he felt and his hatred was increasing with every hour that passed. He had lost them and he did not know why.

They turned south at the next crossroads and walked the horses slowly – partly to rest them and partly because they had nowhere to get to in a hurry. Another horseman approached travelling in the opposite direction. Wybert asked the usual question and received the usual answer. They passed and moved on. Then they heard a call from behind and the horseman came trotting back to them.

"Wait a minute. Yes I *have* seen the people you describe. I went to buy some salt cakes yesterday and I passed the three you mentioned on the road."

Wybert felt himself coming alive again. "Where – when?"

"A couple of leagues east along the road from the Lewys ferry," he said. "It would have been just after midday."

"How far are we from the Lewys ferry here?"

"About five leagues I should think."

"Ha! We'll get there before noon then," he muttered - simultaneously digging his heels sharply into his mount's belly and, as one, the riders took off.

The horseman was left gazing at the cloud of dust left behind. He had noted the man's rudeness and lack of thanks. He sat for several minutes thoughtfully watching the point where they had disappeared. He had not taken to Wybert and was beginning to regret passing on that information. He consoled himself with the thought that it was none of his business.

He turned left at the crossroads and only a short while later met an even larger group of horsemen. As they approached he thought to himself how uncommonly busy the paths were today. History repeated itself as the leader hailed him and asked if he had come across a pack of seven horsemen.

The rider looked at the leader in astonishment.

"Well 'ave ye or 'aven't ye?"

"Well yes I 'ave – but everyone's chasing each other today. If ye go down to the crossroads and turn right - I met 'em 'bout 'alf a league down that way. They took orf like river rats 'n' they're 'eading fer the Lewys ferry 'n' lookin' fer a monk, a dwarf and a boy."

"I don' care 'oo they're lookin' for," said the Hanfelde Taverner, "they've got *my* horses," and they left at a gallop.

--o--

Wybert's party dropped into an easy canter. After a long straight run the track turned to the east and then came to a crossing where they pulled to a stop. Wybert's horse skittered as his rider peered down each path in the forlorn hope of seeing someone from whom he could ask directions. In the absence of this he decided to ride towards the sun, on the basis that by doing this they would cross and recognise their previous tracks. There was no time to waste so he spurred his horse down the valley, closely followed by his men. Wybert's brain and thoughts were so aflame that there was a danger of his riding another horse to its death, but this animal was stubborn and when it tired after a long canter it refused to go faster than a spirited trot, in spite of the constant digging of his heels.   A frustrating half an hour later they found the Lewys road and Wybert, reanimated, gave a shout of triumph as he dragged the horse's head to the east and forced the unwilling beast into another gallop. This ended all too soon. Wybert kicked and shouted at the mare he was riding but all to no avail. To add insult to his fury one of his men overtook him. He shouted an oath and called the rider back with the threat of dire consequences if he was slow about it.

"Get off."

To the accompaniment of a plethora of curses, he commandeered the faster horse and galloped into the distance, leaving his men trailing behind him

--o--

"Seven horsemen?" said Luka putting his own head above the shingle bank, "Yes, so there are."

He watched carefully as they came nearer. It didn't *look* like Wybert in the lead but he couldn't be certain. They turned off behind some huts and were lost to view.

"What do you reckon?" asked Botolph.

"I don't know. It's the right number but I don't *think* it's them. You two stay here and I'll go and look."

He crunched his way quickly up to the top of the shingle bank and ran towards the huts, cursing the loudness of the noise made by his every step. Once he was behind the first building he could move more slowly. He went from hut to hut – stealthily at first but then, when he started to encounter more and more people, adopted a more nonchalant pose. The closer that he came to the quayside the more people there were and with the numbers came a babble of voices topped by the calls of the mercers. He spotted the horsemen. They had just dismounted and were tying their horses to a long horizontal pole that had been placed there for that very purpose. People thronged around them and their faces were hidden.

He worked his way into the crowd and threaded his way through them in order to try to get a better view. This was one of those times when he most despised his size. He was nicely hidden all the time that he was immersed in the crowd but then he had difficulty in seeing past them and if they melted away he would be easily identified.

He caught a glimpse and his heart dropped as he realised that the men were searching for something – he could see their heads turning left and right and noted that they were questioning people as they went.

Suddenly, one of those being questioned pointed straight at him.

--o—

The Hanfelde Taverner and his men were hot on Wybert's trail but knew they had to pace themselves. They also knew that Wybert would be throwing caution to the wind as he drove his men forwards. The blacksmith and his boy were amongst the party. They and a group of Hanfelde villagers had managed to recover the carcass of Wybert's dead horse and had been appalled by the sight of the cruelty that its rump had sustained at the end of Wybert's boot and whip. The Taverner guessed that his seven stolen horses would fare no better and he was keen to retrieve them before they succumbed to the same fate. He therefore had to temper haste with prudence.

When they reached the crossing they automatically took the direct eastern route towards Lewys. It did not occur to them that Wybert might have gone south. They pressed on as fast as they dared and finally trotted down the hill and through the forest into Lewys, momentarily shattering the peace of the village and scattering the crowds surrounding the quayside.   Many of them were known to the Lewys locals.

"What's up?" came a shout.

"I'm looking fer me 'orses," said the Taverner. "Seven of 'em were stolen yesterday a'ternoon.   Evil looking fellow in a black 'at."

"Nah, - seen nuthin' 'ere today."

The Taverner looked puzzled.

"Where've they got to then?" he said.

At that point there came a commotion from the opposite end of the village as seven horses arrived at a gallop and in a cloud of dust.   They were led by a man wearing a black hat.

--o--

Luka froze and waited until a scruffy boy pulling an even scruffier wooden fish-barrow passed between him and the searchers. He furtively sidled close to the lad and kept up with him so that the two of them moved as one across and out of the searchers' view.   The man was still pointing towards the docks but it had clearly not been Luka that he was identifying, since he was now at right angles to the searchers' line of gaze.   The boy and the barrow moved on in one direction and then the searchers, leaving their horses, moved in the opposite direction across towards the docks.   Once they spread out Luka could see clearly that they were not Wybert's group.   For the moment they were safe.

He pushed his way back through the crowd and brought the good news to the waiters on the beach.

"Lord knows if he's still following us," Botolph said to Luka, "but I think the sooner we can get away from here the better.   For one thing we'll then be in Cantium which, being good Christian countryside will not suit Wybert too well and for another he'll be getting further away from his home and might be inclined to give up the chase."

"Hmm," said Luka. "You may be right, but Wybert's a demon with another demon inside him. He's one of those people who, once they've got a bee in their bonnet, won't let go. He'd cut off his nose to spite his face if he had a mind to."

Ash laughed. "You've got some funny sayings today Pa."

Luka looked at him fondly. "Yes - well mebbe I have but I'll tell you one thing for free. It came as a great relief to me to discover that those horsemen were not that maniac Wybert's lot. I agree with you Father. The sooner we get away from here the better."

They made their way to the quayside where several boats were moored. The nearest of them was unloading baskets of fish that the scruffy boy was loading on to his scruffy wheelbarrow. Ahead of the fish-boat lay a small wide vessel with a single mast and three sets of oars. Sitting in the stern was a grey-haired woman with two young girls. A man was standing in the bows ready to take a mooring rope, which at that moment was being untied by another man on the quayside. A third man was similarly loosening the stern line. Botolph approached him.

"We need to get to Folcanstane," he said. "Are you going any where near there?"

"Nay," said the man, "we're bound up the *inside* channel. Once we've crossed the Camber our first stop'll be Bren Sete."

"Ah, that'll do nicely," said Botolph. "Can you take us?"

"Well we're leaving now so ye'd best hop aboard while ye can."

They needed no further bidding and quickly dropped down the wooden quayside steps and onto the boat. The man in the bows motioned them to seats and they settled down on a thwart.

"Where's Bren Sete?" asked Luka.

"Well – surely you remember – it's on the Marsh Wall down a bit from Apuldre."

"Is it? I don't think I've ever been there."

"No I've not been there either, but it's not far from Apuldre and quite close to the place where we rescued Farmer Mosel."

"Hah," said Luka but then his attention was taken as the three men took their place on the rowing thwarts and the boat was pushed away from the quayside.

They pulled out into mid-stream, whereupon the current picked them up and gave them an easy row. On their left side they passed a village nestling on top of a cliff. Below it was a jetty around which a cluster of craft was moored. On the opposite side of the boat there was nothing but a mass of marshland edged by tall rushes. Ahead the river divided and Ash wondered which of the three routes they would take.

"Look," said Botolph pointing, "There's Ox Island and that's where we boarded the ferry for Niwendenne."

"So it is," said Luka. "The boat was full of sheep and goats and the boatman was such a misery that it made you want to pray for him."

"The very one," laughed Botolph. "I wonder how the Mosels are. We really ought to go and see them."

"Mosel'll be alright so long as he's not fallen into any more dykes.[1]"

The boat was by now turning its stern to Ox Island

---

[1] Volume I of the Botolph Trilogy. Chapter 28.

and they focussed their attention on an approaching jetty. Two men, some women and an over-excited boy and girl were standing on the quay watching as they pulled alongside. The grey-haired woman passenger ushered her two girls towards the wet, weedy ladder that they happily clambered up and she followed closely behind. Ash went next followed by Luka and Botolph. At the top of the steps they had to push through a crowd of would-be passengers eager to get aboard.

As Botolph's foot left the ladder the excited boy and girl fought to be first on board. The boy won but as soon as they were on the boat the girl punched him hard and screamed in his face. Botolph, Luka and Ash watched as the rest of the women followed each other down to the boat. One of them cuffed the ears of both children, which set them to yelling even louder.

The sound of their cries was still ringing in Luka's ears as they made their way across the wooden planking and on to the grassy shore.

CHAPTER 8
Cantium

"If this is Christian Cantium," he said, "the children are a lot noisier and less well behaved than those of the heathens of Bradbryc."

The grey-haired woman was just ahead of them and, hearing this exchange, she turned back towards them.

"I 'ope ye're not referring to my granddaughters," she said.

"Never on your life dear lady," said Botolph "and I'm sorry that you should think so. They seem to be charming youngsters."

"Ay, they're that to be sure. Where are ye three bound to?"

"We're making for Folcanstane, - how about you?"

"We live 'ere," she replied. "I 'eard ye talking about Farmer Mosel on the boat. Ye've bin 'ere afore then?"

"Oh yes," said Botolph, "but quite a few years ago. Do you know the Mosels?"

"Aw bless ye yes. They're our closest neighbouring farmers."

Botolph was delighted. "How are they?"

Her face clouded. "The mistress is alright but poor Farmer Mosel has never recovered from the time a few years back when his cart went off the road in a storm and he nearly drowned in a dyke. He only lived because he was saved by God's good fortune when there appeared a couple of monks who braved the storm to rescue him."

There was a very brief silence during which Botolph and Luka caught each other's eyes. Botolph quickly picked up the conversation again.

"Oh dear I'm sorry to hear Farmer Mosel's not well. We must try to get along to see him."

"So ye say ye're going to Folcanstane?"

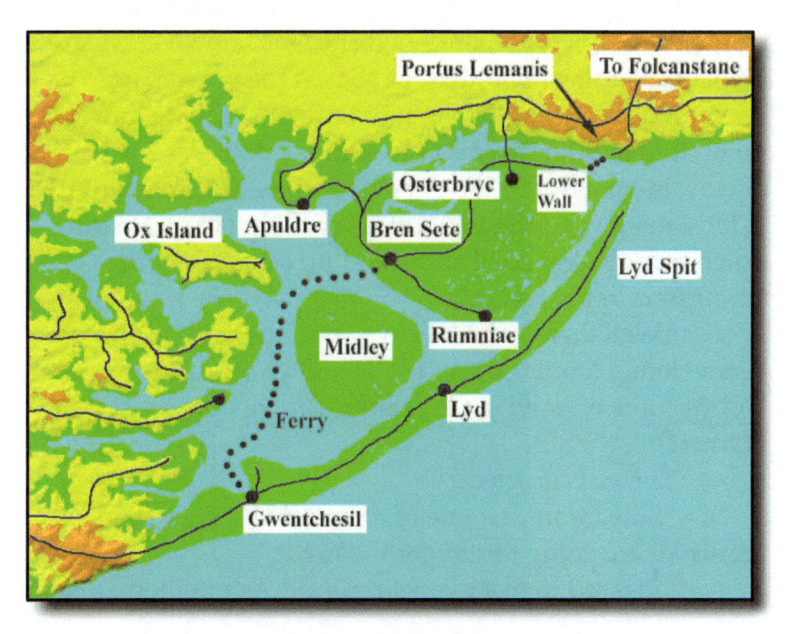

Fig. 6. Gwentchesil to Folcanstane.

They nodded.

"That's another seven leagues, - ye'll never get there by nightfall. Would ye care to stay wi' us fer the night?"

Botolph looked across at Ash who was chatting animatedly with the grandmother's charges.

"That would be very kind," said Botolph, sure in his mind that there would be no objections from his companions, but all the same he looked down at Luka who gave a brief nod with a much longer broad grin. Botolph knew exactly what was passing through his friend's mind; a good meal was one part of it and freshly baked bread was another.

With the little girls and Ash skipping on ahead, they made their way along the path into the village, the grey-haired lady greeting people as they went – and from their responses Botolph gathered that she was known as Mistress Hild. A couple of young dogs sensed the youngsters' excitement and tried to join in with their skipping, but soon grew tired of it and went off to sniff at an interesting clump of wayside grass. By the open door of one of the huts an elderly man was sitting on a stool shelling peas. He put down the wooden bowl and stood up as the skipping youngsters approached.

"Well then, what 'ave we 'ere?" he said benevolently looking at Ash. "I send ye off to Gwentchesil and ye come back wi' a playmate. Did ye buy 'im at the market?"

The girls giggled.

"Silly Gramps," one of them said. "They're our guests 'n' are going to stay fer the night."

"Pleased to meet you sire," said Ash politely.

"'N' I'm very pleased to meet you young man."

The rest of the party caught up and his wife introduced Botolph and Luka, who had given her their names as they walked.

"Well, come in, come in," said Gramps as he turned and picked up his stool with one hand and his bowl of peas with the other. The girls quickly took both items from him and led them into the hut.

--o--

Following a generous meal they all slept well that night and started the next day with a good breakfast. Luka had discovered that the eldest girl's name was Edith and the younger was Winifred. It seemed that they were being brought up by their grandparents because their mother and father had died in the plague.

"That's what killed poor Saint Eanswythe and her father too," said the grandmother as they sat around the table."

"*Saint* Eanswythe?" said Botolph in astonishment.

"Aye, God rest her soul, our dear princess has been performing even more miracles since her death than she did when she was alive."

"How wonderful," said Botolph, heartened.

"Yes, when she died they embalmed her, buried her in the church and erected an altar over her. Ever since that day you couldn't keep people away. They were in and out all the time asking for her prayers for everything from curing sore feet to bringing rain for the crops. She was such a sweet lady."

"You met her then?" said Botolph.

"Aye, many times. We were living in Folcanstane then. My son-in-law was a fisherman."

"How long ago was that?"

"Oh, let me see now," and she counted on her fingers. "I think that must be about eight summers. The plague hit Folcanstane real bad and people were fallin' as quick as leaves in the autumn. Then the king was took ill and the abbess nursed him but he died quite quickly, and after that she took ill and died not long after. Then the girls Ma and Pa caught it and we lost them as well. That's when we decided to come down here to Bren Sete."

"Oh dear," said Botolph, "you have had a bad time of it. But the sickness has gone now, hasn't it?"

"Aw bless ye yes. It lasted about a year. I still get the feelin' that folks are not as 'ealthy as they used to be – but it's just yer usual illnesses and deaths now ... not the 'orror it was."

"So Folcanstane's a bit depleted is it?"

"A bit? I should say. 'Tis nothin' like the place it was. The church and nunnery are still there of course but the fences are all fallin' down 'n' the village is less than 'alf the size it used to be."

"What about the travelling trade?"

"We didn't get 'ardly anyone comin' fer a while. They started goin' up to Dubris but then that got the plague too so they went to Rutupiae. I hear 'tis pickin' up again now though. Mind ye the king don't keep 'is court in Folcanstane no more so there's not the same attraction. There's only really the nunnery fer 'em to stay in."

"Where's the king now then?"

"Oh 'is court's up at Liminge but I don' think e's there that often."

"That's King Eorcenberht?"

"Aye, 'im 'n' Dame Seaxburh. Course they got the two little girls now, Eorcengota's about two and Ermenilda's a year or so."

"You seem to know a lot about them?"

"Well they're our king 'n' queen ain't they? Ever since poor King Eadbald, God rest his soul, was 'ere, the local folks've taken a keen interest in all they do. The villagers were like 'is family then. Course the two princes were young men in those days and both unmarried."

"How was it that Eorcenberht became king then? Surely his brother Eormenred was the elder of the two?"

"Aw, bless 'im yes. Eormenred fell in love with a girl in the north. One day 'e was 'ere and next 'e was gone. I don't know if he argued wi' 'is father or not but 'e just vanished 'n' then when 'is Pa died there was only Eorcenberht left to take the throne."

"Why didn't he stay in Folcanstane?"

"What – wi' everyone dyin' around 'im 'n' 'e likely to be next? Well ye wouldn't would ye? 'Twas said – 'n' I don' know 'ow true it was – but 'twas said that the plague was brought 'ere by one of the sailors on a boat. There was certainly one who was nursed by the nuns – cos I saw 'im meself. Anyway it made sense fer the new young king to get away so 'e went fer a tour round the country introducing 'imself to the other kings 'n' that's when he met 'is wife."

"Where's she from?"

"She's from Engla, daughter of King Anna."

"Oh - I *thought* I recognised the name. She'd be the sister of the two nuns I met at Evoriacum."

This brought the conversation to a standstill.

"Well," said Botolph, "I think that we'd better be on our way. Thanks so much for looking after us. I am sure we'll meet again."

"I do 'ope so," she replied, "but ye'll be hard pressed to get to Folcanstane by nightfall. It's seven leagues."

"Yes, I know, but we're fast walkers and as long as the ferry's working we'll be alright."

"Well, you could always stay at the tavern."

"Tavern? What tavern?"

"The ferry tavern. Ah, of course, if ye've bin away a while, ye wouldn't know about it. It were only built a couple of summers ago. They're alwez pleased to put people up. I tell you what though," she said, "there's bound to be some carts crossing the marsh today – ye'll probably be able to get a ride on one."

And she was right. They had only just got onto the

track when a farm wagon came up behind them and offered them a lift. They accepted gratefully and, having tossed their sacks and sticks in before them, Luka and Ash climbed into the back and Botolph joined the driver.

As was to be expected, he was a chatty creature and did his best to get their life stories out of them before they reached the ferry. Botolph asked hopefully if he was going on to Folcanstane.

"Nah," he said, "I couldn't get across if I wanted to - 'tis not low water until nearly sunset."

"Still no bridge then?" said Botolph.

"Bridge? There's the Osterbryc down there – he waved his arm to the left – 'n' there's several others across the Limen stream. They've built two of three *'ere* in the past - but as soon as we 'ave an easterly storm they gets washed away. 'Tis a waste of time building 'em. The new tavern's bin flooded out several times 'n' I wouldn't give too much 'ope fer *its* chances in the long term."

He dropped them off at the tavern soon after midday. The ferry was on the opposite bank collecting passengers, so they walked across to the seashore and spent a while listening to the whoosh of the waves hitting the muddy banks. It was just before high water and the last of the tide was easing as it sluiced through the sea-gat to fill the marsh streams. Botolph could see the problems a bridge would face.

The day was calm and beautiful with white horsetails of clouds painting streaks across the sky. A steady but gentle breeze was blowing from the southwest. He could imagine the scene in an onshore gale when a bridge would have no protection from waves crashing through the entrance. He turned to Ash.

"This was the Romans' great harbour of Portus Lemanis," he said. See that castle halfway up the hill?"

He pointed and Ash nodded. "That was a signalling station. The Romans would've had a good view of the South Sea from there and, because they could also see up-channel to Folcanstane and down-channel to Gwentchesil and Fairlight, they could give warning of any enemy attack."

"Where's the haven gone then?" asked Ash looking puzzled. "There's no' but a pond here?"

"That's all there is now 'cos it's all silted up. That's why the Romans stopped using it."

They watched as a boat rounded the corner from the northeast. Its sail was furled and its two sets of oars were being pulled lustily by a couple of young lads. An older man was in the stern, adding weight to their passage by sculling with the steering oar. A similar vessel was heading in the opposite direction coming up the river with sail set and heading for the open sea.

The two boats passed in the little estuary, the skipper of the outward bound boat calling "Ye nearly missed the tide then?"

"Aye," came back the old man at the scull, "It's been a hard pull fer the past hour but by God's grace we made it. Fare thee well."

"Oi," came another voice from behind them. "Youse want the ferry or not?"

Botolph had wondered if a now-grown-up Hansa would still be the ferryman but it was another and rather less respectful young lad who took them across. They arrived in Folcanstane late in the afternoon.

--o--

Back at Lewys the Taverner's group unsheathed their seaxes and urged their horses forwards. Wybert, puzzled, unsheathed his seax too and his men followed suit. He looked behind him wondering whether or not to flee, but his path was blocked by villagers eager to watch a scrap. He decided to stay where he was until he had at least discovered what he needed to flee from.

The Taverner waved his seax angrily as he approached. "Get off my 'orse," he shouted.

"This ain't your 'orse," said Wybert "I bought it from . . . "

"I know my 'orses," said the Taverner, becoming even more cross at Wybert's impudence. "Now get off before I put you off."

The remainder of the Taverner's group were beginning to circle round towards the back of Wybert's horses and panic was developing on the faces of Wybert's men as they looked for an escape route. This wasn't what they had joined for. They were totally overawed by Wybert and could easily be browbeaten into doing whatever he said. They each felt big when they were able to regard themselves as his soldiers – ready to fight under his command when facing two or three unruly peasant farmers. But being outnumbered by nearly two to one was a different matter. What were they to do? It looked as if there was a good chance that if they made the wrong decision they were going to die. The Taverner's men continued to close around them while the Taverner himself stood his horse straight in front of Wybert.

Wybert called on his men to move forwards and protect his flanks, but for one thing they were reluctant to do so and for another thing they were already being poked and prodded both verbally and physically by the men of the Taverner's group and being told that if they valued their lives they should get off their horses *now*.

They might have been worthless cowards who had only been bolstered up by their bully of a leader but, if pressed, they could still think for themselves when necessary. To a man, they thought now - reached an instant decision - and, quickly sheathing their seaxes, slid to the ground and, dodging the kicks and punches meted out by the exuberant crowd, ran out of the village as fast as they could.

As a couple of the locals roped up the six horses the Taverner's men completed a circle around Wybert.

"Now put up yer seax," called the Taverner.

Wybert hesitated.

"Put up yer seax 'n' ye'll suffer no more than a long walk."

Wybert did not like long walks any more than he liked being humiliated.

He made his decision and struck at the Taverner, spurring his horse at the same time.

The Taverner let out a yelp of pain as blood spurted out of the arm that he had raised to prevent the weapon cutting into his neck.

Wybert spurred his horse again and yelled wildly, striking out at villagers as they scattered randomly after trying to block his way.

In a trice he was clear of the village, but eleven horsemen were hard on his heels. The natural selection that had occurred when he had swapped horses earlier meant that he had a fine runner beneath him and he began to pull ahead as the horse climbed the hill up on to the ridge.

CHAPTER 9
Folcanstane re-visited.

It was late afternoon when they dropped down the hill into Folcanstane. They left the wider road well before the ford and took a narrow path towards the nunnery.

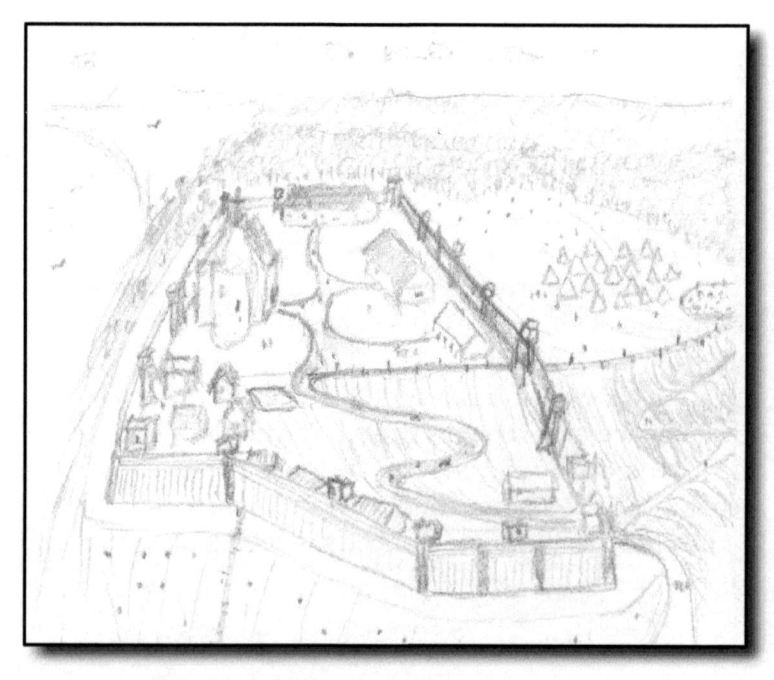

Fig. 7. Folcanstane in Eanswythe's time.

But rather than the proud nunnery they once new, it was the ruins of a forlorn enfencement that greeted them.

A lot of the palisade had broken down and much of it seemed to have been burnt – perhaps by mischievous children. The evil blackness of the charred wood contrasted with their memories of the gentle white holiness of the nunnery.

"It's in a sorry state," said Botolph.

"Not the place it was," agreed Luka. "See there Ash, - that used to be the king's hall. When we were last here it was hidden behind the wooden walls – not all exposed like it is now."

The dilapidations obviated the necessity of their entering by the main gate. Instead, after crossing a hump and a dry ditch, they stepped through a breach and entered the formerly-hallowed precincts of the nunnery grounds.

"Well at least the church is still standing," said Botolph.

"Yes, not only standing but stronger," said Luka. "It was made of wood the last time we saw it but it looks like they've replaced much of that with stone now. King Eadbald must have worked hard at that afore he died."

They went over to the entrance and pulled open a stout oaken door, which was ably supported by two strong iron hinges. Luka expected it to creak but it swung open silently.

"Yes?" said a voice from the gloom.

"Pax vobiscum," Botolph replied in the general direction from which the voice had come – although he was still unable to see the voice's owner.

"Pax in terra et in Folcanstanum," came the disembodied voice.

"Pax quidem in Folcanstanum," replied Botolph hopefully.

A shadow in the corner changed shape and a lightness appeared which resolved itself into a face as it shuffled nearer.

"Who're ye and what d'yer want," it said ungraciously.

"I'm a priest - my name is Father Botolph, this is my friend Luka and his son Ash."

"Oh," said the voice sadly. "So ye've got a son now 'ave ye Luka?"

Luka was startled.

"Who're you?"

"Ha, - wouldn't yer like to know? – but I remember ye when ye were at death's door 'n' the saint brought ye back to life. She shouldn't 'ave bothered."

The unhappy tone of voice rang a bell with Luka but he could still not quite place it – and then it came to him.

"Eric!" he said. "It's old Eric isn't it?"

"So what if it is?"

"Eric," said Botolph. "How good to see you – and how's Martha?"

Silence was the reply.

"Eric?"

"Dead. Dead these eight years 'n' I miss 'er every day."

"Oh Eric I'm so sorry. How awful. Was it the plague?"

The black shadow nodded its head and came further into the light so that they could see that Eric was wrapped in a black woollen habit, his head covered by a cowl.

"How are you managing?"

"Managing? Well I'm managing. I'm alive aren't I? Too old to fish though. Too old to work. Too old to be of use to anyone or anything."

"So what do you do?"

"I beg. I come up 'ere every day. I keep the place

clean. I put out new candles. I light candles for 'em what want 'em lighted 'n' if I'm lucky they'll bring summat for me – a loaf, or fruit . . . or vegetables even. The sisters're very good. They give me a good meal every day but o' course I 'ave to eat it on me own."

His red-rimmed rheumy eyes looked up at Botolph who was not sure if it was tears that he could see or just the natural watering of ancient optics.

"What about your children Eric?"

"The two boys died . . . but the girl's still alive."

His eyes seemed to regain some life at the thought of her.

"How old is she now?"

"Old? . . . I don't know – either fifteen or sixteen summers – summat like that."

"Where is she then?"

"Oh – married – got a little kiddy – nice little fellow. She asked me to go 'n' live with them but I remember what Martha 'n' me were like when we were young – we wouldn't 'ave liked 'n' old failure like me livin' in the same 'ut."

"Where do you sleep then?"

"'Ere."

He jerked his head into the direction of the place previously occupied by the black shadow.

"'Ere. 'Tis comfortable enough. It's out of the wind 'n' rain 'n' it means I can look after the place 'n' keep the villains out."

Luka couldn't imagine him being strong enough to keep a mouse out but was pleased that he had found somewhere that was important to him. He felt quite sorry for him now - although the time when he could not get away fast enough from Eric's pessimistic moaning and groaning was still surprisingly fresh in his memory. He thought back to the way he felt when he lost his dear Clarisse. He and Eric were comrades in arms now. Who would have thought that he would ever have felt such empathy for the old so-and-so?

The door opened again and a young nun entered.

"Pax," she said sweetly and raised her fingers and made the sign of a cross as if blessing and greeting were one.

"Pax Sister," said Botolph, "et pax in terra."

"What can I do for you sires?"

"They wanna bed," said Eric, unexpectedly.

"I . . . ," blustered Botolph but she cut in –

"We shall be pleased for you to stay one night sires. Pray – from whence do you come and what's your destination?"

"We come from the Abbey of Evoriacum in Francia," said Botolph. "We have been travelling for two moons and . . . "

"From Evoriacum? How wonderful. I would love to go there – I hear so much about it . . . or at least I *used* to hear so much about it. Sadly since the death of our Dear Sainted Lady and the King," (she crossed herself), "we see few wayfarers these days."

"Yes," said Botolph. "I was so sorry to hear of their deaths but I'm pleased to hear that Saint Eanswythe lives on in peoples' hearts."

"Indeed she does. It's the end of the day now so I doubt that more will come, but most days we get a number of pilgrims at her shrine," – she turned slightly and opened her right hand to indicate an altar on the south side of the church – "they pray that she will intercede with God for them and grant their petitions – and so many of their prayers are successful. She was such a lovely saintly lady."

"Indeed she was," said Botolph, a lump coming into

his throat, "and will be forever missed."

"You knew her?"

"Aye indeed I did."

"Did you know her well?"

Botolph hesitated, knowing that he could not give the answer which first came into his mind.

"Yes, we were close friends. It was before I became professed. I did what I could to help her in this church."

"You're a monk?"

"I was professed at Evoriacum and later I was ordained and acted as Chaplain to Abbess Fara."

"Oh my," she exclaimed in confused embarrassment. "I am so sorry Father. I had no idea … "

"No reason that you should have Sister. We've been travelling for two months and I am afraid my clothing now looks more like a farmer's smock than a monk's habit, and my tonsure is in sore need of a trim."

"Come then, the visitors quarters are aired and ready." She turned towards the black shadow: "Eric – go and get the visitors' pitcher and fill it from the pond." And then again to Botolph: "We have no other guests tonight. Perhaps once you have settled in, you might come and join us for vespers?"

--o--

Wybert fled along the riverbank, his horse scattering people before him. The path divided and he took the left hand track hoping that the others might go straight on – but, looking back, he could see that they still had him in their sights. He urged his horse up a bank still covered with spring moss and onto the ridge taking to the side verge as he encountered startled wayfarers travelling towards him. He had no time to look behind but sensed that the gap between him and his pursuers was increasing.

He had a good horse but he could feel that it was beginning to tire. He looked around wildly, searching for cover. Out of the corner of his eye he spotted a hut deeper in the forest. There were no other travellers in sight so he reined the horse back, wheeled it around and quickly returned to the spot. He turned off the path and pressed between the trees until he reached the hut where, leaping off the animals back, he pulled it close to the hut's wall so that both were hidden from view.

He did not have long to wait before the sound of their approach filtered through the trees. He hoped the trotting hooves would not bring a whinny from his own horse and he kept his hand over the animal's muzzle while raising his own head to peep at the riders as they passed by.

This gave him time to reflect.

"Curses. Curse the lily-livered cowards who deserted him. Curse the damned priest and the dwarf. Curse the man from whom he stole these useless horses. Why did it have to happen to him? Why did they have to chase him with such a large band? If it had been smaller his men would have stood a chance. Curse everything," . . . and he was hungry.

He could not stay here for long – they would soon realise that he had eluded them and would be back looking for signs of where he had turned off. They would have no difficulty tracking him. In fact they would have no difficulty in tracking him anywhere all the time he had this beast with him. And in any case it was the beast that they were after. Once they had recovered their stolen property perhaps they would forget about searching for him.

He began to regret his attack on the Taverner. The man would always be seeking revenge – particularly if his wounds were severe. There was nothing for it – he had lost his men; they had lost their horses; now he had to lose his – and he had to do it *now*.   There was no time to waste. They would be back at any moment. He ran.

The horse watched him curiously as he picked his way through the trees as fast as he could. A stray sapling sprang back and caught his eye, giving a stab of pain. He cursed again. It was not a good day. He looked back. He could still see the horse and the hut. That was the trouble with woods – they impeded swift passage but still left little slits and cracks that enabled a pursuer to see his quarry. Not only that but it was impossible to avoid marking the ground cover. Any landsman worth his salt would be able to follow his track as easily as if he had been trailing an unrolling skein of wool. There was nothing for it however – he had to keep running and hope that his pursuers would be disinclined to follow on foot.

--o--

The heavy blade smashed into the Taverner's arm causing a searing pain that shot up into his shoulder; his seax fell from his grasp . . . and then he too fell from his horse.

The villagers crowded round him and a wench did her best to stem the spurting flow of blood . . . and then he lost consciousness.

--o--

After the fall of the Taverner it was the blacksmith who took over leadership of the horsemen. He had been made a fool of by Wybert. He had never liked him from the moment he had set eyes on him and he cursed himself for having told the fiend where to find a change of horses. He also cursed the fact that by some quirk of fortune Wybert had ended up on the fastest and strongest horse in the village. They could do nothing but follow the retreating horse's rump as fast as they could ... but they were no match for the speedy animal and they soon lost sight of him and had to slow to a fast trot to save the horses.

"Good horse or not, 'e can't go on at that rate fer ever," mused the blacksmith.

A wagon came around the corner and the blacksmith reined in.

"'Ave you passed an 'orseman travelling at speed?"

"I ain't passed *any* 'orsemen for a while," said the driver.

"Damn 'im. 'E must've turned off into the woods. Back men – 'n' take it slowly now. You five keep an eye open to yer left and you five to yer right. Keep yer ears open too. 'E'll be in there somewhere.'

They found both the hut and the horse quickly enough and the route that Wybert had taken was plain for all to see.

"Right," said the blacksmith dismounting. He pointed: "you three come wi' me. The rest of you go up to the crossing and take the left-han' turning. Y'know the bend jus' afore you reach the Lewys road?" They nodded. "Four of you leave the track there 'n' ride as far as you can into the wood, then leave yer 'orses 'n' continue on foot – got that?" They nodded again. "The rest of you split up and patrol up and down the sea road track and the first bit of the Lewys road – understand?" They nodded for a third time. "Right, now – be quick about it - GO."

He and his men secured their horses and, following Wybert's tracks, ran through the trees and down a narrow valley. When they reached the bottom they found that the trail was obscured and it took a while of casting about before they found that, instead of taking a direct route, he had turned to the left down into another valley where the trees were not so thick. They were able to move faster then and the blacksmith guessed that that would also have been the reason for Wybert's choice of route.

The valley veered round to the right and they saw him in the distance – running for his life. The blacksmith shouted and they increased their speed too – leaping over tree stumps and crashing through old wood. One of the men tripped and fell but was soon up and following again. Wybert fell too but similarly recovered himself quickly. He could hear them behind him but reckoned that, even without the horse, he still had the greater speed.

CHAPTER 10
The Storm

Botolph and Luka were amused to discover that the 'Visitors' Quarters' were where the horses used to be stabled. The nuns had made it very comfortable however. They had taken the 'King's Hall' for their own accommodation and the old Nunnery was now the Infirmary. It transpired that the modest 'sister,' they had met, was in fact the nunnery's current leader - Abbess Constantia.

In spite of their unusual accommodation they had a comfortable night, but were woken early the following morning by heavy rain and howling wind. Luka opened the door a nudge, to be greeted by the sight of tree branches being hurled across the yard by the wind. One of the sisters was on her way from the church to the Great Hall. She was holding her hood to her head and struggling against the blast, but the fact that her habit was blowing across her legs made every step difficult. There was suddenly an enormous gust that both blew the hut door back on its hinges and bowled the young nun completely over - off the path and into the mud. She came to her knees and tried to stand but the wind blew her over again. A section of the palisade fencing tore away and pieces of wood came flying through the air. Luka gave a shout and strode forward into the mayhem. Botolph and Ash rose from their pallets and ran to the doorway. They saw Luka reach the woman. He took her arm and she tried to stand again but another blast came and they both fell. Botolph and Ash went to help them but had to move slowly - leaning at an angle to the wind to stay upright.

Botolph had enough weight to hold him to the ground whereas Ash was so light that he was in danger of being blown like the branches.

"Go back," called Botolph. Ash would have obeyed had it been possible but he was struggling to do *anything*. Suddenly a great ripping sound added to the noise of the general mayhem as the whole of the thatched roof of their Visitors' Quarters was torn away and took to the air like a monster bird.

--o--

Through the trees Wybert could see the road in the distance and knew that he was nearly there. Once he got onto that he would steal a horse from the first rider that came down the track and then he'd be away. His stupid pursuers were now on foot. He had spotted a few behind him and he guessed that the rest had spread out through the forest. Conviction of imminent success spurred him on. He was in good condition and most of the run had been downhill, so he really felt quite exhilarated. He leapt over another branch and came to the edge of the forest. The ground was flatter now and so the running became easier. From behind him came some shouting. Why would they shout? And then he saw them. Two horsemen converging on him from one side and a third from the other and the single rider was closest. He lengthened his stride and felt for his seax thinking that this could be the end – but not if he could help it.

--o--

The blacksmith saw the scene that was developing

on the other side of the trees. He too was fit, and much as Wybert was determined to escape, the blacksmith was determined that he would not. As he reached the edge of the trees he saw that the single rider approaching Wybert was his young lad and deep love drove him faster.

--o--

The boy approached at a gallop and headed across Wybert's path. At the last moment they locked eyes.

The boy's were unafraid, focussed on their duty; Wybert's were as evil as ever, determined to do their worst.

The boy was young. Wybert was a wily and seasoned fighter. He raised his arm with the blade pointing horizontally towards the horse's withers. The boy swung his seax aiming at Wybert's neck – but he saw the blow coming and ducked his head while keeping his arm raised. He felt the blade run along the horse's side and then there was a satisfying thump as it plunged into the boy's belly but the momentum ripped the seax out of Wybert's hand.

The lad fell sideways, narrowly missing him. The horse came to a stop and Wybert turned to catch her bridle but before he could do so the blacksmith with a howl of rage and grief launched himself through the air and knocked him to the ground. The huge man straddled Wybert's winded body squeezing the last of the air out of his lungs. His left arm was twisted under his back and his right arm was pinioned by the blacksmith's knee. Only his legs were free but as he made to move them the blacksmith raised his seax into the air and clasping it with his second hand held it there while the two combatants locked their eyes in mutual hate. Wybert tensed as the black reaper of death sped towards him. He heard the blacksmith's animal roar of execution as the knife plunged down. He sensed the cracking of his ribs as the blade pushed them apart and felt the coldness of the steel as it pierced his thorax. The blacksmith regained his feet and the release of pressure caused a gurgling in Wybert's lungs as they filled with blood. He tried to breathe but was skewered to the ground by the seax. Blind panic overwhelmed him as crimson visions of all those whom he had similarly defiled laughed their way past him as he began his descent to Hell.

The blacksmith left his seax where it was and jumped up and ran to his lad. The boy was unconscious but still breathing. He was losing a lot of blood. The blacksmith pulled up the boy's tunic to get to the wound and then tore off his own neckerchief to stem the flow. The other men gathered round him as he sobbed "Don't die. Don't die. Stay with me. I'll never manage wi'out you."

He looked up at his men. "'E's been wi' me since 'e were a toddler. 'E's bin more like a son than a worker. I can't lose 'im now."

"We need to get 'im back ter the village fast as we can. 'Ow we gonner do that? Shall us sling 'im over one of the nags?"

The blacksmith looked down at the wound. The boy was very pale but, although his neckerchief was soaked, little blood was leaking out of the wound now. He kept up the pressure.

"No, he'll start bleedin' agen if we do that. Cut down a couple of strong saplings - they'll need to be at least ten cubits - and we'll fix a litter a'tween two 'orses. We'll need some rope 'n' some clothes. Take the clothes off that varmint - 'e's not goin' ter need 'em any more."

They did as they were bid and, under his direction, they soon had a litter made up using rope from the harness of the boy's horse and donations of other clothing.

The blacksmith called to the men: "Four of you go

back up the valley and get the 'orses. No need to tie 'em – they'll follow you anyway once ye get goin'. Bring 'em down 'ere. We'll've left by the time you arrive. Sling this corpse over one of 'em and bring it back to 'Anfelde. Two of you go back to Lewys 'n' see if the Taverner's still alive. If 'e is then e'll be pleased to 'ear the news. Whether e's alive or dead, do what ye can to bring 'im 'ome to 'Anfelde. If 'e's too ill to move come back 'n' let me know 'n' we'll sort that out later."

The blacksmith looked down at the lad again. His breathing started to labour as he began to regain consciousness.

"Is that litter ready? I want to get 'im in afore 'e comes round."

"Yes all ready. Bring 'im over."

The blacksmith let go the neckerchief and, placing his arms tenderly under the young body, lifted him up and carried him across to the litter.

--o--

Botolph struggled to reach Ash who was rolling towards the water culvert. The priest leant into the wind, his habit flying. He grabbed Ash's arm and pulled him to his feet. Once erect with Botolph's weight to anchor him down, the young fellow helped where he could, but they made a comical sight if only there had been anyone to see. Botolph's habit blew right across him creating the impression of a four-footed animal leaning at a crazy angle to the wind staggering towards the old King's Hall. When they reached it Botolph hammered on the door and shouted, but if there was an answer it was lost in the wind so, defying polite convention Botolph pinioned Ash against the wall while he lifted the latch and gingerly opened the door. He knew that if he opened it too wide the wind would get behind it and smash it against the other wall. Once the slot was big enough he pushed Ash inside and quickly shut the door again. He turned back into the wind with a view to going to help Luka, but at that same moment his friend arrived in a rush half carrying the injured nun.

Botolph addressed the problem of re-opening the door which needed to be wider this time to accommodate the two individuals. All he could do was to stand downwind and, after pulling it open and letting the couple through, apply all his force to close it again. He repeated the process for a third time and, never letting the door out of his grasp, slipped through and pulled it behind him.

The injured nun was in the far corner being attended to by her sisters. Abbess Constantia came over and genuflected a greeting. Luka and Ash also joined Botolph.

"Thank you so much for rescuing Sister Pachomia," she said.

"I hope she's not badly hurt," Botolph replied.

"No, I don't think so – rather shocked perhaps but otherwise it's only cuts and grazes."

"Is your weather always like this?" asked Luka. "The last time we were here, we were down on the marsh when it rained and blew – but I must admit it wasn't as bad as this."

"No, this is quite exceptional. I've never known it so rough."

"You know you've lost the roof of the Visitors' Quarters," said Luka.

She gasped. "Oh no! I'm so sorry - were you hurt?"

"Bless you no," said Luka, "it didn't blow off when we were in there. I think I must've caused it by opening the door – so best you keep this one firmly shut until the wind subsides."

But the wind did not subside properly for the next two days, and for most of that time it rained heavily. Luka, whose low centre of gravity and minimal top hamper was most suited to survival in such conditions, went out during a lull and retrieved their soaked possessions from the remains of the Visitors' Quarters. He also went down to the pond to fetch some fresh water – but even then he nearly fell in.

"Fine thing that would be," he said to himself as he staggered against the gusts at the water's edge, "if I drowned in the nuns' pond. They'd never be able to drink from it again."

He was soaked to the skin when he returned, but the nuns were well-prepared. They had a good store of logs inside the hall and a blazing fire going in the middle of it. Not having any dry clothes, all he could do was to sit on a bench in front of the fire and steam. Fortunately the rank smell of his drying wet woollens was counteracted by the sweet smell of wood smoke that sometimes went through the hole in the roof, but more often than not pervaded the room. Like everyone else, Luka's eyes were stinging so he just sat on the bench with his head in his hands and his eyes shut, pausing only to cough when his lungs could stand the smoke no longer.

It was most irregular, two men and a boy sharing the nuns' dorter but it was irregular weather and it was a big hall so they managed.

When they awoke on the morning of the third day it was to an uncustomary silence broken only by the happy singing of birds. Luka, as usual was the first up and he gingerly opened the door and poked his head outside. A scene of devastation greeted his eyes. The ground was littered with branches and pieces of thatch and palisade posts and other debris. Two dead seagulls were lying on the sodden grass. He left the door open and went outside to have a better look. The nuns and Botolph and Ash soon joined him.

The church seemed to be undamaged. In fact in general the nunnery had fared well. It was only the roof of the Visitors' Quarters that had gone – the roof of the Sanatorium was still in place. The part which was most damaged was the outer palisade, and the pond was filled with rubbish.

"Oh dear," said Abbess Constantia. "What a mess."

"Never mind," said Botolph. "The Good Lord must have sent us to help you clear it up."

"Thank God," she said. "My grateful thanks to all of you."

--o--

"The thing that needs sorting out most urgently," said Abbess Constantia as she led them through the castle grounds, "is the pond. As you can see it's overflowing and the lower grounds are turning into a quagmire."

"What can we do about that then?" asked Luka. "Is there some way we can divert the in-flow? And where does *that* come from?"

"It comes from a freshwater spring nearly a league away and is brought here through a wooden culvert. When Saint Eanswythe founded our nunnery there was no fresh water at all, so one day three of us rode up into the hills and searched until we found the nearest spring. Our abbess said that it was too low to reach Folcanstane so we spent the next day riding around until we found a higher one. The princess then led us up to the opposite hill and looked first at Folcanstane and then at the site of the spring.

Her eyes and her heart told her that it was high enough for the water to flow to the nunnery but she was not absolutely sure, so we dismounted from our horses there and then and knelt in the field and prayed to the dear Lord for guidance. After that she was satisfied.

"This of course was in the days when the king had his court here and there were plenty of people skilled in woodworking and our lady had only to ask her father for something and it was given. Over the next few weeks a thousand trees were chopped down and Abbess Eanswythe was out on horseback every day directing where the trunks should be laid. It was a massive undertaking."

"I'm sure it was," said Luka.

"Once all the trunks were in place the villagers came to hollow them out. Each family was given three to work on. Once they were ready the craftsmen took over and slotted them together. End to end they led across the hills to the pond which in those days was high up on the headland. When all was ready the topmost gutter was swung across to start catching water from the spring and we waited . . . and waited . . . and waited. Nothing happened. No water. When it became clear that something was wrong the abbess took us into church to pray and then the three of us rode out again. We followed the line of the culvert until we reached a place where it was leaking. This was at about the halfway point. The water was flowing nicely up until there but it would not travel along the next section - it just overflowed. The abbess saw instantly what was wrong and the next day work started to move the lower gutters further down the hill. The trunks were so heavy that they had to use oxen. It was precise and slow work. Do you see?"

They nodded vigorously.

"What an undertaking that must have been," said

Botolph.

"Nearly three hundred had to be moved. It took an awful lot of her time but, as our abbess said, a good water supply was essential, and we and the villagers had put so much effort into it that she would not rest until the water flowed. Her men moved a dozen or so trunks at a time after which they ran the water again to make sure it came thus far. Sometimes it ran too fast and then the trunks had to be moved *up* the hill again. It took a lot of time and trouble. Slowly but surely they made progress and eventually reached the nunnery and where the last gutter finished ... that is where the pond was dug. But there was one more thing ... "

"It needed an overflow," said Luka.

"Exactly."

"And that's the problem now ... the overflow has become blocked up with all the rubbish that's blown into the pond?"

"Precisely."

"So that's what the lower culvert's for – the one that leads down the hill and under the palisade?"

"I'm afraid so."

"Muddy isn't it?" said Luka wryly.

She raised her eyebrows, looked at him squarely in the eyes and nodded - at the same time giving him rather a cheeky smile.

"Great," said Luka looking up at Botolph.

"I'll help you," said Botolph.

"There's no point in two of us getting covered in mud ... and there's less of me than you so I guess that it's gotta be me."

Ash was grinning widely, hugely excited at the prospect of what was going to happen and Botolph was trying hard not to smirk. Luka came to the conclusion that there was no point in stripping down to a loin cloth as his top parts were not going to get wet, so he just took off his boots and stepped gingerly into the quagmire.

The water was only a hand's breadth deep and flowing quite slowly but the mud was rather deeper and every time he replaced his foot the mud seemed determined not to let him have it back. Slowly and painfully he squelched across the bog until he reached the middle when he placed one foot each side of the overflow culvert and climbed up it to the edge of the pond. It was at this point that he came to the conclusion that the loin cloth idea had not been such a bad one.

Since there was no going back he leant forward and lay flat on the culvert so that he could put both arms into the water as far as they would go. He could feel a branch lying across the top end of the pipe. He tried to pull it free but it would not budge. The branch was covered with what seemed to be long strands of grass. Some water was clearly going through the overflow because he could feel the water swirling and it was the suction that was holding the branch in place.

He decided on a change of tactic and grabbed at the grass pulling clumps of it out and throwing it behind him. By the time he had done this a dozen times he could feel the water swirling more powerfully. It occurred to him that if he let an arm get sucked into the pipe he might never get it out. Being sucked to death by a saint's culvert was not the exit he had planned. He tried moving the branch again. It was coming loose. He pulled at one end of it and then pulled again. It seemed to have snagged somewhere. He moved his feet up closer to his body so that, rather than lying flat, he was now in a crouching position which gave him a much better purchase. He grasped each end of the branch and heaved ... and suddenly up it came –

whereupon up he came too ... and overbalanced ... and, falling backwards into the mud, he and the branch rolled down the hill together.

His audience's reaction was initially one of shocked concern but when he stopped rolling and stood up with a cross look on his face they could contain themselves no longer but collapsed with hoots of laughter. Ash particularly was helpless. No sound was coming from his mouth but he doubled up with mirth. Botolph and Abbess Constantia were similarly encumbered. The situation was not improved when he splashed his way towards them – a great mud-ball with two bright eyes supported by two stocky little muddy brown legs.

"Hah. *Very funny,*" he said unsmiling. "Why do I volunteer to do these things?"

"Look though," Abbess Constantia cried – "see – the flooding has stopped – you can now see the edges of the pond. Thank you so much Luka. You will find your place in Heaven I promise."

Luka sighed. He could not stay miserable in the face of such graciousness. He sploshed his way up the path back to the nunnery with them and there, behind a screen, he stripped off his muddy clothes and, having rubbed himself down, put on some clean dry ones while the abbess prepared some hot mulled wine as his reward.

The four of them sat on the benches around the fire. Neither Abbess Constantia nor Ash were drinking but Botolph felt that he should support Luka by having his own horn of mulled wine and he raised it in a toast to his friend.

"To our hero," he said.

"Hah," said Luka.

It took several more days to get the castle grounds back into shape. The biggest job was repairing the palisade. While they were working, village people were constantly coming and going. There was a regular stream of petitioners attending Saint Eanswythe's Chapel and another stream of tradesmen bringing gifts of produce to the nunnery. Quite a few of these had travelled from the Marsh of Rumniae from whence they brought ewes' milk and vegetables.

"We've 'ad a terrible time down on t' marsh," said one of them who stopped to pass the time of day with Botolph and Luka as they were hauling palings into the palisade.

"T' storm broke the sea wall and flooded half t' marsh at Rumniae. T' sea's still pouring in every tide 'n' ye can't see what's goin' t' come of it. Top end's all blocked so ships can't get in or out there."

"What do you men 'the top end's blocked'?" asked Luka. "Whereabouts?"

"Top end – up by t' Ferry Tavern."

"Blocked?" said Botolph.

"Aye – totally blocked. The only way ships can get in now is down by Rumniae. There's a great breach there."

"So what about the ferry – is that still working?"

"Oh aye – t' water still comes up the Liman stream 'n' fills the basin – but t' ferryman has a much easier job now that there's no great waves comin' in from the sea. Don't know how long it'll last though. Pr'aps it'll all silt up so that we can walk across. Now that'd be a good thing from my point of view. Anyway ... can't waste all day talkin' to you two. Wassail."

"We must go and have a look at that," said Luka after he had gone.

"Well I reckon we'll finish this palisade today," said Botolph, "so perhaps we can go tomorrow. If we wait 'til a tradesman comes in from the marsh we'll be able to get a lift and save some foot-leather."

--o--

The boy was conscious by the time they arrived back at Hanfelde but was writhing and moaning in pain. They had brought him back as slowly and gently as they could with one man at each horse's head and another one steadying each side of the litter. The blacksmith walked with them, keeping a supporting hand on the wound and cooing encouragement to the boy. The journey seemed to take forever.

They took him to the blacksmith's house. On the journey, one of the side attendants, who was a carpenter, had been working out how they could make the lad a comfortable bed and disturb him least. He had talked his idea over with the blacksmith and as soon as they arrived at Hanfelde he went off to his hut and came back with two trestles. They first unhitched the front end of the litter which two of the men held while the back end was being unhitched from the other horse. They carried the stretcher into the hut and lowered its ends onto the trestles. History does not record whether the boy lived or died, nor what happened to Wybert's body. It was many years however before Ash's heart stopped skipping a beat when he saw a man wearing a black hat.

CHAPTER 11
Return to the Marsh

That evening they told Abbess Constantia what the tradesmen had said and their plans for a visit to the marsh and at mid-morning the following day a cart arrived and the driver was easily persuaded to carry three passengers on his return journey to the marsh.

As they came down the hill by the side of Portus Lemanis they could see the changes that the storm had wrought. The cart driver stopped halfway to give them a better look.

"That's where we stood only the other day," said Botolph pointing towards the Ferry Tavern. "Where we watched those boats entering and leaving the river there's now no river at all."

"It floods a bit at high water Father," said the carter. "It still looks a bit like a river then but there's no' but a hand's draught of water to sail in."

They continued their descent of the hill and through the ford onto the marsh itself.

"There's no need to wait for low water to cross now then?" said Botolph.

"Oh yes there is Father. 'Tis low water now but the basin still fills up from the Liman. 'Tis better than it was but 'tis still a blessed nuisance. Come to think of it – 'n' I've never done this afore – but it looks as if the ground's hard enough now for us to cross over onto the old spit there. Let's give it a try."

The old horse seemed uneasy about this. They dismounted from the wagon and the carter led the animal gently off the track and onto the new shingle which it crunched across, running its load down a slight slope before sloshing into some mud and then rising up onto the sea wall on the other side.

"There we are," said the carter triumphantly. "Next question will be whether or not we can get off again at the bottom end 'cos we can't now get down to Lyd like we used to."

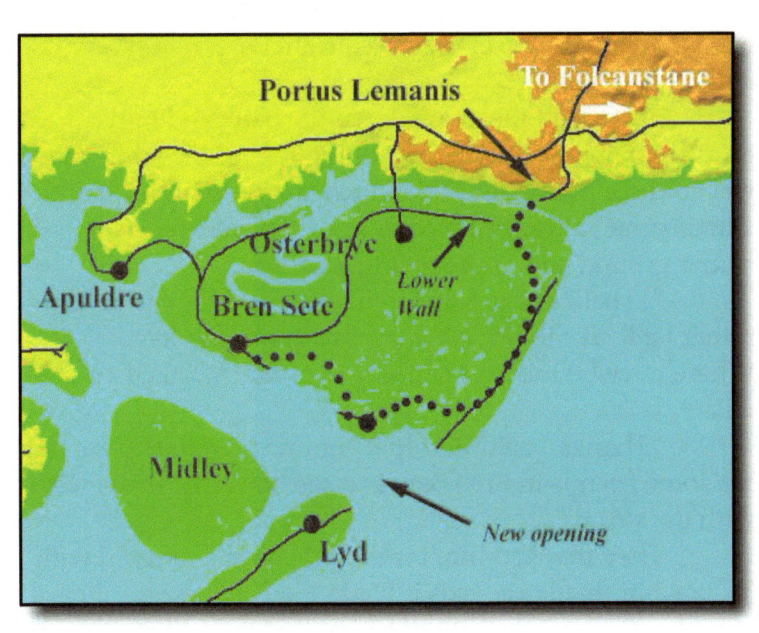

Fig. 8. The Marsh of Rumniae after the storm.

They followed the track along the shingle beach until it petered out, whereupon they came to a standstill and looked forlornly at the great ocean gap where once there was a road. Although it was low tide the water looked as if it still had a good depth.

"The channels around Midley 'ave opened up as well," said the carter. "At full ebb the water rushes out 'ere."

"What's that village over there?" asked Luka pointing westwards across a gulley.

"That's Rumniae itself," he said. "Now comes the test to see if we can get there - 'cos if we can, this is gonna make a much easier road than the one we used to take along the Lower Wall."

"Shall we dismount?" asked Botolph.

"Nah - I reckon we'll be alright here 'n' it'll save getting' yer feet wet."

He turned the horse down the bank and into a muddy channel, which he ran along for a short while until he could see a way out of the ditch and onto firmer land. Skirting then a couple more dykes, they were soon on firmer ground and approaching Rumniae.

"I shall 'ave to leave you 'ere," said the carter "or rather ye'll 'ave to leave me cos this is where I live. Where're ye bound? Ye can stay the night wi' us if ye wish."

"Thanks," said Botolph, "but no – I'd like to go and see some friends in Bren Sete and see how they managed with the storm."

They thanked him for the ride but he retorted with "Nay – but thank *you* - cos if I 'adn't 'ad sight-seers aboard I would never 'ave thought of trying that track along the sea wall."

It was less than a league to Bren Sete but much of the sea wall had been washed away, so they had to pick their route carefully. The water was quietly eddying in the outer bay but as they approached the village they could see that the tide was sluicing strongly past. The little place was full of activity when they reached it and it was not long before Mistress Hild spotted them.

"Wassail Luka," she cried "and Father Botolph and Ash. How good to see you."

"How are you mistress?" asked Botolph, "and how did you fare in the storm?"

"Lucky. We fared very lucky thank'ee. When we heard that the banks had burst we thought we'd be washed away but we were spared, praise the Lord. Now what're you three doing here?"

"We wanted to make sure that you were alright but, I must admit, we also came to have a look at how bad the damage was. Is there a chance we could stay with you for a couple of nights?"

"Lord bless ye yes. The girls'll be pleased to see ye – as will Gramps."

Mistress Hild wanted to know what they had found in Folcanstane and what damage the storm had caused there. It was while Botolph was explaining how they met Eric in the church that their hostess remarked how she wished that they had their own church in Bren Sete.

"It would really make a difference to the village," she said. "Most of the folks here have taken on the new religion, but it'd be so much better if we had somewhere of our own to worship in."

"Are there no churches on the marsh then?" said Botolph.

"Bless yer no ... ah – but now ye're makin' me a liar – I did hear tell there was a wooden chapel somewhere up on t' ridge – but it's too far away to be of any use to us - what we really need is a chapel of our own."

All of this was, of course, music to Botolph's ears but he did all he could to appear nonchalant about it. He glanced over at Luka, who had a mischievous twinkle in his eyes. In the normal way, Botolph would have been afraid that his friend would spoil the magic of the moment by poking fun at him, but at that moment Luka was tucking into a great chunk of newly-baked bread and Botolph knew that food would take priority so he cleared his throat and said, "Well ... if that's what you want and if you have a place you think would be suitable ... and if we can find wood and labour ... I dare say we could soon provide one."

It was Hild's turn to be excited. "What?" she said "But ... how would ye do that. How ... "

"We've done it before," piped up Luka "so I reckon Father B and me could do it again."

"'Ave ye?" she said.

"Yes," said Luka. "Last time we did it, was in a village where half the population *didn't* want a church - so to build one where it *is* wanted would, I'm sure, give the Father great pleasure."

"The problem is," said Botolph "that it needs more than just a church. You're going to need a spiritual leader to follow."

"Well you could do that Father, couldn't you?"

Botolph laughed. "Well of course I would be pleased to do so at the beginning but sadly we can't stay here for ever. I've been offered land in the north to build a monastery and we'll need to press on with that."

"Oh," she said looking a little despondent.

"There must be villagers who'd help though. It'd only take a couple of upstanding young God-fearing lads who I could teach."

"What do you think Gramps?" she said, looking over at him.

Gramps looked back at her somewhat vacantly. Building churches was not really his line of work.

"I'll go 'n' see Alfred first thing in the mornin'" said Hild. "Alfred's our headman 'n' e's well-respected. I'm sure e'll be in favour of it 'n' 'e'll tell us where it can be placed."

She was as good as her word and by the afternoon of the next day Botolph had, under Alfred's guidance and with Luka and Ash's help, hammered marking pegs into a plot of ground on the northern edge of the village.

"What about wood then?" asked Botolph. "Where can we get that?"

"Well," said Alfred, rubbing his chin. "We're always needin' it to build 'n' repair our own huts. We 'ave t' get it where we can. The Tenetwaraden forest is closest but there was a bit of unpleasantness there last summer. There're other forests up on the Folcanstane high ground. But there's a thought: the one at Aescsceaster's owned by the Archbishop. Ye'll need to get 'is permission to build a church so pr'aps e'll give ye permission to use 'is wood as well?"

"Permission?" said Botolph. "I hadn't thought of that. It's not like we're building a *proper* church - it'll only be a field chapel - I wonder if we still need permission."

He looked at Luka who shrugged his shoulders. Permission and Luka had never been close friends.

"Well," said Botolph, "now that I'm back in Britain I really need to go and pay my respects to the Archbishop anyway and it sounds as if that should be our next step. I can petition him then."

He turned back to Alfred.

"What about the walls? When we built the church at Bradbryc we used wattle and daub and I see the same's been done for the buildings here - but lapped wooden walls would be much sturdier."

"Do what yer like. If ye manage to get free wood

it'd be better to make a proper job now rather than patching up the wattle 'n' daub year in year out. But ye've gotta bear in mind the weight o' wood for crossin' the ford. That's thick mud there, 'n' ye'll only be able to manage a few bits at a time or the weight'll sink ye up to yer axles."

Botolph looked disappointed: "So that means twice as many trips then. Oh well it can't be helped."

He turned to Luka: "It looks as if a trip to Cantwarebury is next then."

They walked back to Mistress Hild's in silence. A cascade of thoughts was tumbling through Botolph's mind:

How much material would he need?

Who would provide the ox cart?

How would they negotiate that ford?

It suddenly struck him: 'Why not combine the building of the church with the building of a bridge at Ferry Tavern?' It would take twice the amount of wood but it would only need one permission and the benefit to the marsh would be felt for years. Now that the sea was no longer encroaching in that area of the marsh, a bridge to the mainland would be viable. He shared his thoughts with Luka.

"'Sworth a try," he said.

--o--

The villagers had always been friendly but word of the new chapel had spread rapidly and there was now a constant aura of excitement and, somewhat to their embarrassment, the three of them were treated as if they were the village heroes.

The next day, while Ash stayed at Bren Sete, Botolph and Luka went off to Canterbury on borrowed horses. As they passed the last crossing before the ferry Botolph said, "Why don't we try the bridge that the carter was telling us about and see if that might be suitable for getting the wood?"

They turned about and headed west. After a while they came across the bridge – a poor narrow affair the wood of which was so rotten and broken down that they dare not cross it.

"Can't we ford here?" said Luka.

"Only if you push through that scrub – and then you've got the same on the other side. No – best we go back the way we came and take the ford at the Ferry Tavern. That bridge looks just about safe enough to walk over, but even it were stronger it would still not be *wide* enough to take a wagon."

They turned back to the east. When they reached the Tavern the boatman was doing a good trade but on each side of the bank there were horses and wagons waiting for the tide to go down.

"What's going on?" Botolph asked one of the travellers.

"Well," he said. "We used to know where we was with this ford 'cos the depth of the water followed the 'ights of the sea tide but since the blockage 'igh water's a lot later 'ere 'n' we 'aven't worked it out yet. 'Tis just too deep to cross at the moment."

There was nothing for it but to wait so, tying up their horses, they joined other travellers in the Tavern where Botolph supped mead and Luka had a horn of ale.

"You'll upset the taverner with a bridge," said Luka.

"I was just thinking the same thing. He's doing good business now that the travellers have to wait. Still - we'll never please everybody I suppose."

An hour later they were able to cross. They went over the foreshore and then climbed the steep winding hill up to the village of Lymb and thence onwards to Stone

Street that half a lifetime ago they had known so well. After a pleasant fast trot over flat ground they came to another steep winding hill. When at last they gained the summit they stopped to rest the horses.

"Just look at that view," said Luka as they settled down on the bank. "It's as clear as a bell for as far as the eye can see."

They gazed at the river in the distance below and tried to name the settlements where they could see smoke rising.

"C'mon," said Botolph. "We can't sit here enjoying ourselves all day - there's work to do."

The road was straight and flat from this point on, so they made good time to Cantwarebury where they arrived in mid afternoon.

The ostlers took away the horses and, much to their surprise, they were led straight in for an audience with Archbishop Honorius. They were ushered into a large hall where they waited in front of the Archbishop's chair. Shortly a side door opened and he came through and stood in front of them and extended his right hand.

In turn they knelt and kissed his ring and then rose and stood back a pace while he settled himself into the chair.

"Welcome back my sons," he said.

"You remember us then?" said Botolph in surprise.

"Of course, but how long has it been?"

"Nine years Your Grace."

"Nine? My word – it seems only like a twelve-moon. Well - may I tell you that you have not been forgotten? I have been closely following your progress with Abbess Fara at Evoriacum. I have also heard that you've received two offers of land to build monasteries. I take it you don't propose to build them both at the same time?"   He gave a kind and bemused smile.

"No indeed Your Grace – but I have a more pressing matter to attend to before I can build either, and that's why we've asked for an audience today."

"Tell me my son."

Botolph explained his proposals in detail and included the bridge at Ferry Tavern. The Archbishop closed his eyes and listened attentively until he had finished, and then there was silence.

Luka wondered if the Archbishop had fallen asleep because *he* nearly had.

The silence was becoming overbearing and Botolph wondered whether to cough or make a further comment but the Archbishop suddenly came to life and said, "I have listened to what you propose and I understand all your reasons for wanting to do this. I'm not sure however that I should encourage you to delay your other work which has been commissioned by kings and princes and sounds far more exciting than a marsh bridge and a country chapel.   I will pray about it and let you know. I presume that you will be staying at the abbey tonight?"

"Yes your Grace."

"Alright. Make the most of your time while you're here. You have many friends who will be pleased to see you."

He rose as if to leave but then sat down again.

"*Brother* Luka."

The blood drained from Luka's face. He suddenly had a nasty feeling that the Archbishop had something special for him.

"Yehs . . ." he croaked and then tried again, "Yes Your Grace."

"Brother Luka, you look even less like a monk than when you left us."

"Yes Your Grace."

The Archbishop looked at him sternly and Luka thought that if he had had the sort of knees that knocked they would certainly be knocking now. He was, most unusually, completely over-awed by the great man who had a certain 'presence' about him but he managed not to let his eyes waver. The stern gaze seemed to last for ever but then the eyes twinkled a little, the mouth curled at the edges and the Archbishop spoke in a softer voice:

"I have heard a little of your story and there is much about it that I am not pleased with ... "

He paused and Luka prepared himself for what he thought might be coming next.

"I was so sorry to hear that you lost your wife. Your son I gather is growing up into a fine young man."

Luka was dumbfounded that his life history was known so well and he could think of nothing to say except "Thank you Your Grace."

"However."

"Oh dear," thought Luka, "this is the double feint of the battlefield before the 'merciful despatch.'" He was brought back to earth by the return of the stern voice.

"It will not do. You need to make up your mind whether or not you wish to be a monk and share the same profession as Father Botolph, or whether you wish to simply remain his secular friend. You cannot be half-a-monk. Do you understand?"

"Yes Your Grace."

"Very well, I shall pray for you too Brother Luka and hope that you make the right decision. If you decide to remain with us then I will expect you to regard it as a lifelong decision so I will not rush you but I shall expect to hear from you before the next moon. Will that suit?" he finished with a smile.

"Yes Your Grace."

He stood again and raised his right hand.

"Bless you my sons," he said, "Go now and meet Prior Peter and Brother Idan and all the others who are looking forward to hearing the stories of your travels."

--o--

They received a huge welcome at the monastery which had in their absence been renamed *St. Augustine's* in honour of the saint who had brought the Christian message from Rome half a century earlier. They fed well in the refectory and slept well in the dorter. At least they slept well during the intervals between attending the Holy Offices of Matins, Lauds, Prime and Terce and the Holy Sacrament of High Mass. After Sext they were edified by a reading by Brother Idan as they enjoyed a monastic lunch. Immediately after this they were recalled to the Diocesan Office.

Here they were told that, although he applauded it in principle, the Archbishop was not entirely happy about their project on the marsh because he felt that, as Father Botolph had clearly been called to found a great monastery, he should take up that calling without delay. Nevertheless the marsh projects including the bridge and the church were granted the Archbishop's blessing and a charter was being prepared for the foresters of Selwaraden, charging them with giving Father Botolph every assistance.

The following day being Sunday, they remained at the monastery and attended offices and devotions. Then, leaving at first light on Monday morning in order to catch the ford before the water became too deep, they rode back to the marsh.

--o--

True to the exhortations of Archbishop Honorius we

shall not dwell on the well-coordinated building work that went on for the next few weeks. Suffice it to say that the cooperation of the inhabitants of Osterbryc was obtained; trees were felled and prepared; the bridge was constructed – comfortably wide enough to take an ox-cart and finally the chapel was built and the Archbishop himself came to consecrate it.

At Father Botolph's suggestion, it was dedicated to Saint Eanswythe.

Before the Archbishop left, there was something that Luka needed to do.

"Your Grace," he called, just before the great man entered his carriage.

"Ah, Brother Luka - do you have some news for me?"

"I do, your Grace and I must tell you that I believe that I can serve God best by giving up all thoughts of becoming a monk."

There. He had said it now and he waited for the Heavens to fall upon him.

But the twinkle was in the Archbishop's eyes as he looked fondly down on him.

"A brave decision Luka."

"It was?"

"It would have been cowardly to choose to be professed and then not lived up to the standards required of you."

He handed his crozier to an attendant and placed both his hands on Luka's shoulders saying:

"May God bless you and keep you. May God shine his light upon you and be gracious to you as you serve Him and serve his church in the ways that He will show you."

And with that he entered his carriage and was gone . . . and a great weight was lifted from Luka's mind.

CHAPTER 12
Norflot

Their work done on the marsh and in Folcanstane, the time came for Father Botolph and his two friends to move from the kingdom of Eastern Cantium to the sub-kingdom in the west where King Aethelwald's monastery site awaited him. They had offers of transport but Botolph particularly wanted to walk. He wanted to meet the people. He wanted his spirit to grow into the land.

During the weeks of building work, the three of them had become well-known in the area and they had suddenly become three big fish – although they were in a very small pond. People were particularly impressed by the way Father Botolph would join in with the dirtiest, roughest and hardest jobs. Even Luka began to see his friend in a different light. Botolph had lost his reticence and (dare Luka even think it?) his slight pompousness which Luka had always put down to the problem with his affliction of being so good. As Luka liked to put it: 'he came down from his cloud of ideality and entered the world of reality.' That is not to say that he relaxed any of his principles – if anything they were applied even more strongly.

He had acquired charisma. No longer was he the young priest recently arrived from Francia. He had his own inner force. Even Luka and Ash could see it. He turned heads. Wherever he went people would stop what they were doing and just gaze at him in awe.

They loved to hear him preach. They loved to hear the sensible and loving words he spoke. Nobody could fail to be inspired by him. They hung on his every word and movement.

He prayed with and for the people. He was there when people were ill or injured. He was there bringing God's comfort when they died. He smiled more easily – in fact he smiled almost permanently.

In a private moment Luka and Ash talked about it together:

"The Father's changed," said Ash.

"Aye he has lad - so you've noticed it too."

"So what's happened to him Pa?"

"I'm not sure son. You remember that Jesus and his Pa Joseph were carpenters?"

The boy nodded.

"Well to me it seems as if God's taken our Botolph and suddenly - within the past few weeks - carved and moulded him before our very eyes to be the saint he now is."

"Saint?"

"Well I can't think of any other word for it. You can see how everyone reacts to him and I can't help feeling that way myself. I feel as if I'm in the presence of someone holy."

"He's going bald."

"Ha-ha, you're right - he is that. I'll soon have no need to trim his tonsure for him."

"He's going grey too and his hair is curling at the ends."

"My, what an observant little chap you've become. I shall have to watch what I do or you'll be reporting all my inadequacies. So what do you reckon to me then?"

"Your face is getting wrinkled."

"It's *not*," he said indignantly.

"It certainly is Pa."

"I tell you it's not - I looked in the glass the other day and there was not a wrinkle in sight."

"That's 'cos you don't see too well anymore Pa."

"What? I'm not standing for any more of your insults young man - be off with you and go and do something useful."

--o--

This then was the new man that led his group to the west. And group it was. He had acquired a band of faithful followers both young and old, male and female. As he walked, most of his people followed behind but others went on ahead and proclaimed his arrival to each settlement. They prepared a site – a favoured one being under a tree and close to a stream – where he could preach and proclaim the word of God. The more he preached, the more his eloquence increased. People sat and listened, enthralled. Passing travellers reined in their horses to listen, as did boys driving ox-carts and people riding donkeys.

Even without his forerunners, the word of his preaching was spread up and down the land by the wayfarers who had heard him. Thranes, churls and thralls alike were fascinated by this new travelling preacher who told stories of a god of love who sacrificed his son so that people's sins could be forgiven. The burden of sin was forever present with these people who had been brought up to believe that three-headed devils, fiends and ghouls were a constant danger that would feed upon them and torment them at every opportunity. Now here was a man who preached the word of Jesus Christ and told them that all the sins that they had committed over the years – the rapes, murders, injuries, theft . . . would be forgiven just as long as they were prepared to start again and henceforth treat their neighbours with love and compassion. When they pleaded with him to tell them how they could be accepted by this god he replied "by baptism." He baptised them at the edges of deep rivers. He baptised them in shallow streams. In circumstances where there was no flowing water he baptised them using the precious drinking water from his leather bladder.

It did not hurt and it cost nothing but as Botolph and his group passed onwards, they left behind them men and women, boys and girls, nobles and slaves who felt refreshed and healed by the soothing words that he had brought them.

And so it was that, by the time they arrived at Egensford, King Aethelwald's court was already well aware of his progress. Indeed the Great Hall was agog with excitement - but they found that it was not just Botolph, Luka and Ash that the court would have to feed – there was a small army of supporters of all shapes and sizes, many of whom had already adopted the apparel of the monk's humble grey habit.

--o--

"I see Father, that you already have enough people to fill your monastery and yet you haven't started to build it yet," said Dame Sarre when Botolph was granted an audience the following morning.

"They are somewhat rough and ready at the moment my lady - and they have a lot to learn – but they *are* eager," smiled Botolph.

The king and queen seemed to be a pleasant enough couple, although it was clearly Dame Sarre who was the driving force. She was an attractive lady with startling blue eyes, a purring voice and peach-coloured cheeks -

which were in stark contrast to the ruddy wind-chapped cheeks that Botolph usually encountered.

King Aethelwald was a man of few words:

"When're ye going to get started then?" he asked.

Botolph wondered that himself. He had not yet seen the proposed site. It might not be suitable. How much help would the king give him in terms of labour and materials? Since his sponsor had originally been so reticent, Botolph *had* wondered if, by the time he arrived at Egensford, the king might have changed his mind. Clearly that was not the case and he seemed eager for the project to get underway. Their church building on the marsh and at Bradbryc had made Botolph realise that preparation for such a project was all-important. He would not let himself be rushed into it.

"I haven't seen the site yet sire. Perhaps once I have done so we might discuss what would be needed?"

"Perhaps, perhaps," he said irritably waving his hand as if it would push all discussions aside. "You can talk to Dame Sarre about what you want. Don't make it too much though. I'm not a rich man. Anyway – why don't ye build yer monastery down here by the river – I won't have to go too far to see it then."

Botolph did not like the sound of this at all. He wanted a place that was somewhere remote where he could worship God with his brethren without the world's interference. The prospect of building right under the nose of this king, who was showing every sign of being routinely bad-tempered, was not what he had in mind at all.

"Your sisters suggested a place by the River Tamesis called Springhead," he said.

"Springhead? Springhead? That's where the druids are, isn't it?"

He half-turned to his wife with a questioning look.

"There were some druids there a while ago, certainly," she purred. "Why don't we get Olred to take Father Botolph there tomorrow?"

"I want Olred to go hunting with me tomorrow."

"Well take his boy instead. You said he needs more practice."

He grunted.

"Tomorrow then," she purred again. Olred will take you and your friend Luka to Springhead at first light."

"How far is it?"

"Oh . . ." she looked at the king - ". . . three or four leagues I should think. "You'll be back by mid-afternoon."

---o---

It was a bright sunny morning as they rode between a forest on their right and the River Darent on their left. The birds were singing and the fish were rising. One bird that was not singing was a heron, which was standing stock still at the shallow water's edge, his shiny black eyes motionlessly scouring the glassy water. A dart-like jab - and there was a fish, wriggling in his beak.

Botolph had enjoyed the walk from Folcanstane and rather regretted the fact that today he was on horseback and unable to talk with other travellers.

Olred changed direction and led them away from the river bank into a dark forest - but they could see brightness ahead where the track broke out into bright daylight again and they soon found themselves at the crossing of what once was a handsome road.

"This is Waceling Street," declared Olred, "- the great street built by the Romans, which runs from Rutupiae," (he waved his hand to the right), "to Mercia," (he waved his hand to the left). And that," (he pointed forwards), "is the Roman's Vagniacis - or 'Springhead' as we call it today on account of the fact that the pool in the middle is fed from eight springs."

"What's that structure over there?" asked Luka, pointing to one side.

"Those are the temple ruins," said Olred.

"No, I mean the tall column," said Luka.

"Oh - that's the goddess Epona," said Olred, "A lot of local people still worship her – she's the goddess of fertility, and they come and bathe in the stream and pray to her. Come on. I'll show you one of the places where the king thought you might like to build your monastery."

Crossing the street, they rode along a narrow isthmus and, after passing another ruin on their right, came to a wharf where Olred stopped again.

"Here. This is the place. The king felt that you'd have both easy access to and from the River Tamesis as well as a good road which would take you up to Lundwic or down to Hrofsceaster."

"Yes I can see what he means," said Botolph, "- it's kind of him and I don't want to seem ungrateful but I'm afraid it's rather too close to the main road for my liking and the sea wharf exposes it to the public eye. What I really had in mind was somewhere more desolate – an unused piece of land out in the wilds where we can continue in the service of God without constant disturbances. I'm looking for the sort of place where a visitor would have to make some effort to reach."

"That would include the king of course," said Olred with a knowing smile.

"We'd always be delighted to have our sponsor attend on us," said Botolph – perhaps a little too quickly – "but no - it's more with regard to others - by having somewhere more remote, we would only receive those who had a serious desire, rather than those who were just coming as a matter of curiosity. How about down on the marshes?"

"The marshes are rather wet, Father," Olred pointed out.

"Aye but there must be parts which don't become covered by the tide. How about over there?" he pointed.

"The north side of the Fleet Stream?"

"Yes - if that's what it is," said Botolph.

"We'll go and look if you like."

They trotted eastwards down Waceling Street and, once past the tall column, turned left circling round the marshy ground and then crossed a grassy knoll towards the great river. This took them onto a high peninsula that was free from all signs of habitation both past and present. They rode to the end and dismounted and inspected what they could of the high chalk cliffs which overlooked the junction of the River Tamesis and Ebbsfleet inlet.

"What do you think?" said Luka.

"Hmm," said Botolph, "the headland's spectacular but I'm not sure. I'd hate to think of brothers falling over the edge on dark and stormy nights. The other thing we have to think of is fresh water."

"Ah," said Olred. "If it's fresh water ye want there're plenty of springs further back down the ridge."

They walked their horses back the way they had come and found the springs that Olred was talking about.

"Ah they're ideal, so I think that sways me on the whole site," said Botolph. "Do you think the king will approve?"

"Aw yes he'll be fine with this and ye'll be able to get all the wood ye need from the king's forest yonder."

Botolph looked across the marshy valley towards the forest and was struck once again by the sight of Epona's

Column. He wondered how much conflict there would be between a new monastery and those who still worshipped the heathen gods.

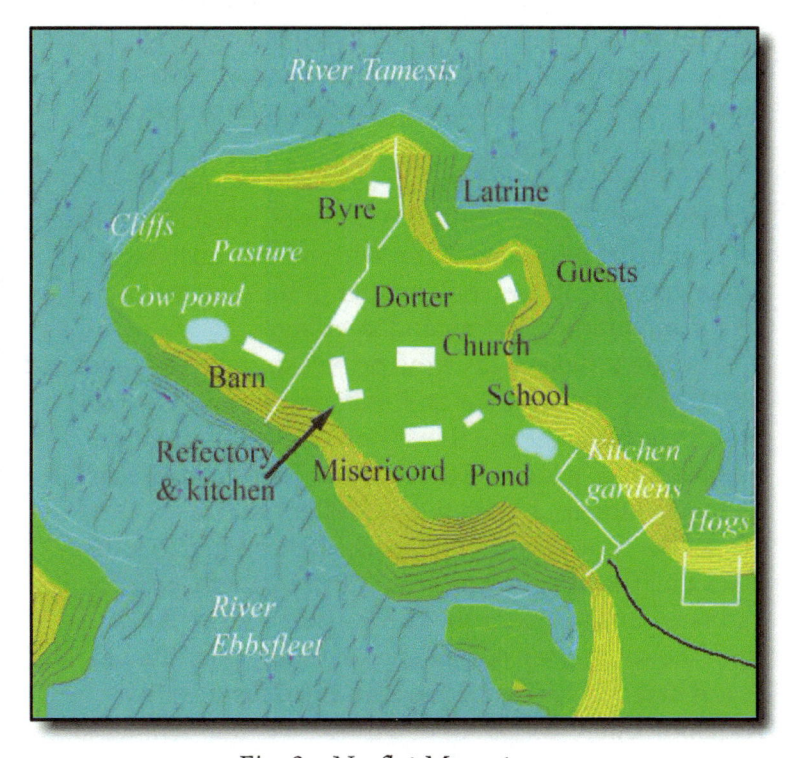

Fig. 9. Norflot Monastery.

He remembered that the Pope had specifically advised Saint Augustine not to destroy the heathen temples but to simply remove the images of their gods and to wash the walls with holy water. He wondered how that would go down with the worshippers of Epona. Still – that was work for another day – they had to start somewhere and it looked as if Springhead was just the place.

--o--

Botolph and Luka arrived back at Egensford at about the same time that King Aethelwald returned from his hunt. Olred described the site where Botolph proposed to build his monastery and Botolph took the grunts that this received to be his sign of approval. Dame Sarre, on the other hand, was ecstatic and as soon as the king left to take off his hunting boots she expressed her excitement with shining eyes.

This was something that she had wanted for so many years. She herself was a devout Christian and had aspirations of becoming a nun whereas her husband was rather cool about the whole matter of the new religion, preferring hunting, eating and sleeping.

Nevertheless, once the project started, he cooperated well by providing labour and materials and so the work progressed quickly and it was not long before Botolph, Luka and Ash were able to leave the Egensford Great Hall and install themselves in the monastery dorter.

As well as building fencing to keep in check the cows that the king had promised to give them, two ponds had been dug – one for the cows – fed by a small channel from the south-west spring and one static pond that looked as if it had been there for years and had just needed widening out.

The building work had taken a few very happy weeks. Most of the labouring had been done by King Aethelwald's serfs, who were pleased to have different work under kinder masters – and they were certainly well-treated by Botolph and Luka. The king also supplied craftsmen for the skilled work of making wooden joints and thatching roofs.

Most of them were interested in the project and several with large families had sons whom they wished to be admitted as novices in the new foundation. When word of this reached Botolph he suddenly realised that a school building would be needed and this was a last minute addition to the plan.

One day, just after sunrise, they were enjoying a hearty breakfast in the refectory with the other workers.

"Well then," said Luka looking at Ash, "we're two moons past mid-summer's day 'n' it's the beginning of the new moon tonight - so what's next then?"

"Um?" said Ash, putting his finger under his chin and looking up to the sky as if hoping for divine guidance. Botolph was sitting opposite and he grinned at the young lad's coquettishness.

"Um ... could it be ...? "

A couple of serfs who were sitting at the same table stopped munching their bread and looked across at the group.

"Yes?" said Luka.

"My ... birthday?"

Everyone laughed.

"How many summers does that make you then Ash?"

"Um ... " - the finger went under the chin again ... "eight!" he said looking at his father who nodded affectionately.

"And what day is it today?"

"Saturn's Day Pa."

"'N' when's yer birthday?"

"Um ... Moon's Day?"

"Quite right son – well done – I thought you might've forgotten it."

"Pa."

"Yes Ash."

"Why do we still name the days after the stars and the *heathen* gods like Woden 'n' Thor? Why don't we have

Jesus Day, Mother Mary Day 'n' things like that instead?"

Luka had been about to pop another piece of bread into his mouth but stopped frozen in mid-action – his mouth still open and the bread still poised in front of it. He slowly rested his arm back on the table again, closed his mouth and turned his head and stared down at his son.

"I . . . "

"Yes Pa?"

"Er . . . "- and then his frown cleared and, as if suddenly inspired, he looked up at Botolph. "I think ye'd better ask Father Botolph that question."

Botolph smiled. "The answer is, young Ash, that the people are happy with those names. By using the old gods' names for the days of the week the people are not doing any harm because they are not *worshipping* them - and nobody can deny that the stars have been important features for thousands of lifetimes. Christ hasn't come to us to change well-used old customs - but to fit in amongst peoples' traditional habits. Understand?"

Ash nodded and turned back to Luka "'N' Pa?"

Once again the bread stopped in mid-flight towards his mouth as Luka wondered what was coming next. Once again he lowered his arm and turned slowly to his son . . . "Yes?"

"Could I have some more bread please?"

--o--

Two days later, when Ash and Luka entered the chapel at sunrise for the service of Prime, they saw that eight church candles had been placed on a central table a little way in front of the altar. During the Latin intonations, which he, by now, half understood, Ash recognised his name being spoken and knew that he was being brought to the attention of God and blessed for his special day. He felt quite a thrill of excitement that *his name* should be included in the prayers and petitions.

There were over a score of people in the church that day. Some of them were men who were still working on the abbey site. There were also four slaves whom King Aethelwald had allocated permanently to the monastery; Olred had arrived the day before and stayed overnight and there were three young boys whom Ash did not recognise - together, of course, with the men and women who worked in the kitchens and on the land.

At the end of the service Botolph came from the altar and took Ash's hand and led him back around the table with its candles towards the cross. He motioned Ash to stand still and then came and stood in front of him, facing the congregation. Ash felt the warmth of his hands as he placed them on his head and then said, in English, so that all could understand:

"O Father we beseech thee to bless this child Ash whom we have brought to you today on the eight anniversary of his birth. Grant him good health, strength, happiness and a long life, and at the end of his days into Thy arms we commend his spirit."

"Amen," they chorused and Luka felt a strange rush of heat go to his head and his eyes filled with tears.

Botolph led Ash back to the table with the candles and then stood to one side. Ash looked at him questioningly but Botolph just smiled and opened his hands gesturing at the candles. Ash took a deep breath and then blew as hard as he could for as long as he could, passing his head from side to side until the candles were all extinguished whereupon he looked up at Botolph with a triumphant grin. The benevolent priest looked back down at his young charge with such an expression of love that Ash could feel it enfolding his body as the smiling abbot clapped his hands together, joined immediately by the rest of the congregation who moved round with their congratulations.

Later, when they were alone, Luka said: "I have a little present for you."

"What is it Pa?"

"Open your hands and close your eyes and you'll find out."

Ash did as he was bid and felt something like a leather pouch being placed in his palms.

"Keep yer eyes closed and tell me what you think it is."

"It's . . . it's a scrip?"

"Aye, it is that. But what's in it?"

Ash squeezed the soft leather and could feel a hard object inside it. He wondered if it was a new knife but it was too small for that. He worked his fingers round the edge.

"Hah!" he said. "It's a strike-a-light!"

"Indeed it is my boy," said his father. "Ye can open yer eyes now and have a good look."

Ash tipped the contents of the scrip out onto the floor. There was the steel itself, a narrow striking stone and some touchwood.

"Can I try it now?" he asked excitedly.

"Of course."

He knelt on the floor and arranged the touchwood as he had seen his father do when he had used his own strike-a-light. He held the flint close and tried to strike it with the steel but without success.

"My hands are all wobbly Pa," he said.

"You're doing alright son," said Luka. "You're holding it right - you just need to practise more. Your hands will get stronger. Give it another try."

Ash's aims were a bit random but suddenly, after a lucky strike a hot spark landed on the tinder and Ash quickly blew it into life.

"Well, what a celebration," said Luka to Ash. "I've never been able to give you a birthday like that before."

"No Pa – but ye've always been with me."

"Aye that I have lad and I'll always try to be."

"Who were those boys Pa?"

"Ah yes – ye haven't met them yet have ye? Their names are Algar, Durwin and Godric."

"What're they doing here then? Are they going to stay?"

"Yep. I reckon so. They're the sons of three of the workers 'n' Father Botolph has agreed to take them on 'n' educate them as monks. In return for that their families have promised to do what they can to support the monastery with work and produce. They only arrived this morning. C'mon - I'll introduce you."

They found the lads with Botolph in the schoolroom, where he was helping them to set up a table and some benches.

"I've brought Ash to welcome the newcomers," said Luka.

"Aye well, here they are," said Botolph. "This one's Algar," he said, pointing to the tall skinny one "and this is Durwin – and here's Cedric."

The boys looked shyly at each other.

"So it's your year day today?" said Cedric, breaking the slightly awkward silence. "I'm twelve."

"Oh," said Ash. "How old are you Durwin?"

"Ten," came the reply.

Ash looked at Algar.

"Eighteen," he volunteered.

"You're all older than I am then. Are you too old to

play?

--o--

Life in the new monastery gradually got underway. Once the bulk of the construction work was finished there were only fifteen mouths to feed each day as opposed to between twenty-five and thirty when the work was at its height. The problem was that when King Aethelwald withdrew his workers the kitchener and the cellarer went with them.

"It looks as if it's down to you then," said Botolph to Luka.

"Aw that's fine. Ye know I'll enjoy being in the kitchen for a while – particularly getting it all set up - but I am not sure I fancy spending the rest of my life being a cook – I'd get as fat as a hog. What are the plans for the future then?"

"Well Olred's just told me that the king wants Foundation Day to be at the beginning of December so there is a lot of work to be done before then."

"Such as?"

"Well, we need to install the livestock – both from the point of view of settling them in and also from the point of view of giving the king's herdsman something to do. He's getting restless. And then the kitchen garden needs preparing and planting before the winter; then we need wax tablets, quills and ink for the novices; wood for the winter fires; we need flour and some unground wheat ... more drinking horns and trenchers ... a stock of straw for pallets ... cattle feed ...

"Right," interrupted Luka "which one of those do you want me to deal with first?"

Fortunately for Luka everything was not put on *his* shoulders since the local farmers had been instructed by the king via Olred to provide all such items - and the king's own farm provided other produce.

There was still a lot for everybody to do. Half a dozen chickens arrived one day and were put into Ash's charge. They were allowed to roam freely in the pasture but nesting boxes had to be made. It was Ash's task to put fresh straw in the boxes regularly and to collect the eggs and take them to Luka in the kitchen.

One day Botolph was in the school giving the novices their first instructions when Ash burst through the door and said breathlessly "Father come quickly - the hogs have arrived and they're digging up Pa's kitchen garden."

The seriousness of this was all too apparent and, with Ash in the lead, followed by Father Botolph and the three novices, they ran down the path towards the pond.

There were three hogs and only Luka and the hog-boy to control them. As fast as they drove one away from the garden, the other two took its place. It transpired that the boy had opened the gate and let them in assuming that their permanent home would be in the pasture, but as soon as they saw the garden crops he could move them no further.

"Get them back through the gate," cried Botolph. "Ash - you open the gate and stand by it. Algar and you others come with me and form a line to drive them through the gate."

The miscreants were soon back in open land.

"I think this is the best place to put the styes anyway," said Luka. "We won't want them in the pasture 'cos that'll be upwind of the abbey and their smell is going to be awful at the best of times. Why don't we build the styes down here near the gate?"

"Good idea," said Botolph.

Similar dramas and potential disasters occurred

regularly during the next few weeks but, as Luka said, although it was two steps forwards and one pace backwards, they were still moving in the right direction and the monastery slowly began to take shape.

Botolph acquired more skills daily and he relished the prospect of facing the challenges and solving the problems. Not only did he have to do all the administrative work for the monastery but, in the absence of another priest, he was the only one who could perform all the rites and services. What he really needed was a prior.

Then, early one morning on a foggy November day a tall dark stranger arrived at the monastery. He was wearing the sandals of a traveller and the habit of a monk – but instead of the habit being the natural grey unbleached, undyed material customarily worn by Botolph and most other monks, the stranger's habit was black; a deep, recently-dyed, uncompromising black. It was complemented above by a strong well-trimmed beard that had no hint of grey and a matching crop of neat curly untonsured black hair. His face showed lines of past pain and yet crows' feet at the corners of his eyes suggested the ability to laugh in times of trouble. His skin was that of a traveller with red crests at the pinnacle of each cheek where it had faced into driving wind, sun, rain and snow. His teeth were even, his breath was pure and his eyes were of the deepest brown.

He stood at the gate near the pig pen, his dark silhouette framed by a grey fog lit from behind by the early morning sun which it obscured.

Ash was the first to see him as he left the dorter on his way to the latrines. At first he thought that his eyes were deceiving him as he looked down the path. Everything else was in its rightful position but there in the distance a monstrous giant stood motionless at the gate. Ash was in the process of stretching when his eyes first alighted on the vision and he froze in half-stretch as he absorbed the sight. At that moment Father Botolph came out of the church where he had been attending to his devotions.

"What is it Ash?"

"I think we have an early-morning visitor father?"

Botolph moved clear of the church so that he too could see the man at the gate.

"Come then," he said, "we must welcome him."

Filled with an inexplicable vibrant and awesome curiosity Ash skipped over to Botolph and took his hand as they walked down to the gate.

The sight of the tall elegant man of the cloth and the boy who held his hand, stirred in the stranger a buried emotion. A tear welled up in each of his eyes and together they rolled down each side of his gentle nose to be lost in the finely-sculptured curls of his moustache.

"Welcome and peace," called Botolph as they approached.

"Veritabile pax," replied the man as he looked in awe at his greeter of whom his first impressions were of the best.

Love, kindness and wisdom exuded from this tall man with the smiling face, who now let go the young lad's hand so that the boy could run the last few steps and open the gate.

To Ash's surprise, as the gate swung open the man fell forwards onto his knees and raised his hands in supplication saying:

"Bless me father, for I have sinned."

Under the fringe of Botolph's greying hair the smile altered to one of concern.

The stranger's head dropped forwards and his body was wracked with sobs.

Botolph continued to walk forwards and, standing in front of the stranger, placed both hands gently on his head, gazed down at him and said nothing. The wrenching of the shoulders gradually eased and then stopped altogether, whereupon Botolph lifted his head and, facing towards the unseen sun, said in a strong loud voice:

"O Lord, bless this stranger who is Thy gift to us. Forgive him all his sins whatever they might be, and confirm and strengthen him in everlasting life."

They stayed together like that for what seemed to be a long time – the priest looking towards the sun, his hands on the man's head, and the man motionless feeling the warmth of Botolph's touch and the calming turmoil of his inner soul as the weight of his sins was relieved.

"Rise my son," said Botolph eventually, leaning forwards to take the man by his arms and help him to his feet. "Thy sins *are* forgiven thee. This is a new day and a new life. Welcome to Norflot Abbey."

--o--

"Father," said Ash a few days later.
"Yes Ash?"
"I have a question."
"Go ahead my son."
"You remember when Brother Selwyn arrived?"
"Yes"
"You forgave him his sins."
"No, not quite. It was God who forgave him his sins, I simply told him that his sins had been forgiven."

"Ah, yes – well I knew that really Father, but my question is 'how could you tell him that his sins were forgiven if you didn't know what his sins were?'"

"I didn't need to know Ash."

"But ... but ... "

"Yes?"

"You always insist that we confess our sins to you before we take the Holy Sacrament."

"Yes, that's right and you are also theoretically right in what you say, but in certain circumstances an open confession is not essential."

"And these were the circum ... "

"Circumstances."

"... the circumstances?"

"Yes I believed they were. What Brother Selwyn needed was an end to his old life so that he could begin his new one, and I felt that he needed that there and then without delay. I hope that in his own time Brother Selwyn might make a full confession to me – but if he doesn't it won't matter because he will have moved ahead and put his old life behind him. Whatever his sins were it seems unlikely that he will ever commit them again. Now, do you have any more questions or shall we go and see how many eggs your hens have laid today?"

Ash jumped up excitedly and, taking Botolph's hand, led him through the gate into the pasture and towards the nesting boxes.

--o--

Brother Selwyn became a great asset to the monastery in general and to Botolph in particular. He was a thoroughly reliable man and seemed to understand instantly whatever it was that Botolph wanted him to do; it was almost as if he had done it all before. Botolph began to wonder if he had served as a prior in another monastery or if indeed he had been an abbot, but Botolph never questioned him and Brother Selwyn never volunteered any information.

He was well-liked by everybody and he and Luka became firm friends . . . although Luka felt from time to time that with *real* friends you usually knew what their innermost thoughts were and what it was that drove them forwards. With Brother Selwyn you never knew that. He kept himself to himself. He was forthcoming but only up to a certain point. He was an enigma.

Word of the new monastery was getting around. Botolph was not sure if this was by general word of mouth or whether King Aethelwald and his court were actively promoting it. Whatever it was, the number of visitors received at the abbey went up week by week. Some were travellers using Waceling Street – seeking a bed for the night and a blessing for their onwards journey – and others were men of all ages and from all walks of life who wished to join the monastery.

Botolph agonised and prayed for many days about whether or not everybody who wished to become a monk should be allowed to do so, but he finally came to the conclusion that he should follow the Lord's maxim of 'seek and ye shall find.' They had sought and so it was only right that they should find. He nevertheless increased the severity of the application process so that incomers were left in no doubt as to what was expected of them and what would happen to them in the event of their failing to comply with the monastery rules. This included punishments in the form of extra duties; a form of solitary confinement; beatings; and, in the most extreme cases, expulsion from the monastery.

Botolph had decided to run the abbey on the basis of the rules devised by the blessed Saint Benedict of Italy more than a century earlier. These rules were somewhat less stringent than the rules of the Irish saint Columbanus under which Botolph had been professed at Evoriacum. Botolph was a man of love and moderation who really felt that there should be no need to punish anyone. But therein lay the problem. There *was* a need because, whereas in Botolph's mind everybody should be doing their best for God and the community, many of the recent arrivals were more interested in doing the best for themselves.

"What're ye going to do about Brother Singer?" asked Luka one day.

Brother Singer had been so-named because of his habit of singing in a loud voice anywhere and everywhere at all times of day and night. In Luka's view he was as mad as a March hare and had been so ever since the day he arrived.

"Well," said Botolph "he doesn't have a *bad* voice."

"Mebbe not Father – but the problem is more a matter of when he uses it and how *loud* it is. Can't we try persuading him to sing softly?"

"I've mentioned that to him," Botolph admitted, "but he insists that he has all this joy trapped inside him and that singing loudly is the only way to let it out."

"How about him just letting it out during daylight hours?"

"I've mentioned that too but he says that he never knows when this joy is going to develop and that it sometimes wakes him in the middle of the night."

Brother Selwyn, who had been listening quietly to this conversation, said:

"What if we tell him that his night-time singing must be done outside and not in the dorter?"

"That's not a bad idea," said Botolph.

"We'd still hear it though," said Luka. "Even if he went out into the pasture we'd still hear it 'cos the wind would be blowing his voice this way. Ah now though . . ."

"What?"

"He could stretch his lungs down by the hog-sties. That'd be down wind and far enough away to give us all a bit of night-time peace."

Brother Singer accepted this new rule quite happily and thereafter he could often be seen to leapt from his pallet in the middle of the night, rush through the doorway, sprint down the path and vault over the gate whereupon his mellifluous tones would inundate the styes – initially to the consternation of the hogs but, being tolerant creatures, they soon overcame their surprise and it was said they even looked forward to their midnight entertainment.

--o--

The monastery grew in size and, according to their various talents, experience and interest, different monks were allocated to different jobs.

At the top of the tree Brother Selwyn looked after the abbey's people in an academic way, whereas Luka looked after the farming side. He had been able to relinquish his position as baker and cook when there was an influx of others who shared some of these talents.

Botolph in the meantime was deeply involved with book-keeping and other administrative duties together with running the religious and educational aspects of the institution. Brother Selwyn was a great help with the latter, having a skilful hand in calligraphy and being fluent in both Latin and Greek.

Where did he acquire these skills? This was a constant question that was frequently asked but the tall elegant man never offered any clues. He was always immaculately dressed and would regularly be seen re-dyeing one or other of the two black habits he possessed.

By the time Foundation Day arrived the number of

mouths being fed in the refectory was close to fifty. King Aethelwald and Dame Sarre came to the celebrations together with a large part of their retinue most of whom had to feast *outside* the refectory since there was insufficient space inside. Holy Communion was celebrated in the church and both the king and the queen received the Holy Sacrament and a blessing from the abbot.

After the ceremony the king gave a short speech from a position mounted on his horse so that he could see everyone and everyone could see him. He congratulated Abbot Botolph and his friend Luka on the abbey's foundation. He remarked wryly that his main regret was that it was not closer to Egensford because he would really like to visit more often.

CHAPTER 13
Visit of the King and Queen

On Midsummer's Day the routine of the monastery was turned upside down when the king and queen made an unexpected visit.

Botolph recognised that his monarch had been more than generous in everything that he had provided, so he could hardly object to such an event although he hoped that the king was not going to make a habit of it. A few words to Luka and monastery duties were rapidly rescheduled while the church was prepared for Holy Communion. As the king and his retinue filed in, Luka closed the doors behind them and then, dropping his 'royal attitude' he ran helter-skelter to the kitchen and issued orders for the ovens to be heated and loaves and vegetables to be prepared. Ash was despatched to the cellarer with a demand for a good quantity of salted fish, wine, mead and beer.

The whole place, which was normally so serene and peaceful, became a scene of frenzied activity outside - while inside the church tranquillity and order took over as usual.

Weeks of teaching and training paid a dividend and the calming sound of the brothers' plainchant percolated through the church's walls and gave encouragement to those who were struggling at short notice to prepare a feast.

All too soon for those outside, the great doors were opened and the congregation spilled out onto the campus. The king indicated that the others should go to the refectory while he turned to Botolph and told him that he had a sin that he wished to confess.

The two returned to the church and Botolph closed the door behind them. As they walked towards the altar Botolph said: "Well my lord?"

"Well Father Botolph, it is only a small sin I think."

"Would you like to make an orthodox confession?"

"No Father, I will tell you now ... I have built a church."

This was not what Botolph had been expecting and uncharacteristically he struggled to find words.

"A ... a church?"

The king nodded with a wry smile.

"What? Where?"

"At Egensford."

"But where's the sin my lord?"

"My sin is that I didn't consult you first – in fact I swore my people to secrecy."

"Hah! But that is no sin my lord – I'm delighted."

"Well I hoped you would be but I wanted to build the church my way and close to the Great Hall. I think that I have perhaps committed the sin of pride – or something like that."

Botolph had never seen the king in such a light before and, for the first time, he saw more than a glimpse of humility. The king looked vaguely embarrassed.

"There is another matter."

"Yes my lord."

"My church needs a priest."

"Ah."

Botolph's heart sank while he fought to find words to say. He could not leave Norflot now and serve the king at Egensford. Is this what the king was expecting and might perhaps command him to do? He remained silent and issued a mental prayer to his other Lord in Heaven with an urgent request for guidance while he continued to fumble with his thoughts to come up with an answer that the king would accept.

"I had hoped . . . "continued the king.

Botolph's heart dropped further.

"I had hoped that you might be able to spare one of your brothers to come and work for me."

Botolph's spirits lifted a little but then shifted rapidly sideways. Brother Selwyn. He would be the obvious answer but he was such a kingpin in the monastery's organisation that his loss would be a catastrophe. He issued another urgent prayer while furiously plumbing the depths of his mind to find an alternative solution.

--o--

Luka was in his element. The king's unexpected arrival had caused consternation but Luka worked well under pressure – indeed he thrived on it. The slaves, workers and brothers all leapt at his commands. They bore no resentment – indeed they too were pleased to have a break from their normal routines and responded well to the demands that were made of them.

As the first of the guests approached the refectory Luka barked out a few more orders and his people stopped rushing about like frightened ants and presented an orderly appearance to those who entered.

The first was Dame Sarre whom Luka greeted at the doorway and escorted to a table at the head of the hall. Other tables and benches had been rapidly moved down to make a space for the king's table; Luka would have liked to have been able to have placed it on a raised dais but sadly it had been impossible to provide one in time. He made a mental note to prepare one for future such events.

The others gradually filed in and took their places. Luka cursorily scanned the scene to ensure that his orders were being carried out and that ale and platters were being distributed promptly.

He turned his attention back to the queen and settled her at the table, wondering what had become of the king and Botolph.

"How is your son?" asked Dame Sarre.

"Well - thank you my lady."

"How old is he now?"

"He'll be nine in a couple of moons. It hardly seems long since his last birthday but time marches on at such a pace. Here he comes now. Ash my boy ... come over here and entertain Dame Sarre while I go and see what the delay is with the bread. If you'll forgive me ma'am."

--o--

"I think, my lord ... "

"Yes?"

"Well ... before I tell you what I think, can you tell me how soon you will need a priest?"

"The hall is built and the roof has been thatched but there is still some finishing work to do inside – and then, I presume, we shall need to have a consecration service?"

Botolph nodded slowly: "Have you thought of dedicating it to a particular saint sire?"

The king shook his head: "No ... why? ... should I?"

"This does seem to be customary these days. It helps those who come to the church to pray, if, rather than making direct contact with God, they have some earthly saint who lived a good life whom they can ask to intercede with God for them.

"Have you any saint in mind?"

"It seems to me sire that you might like to have a saint who was a soldier."

"A soldier eh?"

"Aye. A soldier who we now know as 'St Martin.' He was a Roman legionnaire who was ..."

The king held up his hand: "I'm sorry to interrupt you father but this sounds like a long tale and I'm famished – besides which I think that Dame Sarre might also like to hear the story from your own lips, so shall we save it until a little later?"

The feast was enjoined and enjoyed. It transpired that the king had brought a mountain of extra food with him – although whether that was out of kindness or because he did not expect to care for the food that the monastery would be able to provide, Botolph never discovered.

Afterwards, while the abbot, Luka, Ash, Brother Selwyn and the royal party were relaxing, the king brought up the subject of his new church's dedication once again:

"So, Father, you were going to tell me about Saint Martin."

Botolph had noticed that Luka had been joining in fully with the spirit of relaxation to the extent that the contents of ale-horns disappeared almost as soon as they were placed before him. He thought therefore that a distraction might be beneficial so he said:

"Luka's really the expert on that ... aren't you Luka?"

"Err – what's that?" said Luka, spinning round on a slightly eccentric pivot.

"Saint Martin," said Botolph. "You will recall the story told us by Marcus, King Dagobert's Capellanu when we were travelling across Francia."

"Aah yesh," said Luka, struggling to remember.

"Marcush – lovely fellow – carrying a locked box that had no key. Went to war with it. Alwez stayed close to the king. Right?" he said settling himself opposite King Aethelwald but looking deeply into the eyes of Dame Sarre who was watching him with an amused expression.

"The box," said Luka slowly as he struggled to regain his faculties, "contained one half of an *enormoush* black cloak which used to belong to a Roman Legionnaire called Martin. Now this Martin came from a family of *life*long committed pagans who had become quite upset when he said he wanted to become a Christian. So what did they do?"

He looked round expectantly but received no answer.

"Well – they sent him off to join the Roman Army in the hope that he would forget about it. But *did* he forget?"

The king and queen remained regally immobile but others in the party who were both fascinated by Luka's dramatic rendering and almost as inebriated as he was, shook their heads in unison with his.

"*No!* You're quite right. He *didn't* forget and one *cold winter's* night while he was patrolling the battlements at a Gallic fortress called *Samarobriva* . . . "Luka enunciated this name with relish . . . "he noticed a shivering nearly-naked beggar *huddling* in a doorway. So what did he do?"

His listeners offered no opinion.

"Well – he *ignored* him, didn't he? He was a Roman Legionnaire wasn't he? He didn't want to talk to any *dirty* beggars. So he turned his back on him and walked away."

By this time, more and more people, including some of the brethren, were crowding round watching and listening intently as Luka's drama unfolded.

"But he couldn't forget him. The picture of the soul

cowering in the corner kept haunting his mind . . . so he turned back to the creature. When he reached him . . . "Luka spun round and stood up – lurching only slightly.

"When he reached him he *drew* his sword and raised it in the air," Luka lifted his arm but then crouched a little and scanned his watchers' faces from left to right.

" . . . This sword was a sharp as a razor – run your finger along its edge and your finger'll bleed like a fountain. He unclipped his cloak and *swirled* it ahead of him, placing his foot on its hem and saying: 'There is enough material here to keep us *both* warm tonight' he *ran* the point of his sword across the middle, cutting it perfectly in half and, re-sheathing his sword, he pressed the cut half of the cloak into the hands of the beggar and resumed his patrol . . . BUT!"

Luka's eyes opened wide and his right hand pointed upwards as he stage-managed an impressive pause.

"BUT . . . the story doesn't end there because at the end of his shift and when he was fast asleep in his pallet, he had a dream where he saw *Jesus* wearing the torn part of his cloak and saying 'I was given this cloak by Martin - a Roman soldier who has never been baptised.' There was no stopping him then . . . " Luka scanned his audience again, " . . . he became baptised, got himself discharged from the army, went on to become a bishop, performed lots of miracles and then . . . *on his death* . . . they built a great tomb above his grave and made him a saint. Still, *to this very day*, if you go to his tomb and pray to him, your wish will be granted! . . . And *that*," he said with a flourish "is the story . . . of St Martin."

Luka spread his arms wide and bowed his head . . . to the sound of rapturous applause and cheering.

"Well thank you Luka," said the king, laughing, "I

have no doubt that today is not the last time that you will be asked to narrate this story," and - turning to Botolph: "I am persuaded, Father Abbot. We will dedicate Egensford Church to Saint Martin."

--o--

For the next two months Botolph spent much of his spare time training four of the monastery brethren to look after the Egensford church. He selected four on the basis that first of all he would send one pair for six months. They would then return to the monastery for further training and respite, while the second pair took over for the next six months whereupon the process would be repeated.

He did this partly because *he* wanted to maintain contact with the brethren and also assumed (rightly as it turned out) that *they* would want to maintain contact with Norflot - and partly because time had been so short that, although they were competent, he felt he had not really given them as much training as he would have liked to have done.

The church was consecrated at the end of August. The festivities at Egensford were far more elaborate than they had been at Norflot, but that came as no surprise to Botolph. This was the king and queen's personal contribution to Christianity and it was only right that they should choose how to mark the occasion.

--o--

After the founding of St Martin's at Egensford, Botolph returned to Norflot re-inspired and re-invigorated.

The celebrations had been a revelation to him. He had been treated with great respect and he could not get away from this. It worried him slightly because he was well aware of the danger of succumbing to personal pride.

His soul, however, was irrefutably humble and he valued this and intended to never let it go. He realised that what came across as personal respect was simply a sign that people had confidence in him to carry out God's work, and of that he was grateful. He was suddenly in a position of power and people were coming to him asking what should be done. He believed he knew very well what should be done. It was as if his eyes had been re-opened to see the answers to mysteries that had previously been hidden from him and would remain hidden to most men. He had the firm backing of his local lord and a free hand to carry out his vocation. He had no doubt that it was God's will that he should press on with all speed to do His work.

His vision was to establish churches throughout the country. He would do as much as he could from Norflot before taking up King Anna's offer in Engla and then gradually work his way up to the north.

He had already started to teach his young brethren in such a way that they would each be capable of setting up a small chapel and running it so that they could both preach and administer the Holy Sacrament to their congregations while gradually gathering around themselves boys and young men as fledgling monks.

--o--

Luka wanted a boat. He had been badgering Botolph about this for weeks – constantly bringing up ever-increasing and diverse reasons as to why such a vessel was a necessary part of the monastery's equipment. Botolph could on one hand see the sense of Luka's argument but on the other hand he suspected that the main reason that Luka wanted a boat was so that he could play with it. Luka became bored easily and there was a distinct likelihood that he would, after a while, become bored with a boat too, but the more irons he had in the fire the more choices he would have as to which one he would choose to play with on any particular day.

Botolph knew that variety was good for Luka and for the running of the monastery because he would throw himself with renewed vigour into any project that Botolph gave him – as long as the project did not go on for too long. Fifteen months had passed since the abbey was founded and it now supported nearly a hundred people, three quarters of whom were monks at varying stages of their profession and the other quarter were labouring and administrative staff – of whom Luka was but one.   There were plenty of people therefore, who could take over from him as he hopped from job to job.

On the subject of the monastery's size, Luka had a favourite pun that he used on every possible occasion.   The first time that he produced it, it took Botolph quite a long time to work out what he was talking about. It occurred a few months earlier when they were standing in the pasture with Ash and Brother Selwyn.   Botolph had remarked to Luka that the abbey had nearly 150 mouths to feed.

"That's a Norflot of people," said Luka innocently.

"Yes it is," Botolph had agreed.

Luka's face broke into a beam and he looked up at Brother Selwyn and nudged him.

"D'ye get it?" he said.

"Get it?"

Luka nudged him again and could scarcely contain his mirth.

"A *Norflot* of people," Luka said, slapping his thigh and guffawing with laughter.

"A what?"

"A *Norflot* – you know- *Norflot* – an awful lot – a . . . large number . . . a . . . "

His voice trailed off and he stopped laughing as they all stared at him.

"Ah - I see," said Botolph with a laugh, "a *Norflot* - an awful lot - yes very clever Luka - thank you for sharing that with us and thereby enriching our lives. Now if we could just get back to the subject of how much cattle feed we are going to require this winter?"

A grin returned to Luka's face and he nodded at Botolph and looked across at Ash who had understood what he was talking about almost as soon as the words were out his mouth. Ash glanced at his father with a mixture of amusement and tolerance. Brother Selwyn however was shaking his head and looking at the ground saying:

"An awful lot of people - an awful lot . . . "

CHAPTER 14
An Expedition

Botolph was ready for his first expedition. He and Luka had been exploring the local surroundings for several weeks and he had identified a small settlement nearby as being ideal for a field chapel.

The people were friendly. Like at Bren Sete they were eager to be baptised and to have a church. Botolph had selected two of the brethren whom he believed were well qualified to look after the community's spiritual needs.

King Aethelwald had given his permission - both to cut the timber and to build the church.

It lay only three leagues to the southwest of Norflot at the edge of a wood high above the River Cray at a place they called Rookslea because of the hundreds of noisy black birds which lived in the surrounding trees.

The time came for the felling of the timber and this brought a multitude of objections from the flying residents. The local people hardly seemed to notice them and they just chuckled when Luka grumbled about the noise. The rooks seemed to know that they irritated him. Several of them would take turns to mob him – swooping close to his head before climbing high into the sky with a mocking "caw caw caw."

"Ye see that bunch of them over there," said Luka to Ash one day.

Ash nodded.

"*Those* are the varmints. There's a whole family of

them. Look at them now – they're sitting up there looking down at me and waiting their chance. Once I've got me back turned and start working on something they'll swoop down and frighten the daylights out of me."

He held out his hands: "Look ye 'ere - I've got no end of cuts and grazes where they've startled me while I was using me tools. It's no good you laughing young Ash."

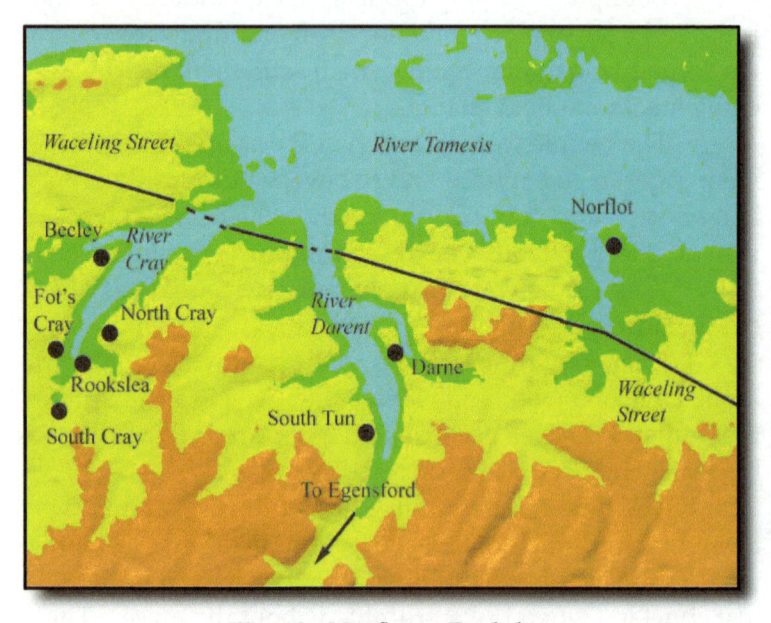

Fig. 10. Norflot to Rookslea.

His son by that time was bent over and had his hands on his knees trying to get a breath as his stomach convulsed and the tears ran. He raised one finger and pointed at his father and tried to speak but collapsed into laughter again. Luka loved to see his son's mirth and he well knew that the sterner and crosser he looked, the funnier Ash found it, so he was careful not to let his demeanour slip. As he continued to rant and rave some of the villagers stopped their work and came over to see what the fuss was about. They too began to giggle as Luka carried on his tirade.

He eventually calmed down, allowing Ash to regain his breath and composure.

"Well if you can't do anything better than laugh son, I suggest you take that barrow over there and put your energies to good use by collecting some more poles for me. Get on with you now," he said with false grumpiness and turned back to his work, grinning inwardly.

Botolph had selected Rookslea because it was centrally placed between three other settlements – namely North and South Cray, which were on the same side of the valley, and Fot's Cray which was level with Rookslea but on the other side. It was also at the head of the river, which meant easy access for people and produce as well as a good supply of water, mud and rushes.

The little wooden chapel was quickly built. All the materials were readily available and a fortnight later Abbot Botolph installed the two incumbents. They already knew the local people well, having worked alongside them during the building process. This was no accident and it was one of the principles that Botolph continued to employ throughout the rest of his chapel-founding life. During the two weeks that the construction had taken, Botolph had attended four times on the pretext of overseeing the work. He had made sure that a good meal of bread and broth was available for the workers at noon. The villagers were happy to prepare this themselves – for after all they were getting a new hall which would not only serve their religious needs but would also provide them with a community centre and extra shelter.

During these meals Botolph would surreptitiously study the way his two intended incumbent monks interacted with the villagers. There would be circumstances in the future when he would have to make substitutions due to monks becoming over-familiar with their charges. The abbot was a good judge of character and as this skill was honed further he became adept at quickly identifying those monks who were going to cause more harm than good. These were quickly weeded out.

Another of the wise conditions that he imposed was that only water from the local sweet-running stream would be served at lunchtime, on the basis that mead or ale would be counter-productive to the afternoon's work.

The workers were a selection who came from all four vills. Each day started with the two incumbent monks praying with the whole gathering, asking God to help everyone to use their skills to the best of their abilities and to protect each other from injury. The potential for the latter was enormous with so many people working on one site.

Grace was routinely said at lunchtime. In the evening before the workers dispersed there were more prayers thanking God for the progress made during a successful day.

The day of the chapel's inauguration was different however. The celebrations were led by Abbot Botolph himself. The previous day over fifty monks had travelled up from Norflot monastery. They divided up to be billeted in each of the four villages.

At sunrise on the day of the inauguration each of the groups, led by one of their number carrying a high cross, started their procession to Rookslea. Behind them came the men of the village and behind those came the women and children. The monks chanted as they went and some of the villagers joined in as best they could.

At Rookslea itself the procession also started at sunrise but this was a rite where the long line of people beat the bounds of the village and marked out the Rookslea territory. By the time the procession returned to the church, the other groups were arriving too, and the chanting of the four sections joined in unison.

There was no way that the little chapel could accommodate the great mass of people who had come to the ceremony, but the abbot had made it clear that the villagers would have pride of place - leaving just enough room for himself and the two incumbents; the rest of the monks would stay outside.

Even so, by the time everybody was there, the chapel was crammed to capacity and hordes were outside trying to get a view. When Botolph saw this, he realised that some modification was necessary and he made the instant decision that the bulk of the ceremony would take place *outside* the chapel. Only at the last moment would he, the two incumbents and the village elders enter the new building to bless and sanctify it.

There was no time to construct a dais but two wheelbarrows were crudely lashed together with some planking on the top and, much to the crowd's amusement, Abbot Botolph was helped to ascend this rather rickety platform.

He raised his hands and the laughter and chatter stopped and there was silence. He said nothing at first but, hands still raised, he swung slowly round.

At first he looked at the chapel . . . and then over the heads of the people to where wisps of smoke were rising in the distance. His gaze followed the wisps downwards to its source which he saw was a pig roasting on a spit.

Swinging further round he noted the Cray river flooding past North Cray village.

His final vista was the edge of the wood from whence came the timber to build the church.

"My friends," he said – there was a murmur.

"My friends," he repeated. "It gives me great joy to see you here today. It gives me great joy to see that Christianity brings unity to your four villages. It gives me great joy that you have built this chapel in the service of Our Lord Jesus Christ."

The consecration service proceeded with prayers, responses and readings from the Old Testament and the Gospels and then came the time for the abbot to bless the holy water ...

"*Exorcizo te, creatura aquae, in nomine Dei Patris omnopotentis, et in nomine Jesu Christi, Filii ejus Domini nostri ...* " his voice rang out across the gathering.

It was not necessary for them to understand the words. One of the servers poured water from a pitcher into the aspergorium and Botolph raised his hands in supplication as he uttered the incantation, finishing

"*... ut salubritas, per invocationem sancti tui nominis expetita, ab omnibus sit impugnationibus defensa. Per Dominum, amen.*"

The other server raised the aspergorium and Botolph dipped into it a holy besom brush made especially for the occasion and sprinkled it, first to the right of him over the crowd:

"*In nomine Patris ...* "

... and then straight in front of him ...

" *... et Filii ...*"

... and then to his left ...

" *... et Spiritus Sancti ...* "

At his final word the servers moved away and eager

hands helped him step down onto the ground whereupon he and the aspergorium bearer, moved towards the chapel where the abbot similarly sprinkled the south, east, north and west walls while repeating his incantations.

At the west doorway he placed the besom into the aspergorium and bowed to the server, who moved to one side. The other server handed him an iron chisel and a mallet. The abbot moved to the right hand side of the doorway where, etched onto the timber was the sign of a consecration cross which had been half-cut by the carpenter. Botolph placed the sharp edge of the chisel onto an etch line and gave it a smart tap with the mallet causing one limb of the cross to obediently break away. He repeated the process with the other three limbs until the white cross was fully exposed on the dark wood. He moved to the left hand side of the doorway where another cross had been similarly prepared and did the same thing there.

Handing the mallet and chisel to the server, he turned to face the people and said in a loud voice:

"Your church has now been consecrated. Praise be to God."

"Praise be to God," came the thunderous reply and Botolph turned and entered the chapel followed by the two servers, the two incumbent monks and the elders of the four villages.

On the Mass Table were two large loaves, a large earthenware flagon of wine. In the centre were two sizeable drinking horns. Botolph stood in front of the altar and looked across the congregation to the crowd he could see standing outside. Two hassocks had been placed before him and he gestured to the incumbents to kneel on them. Placing a hand on each of their heads and looking high up into the timbers of the new chapel he prayed:

"Almighty Father, I bring before you these Thy loyal servants. Bless them and guide them as they serve this community as Thy shepherds. Grant them wisdom and foresight, compassion and kindness, strength and perseverance. Keep them from temptation and help them to bring all their flock safe and intact to Thy Heavenly Kingdom. Amen."

"Amen," the congregation repeated.

Removing his hands from their heads he gestured to them to rise and face the congregation.

"People of the valley of the River Cray," he intoned, "I give you your two new shepherds, Brother Zacharias and Brother Benjamin. Praise be to God."

"Praise be to God."

The sound echoed round the chapel and then out into the countryside, where the call was repeated by those standing outside. "Praise be to God; praise be to God."

The abbot turned and moved behind the Communion Table with the brothers standing on each side of him. He continued with the prayers of the Holy Communion service.

When the time came for him to break the bread he held one loaf aloft and broke it in half. The whole flagon of wine was consecrated and the two drinking horns filled from it. Botolph took Communion himself and then administered it to the two brothers after which he gave each of them one of the two drinking horns and, with the abbot carrying one of the loaves, the trio moved to the front of the altar where Botolph stood between the two, facing the congregation.

"I invite all ye who have been baptised in the name of Christ and have confessed your sins, to come forward and take this Holy Sacrament to your comfort."

The servers took on the role of ushers and after

taking Communion themselves they set about creating an orderly flow between those who had taken the sacrament and those who were about to take it. The latter came forward two at a time and stood before Botolph who administered the bread while the incumbents administered the wine.

Outside the chapel Luka and half a dozen monks had the task of controlling the crowd. Ash, who was generally by Luka's side, was sent scampering off from time to time with various messages. Luka finally herded the last of the communicants in.

Botolph caught Luka's eye and raised the bread questioningly. There was a pause and time stood still for them both – their eyes locked in combat – Botolph's pleading with Luka's to accept the sacrament and Luka's pleading with Botolph to forgive his inability to do so. He shook his head – ever so slightly – their eyes remained locked. Botolph felt a lump come into his throat and Luka felt his eyes beginning to water. He broke the contact and quickly left the chapel and vanished from Botolph's sight.

The abbot and the incumbents finished the ablutions with the help of the servers and the holy water from the aspergorium was used to wash the drinking horns and the wine flagon. The contents of the aspergorium were then poured onto the soil over which Botolph made the sign of the cross.

And then the festivities began. Botolph looked for Luka but he was nowhere to be seen.

--o--

Luka strode swiftly out of the church and then followed the outside wall round to the east and broke into a run as the forest swallowed him up. He felt sick. He ran blindly at full speed, relishing the pain of muscles working at full stretch – but there was no path – he tripped on a branch and his face smashed onto the solid ground that lay beneath a carpet of thin leaf mould. He picked himself up and started to run again. He had nowhere to go. Blood ran down his face making it difficult for him to see out of his right eye. He fell again. He rose again and ran again. He fell for a third time and this time did not rise but sobbed and sobbed and lay there sobbing.

Slowly the tears subsided. What was he *doing*? He was strong. He could stand any amount of pain without flinching. Why was he lying here crying like a foolish maiden?

He felt like a traitor. He had let down his dearest friend in the world. He had failed him. He couldn't do it. He couldn't take Communion. Why?

He had lost his faith.

He sat up and pushed his back against a tree-trunk – raising his head to stare disconsolately into the canopy of trees above.

Why? What had happened to God? Where was He?

He wasn't there. He wasn't where He should have been.

Was He ever there?

Luka thought and wondered.

Was he ever a proper Christian?

He had liked the idea of God. He had liked the idea of Christianity. He believed that Christ had lived. He believed that Christ was holy and had lived the sort of unselfish life that we all should live. He believed that Christianity had brought peace to a Britain that had previously had been a country of mad dogs – all snapping and trying to steal each other's food and possessions. The country had been full of hate and selfishness. Nobody had felt safe, neither kings, queens nor peasants. Raiding parties would come from nowhere and rape and kill. His own tribe had been the rapists. His father had been a hard and cruel man and he grew to hate him for it. Luka had escaped to Cnobersburg where he had met Botolph whom he had also hated. He had hated the whole world. He had no wish to live like his father.

With Botolph he had started a journey to enter the church – but why? Was it just somewhere to go? A journey to take? Was it hero worship of Botolph? Did he admire Botolph because he was a Christian - or was it something else?

No - he admired Botolph because he was Botolph. Because their personalities merged and harmonised with each other. He could no more consider giving up his friendship with Botolph than Botolph could consider giving up his relationship with God. Botolph never had any doubts. Botolph was wedded to God and Luka admired him for it and wished that he too could be like his friend.

But he could not.

He did not have Botolph's conviction. Luka could not *see* God – he could not *hear* God – he could not *sense* that God was there. It was not a case of disbelief. He was quite ready to believe that God existed but he was unable to *feel* him.

Botolph could. Botolph had no doubts. Botolph was relaxed whereas Luka was in torment. Luka wished that he had Botolph's faith. Was such a wish half a step to becoming a Christian? Half a step it might be but he doubted that he would ever be able to take the other half of the step.

What should he do? There seemed to be no other choice. He had to go.

--o--

"Where's Pa, Father?" asked Ash.

"He's had to go off on a journey," said Botolph.

"Did you send him?"

"Well, in a manner of speaking I suppose I did."

"When will he be back?"

"As soon as he's found what he's gone to look for."

"What's that?"

"Well my son – that's difficult to explain, but I suppose he's really gone to look for himself."

"Himself? Oh ... I see."

"You do?"

"It's God, isn't it Father?"

"What do you mean?"

"Pa's always had difficulty with God. He says he can't talk to Him 'n' he's never sure if He's listening or not. I've asked him about it lots."

"You have?"

"Yes, he says that he's glad that I'm like you and that you never have any doubts about God."

Botolph put his arm around the lad and hugged him, marvelling, not for the first time, at the perspicacity of the young.

--o--

When the consecration party arrived back at Norflot they were greeted by the familiar sight of a short sturdy man cheerfully raking the kitchen garden and whistling as he worked.

It was Ash who saw him first. He ran ahead and threw himself at his father.

Luka staggered back: "Well where've you been?" he said.

"Never mind that," said his father's son, "where've *you* been Pa?"

"I've been working here. This place won't run itself you know. 'Tis all very well you lot going off and consecrating and celebrating ... but the weeds still keep growing and the hogs still need feeding."

Ash stood back, realising that he was doomed to get nowhere with this conversation.

"Well I'm glad you're back Pa. I thought I'd lost you."

"Ha!" said Luka. "You'll not lose me that easily son. You're stuck with me. I'll never leave you."

"What's that?" called Botolph catching up with Ash.

"I was just telling Ash that one of the hogs seems to have a bit of foot rot which needs treating."

"Oh - that," said Botolph with a happy grin. "Well I've no doubt you'll look after it."

CHAPTER 15
The Voyage of *The Ganot*

Rookslea was a great success and became a thriving Christian community that flourished further as the banks of the River Cray became more widely populated. The abbot was able to create several more such communities both further down the Cray valley and also along the southern parts of the River Darent.

Feeling that he had done all he could on the southern shore of the River Tamesis, Botolph turned his attention to the north bank. King Aethelwald had provided him with a large trading vessel, together with a skipper and two hands. The skipper had sailed the River Tamesis and its reaches for many years and he was well versed in the capriciousness of its tides.

The skipper brought the boat into the Ebbsfleet river mouth and moored alongside the low west quay while he waited for the abbot to make his final preparations.

Luka was fully back on form and fussed about ensuring that the boat would be well victualled. He did not go along with the theory that 'God will provide' as, in the past, he had discovered that he had often become quite famished before God had got around to providing. He took it into his own hands therefore to collect together enough food and ale for a week. Anything extra that God might choose to provide, Luka told himself, he would be grateful for.

Botolph was kept busy too. On the day of their

departure he was up before dawn finalising arrangements to ensure that the monastery continued to function properly during his absence.

It would have been more convenient if the boat had been able to moor closer to the monastery, but this was precluded by it being surrounded by steep cliffs on one side and marshy ground on the other – neither of which was conducive to safe mooring for the boat or safe embarkation of the passengers.

Soon a long line of bundle-bearing monks preceded by Luka, a scampering Ash, and Botolph carrying his crozier, could be seen silhouetted against the morning sky as it made its away along the ridge from the monastery to Waceling Street. Behind them came the monastery's horse-drawn cart carrying the tents they would need. Other wayfarers were already travelling along the dusty road and, depending upon their inclinations, they either ignored the abbot and his group or greeted them with reverence and respect.

Once past the springhead they turned off the road and followed a track along the edge of the muddy banks of the river to where the good vessel *Ganot* was wallowing in the shallow water and bouncing occasionally off the edges of the wooden wharf.

The skipper, helped by his two swarthy crew, took the bundles and tents and stowed them away before helping their passengers aboard.

"Is that it then Father?" asked the skipper. "We still have the last of the ebb to help us out into the river so if it's all the same to you we'll push off now afore we lose it."

"Yes indeed my son, that's all of us, so let's proceed. My brethren are all eager sailors so if they can be of any assistance to you then they'll be glad of your request."

It amused Ash to hear the skipper calling the abbot

'Father' and to hear Botolph referring to the skipper as 'my son' - since the skipper looked old enough to be Methuselah himself. He was of a stocky build with a full white beard and a complete absence of teeth. His cheeks were ruddy and wind-worn and his wild white over-generous eyebrows were composed of hairs that gave the appearance of being continually in battle. Ash imagined that in strong wind or spray, he would simply have to frown a little and his eyes would be protected by an impenetrable hemp-like curtain.

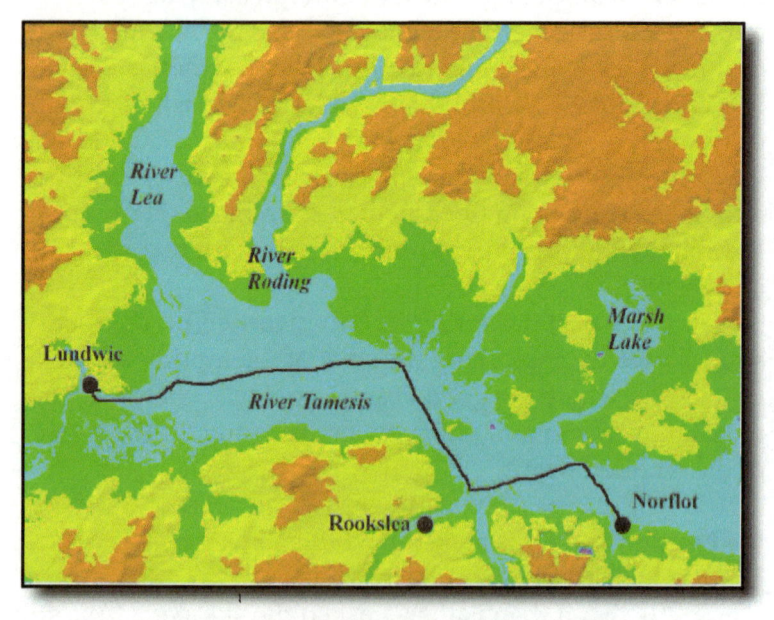

Fig. 11. Voyage from Norflot to Lundwic.

The short fingers of his hands were gnarled and calloused. As well as the seax at his belt he also had a short knife tucked into the top of his gaiters – a clothing feature that was unfamiliar to Ash. In spite of his great age and serious appearance he seemed to lack neither humour nor agility.

There was a light southwesterly breeze blowing – not exactly the wind direction one might have chosen for a sail up the River Tamesis to Lundwic, but it served well to lift the boat away from the Norflot quayside as the crew unlashed the spar and hoisted both it and the square woven sail.

As they passed the abbey headland, brother monks working in the pasture called and waved and a short while later they passed through the poppled water of the great river as the mischievous currents of ebb and flow fought with each other at the confluence of the Ebbsfleet inlet.

The skipper, perched on the stern clutching the steering oar, set a course for the northwest but, although the sail was full, it gave them little speed in the light wind. At his call the two crew unshipped their oars and bent to their labour of rowing the vessel up and into the fairway, where the tide would scud her up the river.

He did his best to keep the sail drawing but this was sending them too close to the north bank so he gave up the unequal struggle and, once the sail had been dropped and gasketted, the task was given over to the rowers and the current. It was not in the nature of Norflot monks to sit with idle hands and first one offered his services and then another and it was not long before the four empty rowing positions were also soon occupied and the craft was making good progress to the west.

They came to a wide bay and, following Ash's question about where they might be, Botolph had to admit that he was completely lost. He suggested to Ash that he should go and ask Methuselah. After threading his way aft, skirting around the rowers and other bodies and packages, Ash posed the same question whilst also wondering how long it might be before they arrived.

"Ar well. That's Lundwic over there," he said, pointing slightly to the right of their direction of travel.

"D'ye see the dip between the hills – where the land goes flat? That's where the Lundwic River picks its way 'tween the marshes as it heads to the west."

"I thought the river was the Tamesis."

"Aye, so it is. That's its proper name but, particularly in these reaches, us seamen call it by its other name. If you look over there ... " - he pointed across to the right – "ye can see the great River Lea as it heads up to the north. The tide's doin' its best to swirl us up there 'n' that's why we're heading a bit to the south ... to get out of its grip, so to speak. Would ye like to try yer 'and at steering?"

Ash nodded and they changed their positions on the helmbox.

"What do I have to do?"

"Nothin' much, most of the time, 'cos the rowers have got her quite even at present, but they'll gradually drift off course and then'll come the moment when ye'll have to give her a great heave on the steering oar – I'll lend ye a hand when the time's right."

The wind went round to the south and picked up a little so they hoisted the sail again giving the rowers an easier run. It seemed no time at all before they found themselves approaching a wide marshy inlet. A few huts appeared on the south bank but the skipper steered towards the northern edge and, with the bow wave susurrating softly against the ship's side they watched in wonder as the ruined city of Lundwic came slowly, silently - and somewhat sinisterly - into view.

The skipper pointed out the crumbling walls of the old city and then the place where the relics of the old

Roman bridge still scrambled up onto the shore. Just past that came a ruined palace where a lone figure waved to them from the river bank. Then there was a wide inlet with two vessels tied up alongside.

"That's the Wall Brook," said the skipper. "It runs under the north wall of the city and drains down here into the river. It used t' serve as both water supply and washerwoman for the big city. Ye see that ruin up there?"

Ash nodded.

"That's a temple. A *Roman* temple to the God Mithras. We'll go 'n' see it later if ye like?"

Ash nodded enthusiastically.

"'Ere we go then. Let me 'ave the oar back boy. Ye've done a good job. Get ready to let that sail go," he called in a louder voice as he turned the craft northwards into a sizeable river with a wharf on the right hand side.

"This be the River Fleet," he said briefly before adding more loudly again "down with that sail now. Avast rowing. One man on the bow with a warp."

An expectant silent pause as the wind and tide pushed the boat nearer to the quay and then "ship oars," and the passengers shuffled their bodies out of the way as the wet blades dropped alongside them.

The skipper stood acrobatically on the ship's side and deftly looped a rope over a wooden post as they glided past. He skipped back and allowed a coil of the inboard end of the rope to surge around the vessel's sternpost until they came to a gentle standstill.

"Very neat!" called Luka admiringly to the nods of the other passengers. The skipper gave a triumphant toothless grin and made a mock bow before setting about securing the boat properly.

--o--

A small community had made their home just outside the former city wall. They were farmers, fishermen and opportunistic traders who welcomed ships to the quayside in the hope of profitable business. They were led by a senior elder who, as a mark of respect, was known as the 'Aldor.'

Some of the traders had made their way down river from the narrower reaches of the Upper Tamesis. A few were ultimately destined for Gaul; others were bound for the wide mouth of the river estuary where they would turn north towards the ports of Britain's eastern seaboard.

Smaller ships ferried passengers across the Tamesis from the south bank. Many of these carried traders who had landed on the south coast and were making their way overland to the north. Some would not be separated from their horses, in which case they had to travel in special cattle boats where the animals could be seen standing stock still with fright, surrounded by similarly petrified sheep and goats. Others left their hirelings on the south bank in the almost certain hope of obtaining a replacement on the other side.

This was all good business for the settlers of the outskirts of Lundwic, who did their best to cater for their customers' every need.

Some of the wayfarers were too poor, too mean or too principled to do anything but walk. But at the same time there were others who were too rich, too lazy or in too much of a hurry - and these often chose to hire a fast cart.

The enterprising merchants of the new Lundwic had products to cater for everyone's needs and Botolph had no difficulty in obtaining the services of a decent-sized cart to carry the tents up to a hillside just north of the city walls. They pitched them near one of the springs that supplied the Wall Brook and finished just as the sun touched the horizon.

Early the following morning the villagers woke to the sound of plainsong as the monks chanted their morning litany during their procession to the quayside.

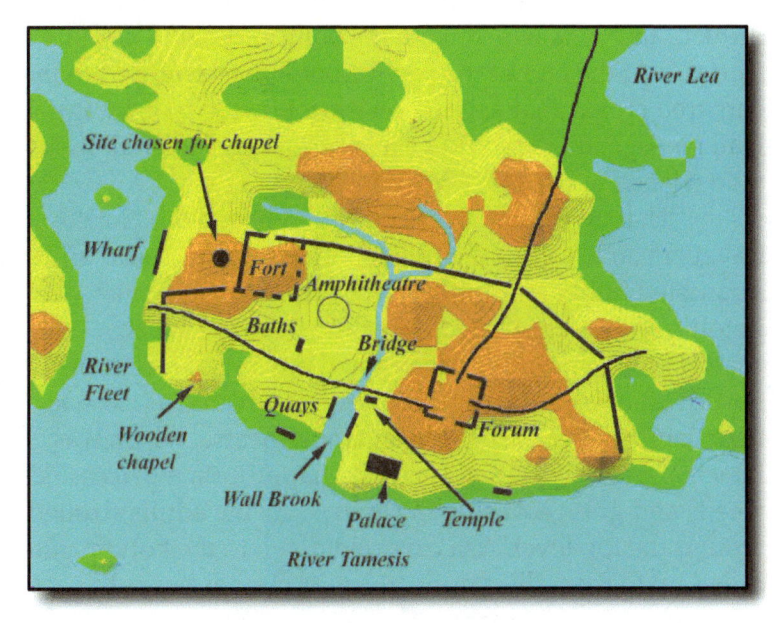

Fig. 12. Lundwic.

The locals rose hastily from their pallets and ran from their homes to see and hear this spectacle which, for some, was their first experience of Christianity.

Botolph was at the front of the procession, singing with a good strong voice while using his crozier as a walking stick to steady himself on the uneven ground, but the actual leader was Ash, carrying a simple wooden cross that he held high in the air as if proclaiming that Jesus himself was coming to visit.

Following a prompt from the abbot, Ash came to a

standstill at the quayside and the group formed a semicircle around him. The singing continued for a short while longer and then the Sacrament of Holy Communion began. At the appropriate moment, all present who had been baptised were invited to eat of the broken bread and to drink of the wine which were the body and blood of Jesus Christ. At the end of the service Botolph announced to the gathered crowd that at noon on the following day, by the water's edge, there would be a baptism service for all those who wished to become Christians.

That afternoon, the skipper conducted the Norflot travellers on a tour of the ruined city. Ash ran ahead and scrambled hither and thither over broken walls while Botolph and Luka strolled down the deserted streets, chatting to their guide. He pointed out an old fort in the northwest corner, the opposite edge of which was close to their campsite. Nearby was an amphitheatre, which was intact apart from trees growing in inappropriate places and weeds and grass covering the arena. As the adults strolled around the top level, Ash cavorted down to the bottom and called up to them, his young voice, as clear as crystal, echoing around the place. The skipper showed them the sunken baths and the hypocausts with the fire ovens and then they crossed the remains of a small rickety stone bridge to what was left of a once-handsome stone building with a tiled roof.

"This is the temple of Mithras," said the skipper pointing to the floor where a mosaic showed a powerful god thrusting a knife into the side of a bull.

Botolph studied the ruins closely. It was much like the stone church that he would like to build and it crossed his mind that, although it was a Heathen temple, there might be a possibility of their following Pope Gregory's suggestion and turning it into a Christian church.

He saw three things against this though. The building was back to front – its altar was in the west; the Heathen mosaics were inappropriate but it would be a shame to dig up the floor. The third obstacle was its position within the city: his countrymen were happy to plunder stones to construct their own buildings but they were traditionally opposed to converting whole Roman homes to their own use. Whether it was out of respect for their former masters or something else he was not too sure. He had seen the same situation at Cantwarebury. People were happiest outside the old city walls and that was where he too would build Lundwic's chapel.

--o--

The next day, while everybody else was taking part in the baptismal sacraments, Ash wandered back into the ruined city with a view to exploring on his own. On the previous day's tour he had particularly wanted to see the old palace, but by the time they had looked at the Temple of Mithras it was close to lunchtime and the prospect of food had overcome other interests.

Ash made his way along the city wall and in through the west gate. On the brow of a hill to his right stood an un-roofed wooden building, which was in the process of being consumed by trees. He climbed the grassy slope for a closer look. Clearly it had once been a building of note. Was it an old Christian chapel? He resolved to tell the abbot about it later. Skipping onwards over a gulley he ran back to the road and made his way across the rickety stone bridge following the path past the temple until at last the ruined palace lay before him.

It looked like a spooky place and he wondered if fiends and goblins lived there. Again there were trees and plants growing everywhere they shouldn't – rather (he thought) like the hairs that grew out of Pa's nose and ears.

He threaded his way through the trees looking for a door – and eventually he found one. It was secured by a once-handsome but now-rusty immoveable iron latch. He turned away from the door and went to search for a stone that might be used to free it. There were plenty nearby at the base of a collapsed wall and he suddenly realised he did not need to open the door as the breach in the wall provided easy access to the palace's inner corridor. Once within he hesitated for a moment - getting his bearings and wondering where to start.

Murals had been painted on the walls but dirt and damp had taken their toll and it was difficult to work out what the pictures had shown in their glory.

'Bang!' A loose shutter made him jump. The wind was freshening. Goose-bumps tingled down his spine and he suddenly felt a little scared . . . but brave enough to go on – and so he did – while his mind was still resolute.

He noted that much of the roof was still intact.

He worked his way along the corridor, stumbling past wooden benches and pieces of broken furniture.

'Bang!' The shutter frapped in the wind again. He shivered once more – and then suddenly jumped as, with a squeal, an object darted out of a corner and shot between his legs. More goose-bumps spread across his back as wide-eyed he spun round to see what it was. A dirty brown piglet was standing a few cubits away, sniffing the air and looking at him warily through tiny pink eyes. He bent down and extended his fingers:

"C'mon little hoglet. I won't hurt you. What are you doing here? Are you on your own?"

He crept forwards a little but the piglet had an inborn terror and it shimmied further away. He advanced again, having another try:

"C'mon little hoglet ... " *Bang!* went the shutter again, making them both jump and the piglet vanished from sight.

Ash gave up and continued with his exploration. Draughts coming in through holes in the walls warned him that the wind was freshening further. Gloom descended as the sky became ever darker. He wondered if he should go back to the camp now - but a child's foolhardiness made him press on further.

--o--

The baptismal ceremony having reached its end, a feast of celebration had been arranged by the villagers.

"We shall all be able to eat together of the magic white bread," said the headman to Botolph.

"Ah, well it's not magic – it's holy," said Botolph.

"Yes yes," said the headman, nodding his head happily. "That's what I mean – *holy* magic bread. It makes us strong. It gives us special powers. We're lucky to be able to have it."

Luka was standing next to Botolph with his face showing the suggestion of a smirk.

"Well then Father," he said after the headman had left. "Magic powers is it?"

"I shall have to pray about this," said Botolph.

"Does it really matter? I mean there's only a very narrow gap between 'holy' and 'magic' isn't there?"

"No there's not – there's a huge gulf between the two."

"Well I understand what you're saying, but if they're keen to become Christians because they will then be permitted to eat the holy bread which they believe gives them special powers – isn't that what you want?"

"No it isn't. The Holy Bread fills them with the body of Christ and gives them a reason for loving their neighbours and doing good things to those that hate them and living a Christ-like life."

"Well aren't those special powers?"

Botolph sighed as he looked down at his incorrigible friend. "Luka, you know what I'm talking about. Magic is deceptive – magic is sinful and magic comes from the pagans – what we're talking about here isn't magic but *real*."

"Well," said Luka, "all I can say is that if anybody asked me what the advantages were of being a Christian, I would find it much easier to praise the privilege of being able to eat the magic bread, than I would to praise the notion of turning the other cheek when your enemy was punching you."

"Well both indeed are worthy of praise," said Botolph, "although I would still prefer it if you referred to the bread as being 'Holy' rather than 'magic'. You are turning into quite a philosopher Luka."

"Oh am I? Well, all this philosophising is making me hungry so, if it's alright with you Father, I'm off to find Ash and get something to eat."

But Ash was nowhere to be seen and the skies were lowering.

He looked to the west and sniffed as he always did. The air carried the smell of the rain that was travelling behind it. A violent gust of wind came from nowhere and went back there just as quickly. Low black clouds scudded towards him and, as they passed overhead, their shadow enveloped him in a mantle of foreboding. For no apparent reason, he suddenly felt a sensation close to panic – and the fact that panic was foreign to him made the feeling all the more alarming. Something was wrong. Butterflies cavorted in his stomach. Ash. Where was he?

He ran to the village - vigorously scouring it - and then the river bank - running backwards and forwards like a lost dog. He clambered up to the tented area and searched through each of the flapping doorways calling Ash's name. The tents were filling and lifting and leaning and broaching as the wind caught them and he knew that they should be secured against the rising storm - but there was no time for that. He ran back down the hill ...

--o--

Ash stepped over a rubble of broken tiles and beams as he explored the rooms in the villa's west wing. The roofs had all gone – lost, he guessed, because they were on the side of the building that was first to be hit by the prevailing wind which even now was doing its best to wreck the place further. Four strong gusts sent more tiles crashing to the floor. It seemed that the old palace was collapsing around him. He gulped. Spatters of rain came through the open roof; thunder rumbled in the distance and then alarmingly vicious raindrops started to pummel at his arms. He picked his way quickly across the mosaic-floored atrium and into the east side of the villa searching for shelter under what was left of the remaining roofs.

He stood shivering in a hallway feeling the cold chill of his newly-dampened tunic. Then, with a crash that made him jump, a beam fell from the roof and landed on the mosaic over which he had just walked. He leant instinctively on a nearby door which, to his surprise, opened easily to his touch and gave him access to another room. He stepped inside closing the door behind him. This quieted the noise and offered some semblance of peace though he could still see the wildness of the weather through a square opening on the opposite wall where a window had once been. Rain lashed down in alternating light and heavy bursts as it swirled backwards and forwards buffeted as it was by the wind. Thunder crashed again.

He looked around him. The room was lavishly decorated. On one wall was painted a large circle. In the centre of this was a cross – not the Christian sort of cross with which he was familiar but a cross on its side with another line running up the centre finished by a loop at the top. He wondered what it could mean. On the opposite wall was a picture of six men, each with their arms outstretched. They seemed to be floating in the air. Each was wearing elaborate clothing. Their clothes were all different but each had a cross on the front. In the centre of the room was a stone altar upon which lay the remains of two candles in their holders. Was this a private chapel?

To one side of the room were some stone steps which seemed to be beckoning him downwards. Ash felt for the scrip which he had carried on his belt since his eighth birthday and found the strike-a-light his father had given to him. Since that day he had practised with it often and now he had no trouble in getting the touchwood to glow. He transferred the flame to one of the candles, snuffed out the touchwood and replaced both it and the strike-a-light in his scrip. With the rain hammering on the tiles and the wind howling at the window he grasped the candle holder in his right hand and, shielding the flame as he went, made his way towards the steps.

Gingerly he worked his way downwards, whereupon he found himself in an underground cellar. Its floor was also mosaic. The walls carried all sorts of strange inscriptions and paintings of water-bearers. In the centre of the room was a square-rimmed hole surrounded by four wooden benches.

Then came the sort of thunder that has the unmistakable signature of a thunderbolt. The crackle started well up in the sky and Ash held his breath as he heard the lightning's rattle crash on each of a thousand ethereal steps before exploding venomously immediately above him. Reverberations, bangings and shockwaves continued as the wind ripped off the villa's roof causing the west wall to cave in and land right across the top of the stone steps. The final crash was so violent that Ash squealed like the piglet that he had just met, and the room that had been his haven suddenly turned into a prison cell full of thick choking dust.

--o--

Luka ran back to the site of the feast, where he found Botolph talking to the headman about the prospect of building a chapel.

They looked up as Luka approached and Botolph immediately saw the concern in his eyes.

"I can't find Ash," he said tersely.

Botolph jumped to his feet, intuitively understanding that this was no casual worry. He placed a hand briefly on his friend's shoulder.

"I'm sure he'll be alright but we'll start a search."

"What's the matter Father?" asked the headman, sensing urgency.

"Luka's young son's gone missing."

"The little lad who carried the cross?"

Botolph nodded.

He wasted no time: "I'll get some men."

He was as good as his word and within a few minutes a search team was assembled, consisting not only of local men but including the monastic brethren as well as the skipper and his two crew.

"Where shall we start Aldor?"

The headman looked at Luka who shrugged his shoulders despairingly.

"He could be anywhere," he said. "He might have gone exploring up to the north or he could be in the old city. I've looked all along the river's edge – he's not there – and the weather's coming in."

As if to underline his words there came a crash of thunder and the first drops of rain.

"Right," said the Aldor. "Half of you spread out and head for the north of the old city – there's some wells and sump holes that he could have fallen into. The skipper here'll be your leader. Now go! The rest of you come with me ... What'll you two do?"

"I'll come into the city with you," said Luka.

"Right – off you go then," said Botolph "and may God go with you and bring you success."

"So what are you going to do Father?" asked the Aldor, surprised that he was not coming with them.

"I'm going to pray," said Botolph "Now go."

"As you wish Father. Come on men ... Luka."

Luka miserably clasped his friend's arms. He felt no sense of betrayal. He understood Botolph's way of working and realised that his few minutes with God might well save them hours of searching. He turned and chased off towards the west gate with the others in hot pursuit.

As they ran the black thunderclouds came lower still and increased their intensity. The wind began a fiendish howling and great gobs of rain pelted their retreating figures. It occurred to Luka's fertile mind that it was the great Thunder God who was trying to steal his son away from him for a sacrifice – and Luka was not having that. A picture flashed through his mind of the Goliath Thor with Ash in his clutches and Luka standing before him with slingshot and seax determined either to save his son - or die in the process.

Normally the Aldor would have led his men but Luka immediately assumed command and the Aldor yielded to him without demur.   The first ruin they passed was the old fort and Luka sent him in to search with four others and told him to re-group afterwards at the Temple Bridge. Meanwhile Luka divided the rest of the group. One section he sent to search the Tamesis river banks round and up to the bridge.   He himself led his group to search the baths, the amphitheatre and the west side of the Brook.

--o--

As Botolph strode back to his tent the wind pushed and plucked at his habit, swirling it between his ankles like a snapping dog. He stumbled several times but managed to reach the tent without falling, and ducked inside.   He needed to think. He needed God's help. Ash was such a dear child and so important to all of them. It might of course all be a mistake. Ash might be quite safe – just hiding from the storm somewhere – he hoped to God that was the case but, in his bones, he doubted it since, like Luka, he felt an inexplicable sense of foreboding.

"Dear Lord," he started as he fell on his knees, facing to the east . . .

His supplications brought no revelation of Ash's whereabouts – nor had he expected them to. The urgency of his prayers had been more in the line of pleading with God for Ash's life. He was a resilient little chap and this would be neither the first nor (Botolph fervently hoped) the last time that he got himself into scrapes. Such adventures would ultimately make him a stronger person and a wiser man and this was what Botolph wished for him. He had asked God for guidance as to where he should search but since no inspiration had been forthcoming he decided to catch up with Luka's party and prayed that God would guide his feet.

On leaving the tent he was lashed by the driving wind and rain while he tried to close the opening. His prayers had composed him. He knew what his mission was and he too was prepared to give his life for young Ash, should that be necessary. All he needed was to be guided to the boy and then he would give whatever was asked of him.

Striding quickly into the tempest he hardly felt the wind and rain as he brushed aside the half-gale and turned into the northwest gateway of the old city. He saw the Aldor and his men searching the old fort as he passed by, and he felt sure that Luka and his group would be working their way methodically through the western half of the city, so it seemed logical to him that he should go to the eastern side.

The wind and the rain drove him quickly to the stone bridge. He calculated that, as they had already had a guided tour of the Temple, it would not have held much further interest for Ash, so he went straight to the ruins of the forum.

As he clambered over the outlying building he was appalled by the size of the search area. There had been an enormous building on the northern side that looked as if it might have been a basilica. There were so many nooks and crannies there that it would take a vast quantity of people to search it. Nevertheless he ran around the internal perimeter calling Ash's name and then stopping to listen for a reply, but it was pretty hopeless because of the weather's noise. He decided to leave it to Luka's team and head for the old palace which, during a lull in the rain, he had spotted down by the banks of the river and which looked more within his capabilities.

This meant fighting his way back into the wind and there were several gusts that threatened to blow him off his feet. As he approached, one of the palace walls collapsed and tiles and wooden pieces tumbled threateningly towards him. He veered away upwind of the building with a view to approaching it from a safer angle. Loose tree branches were rolling across the grass and many were coming to rest against the villa's western wall. Botolph skirted around each hazard as it presented itself and, after following the banks of the Wall Brook, climbed up the villa's outside steps onto the rubble-strewn portico just as the skies were lit up by another double flash of lightning. Lundwic was under attack from alternating flashes and thunderclaps, which seemed bent on her destruction.

He saw that much of the portico's roof had been torn away– either in this storm or in a previous one – and a large section of the wall of the east wing had gone. The west wing and the atrium were relatively intact. He went through a doorway into the latter and shouted as loudly as he could: "Ash ... Ash ... Are you there Ash?

There was no reply and he thought miserably to himself that even if Ash were in here he might be unconscious, and what hope would there be of finding him then?

--o--

Luka was frantic with worry. He had a nasty feeling about all this. It was not like Ash to be away for so long without good reason. Since his experience with the slave trade in Gaul it had been a constant concern for Luka that his son might one day be similarly snatched. Although Lundwic was only a small vill there was a constant flow of people through it – both British and foreign – perhaps one of those had taken Ash – perhaps he was looking in the wrong place?

It had not taken them long to cover their search area and they were the first ones to arrive at the bridge.   He was not surprised because the Aldor and his men had a much greater task searching the fort and its complicated mix of broken down buildings, wells and ditches.   In view of their local knowledge it had seemed sensible to send them there however, since they would be able to cover it more efficiently and quickly than he could have done.

Glancing down the river he saw that there were two vessels lying against both the west and the east quays.   He considered sending men to rummage each of the boats while he pressed on to the Forum.   On reflection he decided that *he* would do it since, considering himself a good judge of character, he felt that he would know if the crew were lying.

The meeting was not a happy one because the boaters had enough of their own problems keeping themselves dry and the vessels safe in the stormy conditions.   They could do without the interference of a bunch of thugs to add to their miseries.   Nevertheless the inspections were carried out fairly quickly without bloodshed – although it was a close run thing when one of the captains decided to defy the wishes of this short intruder.   Luka's seax was at his throat in a flash and it was quite clear that he would have had no compunction about using it.   The result was a hasty change of mind by the captain and a thorough turning over of the inside of his boat by the searchers.

Although the Aldor's party had still not arrived, the river bank team were there and they rejoined the main group.   Luka could not bear to stand around so, leaving a messenger at the bridge, he led the men at a run to the

Forum where he sent one group to the left and the others to the right saying that he would take his team straight up the centre of the Basilica.

By now they were all soaking wet and had their straggly hair sticking to their faces and clammy clothes clinging to their skin. Their woollen garments were getting heavier as they soaked up the rainwater but Luka spurred them on, infecting them with his sense of urgency and they willingly ran between the columns and poked into holes with sticks, calling Ash's name.

Several of them had the same experience as Ash, as a group of pigs that were sheltering from the rain suddenly took off in fright.

The Aldor's team arrived and Luka sent them to search the eastern edge of the forum while he, taking a dozen men with him, ran down towards the palace ruins. Half his men he sent to comb the river banks of the Wall Brook confluence and eastwards along the banks of the Tamesis. He had visions of Ash having slipped down a river bank and perhaps holding onto a tree branch in the face of fast-rising flood water. He wanted to go with the men but he could not be everywhere at once so he gritted his teeth and clambered over the rubble of the north wall and entered the palace.

As they spread out and began to search there came a crash as some heavy masonry fell down, and then another crash for a similar reason.

"Christ," said Luka "the whole place is falling apart."

Another two crashes followed in quick succession, confirming his fears.

"Out!" he shouted. "Everybody out! Quickly! We can't search here now – the walls are unstable. We'll have to leave it until the wind drops ... Out! Out!"

The men came running from all parts of the building but one was struck to the ground by a falling tile. Luka and another man ran to the unconscious villager and grabbed him by the arms dragging him unmercifully across the rubble into relative safety.

"Is everybody out?" he yelled against the noise of the wind.

They nodded their affirmations. He took a quick look at the injured man, who had blood pouring from a wound in his scalp. The still-heavy rain was washing it away as quickly as the man's pumping heart could produce it, and a crimson stream flowed down his neck and onto Luka's tunic as more crashes emanated from the doomed building.

--o--

Ash's underground prison cell was filled with thick choking dust so that, in spite of the candle flame, he could see nothing of his surroundings. He walked forward and tripped over something that had not been there a moment earlier; he fell heavily to the ground and, as he did so, the candle dropped from his hand and extinguished itself. His right knee hurt so badly that he stifled a sob but then had no choice but to forget his pain as dust filled his throat and he coughed and retched in the all-obtrusive atmosphere. Still coughing and retching he forced himself to a kneeling position and for a short sweet moment the air *did* seem to be clearer. He tried to stand but the floor was covered with boulders. He crawled across them, scraping his skin and hoping that he was heading in the direction where the stone stairway had been. He was in total darkness. He could see nothing at all. His head hit something solid. It was a wall. He held onto it with his fingernails and slowly and painfully pulled himself to his

feet and leant against the wall coughing and gagging.
--o--

    Botolph had gone from the atrium into what looked like the west bedchamber. He had called Ash's name and then stayed quiet - listening past the noises of creaking and whistling, hoping against hope that he would hear a reply. When he did not, he had called once again and listened briefly before moving on to the next room. Here again there had been a state of turmoil and chaos and he had repeated his calls, begging God to bring him an answer ... and 'nothing' was the answer he received. He had called again and listened intently but unless Ash was lying unconscious - buried under that pile of rubble, he was not there.

    And then he had heard shouted voices. They seemed to be coming closer. Help was at hand. It must be Luka. He had turned to go and join them but had only just made it as far as the atrium when from above him there came a loud ominous drawn-out creaking sound. He had only had time to glance towards the sound when a great shadow passed across his vision and he knew no more.
--o--

    Ash had thought that he had heard a shout above the cacophony of noise and he had tried to call back but as he had drawn breath all he had been able to expire was a hoarse cough, due to the dust in his throat. The only thing that he had known for certain was that he was touching a wall. With difficulty he had managed a feeble shout of "Help!"

    He thought he had heard some distant shouts but then there came an enormous crash from above his head and rubble had rained down on him, knocking him to the bottom of the wall. He had clenched his eyes tightly as another paroxysm of coughing had started. Without waiting for this to stop, shaking himself clear of the latest onslaught of masonry, he had resolutely fought himself upright once more, using the wall for support. He had wiped the dust from his hair and eyes and cautiously allowed them to open, blinking clear the last traces of grit.

Light! A shaft of light came from above his head. A tiny beam that spread out in the darkness to reveal a fog of yellow particles rising in it. It was too far above his head for him to reach it but at least he could now look around his cell - but what he saw terrified him even more than the darkness.

"Help ... help," he screamed. "Please ... someone help me."

--o--

Consciousness and a throbbing headache slowly returned to Botolph. It took him a few moments to remember where he was but then the memory of Ash came flooding back to him and he tried to stand up, but a great wooden beam was pinning down his legs. Suddenly he heard Ash's cry.

"Ash? Ash – is that you?" he called back incredulously.

"Father?"

"Yes, Ash it's me. Where are you?"

"I'm sort of underground. Come closer and I'll shout again."

Botolph was silent for a moment.

"Ash, I can't get to you at the moment because I'm trapped by a wooden beam. I'll try to free myself and get to you as soon as I can."

There was no reply because, unheard by Botolph,

Ash was sobbing.

"Ash, - is that alright?"

"Father?"

"Yes Ash."

"I don't think I have much time."

"What did you say?   Shout louder Ash."

"I don't have time."

"Why not?"

"Water."

"What?"

"Water.   It's pouring in from every corner.   I've climbed up as high as I can but it's filling the room.   Help me Father."

"Hold on Ash, - I'll get you out of there – trust in God," and he heaved away at the massive beam but it would not budge.   And then there was another crash as more masonry blew down.

"O God help me," he prayed, "help me to save the little lad.   I ask this in the name of Your Son Jesus Christ!"

--o--

The Aldor and his men had searched the Forum and the Basilica as fully as they could so, still at the run, they made their way to the palace, where they arrived at the same time as the other party which had been searching the banks of the river.

Luka stood to greet them.

"No luck?"

They shook their heads.

"Well there's no point in us staying here – the palace is falling apart."

As if wishing to confirm his words another squall swirled viciously in and tiles and debris hurtled towards them.

"Best we get back to the village," Luka shouted

above the racket.

"This man's unconscious and bleeding. We've found an old door to rest him on and the men will carry him back on that.

The Aldor nodded.

"Right men, we've done all we can. Six of you support that door and let's get back as soon as we can. Smartly now ... "

They lifted the casualty as gently as they could and set off towards the bridge.

Luka sighed and turned to take one last look at the palace and then turned back and followed them.

--o--

The water had reached Ash's waist. It was cold and evil-smelling and it swirled and buffeted him as it rose ever more quickly.

--o--

The beam would still not move. In spite of Botolph's best efforts he could not even shake it. It was if it was pinioned somehow at each end. He thanked God that his arms at least were free.

"Are you alright Ash?"

"I'm nearly drowning Father."

"Hold on boy. I'll soon be with you."

He hoped that was true. He tried another method, putting his hands below him and pulling at the stones. One gave way under his thigh and then another. He was afraid that the beam might fall further but it seemed secure at the moment. He pulled the stones upwards and then reached down again to loosen more under his left knee. It would not loosen at first but then it suddenly did and he could move his left leg a little. He tried again with the right leg, working slowly and painfully from thigh to knee and then towards his calf, trying to wriggle his legs free as he did so.

At last they seemed to be fairly loose. He pushed down on his arms and tried to move backwards. He managed half a cubit but then could move no further because there was a wall behind him. He nearly cried with frustration but forced himself to remain calm.

"Father," came Ash's cry again. I can hardly breathe."

"Hold on Ash, I'm nearly free."

He rolled over to one side and curled into a C-shape and kept moving forwards, his legs obediently following. One last pull and he was out.

His instinct was to go straight to Ash but he was not sure he could dig him out on his own, so he took a chance and headed back into the atrium and into the west corridor where, over the top of the ruined wall he could see the backs of the men as they left.

--o--

As he sorrowfully forced his way back into the wind, following the retreating figures of the other men, Luka thought he heard a shout. He stopped and looked back but could see nothing so headed forwards again. But he was unsure.

"Wait!" he called to those in front of him. "There's someone there. I'm going back – some of you come with me."

As he ran back, the cry came again and he saw a white ghostly figure waving from inside the wall of the palace. It crossed his mind that it was a Bog Devil luring him to his death but his fear for Ash made him reckless. By the time they reached the ruins the ghostly figure had disappeared and Luka hesitated – but only for a moment.

"Wait here," he said to the men who were hard on his heels.

"Sire," said one "you can't go in there, you'll be killed."

"You stay there," he said. "I'll be back."

He shinned over the wall and into the maelstrom of flying and crashing stones, mortar, tiles, rain and dust.

--o--

Once he saw that help was coming, Botolph went back through the corridor to the atrium, stepped over the beam that had pinned him down, and then entered the chamber from which he thought Ash's voice had come.

"Ash?"

There was no reply.

"Ash."

Still no reply but he saw a movement out of the corner of his eye. A stick. A stick was waggling frantically between two stones. He pulled it gently. A nine-year-old boy who, for some reason could not speak, pulled it back.

"Don't worry Ash. I'm here now and your Pa's coming. We'll get you out."

He had only moved about three stones when Luka was at his side.

"He's down there Luka, and the cellar's filling up with water– we don't have much time."

Feverishly they began to lift stones and debris off the area where the stick was poking through the hole and each one they threw to one side landed with a 'clunk'. But then, only a short while later there came a time when one landed with a 'splash.' They looked at each other with alarm. The water was still rising fast and was now seeping into the upper floor.

Suddenly eight more hands appeared around them as the four men that Luka had ordered to stay outside came to their aid. No words were spoken but knuckles were grazed and fingers were torn as the material was pulled out from around the stick. At last Luka heaved out a massive stone that sent him rolling backwards and Ash's head appeared - gasping for breath.

"Thank God," said Luka through crumpled eyes as tears ran down his face.

They were by no means finished yet though. Ash had lost the handhold he had been using and the hole was not large enough for his head and an arm. He was treading water furiously with his legs, and if he stopped he would sink.

Botolph saw the problem and grasped Ash's long hair, which brought a squeal from him – but there was nothing else for it. At least he could breathe – although that brought with it a mixture of coughs, burps and retches.

The hands continued to clear away the rocks around his shoulders, but by now the men were ankle deep in rising water. At last Ash could get his hands over the edge of the opening and Botolph could relax his grip on his hair. Then, another couple of boulders and with Botolph holding one arm and Luka holding the other, they pulled the boy out of his watery near-grave.

"Well done men," said Luka "Now out with you all as quick as you can."

They needed no further bidding and with Ash being half carried and half running they stumbled across the debris and over the ruined wall and out into the soggy field.

The rain had stopped and the wind had eased. They were all soaking wet and Ash was shivering uncontrollably.

Luka picked him up and told him to put his arms around his neck. He hugged him tightly to his chest, covered as it was by a soggy woollen tunic. He held his legs tightly wrapped around his body and Botolph took off his own tunic and wrapped it round them both, holding it pinched together behind Luka as they made their way back to the camp. By the time they arrived Ash was asleep and to all intents and purposes he stayed that way while Luka stripped off his wet clothes and laid him down on a dry straw pallet before covering him with a warm woollen blanket.

He left the tent and went across to one of the trees in the adjacent wood where he crouched down, rested his back against the tree, placed his hands over his face and shook with sobs until his body was drained of tears and his soul was drained of emotion.

He took his hands from his face just in time to see a re-clothed Abbot Botolph coming towards him. He stood up and they just looked into each other's eyes, clasping arms, saying nothing with their lips but speaking volumes with their hearts.

Botolph was the one who eventually broke the silence.

"Come and have a horn of warm mead."

"I don't mind if I do," retorted Luka with as much jauntiness as he could muster. "And if you've got the cow that the horn came from . . . I could probably eat that as well."

--o--

The hurricane – for so it proved to be – gave way the next day to gentle sunny weather, albeit with some rather strange, long, tubular clouds.

It was not only the Palace of the former Roman Governor which had been wrecked – the countryside was generally in a mess with uprooted trees here and there and all sorts of other structural damage. Most of the huts in Lundwic village needed to be either repaired or rebuilt and everybody - even visitors - were expected to work together to achieve this.

Luka, Ash and Botolph owed a great debt of thanks to those villagers who had risked their lives in the previous day's search and they were delighted to be able to show their appreciation in a practical way.

Botolph had, at the baptism service, already broached the idea of building a chapel in the settlement, and on this day the Aldor came to him and suggested that it might be appropriate to start the work now. Not only that but, since the repair of the dwellings would involve a fair amount of tree-felling, thatching etc., if the work on the chapel was combined with it there would be minimal disruption to all.

Botolph was of course delighted with this, since a Lundwic Chapel had been his ambition from the beginning. He and the brethren set to work with enthusiasm and started by helping the villagers to repair their houses. They enjoyed this almost as much as their next job, which was building the chapel. Every evening there was a feast to which everybody contributed some food. The main feature on the first day was spit-roasted hog – a great pleasure for the brethren for whom meat was deemed a luxury only to be enjoyed rarely on high days or holidays or times of illness.

As the brethren worked, Botolph kept a close eye on them trying to work out which pair he would choose to leave behind to administer the chapel. He was looking for two who appeared to have formed a 'professional bond' with the villagers. There were two who gave the impression that an *unprofessional* bond might be more to their liking as they had shown more than a passing interest in a couple of the village girls. Not only were these monks discounted from Botolph's selection but he also felt duty bound to have a strong word with them.

At last the chapel was built and consecrated and the two chosen brothers inducted and charged with overseeing the Christian welfare of the village. The Aldor had not only given land and materials for the chapel but he had also provided sufficient extra land that the brothers could till and use to support themselves.

Satisfied that everything was well in hand Botolph, asked the skipper to have the *Ganot* ready to sail the following day.

As Botolph and the Aldor stood chatting on the quayside just prior to departure, the latter asked about his future plans. Botolph replied that he intended to visit the eastern side of the River Lea where he hoped to find other communities ready to receive the Word of Christ. The Aldor pulled a wry face.

"Do you see a problem with that Aldor?"

"Here in Lundwic we are under the Lordship of King Eorcenberht of Kent and of his uncle sub-King Aethelwald. Ever since the times of Eorcenberht's grandfather this whole region has been Christian – although ... " he chuckled, "Bishop Mellitus received short shrift when he tried to impose his Christian will on us."

Botolph felt it was politic to keep his views to himself on that subject.

"The scir of the East Saxons is a different matter altogether. Those people are ruled by the pagan King Sigeberht, who's never shown any interest in adopting the new religion."

"He's not against it though –is he?"

"The word is that he's not *violently* against it. He apparently just doesn't see the point in changing from the old ways which have worked well for centuries."

"But doesn't he see that by converting his people to Christianity they will be much more loyal to him?"

"I don't think he does. I don't think he cares. He has been king now for getting on for thirty years and he's set in his old ways. You might be able to change his mind. Who knows? I've seen him – he came to Lundwic once - he's old and rather short. You're tall and young so I suppose that there might be a chance that he'll listen to you as having a new and progressive voice . . . but I'm bound to say that I doubt it."

"Oh dear," said Botolph, "so what do you think his reaction would be if we managed to convert any of his people to Christianity then?"

"I shouldn't think you'd get any reaction. From what I understand of him I shouldn't think he could care less but - like the leader – like the people . . . you might find you'll have difficulty getting a spark out of them too."

"Well," said Botolph, brightening a little, "it sounds like another challenge, but that's what Christianity is all about."

"Good luck then Father," said the Aldor with a grin as they clasped arms bidding each other farewell.

Botolph glanced behind him and saw that the *Ganot* was ready to leave so he stood back a couple of paces and raised his right hand in blessing, made the sign of the cross and called loudly above the crowd:

"May the Peace of God be with you all and guide you in the ways of his Son Jesus Christ."

By this time most of the crowd had fallen to their knees and, with their thumbs, they made the sign of the cross on their foreheads as they replied eagerly:

"Amen."

The abbot strode across to the two monks who would be conducting the progress of Lundwic's Christianity and embraced each of them before turning back to the *Ganot* and, stepping aboard, he gave the skipper the formal order to cast off from the quay. The vessel, fully re-provisioned for another week's sailing, slipped away from her berth, hoisted sail, and made her way down to the River Tamesis. Here they gybed the sail to the southwesterly wind and headed towards the river's confluence with the River Lea.

As they passed the Roman Governor's Palace they could see that it was now totally ruined - a complete contrast to its appearance of only a few days previously. Botolph and Luka watched it silently – reliving their horrors. Ash said:

"I was nearly done for there Pa. I didn't think I'd get out of that alive." He shivered involuntarily.

Luka put his arm around him and hugged him.

"No, we nearly lost you then and . . . "looking up at Botolph, "I'm so grateful we didn't."

Botolph put his arm round his old friend and said nothing with his lips - but gave a silent prayer of thankfulness in his heart.

CHAPTER 16
The River Lea

They soon reached the River Lea where they gybed the sail and the skipper moved three-quarters of the crew over to the larboard side of the boat so that it was better balanced.

As they worked their way upriver Botolph scanned the banks on each side, looking for a substantial group of huts that might represent a shore-side community large enough to support a new chapel.

After a few hours he thought he might have found his target when they came across a settlement at the base of some foothills.

"What about over there, skipper?" he called.

"Aye Father – that's Wealdham. Do ye want to go ashore?"

"It looks ideal," he answered. "Do you know if they're Christians?"

"I've no idea, but we'll soon find out."

The sail was doused and the rowers took over as the skipper guided the boat through shallow water dotted with grassy islands. They moored up at a rough jetty within a C-shaped natural harbour. One of the locals took their lines.

"Ye know the craft will take the ground at low water?" he warned.

"Aye, thanks – I know that – I've been 'ere afore – though 'twas a while ago."

"I see ye've got quite a shipload. Where're ye from

'n' whither're ye bound?"

A crowd was gathering at the end of the jetty as the monks tumbled out onto dry land.

"Ye'd best talk to the Father. He'll explain it better'n I can."

Botolph came across to join in the conversation: "Peace be with you."

"Peace be with you Father. I 'spect ye'll want to come 'n' meet our Aldor."

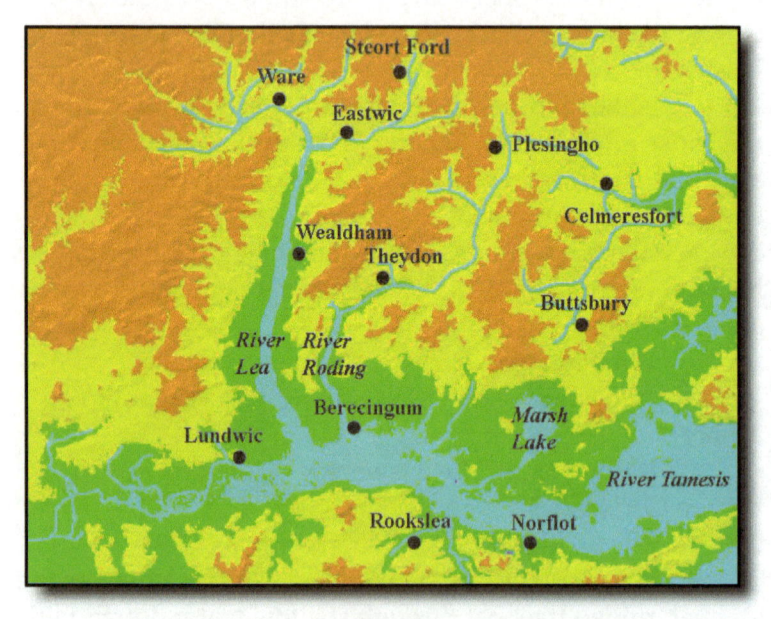

Fig. 13. The River Tamesis and its tributaries.

Botolph happily accepted the offer and he selected two of the monks to join them as he and Luka allowed themselves to be led along the grassy causeway to the shore.

Curious eyes watched them as they walked through

the village. The Aldor's hut was no different to the others, but he himself was a wizened old man who seemed quite uninterested in anything that Botolph had to say. His favourite word seemed to be 'No,' and they made their way back through the village to the duller stares of the same curious eyes.

Disappointed, they set sail again and a few miles further on called briefly at another village - where they received a similar response.

They then reached a point where the river divided and the skipper announced that he would take the right-hand fork towards Steort Ford. As they rounded a bend another group of houses and a quayside hove into sight on the left-hand bank. Undaunted, Botolph decided to try for a third time. They discovered that the village was called Eastwic and that the people there, though not at first as enthusiastic as Botolph would have liked, nevertheless warmed to his theme after he had preached to them a sermon which Luka and the monks agreed was one of his best.

They stayed for several days. There were only two villagers who were Christian so a mass baptism was held at the banks of the river, and a small chapel was constructed. Botolph was a little worried about leaving two of his monks in an area which, in view of King Sigeberht's pagan propensities, might be regarded as hostile country. The chosen monks had quickly formed a good relationship with the villagers however, and since the monks themselves seemed quite happy with the prospect, the abbot's trepidation was assuaged.

They continued upriver towards the 'steort' – a constriction of the river caused by the bulging of two tongues of land into it. The skipper doused the sail as they approached the first tongue. They skirted this one, which was on the eastern side, and then swung round the other way as they tackled the second tongue, which protruded from the western bank. This looked as if it had the ruins of a fortress at its peak. Once past, the skipper called out:

"What do you think Father? It doesn't look as if there's much point in travelling any further up river."

"No," agreed Botolph, "there doesn't seem to be much here for us at all. If we turn back now is there somewhere else we can reach before nightfall? How far's the River Roding?"

"It's a few hours but we'll make good speed down the river on the ebb. We should be able to make Berecingum by nightfall without too much trouble."

They turned the craft around and headed back downstream, waving to their friends at Eastwic as they passed. There was little wind and what there was blew from dead ahead, so they had to rely on the tidal flow and the rowing abilities of the monks. Once they reached the wide expanse of the Tamesis they hoisted the sail and turned to the east, giving the rowers a brief but welcome rest. All too soon, from the rowers' point of view, they were approaching the confluence of the Roding and the oars were brought to bear again to prevent the tide sweeping them past the entrance. As they entered the river the sun was settling onto the horizon and they glided thankfully alongside Berecingum quay.

---o---

Like Wealdham, Berecingum was on low ground and although it did not seem to be at all marshy, Botolph's natural instincts made him shy at the thought of putting a church so close to the high tide level. The locals were friendly enough but, again like Wealdham, the Aldor's attitude was very negative. It did occur to Botolph that these were perhaps the very people with whom he should be making the effort to change their views from negative paganism towards positive Christianity. He prayed about it that night and again the following morning but came to the conclusion that they should move on.

The following day there was a gentle breeze from the southwest so they left early and had a pleasant sail up the River Roding scanning the banks as they went until, just before noon, they caught up with a cockleshell of a skiff that was sailing in the same direction.

The skipper was steering the *Ganot* close to the west bank but the cockleshell was on the other side of the river and was so small that she could hardly be seen against the backdrop of dark green foliage. Ash was the first to spot her and he made his way excitedly up to the bows. He could see that three children were sailing her and he cupped his hands to his lips and called across to them.

The young lad at the helm of the skiff stood up. This looked quite alarming in such a small craft but the boy and the boat were joined as one, and he waved cheerily and pushed the steering oar down so that the boat headed towards them. For all its minimal size it was going faster than *Ganot*.

As they approached, Ash could see that there were two boys and a girl in the boat together with a wicker-lidded basket that contained a mass of squirming eels. As the skiff nudged up to them the girl caught onto one of *Ganot's* thole pins, the young boy left the helm and he and the other boy followed their sister's lead and leant on the ship's side and all grinned happily at Ash.

"Where ye goin' then?" said the boy.

"Dunno," said Ash. "We're strangers in these waters – we come from Norflot on t'other side of the Tamesis."

"Ain't bin there. So what ye doin' 'ere?"

"Explorin'," said Ash. "We've been up the River Lea as far as Steort, 'n' now we're explorin' the Roding."

"There's a lot of ye to go explorin'," said the boy. "Why've ye got all those monks with yer?"

Ash looked back towards the stern where the skipper, Botolph and Luka were watching the proceedings with amusement.

"That's Father Botolph," said Ash pointing backwards, "'n' next to him's my Pa. We're on a mission. We're explorin' the river to see if there 're any people who need our help to build a church."

"A church?"

"Mm."

"Is it free or does it cost silver?"

Ash laughed. "Nah – it's free."

"My Pa might like a church," said the lad looking at his siblings. They nodded vigorously. "Why don't ye come 'n' stay wi' us for a bit – I'm sure my Pa would like to meet ye – 'n' we could play together."

Ash had taken a liking to this young man and it seemed that it was mutual. It warmed Luka's heart to see them both grinning at each other. Ash needed someone of his own age to play with. Luka glanced up at Botolph who gave him an almost imperceptible nod as the wordless message passed between them. They did not move however, but left everything to Ash – he seemed to be doing quite nicely without their help.

A split second later, Ash looked across at Luka and an almost identical silent message passed between them as Luka nodded in his turn.

Ash looked back at the boy.

"Yes, we'll come. Where is it?"

"I'll show ye," said the boy gleefully as he jumped

back to the steering oar.

The other boy let go the side of the boat and the girl skilfully twisted the little craft round at right angles to the larger vessel and pushed off; the sail filled as the boy bore away. Once his boat had gained speed he brought her a little closer to the wind again and overtook *Ganot* piloting them northwards.

A bend in the river took them to the northeast and the slow lumbering *Ganot* fell behind as the cockleshell slid easily across the rippling water.

Ash, who was up in the bows intently watching his new friends, suddenly turned and announced: "They've brought her up."

The skipper had been watching too and said: "Aye, they're going into Theydon Bay," whereupon the little boat disappeared from sight, hidden by a headland.

It was not long before they reached the same headland and, as the bay opened to their view, they saw the skiff alongside an old wooden quay upon which the children were standing. They started waving excitedly and Ash waved back with equal vigour as the *Ganot* sailed into the reach.

As they approached the quayside the skipper began to spill wind from the sail so that the boat gradually slowed. A man and a woman left one of the huts that they had just sailed past, and ran lightly to the quay as another two men walked onto it from the opposite direction.

One of the men held out his hands and Ash, who had the bow line, threw it to him while Luka threw the stern line to another helper. At the skipper's order one of the monks had already lowered the sail and they made their final approach and glided gracefully to a standstill as the creaking ropes arrested the boat's motion.

More curious onlookers were arriving. The three

children suddenly spotted a wizened white-bearded bent-over old man who had just appeared on the scene. They ran over to him and the girl took his left hand, his right hand being occupied by a long staff that he was using as a walking aid. The elder boy was skipping backwards in front of him, chattering away as he told him of meeting *Ganot* on the river. The younger boy ran in circles around the trio whooping and skipping like an excited dog.

As the group approached the *Ganot* the crowd parted and let them through. Botolph had moved down to the middle of the boat but, as seemed politic, remained where he was until the welcoming party was in place.

The wizened man was clearly the much-loved leader of the community. Bent over as his old body was, his staff kept him steady as, with piercing blue eyes, he looked penetratingly into those of Botolph.

The laughter and the merriment had stopped while the leader's judgement was awaited. Behind him stood a semi-circle of well-built younger men whom Botolph guessed were probably his sons. While Botolph's eyes were occupied, Luka's were not and he was able to scan the village. He noted that not all the working-age men were at the quayside – there were others who were spaced about standing between the houses but looking intently at the *Ganot*. A large group of older women and young children were making their way out of the village towards the west. Two more groups of men had positioned themselves away from the quay but ahead and astern of the boat. The seven sons had their hands on the pommels of the seaxes that swung from their belts.

Luka tensed as the thought occurred to him that they might have been lured into a trap by the children. But what did they want? They had nothing of value but the boat.

But then the answer came to him. It was the other way around. They thought the *Ganot* and her large crew might be a assault party. with raiders disguised as monks. These people must have been attacked before and arranged a well-rehearsed plan for future defence.

The old man remained silent as Botolph gazed back steadily, allowing the piercing blue eyes to penetrate and explore his soul. The time came when it seemed that the antennae should by then have found the answer to whatever questions they were asking, and Botolph concluded that it was he who should make the opening gambit. He was about to do so when the man nodded his head as he said quietly, "Welcome to our shore Father."

That was all it took. The atmosphere changed immediately. The sons took their hands from the seaxes. As a result of some sort of mystical signal the women and children turned back into the village and smiles returned to everyone's faces.

The incident must have been over in a short time but to all involved it had seemed to last forever.

"Peace be with you my children," said Botolph raising his hand in blessing. "I bring you the Peace of God and of his son Jesus Christ."

The old man extended his left hand and Botolph climbed out of the boat slowly followed by the rest of the crew.

Their time in Theydon was as happy, peaceful and productive as Botolph could have wished. Two weeks and nine of Father Botolph's sermons later they left behind them a new field chapel with two of the monks to run it and a whole village of newly-baptised people, all eager to serve the Lord under the monks' guidance.

When they left they took with them fresh produce and gifts for a community further up the river at the smaller village called Plesingho. Such an introduction made the whole process much easier. The villagers were as keen to hear Botolph preach as he was to do so and by the time the ebb tide flushed them back down the river only four out of the original twelve monks were on board.

CHAPTER 17
Engla

It was March in the year 651. Botolph had been back in Britain for four years, two of which he had spent at Norflot. The monastery was now well-established and thriving. When he returned after his Lundwic mission he found that Prior Selwyn was running the monastery more smoothly than ever, and this left Botolph with little doubt that it was the ideal time for him to leave matters to Selwyn and continue his journey to the land of the Engles.

--o--

They followed the same road to the north as they had taken some 25 years previously. On that occasion the first part of their journey had been in a fish cart from Cantwarebury to Lundwic. After two changes of wagons they had eventually arrived at Cnobersburg. This time they were not planning to go that far. They were heading for Rendelsham, which had been the hall of Englan kings for as long as anyone could remember.

As they turned east off the Venta Icanorum road the countryside became flatter and it was not long before they could smell the sea. Some hours later there were increasing signs of habitation and the royal encampment soon appeared before them.

"Good evening Father," said a young soldier respectfully as they approached the main hall.

"Peace be with you my son," Botolph replied. "My

name's Father Botolph and I come to see King Anna."

"I'll tell him Father, if it will please you to wait here," and he strode into the hall.

Botolph turned to Luka.

"A polite young man."

"Yes," said Luka, "What's wrong with him? Bonitius alwez told us to be wary of people who were polite."

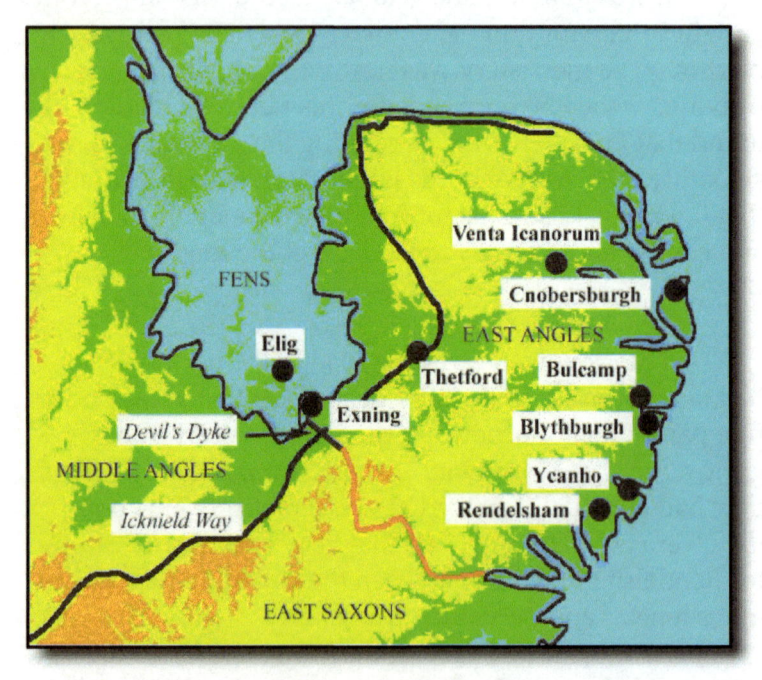

Fig. 14. Engla.

Botolph laughed.

"Ah but Bonitius was a Gaul and a criminal so he wouldn't expect people to be polite to him. It's different here ... Ah ... "

He turned back as the young soldier reappeared.

"The king will see you Father - please come this way."

As they followed him into the hall's smoky interior the smell of hot tallow saturated their nostrils. Candle flames flickered and bowed at their entrance and as their eyes became accustomed to the darkness they saw that trestles were being laid for the evening meal.

King Anna was in a corner conversing with some of his henchmen but he broke away when he saw the visitors and came across to greet them.

"Young Botolph and Luka," he said - "now *Father* Botolph who I have to treat with respect."

They all laughed.

"We weren't sure whether you'd be here or at Exning sire," said Botolph, "but we thought we'd try Rendelsham first."

"Quite right," said Anna. "We move about quite a bit depending on weather and circumstances but most of the time we spend the summer at Rendelsham and the winter at Exning. In fact you're lucky - we've only just come back from Exning now. Do you remember my daughter Etheldreda?"

"Er - no, I'm afraid not sire."

"No of course not, she wasn't even born when you were last here. Anyway she's a lovely girl of nineteen summers now and has just married Prince Tondberht of the Fens. Have your heard of him?"

They shook their heads.

"He's a good man and chief of the South Gyrwas but he'll have his time cut out with Etheldreda because she's sworn to remain a virgin."

He laughed.

"It's taken me this long to get her married off. We'll see how long it takes before he gets her pregnant.

Now Father, - I guess you've come because at last you're ready to build your monastery?"

"Aye we have sire - if you've not changed your mind."

"Never on your life Father. 'Tis something Lady Saewara and I have wanted for a long time. Now I suggest you go round to the guest hall and find yourselves a pallet each and then tomorrow we'll go out and decide where your monastery's to be."

Botolph was listening keenly to the king's every word but Luka's attention had been taken by the sight of a hog roasting on a spit in the centre of the hall. It was attended by two slaves, one of whom was turning the spit while the other basted the carcass with oil that fizzed and spluttered as it caught the flames, filling the air with the sweet smell of bacon. Luka's nostrils flared a little as he savoured the aroma. He gave an anticipatory swallow.

"Hungry as ever Master Luka?" said the king.

"Eh - what? Oh - sorry sire . . . yes I'm afraid so . . ."

The king laughed. "Away with you now to the guest hall. Come back in an hour and you will be able to feast on as much hog as your stomach will take."

--o--

They slept well that night and woke the next morning to the sound of rain pattering on the thatched roof. A small rivulet had found its way into Luka's pallet and he was the first to rise - muttering and cursing about being wet. He dragged the pallet away from the wall, pulled out the wet straw and threw it into a corner in disgust.

Ash opened the door and they looked out into the drizzle.

"Not a good day for monastery hunting," said Luka.

"No, sadly not," replied Botolph from his pallet, "perhaps it will clear up later."

Clear up it did and as they rode out from Rendelsham the sun burst through the clouds, and it was not long before steam started to rise from the wet grass.

They started by heading south and were soon skirting round the end of a narrow muddy creek. The king and Botolph were riding side by side while the royal guards rode ahead and Luka and Ash trailed along behind.

"I had in mind," said the king, "that you would want to be far enough away from the court so that you were not unduly disturbed, but in an area where you would be dry and safe from floods. You would want though, a good freshwater stream nearby."

They passed a couple of crofts and an elderly couple raised their hands in greeting as the horsemen turned a little more towards the east.

"I thought, perhaps, somewhere here," said the king. "Maybe over there - down by the water's edge."

They stopped at the end of a promontory and Botolph gazed across at the sea as it funnelled into a cove. There was a small island right in the middle of the gap.

"How about over there?" said Botolph.

"That's Gullney," said the king. "I don't think that would be large enough for your monastery - besides which you would find it difficult to get supplies - there's no way of getting ashore other than by boat. Why not here on the mainland - it's good fertile land for growing crops, so with land like this your monastery would be self-supporting."

"Well that's part of the problem really," said Botolph. "I don't want to take away land that a proper farmer could use. I'd rather have waste land that nobody wants and then by God's grace make it arable."

"Well," said the king, "you don't like making things

easy for yourself do you? But if that's what you want, let's go and see if there's anything that appeals to you over at Subben."

They retraced their steps and picked their way around the creeks until they arrived at the small settlement that King Anna had in mind. Once again Botolph felt that the land was too valuable for his humble needs, but the king took him through the village and pointed out an off-lying island.

"How about over there?" he said. "At low water you can walk across from Subben and at all other times you will be nicely isolated."

Botolph was beginning to get a little embarrassed about having to refuse King Anna's kind offers but once again it just did not *feel* right.

"What about easterly gales?" he asked.

"Ah, well, you have a point there. We don't get strong winds from the east *that* often but when we do the sea certainly pummels that island. Perhaps you're right. Let's go round a bit further."

They turned away from the sun and were soon facing a wide waterway which Anna told them was known as 'Old River.' The land was very flat and desolate and there were few signs of habitation.

"Where are we?" asked Botolph.

"We'll not stay here for long. 'Tis called 'Ycan' and it's an awful place that's famous for fiends, goblins and all things evil. For centuries there've been stories of strange goings-on here. It's not the sort of place you'd want to tarry in. People keep as far away from it as they can. The place I have in mind to see next is further along . . . "

"A moment sire - if you'll forgive me. I'd like to go and take a closer look."

"What, *here?*"

"Yes. Can we go and see?"

"Well, yes, if you want to."

He turned his horse towards the river and called to the guards to follow them. A short while later Luka noticed the horses beginning to spook and at first he wondered if it was just due to the prickly gorse they were walking through.

But the lead horse suddenly reared up, nearly throwing the guard who shouted a curse and, kicking his heels into its ribs in punishment, he pulled savagely on the reins. The animal turned sideways across the path frantically bucking and kicking. The rider was standing no nonsense and he had shortened the reins holding them so tight that the animals muzzle was pulled up hard against its neck. Its steaming flared nostrils flushed in and out with every panicky breath it took and its eyes were wild.

The rider of the second guard horse spurred his animal past the recalcitrant beast and the rest of the party followed suit. Luka wondered if a thorn had somehow penetrated the sensitive part of the horses hoof. He turned to look back - but at that very instant the rein snapped and with the now helpless rider clinging to its neck the horse took off the way it had come as fast as an arrow flies from a bow.

"No trouble when its hooves are going in that direction then," thought Luka turning to face forwards again.

The rest of the horses seemed to have settled down and all was going well until the new lead horse suddenly jerked sideways as if it had been struck by a rock. Squealing eerily as it did so it fell sideways into the gorse, dismounting its rider. He kept a strong grip on the reins as it scrambled upright again. It showed every intention of chasing after its mate but he pulled the animal towards him and calmed it down.

King Anna had seen a lot of strange things in his 51 years and he was a kind, tolerant and compassionate man - so rather than berating his guard as others might have done he simply said, "I suggest that you just walk your nag back the way we came until she settles down enough for you to mount her, then go back to the Rendelsham path and wait for us there."

The white-faced guard seemed as frightened as his horse but he nodded his thanks and stumbled away from them, still struggling with the beast.

"Well now," said Anna quietly to Botolph so that the others could not hear, "what do you make of that? I think we ought to turn parallel to the river again and follow it up towards the bridge rather than getting closer."

Botolph was staring straight ahead to where the gorse spread into thicker clusters. Beyond that, on a rise, he could see a group of trees.

"What's that?" he said.

"That's the Hoe," replied Anna. "It's a section of land that projects out into the river making a nightmare out of the eddies and swirls that rip around it. To tell you the truth I've only seen it properly from the river itself but the saying goes that if you take a boat too close at mid-tide, you'll get caught by the edge of an eddy and if there's any wind from the east you'll be over and drowned in a flash. We've lost several there over the years."

Botolph had kept his eyes firmly fixed on the clump of trees all the time that King Anna was talking.

"Oh," said Botolph vaguely - his gaze still not wandering.

All fell silent and the king waited patiently. At last he could wait no longer.

"Right Father," he said, "the sun's falling and we

need to find a suitable site for your monastery by nightfall."

"I think we've found it," said Botolph, dragging his eyes from the Hoe towards the king, "I think we've found it - God be praised."

"What?" said Anna. "Not *there*? Surely you don't want to build a monastery *there* in that God-forsaken place."

"I don't think it *is* God-*forsaken*," replied Botolph, "I think that is exactly what it is not. I think it's a place which needs God's help - and I think I'm the one He's asking to help it. Would my lord grant it to me?"

The king looked at him in astonishment. "Well," he spluttered, "it's the last place I would have thought of offering you but if that's what you want then so be it."

"Thank you sire, - it is *exactly* what I want and I think you will be surprised at the success God makes of it."

"I'll be surprised if you don't kill yourself in the process," thought Anna but then, aloud, "we'll get back to the hall and I'll have the deeds drawn up tonight."

--o--

True to his word, Anna set his scribe to work as soon as they returned, and Botolph started planning his attack on the gorse-infested scrubland.

"So how do you think you're going to get a monastery built there?" said Luka.

"Well I'm obviously going to need a lot of hands, so I shall have to ask King Anna if he will lend me some men for a few days."

"You're never going to get men within half a league of that place," said Luka. "It's evil - you've seen the effect it had on the guards as well as on the horses."

"Yes, that was *interesting* wasn't it?" agreed Botolph. "I shall have to pray about it for a while, - the Good Lord will guide me."

The next morning they were breaking their fast in the great hall when there was a sudden commotion outside and a messenger burst in and ran to the king's table.

"Sire," he gasped, "Lord Penda's army is invading."

The king threw down his food and jumped to his feet.

Thrusting his right arm at the table nearest the door, he shouted, "Sound the alarm. Prepare the horses and collect your weapons."

The men leapt from their seats - some of them managing to bolt the last of their food as they did so - and then all rushed from the hall back to their billets to collect their war gear.

Anna was clearly perturbed but he found time to put his hand gently on the shoulder of the messenger, whose breathing was slowly easing. He was trembling violently with pent-up emotion.

"Where were they and when?"

"Exning, my l-l-lord. D-D-During the n-n-night one . . ."

"Sit down man. Take your time and just tell me the story slowly and clearly, trying to leave nothing out. Meg - bring this man some mead."

The young lad collapsed onto a nearby stool and began his story again.

"One of the scouts came in to warn us that they'd made camp further down the Icknield, so we barricaded Devil's Dyke and prepared as well as we could. We got the women and children away into the Fens and . . . and . . ."

"Take your time. Look, - here's your mead - have a good swig of that and then . . . slowly."

"Thank you sire . . . and then a few of us waited to make sure they intended to attack. Sure enough, even before the sun was up they came at us from the forest. There was no point in just watching them so we backed away from the barricades and the rest of the men took to the Fens while I rode the fastest horse here."

"You did well," said the king, "but you must have ridden like the wind."

"I had to change horses sire - once at Beodricsworth and then again at Combretovium."

"Not only valour but wisdom too. I thank you for your loyalty - now get some vittals down as fast as you can 'n' come 'n' meet us outside."

In the camp there was pandemonium with people running hither and thither and Anna's henchmen sending riders in all directions to call the fyrds to gather at Rendelsham. Meanwhile scouts were sent out in pairs to spy on all the tracks from Exning, to bring word of the heathen army's progress.

"Sire!" called a be-helmeted soldier to the king, "What about the monastery at Cnobersburg?"

"Oh God," said the king. "I'd forgotten them. We must go there with all speed. Their boats'll be ready but it's not only the monks who need to get away - we're going to need time to collect the manuscripts and other valuables too."

"What about the womenfolk and children lord?"

Anna thought for a moment and then spun round until his eyes found Botolph's:

"Father - you, Luka and Ash take the women and children to Bishop Thomas at Dommoc - he'll look after them.

"Where's Dommoc?" asked Luka.

"Oh don't worry about that," said Anna, "someone

in the cart will know the way."

Then, turning back towards his soldiers:

"Now come on - there's little time - we need to keep up a good speed - so as fast as you can."

His horse was waiting outside the Great Hall, held by an ostler. He ran towards it, swung himself onto its back and with no more words kicked his heels into its ribs and cantered out of the village closely pursued by a cavalcade of horses carrying his fighting men. The hogs and chickens that had been released from their pens scattered in front of them. The animals would have to fend for themselves until the court returned.

"What do we do now Pa?" asked Ash, gazing at the continuing activity in front of him.

"Well, we'd better find out which carts are going where first I guess," said Luka, "and separate those that are taking the womenfolk from those that are taking the war goods."

CHAPTER 18
Flight

They ran over to three carts that were feverishly being loaded with, amongst other things, spears, axes and war clothing.

"You ready yet?" called one of the men.

"No, not yet, there's more stuff in the hall."

"Well come on - get on with it."

"Which are the wagons for the womenfolk and children?" asked Botolph.

"Eh? - Oh, it's you Father. The womenfolk? You're taking them are you? Well you'll 'ave to use those over there. You can't take all the women - some of 'em 'll be needed for the cooking and tending to the wounded - but they'll know who they are 'n' they'll come in the war wagons wi' us. The rest're yours and good luck to you."

Botolph gave a questioning frown and started to say, "What you mean by that?" but the man had turned away from him and was busily answering somebody else's question.

Luka had been looking about wildly, understanding the need for urgency and wondering how he could speed things up.

"Ash, d'ye see the womenfolk over there - most of them are royals but they've got maidservants and slaves with them. See if you can find out who knows the way to this Dommoc and start preparing them to get in the carts.

I'm going off to get some nags."

Ash ran one way and Luka ran the other - over to the paddock gate, which was in the charge of an ostler.

"We need horses for the womenfolk's carts," he said, "but it might be a good idea if we had three good fast riding horses too. Any idea which'd be best?"

"That one, that one and that one are good riders but there's no shortage - they've all got to go 'cos we won't want to be leaving any for the enemy. It looks as if you're going to be the last to leave 'cos I'm about to go myself. We'll take as many as we can with the war-wagons, but you'll need take any that are left. Just hitch 'em onto the backs of yer carts. Now off you go and get those you need 'n' I'll get the three riders and tie them onto the rail 'ere so they're ready for you. I'll be on my way in a minute so the last bit's up to you. But look sharp - it's time you weren't here."

Luka ran into the field. The horses were already roped up with harnesses so they were not difficult to catch. The ostler had already been as good as his word with the riders and he opened the gate for Luka to lead the cart horses out.

At that moment Botolph and Ash came running up and they each took a horse and led it towards the wagons. A couple of the slaves saw them coming and made themselves useful by manhandling three of the carts and turning them ready for the horses. They held up the shafts while they were roped onto the neck collars.

Across the way they heard the ostler with the war-wagons shout, "Come on now - are you ready? You got everyone? Right. Go!" He slapped the horse's rump as the first cart took off. "Now you. What are you waiting for? Go!"

Although they could hear all this commotion going

on they had but little time to look, because they needed their eyes on the job in hand.   After a while Botolph realised that it had gone quiet and that they were the last ones left. He glanced back towards the track down which they had come when they arrived only a few days previously, wondering if he might see a plume of dust announcing the arrival of the Mercians. He noted with relief that the road was clear - but not for long perhaps.

With fumbling fingers they fixed the horses in the shafts. The womenfolk were chattering excitedly but there was no sign of laughter as they quickly helped each other into the carts, while the slaves held the horses' heads.

"We've got to collect the other horses afore we leave," said Luka. "Who is it who knows the way to Dommoc?"

"That's the wench there Pa," said Ash.

"Right lad, you drive that one over to the paddock gate as fast as you like and let me hitch a couple of nags onto the back then make the best speed you can and follow the wench's instructions 'n' we'll be close on yer heels. Drive like the wind and don't stop 'til you get to Dommoc. Got it?"

"Yes Pa."

"Good lad. Off you go then. Father - perhaps you'd come with me . . . and you slaves - lead those horses over to the paddock. Come on - let's go."

Luka and Botolph ran to the paddock. The three rider horses were tied to the rail outside and they attached two of these to Ash's cart and sent him on his way. While Botolph took the third down to the other cart, Luka went into the field to get the other three. Fortunately they all seemed eager to leave and as Luka pulled one through the open gate the other two followed just as Botolph arrived with the second cart.

"Go then Father," cried Luka. "Fast as you can."

The rope reins cracked on the horses' backs and the cart took off.

Luka ran the lead horse down to the third cart and he had just lashed it on when he threw a quick glance down the track and to his horror he saw an unmistakable cloud of dust building on the horizon.

"Oh, Christ no! Get on," he shouted to the slave who was about to attach the third horse.

"But I haven't . . . "

"Leave it - there's no time - grab those reins and drive. Leave these two to me. I'll catch up with you."

The slave did as he was bid and Luka mounted one of the horses as the cart picked up speed.

He looked behind him - the cloud was getting noticeably closer. It would not be long before he could see the riders and from the size of the cloud there were going to be a lot of them.

He dug his heels into the horse's flanks. It ambled casually forwards. Luka saw the third cart disappear behind the trees.

He dug his heels in again: "C'm on - you've got to do better than that. Get up with you."

The stupid nag would not have it - in spite of his digging heels and urgent commands. Suddenly Luka felt very much alone. The carts and the only decent riding horses were out of sight. The enemy was almost upon him. The horse would hardly move. He looked wildly around. What could he do?

--o--

Ash and Botolph were having better luck. Their willing beasts were covering the flat land at a fast trot. Whinnies from the trailing animals encouraged the pulling beasts and Ash was relishing the challenge of his mission to get his cargo to the safety of Dommoc. Their headlong flight was marred only by the prospect of the shadow of death behind them and the fact that, being at the back, his Pa's cart would be the first to be mown down if the enemy caught up with them. He wondered if the host was in view yet.

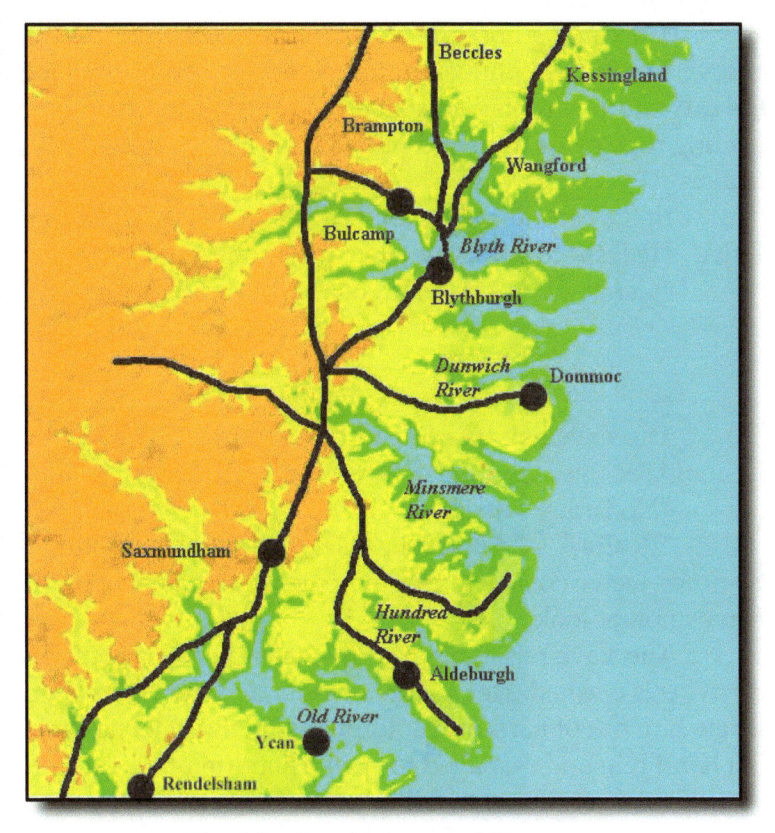

Fig. 15. Rendelsham and Dommoc.

He stood and, leaning slightly backwards so that his

legs were braced against the front edge of the driving seat, turned to look behind. They were on a long straight treeless stretch and he could just make out Botolph's tall figure driving the second cart . . . but he could see nothing behind that. He was worried - but Pa had said to press on with all speed so he pushed bad thoughts out of his mind and flicked the tail of his whip across the mare's rump spurring her into yet greater effort.

The trailing horses were enjoying the exercise and every so often they pulled out to one side trying to overtake the cart but they soon discovered their mistake when their leading rope came tight and pulled their heads round again.

In the second cart Botolph was *also* worrying about Luka. He leant towards the slave next to him.

"Can you see Master Luka's cart behind us yet?"

The slave half turned and raised himself up so that he could see over the heads of the passengers.

"No Father - no sign."

"Really?" said Botolph. "They should be in sight by now - we've come a long way since we left the woods. Have another look."

The slave raised himself up again - just as one of the cartwheels crashed over a large boulder and the violent jolt threw him out of his seat. Botolph instinctively let go the left hand rein and managed to grab a handful of his tunic but the man continued to fall until he was between the cart and the horse's hooves. Botolph could not let the man go but could not pull on the rein in his right hand or the horse would veer to its right whereupon the cart would overturn, the man would be crushed and the rest of them injured if not killed.

The women in the back took to screaming as the now out-of-control cart plummeted helter-skelter down a hill. The screams and the back-weight of the cart brought the horse to a state of panic and it started to bolt with no sense of rationality. Botolph was left with no choice but to let go the right hand rein and concentrate all his efforts on pulling the victim back. The man was screaming as the prospect of imminent death drew nearer and his eyes were open wide in fright as he looked imploringly at the priest who was his only link with life. Both his hands were gripping Botolph's left arm so tightly that they were drawing blood. With every jarring bump Botolph had slid further along the seat and was now perched right on the edge. One more bump and he would be over. His feet searched wildly for something to grip on but without success. His right hand had a tenuous grasp on the edge of the seat, but if he let it go and turned to grab the man with it he would be entirely unbalanced and disaster would be inevitable. He could not let go the man because the man had such a tight grip on him. Something made Botolph take his eyes away from the man and look ahead. To his horror he saw that in their downhill flight they were racing towards a sharp bend.

--o--

Ash successfully navigated the left hand bend and shortly afterwards they trotted briskly through a village that seemed totally deserted. Ash guessed correctly that Anna, on passing through it, had grasped the opportunity to take the men with him and had sent their women and children to Dommoc. The horse was tiring now and as the incline became steeper the animal slowed almost to a stop. Ash coaxed it onwards but it refused to do any more than plod slowly up the hill - snorting with displeasure as frothy saliva spewed from its steaming mouth. Ash knew enough about horses to let it take the hill at its own pace and once they reached the flat ridge he was able to goad it into a gentle trot again.

By the time they reached the other side of the ridge and started down the hill the horse had gained its second wind, pushed as it was by the weight of its following load, and it kept up a good trot as they crossed a track at the bottom of a river valley. A little further on they met the beginnings of another hill and, once again, the horse slowed to a walk.

"Driver," called one of the girls.

"Aye?" said Ash.

"Ye'll come to a crossroads in a few minutes. Take the right hand one - that's the road to Dommoc."

The path flattened and the horse started to trot again and, sure enough, there was the road ahead. They were nearly safe.

--o--

Luka was by no means safe. He vaulted off the first horse, clambered onto the other and dug his heels in again. This time he was at least rewarded by a gentle trot but it was only a little faster than he would have been able to run. He urged the horse towards the trees and as he did so he looked behind him at the smoky horizon. He reasoned that if he could not see *their* horses they would not be able to see his. The idiot nag was following close behind having discovered that it could trot after all. He dug his heels in again trying to urge a gallop or at least a canter but the stubborn animal had its own pace and was not going to offer more.

"How is it I manage to pick the slowest horses in the team?" he thought to himself and then he answered his own question. "I should have known that, being the last ones left, they would be the dregs."

The next question was whether the Mercians would stop at Rendelsham or carry on northwards.

It was still early in the day. The sun was on his right hand side behind him but still rising. He reasoned that Penda and his men would probably burn the Rendelsham settlement and then press on to the north. He would know where he stood as soon as black smoke started to show itself in the morning sky.

The horse slowed to a walk and kick as he might the animal just ignored him. This was not going to work. The thought had just passed through his mind that he was a sitting duck for the Mercians to pick off at their leisure when his mount stopped completely and started to graze.

Luka wasted no more time on the faithless creature but slid off and ran to the cover of the trees that lined the western side of the track. He made as rapid progress as he could but the thick undergrowth made it impossible to run. He wondered how he was going to find Dommoc.

--o--

The sight of the bend spurred Botolph into taking drastic action. He knew that he had to retrieve the man and stop the horse's headlong flight or, sure as chickens' eggs were chickens' eggs, the cart would capsize on the corner.

He threw his right arm backwards and locked it under the rail at the front of the wagon. This at least kept him from falling off the seat although by this time he was teetering on its left edge. He only had a few seconds to act before both of them would lose their strength.

"Hold tightly," he yelled at the man. "Ready?"
The slave showed no sign of comprehension and Botolph

prayed that his tunic did not tear as he gave an almighty wrench with his left hand and pulled the man upwards and across his knees. The man was on his back but he released his grip on Botolph's arm and, turning himself over, scrambled across Botolph to the opposite side of the seat. Unencumbered, Botolph grasped the reins and started to bring the horse under some sort of control but he had left it late and they were still approaching the corner far too quickly.

"Brake," shouted Botolph at the former victim.

"What?"

"Brake. That lever on the side. Push it down. Lean on it."

It was only then that the man saw the nearness of the corner and, in spite of all the indignities and terror he had suffered, he still retained just enough wit to carry out Botolph's command and he leant on the wooden lever with all his might.

As the cart slowed one of the trailing horses was unable to stop in time and as it hit the back of the cart with a crunch and a squeal there suddenly came the rich but putrid smell of burning apple wood as smoke poured out of the scorching brake block. The braking system was notably inefficient, but a combination of that and Botolph heaving on the reins was just enough to keep the cart on the track and they rounded the corner safely and then came to a standstill. The horse stood shaking and steaming.

Botolph jumped down and had just patted its withers in an attempt to calm it when the third cart came round the corner and stopped behind them.

"Where's Master Luka?" asked Botolph, surprised not to see him in the driving seat.

"He's back there Father, and the Mercians are not far behind him. We saw black smoke behind us just afore we came down the hill."

So Penda's men had fired Rendelsham and it would not be long before they passed this way.

"But where's Master Luka?"

"He's on horseback sire. He said not to worry he'd catch up but to press on with all speed."

Botolph reluctantly ran back to his cart, clambered aboard and urged the horse to a fast trot.

The two carts passed through the deserted village and up onto the ridge. Botolph looked back from the greater height to see if he could see any signs of a lone horseman who might be Luka but all he could see was an empty cart track and black billows of smoke building behind the bordering trees.

Half an hour later they dropped down to the river valley and found Ash's cart waiting for them at the corner.

"Where's Pa?" asked Ash.

"There's no time to tell you now," said Botolph. "He's on his way but we have to get these carts to safety, so Go!"

Ash reluctantly complied and within another half an hour the three carts had driven along the wood-covered narrow isthmus that led them and their passengers to the settlement. They arrived just before the sun reached its zenith.

Ash immediately released one of the rider horses from the back rail and mounted it.

"Where are you going?" asked Botolph as if he didn't know.

"I'm going to look for Pa."

"Wait, I'll come with you. We'll take all three horses."

Ash was galloping back towards the wood before Botolph's feet had even touched the ground. He quickly released the other two rider-horses, mounted one and pushed on in pursuit of Ash as fast as he could - leaving the passengers to sort *themselves* out.

In the distance he saw the boy turn to check that he was following.

"Wait," called Botolph.

He was too far away for Ash to have heard him but even so the boy's horse slowed to a trot while Botolph galloped on to catch him up.

"Ash, wait. We have to plan this. Did you know they've fired Rendelsham?"

"Yes, I saw," said Ash.

"That means they won't be staying there but will be following in our tracks within the next hour or so."

"That means they'll catch Pa."

"Not necessarily. He'll have seen the same signs that we have and will have left the road. That's why he's late."

Ash saw the logic in this.

"So what do we do?"

"Well if we go headlong back towards Rendelsham we'll ride straight into the enemy and probably get ourselves killed, and that's not going to help your Pa or anyone else."

"But Pa might be running in front of the Mercians and he won't know which is the road to Dommoc."

"Well that's exactly it. We need to get close enough to the turning to be able to watch the main road and guide your Pa in. If the enemy host arrives without your Pa, we can wait until they pass. If they don't pass but turn towards Dommoc then we're all in trouble - but if they continue onwards we can wait until they've passed and then go and look for your Pa in relative safety."

"So?"

"So I think we ought to tie our horses here and continue on foot, keeping to the north side of the bank so that they can't see us on the skyline."

They stopped at the forest's edge and lashed the horses to a fallen tree trunk where they could graze comfortably. Going as fast as they could they dropped down into the long grass following the river's edge and made their way quickly towards the main road, continually looking ahead for signs of Luka.

They kept close to the edge of the ridge and every few minutes one of them would venture further up to see if they could see any sign of the enemy. There was no column of dust this time. The army was travelling more slowly - tiring perhaps after their long journey and the efforts of firing Rendelsham. The first they heard was voices and this was soon followed by the appearance of a long train of horses carrying men with shields and spears.

Ash and Botolph were close to the turning and they kept their heads well down in the long grass as the army approached.

"Now we shall find out," Botolph whispered. "Is it to be Dommoc or further north?"

It came as a relief when the leaders continued on their way. Behind them came more wagons - some containing men and others with tents and supplies and then right at the back came another long double line of armed horsemen followed by a rabble of walkers and dogs. Finally, as they receded into the distance, all went quiet.

Botolph had wanted to get a look to see if there were any prisoners, but had been forced to keep his head down most of the time catching only a few glimpses none of which showed any sign of captives. That was not entirely reassuring, Botolph thought. It might well be Penda's policy to kill rather than capture. He hoped that

Luka had suffered neither. They waited until the last of the stragglers was out of sight and then climbed up onto the track and ran back to collect their horses. They mounted quickly and headed back to the corner, turned to the left and alternately cantered and trotted towards the south where billowing smoke was still doing its best to blot out the sun.

As they approached the ridge they realised there were *two* lots of smoke. The deserted village had *also* been torched by the marauders as they passed through.

"Ash," called Botolph.

Ash responded by half-turning his body towards him as Botolph drew alongside and they stopped.

"I think we should slow down a bit now. It's several hours since your Pa left Rendelsham and even on foot he should have been able to cover a couple of leagues by now. We don't want to ride right past him."

"Oi!"

They spun round and there was Luka behind them.

"Where are you two off to then?" he said. "Are you going for a jolly or might there be a chance of an old father getting a lift?"

--o--

They returned to Dommoc a lot happier than when they had left. They had Luka back again and, at least for the moment, the Mercians were not an imminent threat.

Thomas, Bishop of Dommoc, was an affable man but not, by all accounts, anything like as dynamic as his immediate predecessor now revered as Saint Felix, whom old king Sigeberht had brought over from Francia in order to convert his people to Christianity. Until Bishop Felix arrived only Cantium and Northumbria were Christian, but Felix had worked miracles in Engla.

Botolph had first heard of him at Evoriacum Abbey. The stories of his great works were legendary and he had been looking forward to meeting him but then, three years ago, came the sad news of his death.

Botolph was full of admiration for the work that he had done and saw it as a fertile basis upon which *he* could build Engla's *second* layer of Christianity. He had long cultivated the notion of spreading God's word in the same way that He spread His plants. That is to say planting trees here and there with sensible gaps between them. Instead of trees, Botolph would plant churches and hope that with God's love they would thrive and prosper producing fruit and seeds that would, in due course, grow into other trees resulting in a forest of Christianity across Britain.

He had tried this in the land of the South Saxons and in Cantium with some success, although for some time now he had been worrying that the Christian communities he had founded were perhaps not obtaining as much nourishment as they needed. He had given them little or no hope that he personally would, like a conscientious gardener, return from time to time to bring them nurture. Although he had tried to leave behind him responsible and devoted Christians who would lead the churches forwards, he, to all intents and purposes, had deserted them. He resolved to try to remedy this by following the example of Saint Paul and write them letters of encouragement and guidance and then, once the Ycan monastery was well established, he would go and visit them.

He tried to discuss these ideas with Bishop Thomas but was unable to capture his imagination. The old man, who had been born and bred in the Fens, was content to sanction anything that Botolph wanted to do but, for himself, he intended to concentrate on doing God's work at Dommoc.

He was pleased about the arrival of the womenfolk from Rendelsham however. They had livened things up considerably and their voices contributed delightfully to the plain chant of the nunnery.

--o--

"Where do we go from here then?" said Luka later that day.

"Well," replied Botolph, "We've done what King Anna asked of us so I suppose we're now free to make our own choices."

"I was hoping that I'd be able to join in the fighting."

"Yes I expect you were but it seems that God doesn't want you killed yet."

"I wouldn't have been killed. I'd 've shown those Mercians a thing or two."

"Yes I expect you would have - but clearly it wasn't to be."

"I wonder if they've joined battle yet."

"Why do you ask?"

"Well," he shuffled, "I just wondered."

Botolph could see that if Luka had his way the three of them would be riding north and risking their lives in the melee but he accepted Botolph's decision to remain at Dommoc for the moment.

Only two days later, however, they were called urgently to the Chapter House. Botolph and Luka arrived to find that three horsemen had just delivered some unwelcome news to the bishop. Botolph recognised one of the horsemen as the Anna's man who had supervised the loading of the carts at Rendelsham but he was far less ebullient than he had been on that day, and it was clear he had been wounded.

"I'm afraid I bring bad tidings Your Grace. We lost the battle of Waif Island and I come here as a prisoner. These two are my guards," he said, nodding at the other two.

"Is King Anna dead then?" asked the bishop.

"No, Your Grace, he's not dead but he and the few of us who've survived are to be exiled to the west on pain of death if we ever set foot in Engla again."

"When do you leave?" asked the Bishop.

"Tomorrow. I've come to collect Lady Saewara, the young Prince Jurmin, Lady Wendreda, my wife and any other womenfolk who may wish to come with us. This is a delicate matter Your Grace. Many of the wenches you have here in Dommoc still believe they have husbands but the truth is that most of them are widows."

It was a gruesome time with much sobbing and wailing. Many of the new widows opted to stay at Dommoc, but several who were of royal birth decided to go with the king.

"What are we going to do Father?" asked Luka.

"Oh dear - I'm not sure. Of course my choice would be to stay and get on with building the abbey at Ycan but I wonder if that would be feasible without King Anna. He would've helped with providing labour and building materials, but it sounds as if Penda's our king now and we know that he barely tolerates Christianity. I certainly can't see him being at all helpful. Disappointing as it is I think I'm going to have to abandon the idea for the moment."

"So what shall we do?" Luka repeated.

"Well it seems to me that our loyalty lies with King Anna. His court's severely depleted and wherever he goes in exile he's not going to be living the kingly life he lived here. We also have Lady Saewara and the rest of the family to consider. It seems to me that God's calling us to go with them and give them what comfort and protection we can."

"'S'fine with me," said Luka. "I'm getting bored with this place anyway. There's not enough oomph in it for my liking."

"What d'we do about the slaves Father?" asked Ash.

"Hmm - a good point. They and their children belong to the king, so they'll have to come along too."

"Well we're going to have to use at least two carts then," said Luka, "one won't be enough."

"No - and for a long journey like this we'll need to use good solid wains with four wheels to make the ride less bumpy. That'll use up more of the horses because we'll have a pair in each of the shafts as well as towing a couple of rider horses behind each wagon."

By noon the wains had been prepared - with a liberal amount of straw in them to cushion the ride. The passengers climbed aboard with what few belongings they had. The backboard of each wagon was locked in place and then under the stern gaze of the escorts they crossed the isthmus, turned right onto the main road and headed to the place where Penda's victorious army and Anna's defeated men were waiting for them.

CHAPTER 19
Journey to the southwest

The next day they started the long slow plodding trail which would take them 60 leagues down the ancient trackway that led to the southwest.

"Where're we going?" Luka asked one of the few soldiers who had been allowed to join the party.

"To the Gewisse in Wessex," came the reply.

"Who's king there then?"

"Cenwaller. 'E and King Anna are good friends, so that's why we're going there. In fact e'll be returning a favour 'cos 'e and 'is court came to us for asylum in Engla a few years ago."

"Why was that then?"

"What?"

"Why was King Cenwaller seeking asylum?"

"Oh ... Cenwaller divorced his wife - which would 've been alright if she 'adn't been Penda's sister. Penda wasn't 'appy about it so 'e punished 'im by driving 'im out of 'is kingdom."

"He seems to make a habit of sending kings into exile then?"

"Well 'e's trying to expand 'is territories ain't 'e. 'E drives the king out and puts his own men in. Trouble is 'e ain't got enough men 'e can trust so instead of getting stronger by gaining more territories 'e ends up weaker 'cos 'e overstretches 'imself."

Luka stayed silent while he considered the

commonsense of the words themselves and the fact that they were uttered by a man who was no more than a humble soldier.

As they moved slowly but inexorably down the ancient trackway the extraordinary group became the subject of stares, finger-pointing and open-mouthed wonder of other travellers.   It was a large party and the armed guard was a notable presence. Whereas in most cases passing travellers would have asked each other for news and exchanged stories, in these circumstances they thought better of it and either stood to one side and stared or   kept their heads down and avoided making eye contact with anyone in the dour procession.

After three nights of making and striking camp, they arrived on 15th April at the crossing of another great highway, which they later decided must have been Waceling Street. It was here that the guards unleashed King Anna's wrists for the last time.

"You're on yer own now," they told him. "Our orders are to tell you to make sure you keep to the track well into Gewisse territory.   If you come back, King Penda has sworn that he will kill you."

The guards remounted their horses and stood to one side and then watched the group as it crossed over the highway and gradually dissolved into the distance. They then turned and headed back up the trackway towards the northeast.

With the departure of their guards a new spirit entered the souls of the travellers.   King Anna, great leader that he was, wrenched at the cloak of despondency that had engulfed him since his defeat and cast it away. He reined his horse's head to one side, pulled out of the procession and rode back towards Botolph, Luka and Ash.

"Hey up," said Luka "it looks as if we might be

getting a visitor - and he has a smile on his lips today."

"Good morrow," said the king.

"Good morrow sire," they replied in unison.

"Let me ride between you, - I wish to talk."

They moved apart and he rode into the gap.

"What is it, my Lord?" said Botolph.

"I'm afraid I've been poor company these past few days."

Fig. 16. Route followed by the Icknield Way.

"We've none of us been in the best of spirits sire."

"No ... Well today is another day that God has spared us to live and we must do him justice and live to the best of our ability."

"Sire?"

"We will lie up early tonight to allow time for

merriment. Once the fires have been lit and the food has been served, I shall get the scop to sing to us. I want to bring joy back into our little party. We must put our troubles behind us and look forward to arrival at our destination."

"Ah," said Luka. "Our destination . . . and where might that be sire?"

"That rather depends upon where the Gewisse court is at the moment. We're out on the borders now but once we get deeper into their territory I am sure we will find travellers who will be able to direct us."

"Have you any idea where the choices might be?"

"Well they might be right across to the west of course and that would be a long way to go, but if we're lucky they'll either be at Dorceaster or Wintanceastre . . . or they could be at Calleva. Any of those would be easy."

"What're your plans in the long term sire?"

"Well, I've not thought that far ahead yet. Clearly I can't stay with the Gewisse for ever. I've got to get back home as soon as I can."

"But his guards said that if you try then Penda will kill you," said Luka.

Unexpectedly the king laughed.

"Hah! Yes I expect he'll try but with any luck God'll be with me and it'll be Penda who dies - although if, when the time comes, the Good Lord is ready to grant me a space in Heaven then so be it. Better to die battling the forces of evil than to languish timidly in a foreign land."

--o--

In the event it was at Wintanceastre that they eventually received a good welcome from King Cenwaller and, by the end of April, they had become well-settled in his court there.

Ash was delighted to find that King Cenwaller had a son, Merewalh, who was only a few months younger than Ash, and they became firm friends.

Three months later Luka had a surreptitious visit from one of King Anna's servants asking him to attend the king as soon as possible - but to tell nobody - not even Father Botolph. Luka was intrigued but did as he was asked as soon as he could find a time when he could excuse himself easily.

He found the king alone in his unguarded tent - the absence of King Anna's usual retainers surprised him.

"Thank you for coming Luka. I have a proposal for you."

"Sire?"

"I want you to take your son and Father Botolph back to Engla."

Luka did not know whether to laugh or cry. The Gewisse were not such a bad bunch and he had been having a good time in the camp. He had been looking forward to fighting for Cenwaller in border skirmishes. It was not just that he enjoyed a good scrap - although that was a pleasing prospect - but it would also give him the chance of making some money. Penda had confiscated all their weapons before they had left and at the moment he did not even have a trusted seax to his name.

King Anna must have read his thoughts because he turned and picked up something from the table behind him. He handed it to Luka whose eyes lit up. It was a seax - but not just any old seax - it had been beautifully hand crafted with a pattern on its blade. Luka felt the edge - it was as sharp as a tonsure razor.

"This is for you Luka, and . . . "

He turned to the table again and handed him a smaller package.

" . . . this is a dagger for Ash. Both are from me in grateful thanks for what I am going to ask you to do."

By now he had gained Luka's full attention. This sounded more like it.

"I want you to go back to Engla. That in itself has its dangers and you might well have need of your new seax to defend yourself and Father Botolph. Take the trackway back to the northeast. Do you remember the great highway we crossed after the guards had released my bonds?"

Luka nodded.

"Well that highway was The Waceling. Don't cross it into Mercia but follow it to the southeast."

"The Waceling?" Luka interrupted.

This time it was the king who nodded.

"That was also the name of a road which passed through Cantium," said Luka.

"It's the same road," said King Anna. "It runs right across the country from the old Roman port of Rutupiae. I want you to follow that down towards the mid-morning sun until you are in the land of the East Saxons. Then turn towards the east until you get to the coast and follow the water north to Rendelsham."

"What if we meet any of Penda's soldiers?"

"I very much doubt they'll be interested in you but if they are then I'm sorry but you'll just have to make the best of it. Of course you'd attract less attention if you weren't riding horses and that's why I'm suggesting you avoid passing through Mercia."

"Ah - we get horses do we?"

"Well I can't expect you to travel all that way on foot."

Luka nearly retorted that he thought that would suit Father Botolph very well but he quickly bit his tongue.

"So what do we do when we get there sire?"

"I want you to make your way back to Ycan - you remember - the place the Father chose to build his abbey?"

Luka nodded.

"You'll find several old disused byres near there. Find one that you could make reasonably habitable and use that as your base while you start clearing the monastery site of scrub."

Luka's heart sank. Is that what he was being sent back for - to clear that rotten spooky place of scrub? He had not liked it when first he saw it - there was something about it that had made the hairs on his back stand up on end. Even the thought of it now made him shiver. King Anna noticed this and laughed.

"You don't like that place much do you?"

"No I don't sire - there's not much that scares me but that place gives me the creeps, and I can't for one moment think why the Father should have chosen it."

"I know what you mean. It's had a bad name for years and I generally can't get anyone to go near it. There are all sorts of tales of terrible smells coming from there - and noises that can be heard from miles around. When local children are naughty their parents often threaten that if they don't behave they'll send them to Ycan and that usually solves the problem. People who *have* been foolhardy enough to venture there have often died. The bodies get washed down the river and are found to have all sorts of horrible injuries that look as if they have been made by giant claws."

Luka shivered again and thought to himself that he could have done without hearing that. It was typical of Father Botolph to choose to build on the most inhospitable and difficult site that Engla had to offer. But then he realised that that was the answer. It was precisely because it *was* so difficult that his friend had chosen it.   He groaned.   King Anna raised his eyebrows.

"I'm sorry sire but I think I'd rather stay here," he said - and, turning the handle forwards he offered the beautiful seax back to the king.

Anna shook his head and lowered his voice confidingly.

"I can understand your concerns but clearing scrub in the land of Hell is not why I want you to go."

Luka's spirits rose hopefully from his boots and made it as far as his knees.

"It's not?"

"No, I've a much more important mission for you.   I flatter myself that since first we met I've come to understand the Father well, and I suspect that once he gets to Ycan he'll become so entranced by the prospect of his new foundation that he'll be interested in nothing else but getting it built.   If anyone can purge the place of its evil then Father Botolph's the man - but I have little doubt that he'll want to be left on his own and will consider your presence and the presence of anybody else a distraction that he'd rather not have.   That is where *your* mission begins."

--o--

They left at sunrise in early August.

All were excited but for different reasons.

Father Botolph was excited because his prayers had been answered.   He had seen the dream of his new monastery disappearing further from the realms of possibility and thought that he was going to be incarcerated with the Gewisse for ever.

Ash was excited because, if he was honest, he had become bored with life at Wintanceastre.   There were not many children in the town and those that there were stayed tied to their mothers' apron strings. Even his friendship with Merewalh had soured a little. He enjoyed being with his father and Botolph and looked upon the journey back to Engla as being another adventure.

Luka was excited because he had a project that was his very own and that he somehow had to fit around the smokescreen of Ycan. He had told the other two only as much as they needed to know. This bothered him a little because he had previously always been totally honest with them both, but for their safety there was only so much that he could tell them.

"What do we say if we're questioned by any of Penda's soldiers?" Ash asked as they rode three abreast along one of the wider parts of the trackway.

"I'm hoping we *won't* meet any soldiers this side of the border," Luka replied.

"Well what if we do?"

"We'll tell them we're going to Cantium."

"Cantium?" Botolph expostulated in surprise.

"Yes, Cantium. You know that road that we crossed just after the guard released us?"

"Y-e-s?"

"That was Waceling Street."

"What - the one that went through Norflot?"

"The very same. Well we're going to turn onto that and if anyone asks us then Norflot's where we are heading."

"But we're not going there?" said Ash.

"Nope. Once we get into the land of the East Saxons we'll be clear of Penda's jurisdiction and we can turn off the Waceling and head east. There won't be much danger from Penda until we get back into Engla and even then I guess his men'll be thin on the ground."

--o--

God seemed to be with them for the journey. Perhaps this was due to Father Botolph's constant prayers. The weather stayed dry and their sturdy horses plodded along unfalteringly. They met plenty of travellers and were asked many questions, but Luka did most of the talking and their story was plausible. Once they turned off the Waceling, Luka announced to anyone who cared to ask that their destination was Colneceaster and after that it became Gippeswic by which time they were back in southern Engla. As they crossed the ford west of Ycan, Luka's back gave its customary shiver and he recalled the feeling of relief he had felt when King Anna had made the suggestion that *Dommoc* would be the best place for them to make their base.

They rode across the isthmus to Dommoc Abbey just before sunset on 14th August and, after bedding down the horses, they were soon asleep themselves.

The following morning they received warm welcomes both from Abbot Thomas and, as Luka called them, the 'Widows of Rendelsham' who by then had become well established in the community of nuns. Abbot Thomas guessed that Botolph's early return was so that he could get on with building his abbey four leagues to the south. Far from being upset about it, he welcomed the prospect. From his point of view it was a case of 'the more monasteries the merrier.'

"There is a problem however," he said.

"What's that?" said Botolph.

"The countryside's full of Penda's soldiers and although he's so far left us in peace, both you and Luka are well-known as King Anna's men *and* you are both easily recognisable. I don't think he'd tolerate your starting to build now. In fact I'm concerned for your safety. I'm amazed you managed to get this far without being taken."

"Ah. It's as bad as that, is it?" said Luka.

"I'm afraid so. In fact your very presence in the monastery poses a threat to us. I'm not saying you can't stay but I'd rather that the news of your presence didn't get out."

"Hmm - we must move on then," said Botolph.

"Well even that'll not be easy. You've somehow managed to get here - right in the middle of enemy territory - and whichever way you go now you'll have to pass through hordes of the occupying army. And in any case - where would you go?"

Botolph and Luka looked at each other questionningly. Luka was hoping that Botolph would be the first to speak but when he didn't Luka said, "North I think."

"That's fine with me - but any particular reason?"

"Well," said Luka, "if we went south we'd be retracing our footsteps; if we go west we'll be getting closer to Penda's court; we've come as far east as we can ... so that only leaves north."

They laughed at his concise logic and even Abbot Thomas managed a dour smile.

"I'm not sure how much Penda's infiltrated the fens," said the abbot "but, as I believe you know, that's where I was born and King Anna's daughter Etheldreda recently married Prince Tonberht so you might find a welcome there - unless Penda's taken that over too."

"From what you say, I don't think we can risk going cross-country," said Botolph. "It seems that our best chance would be to take a boat."

The abbot nodded.

"We could go up to Lotha's Croft and get one

there," said Luka, remembering their days on Waif Island."

"But it would be *getting* there that would be the problem," said Botolph. "Don't any boats come in here Father?"

"Oh we get one from time to time, but Luka's right, somewhere up near Lotha's Croft would seem a good idea but that'll mean crossing the river. It would be better to stay on the south shore. You could go up to Hethburh in our fish cart tomorrow."

"Hethburh? Where's that?"

"It's a cove which is a couple of leagues to the west of Lotha's Croft but you'll easily get a boat there - and you won't be as exposed as you would be at the main port. You'll need to disguise yourselves though, in case the cart gets stopped."

CHAPTER 20
Enemy Territory

Much to his annoyance the disguise chosen for Luka was that of a fish-wife. Disgruntled he climbed onto the back of the cart wearing a shawl around his head and a long scruffy peplos that had been rubbed with fish-waste and smelt truly awful. He insisted on carrying a bag containing his own clothes and was looking forward to changing into them at the earliest opportunity. He had drawn the line at being separated from his seax and that was attached to a cord around his waist. Both cord and seax were covered by the peplos however, and he had no idea of how he would get to the seax if he needed it quickly.

It was a long while since Botolph had had his tonsure properly shaved, so by good fortune he looked less like a monk than usual. He too had bundled up his habit and put it into Luka's bag while he donned a tunic and trousers. Ash was less of a problem but was warned to keep himself to himself during the journey.

Ash clambered into the back of the cart beside Luka saying:

"Alright if I join you Ma?"

Luka gave an unladylike scowl and turned away.

Botolph sat alongside the driver and they started off across the isthmus and then turned right along the track to the north.

There were plenty of travellers going in both

directions. Every so often they would come across a squad of warriors who were clearly in the fyrd of Penda but nobody bothered them until they came close to the Waif River.

"What's going on there?" Botolph said to the driver, pointing to a gaggle of carts and people in front of them.

"That's the ford. It looks as if soldiers are checking people before they cross."

"What should we do?"

"We don't need to cross but our road leads close to the bank before it turns right so we've no alternative but to push our way through the crowd and hope for the best."

Botolph leant over and told Luka and Ash the good news saying:

"You'll need to put on your sweetest smile Luka," but this brought no more than a grunt in reply.

The driver was as keen as the others to get through undetected since he too would be in trouble if he was found to have miscreants in his cart. He gently pushed the horse through the crowd trying not to create too much of a disturbance. They were nearly through when there came a shout, "Oi - where d'ye think ye're goin'?" and four ruffians purporting to be soldiers of the king, gathered around the cart. One of them held the horse's head and another accosted the driver.

"Well?"

"We're going to Hethburh to get our fish."

"Are ye now? 'N' why does it take four of ye to do that?"

"Well the wife's the expert at choosing the freshest fish at the best price, the boy does all the carrying and carting and we two are needed to make sure our purchases don't get stolen on the way home."

"Where're ye from?"

"Dommoc," he said without thinking and then bit his tongue in annoyance.

There was a long pause while the soldier studied him closely:

"Never 'eard of it."

One of the other men walked round the back of the cart and looked first at Ash and then at Luka. Luka said nothing but put on an endearing smile.

"You've got lovely eyes," said the soldier.

Luka smiled a little wider and shook his head coquettishly while thinking that if he had easier access to his seax he might have been inclined to stick it into the man's neck.

"Off you go then," said one of them, "and buy some extra fish to give us on the way back."

Half an hour later they arrived at Hethburh.

"You've got lovely eyes Ma," said Ash as they scrambled out of the cart - and then ducked as Luka aimed a cuff at his ears.

--o--

As predicted they found a trading boat easily at Hethburh and, having discarded their disguises, were soon in the German Ocean, hugging the coast in a brisk southwesterly wind.

They huddled together in a corner as the boat headed first to the north and then gradually turned to the northwest.

"What's the plan then Luka? What do you have in mind for us now?"

Luka grimaced: "I'll admit I don't really care much what we do as long as I don't have to dress up as a pesky fishwife again - I've still got that smell of her clothes up my nostrils."

Ash chuckled and Luka leaned forwards and continued conspiratorially in a low voice: "Safest place for us might be up north."

"North?" expostulated Botolph. "Why would we want to go all the way up there? I need to be as close to Engla as I can so that as soon as the king gets back I can start building at Ycan."

"Ah, yes Father but ... but ... "

One of the sailors looked over at them.

"No, of course Father - silly idea of mine ... we'll go where we can and bide our time."

"Yes, that sounds good," said Botolph - and the subject was dropped.

It was two days later, soon after dawn, when the boat finally tacked into a river and slid alongside a jetty.

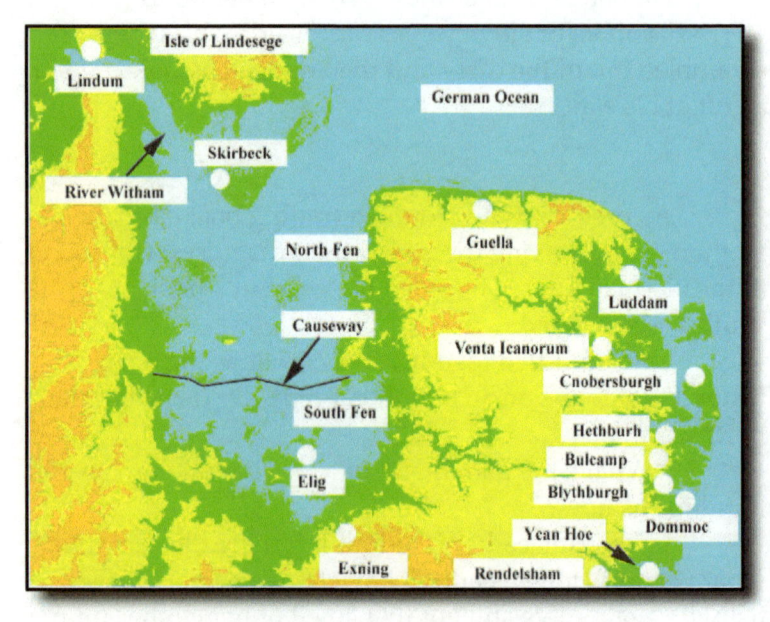

Fig. 17. Engla, the Fens and Lindum.

The port was a busy little place and ships were constantly arriving with fish, furs, oil and wine. Outbound vessels were loading with corn, cloth and wool. Merchants were strutting here and there and calling out their wares.

They disembarked as quickly as they could but stood on the quayside watching, fascinated, as their own skipper began to call out his cargo. Before long a group of traders had gathered round him haggling for the best price. The three fugitives moved away. Although they were clear of Penda country there would still be spies everywhere, and the less they drew attention to themselves the better. They needed accommodation.

"There's bound to be somewhere we can get our heads down," said Luka, "like there was a Bradbryc. We need to find a tavern - there'll be someone there to give us advice."

Sure enough, a beer or two later, they were sent to a place just a road or two back from the jetty.

"Let's drop off our dunnage at the billet then," said Botolph, "and then wander round and get our bearings."

They took the river path to the north.

"Where are we?" asked Ash.

"You're 'ere," said Luka.

"You know what I mean Pa - what's the name of the place?"

"Now there's a good point. I'm blessed if I know - we'd better ask someone."

"Skirbeck," came the answer from a passer-by. "Skirbeck on the island of Lindesege."

"Island?" said Luka, his heart suddenly dropping. "Oh no, we're not on an island are we?

"'Fraid so. Is that a problem?"

"Well - how far away's the mainland then?"

"Just over there," said his informer pointing to the

other side of the river.

Luka's spirits rose again. "Oh - that's not so bad then - I thought that was perhaps all part of the island and that we were in the middle of the sea somewhere. What's the mainland like?"

"S'alright if you know where you're going but there're few people who live there - it's all marsh."

"Where's the nearest settlement then?"

"Your next big place is up the Witham at Lindum."

"Is Witham the name of the river then?" piped up Ash.

"Yes it is, young fellow and Lindum's the biggest town on Lindesege but this 'ere Skirbeck's the main port."

"Can we walk to Lindum?"

"Aye ye could but its nearly ten leagues - 'n' for two of those ye'd be walking across nothing but marshes afore ye reach the wolds. Ye'd be far better to take a boat - that's what most folk do."

They thanked him and continued to explore, walking out of the village and surveying the marsh in front of them.

"It don't look too attractive," said Luka "the land's as flat as a cow pat. I can just imagine what it'd be like if a fog came down - like we had that day in Calletum Father."

"What happened then Pa?"

Luka and Botolph grinned at each other.

"We were both eighteen summers at the time and we'd just sailed across the sea to Gaul when we ran aground in thick fog. If you remind me, I'll tell you the tale when we're sitting round a nice cosy fire one evening - alright?"

Ash nodded.

"Well what do you think, Father?"

Botolph stood gazing across the land to the north

and then turned to study both the river and the land to the west before he answered:

"I think it'll do very nicely for the moment Luka. At least we're out of Penda's clutches and can relax here."

A couple of walkers passed them by.

"Let's wander a bit further out onto the marshes Father."

"Why? We're not going to be able to see anything different however far we go - unless you're proposing to walk to the wolds now?"

"Err no ... I just fancy a bit more of a walk. Communing with nature you might say."

"Communing with nature Luka? I've never come across you wanting to *commune with nature* before. What're you up to? ... Oh, very well. Have it your own way."

They walked for another half an hour until the sun was high in the sky. Every so often Luka would turn and look behind him - otherwise he gazed ahead watching travellers coming from the north.

Botolph began to realise that there was something in the air apart from the geese and ducks which occasionally passed overhead.

Eventually Luka was satisfied with the gap in the traffic. There were two travellers gradually catching up behind them but otherwise the path was clear. He cleared his throat and Botolph waited expectantly.

"I have a confession Father."

"Is this suitable for Ash's ears Luka?"

"Oh aye - in fact he *needs* to know. I'm afraid I've been keeping a few things back from ye both since we left Wintanceastre."

"Huh. That doesn't surprise me," said Ash. "What is it Pa?"

"King Anna's charged me with a secret mission."

Luka glanced behind them again but, satisfied, continued:

"He asked me to come back to Engla so that I could find out how thickly Penda had planted his men with a view to his returning as soon as possible."

"Oh?" said Botolph.

"So you're a *spy* Pa."

"Well, yes I s'pose I am - but on the side of good."

"So how would you get the word back to King Anna?" asked Ash.

"Ah - well he offered me several alternatives but ideally he wanted me to go back and report to him personally."

"So what are we doing all the way up here Pa?"

"The first reason we're here is because going back to Wintanceastre would have been too dangerous - I think we were lucky to get away with our journey east. The second reason we're here is because King Anna said that if I found Penda's troops to be thickly spread - which indeed they are - I was to follow an alternative plan."

"Ah," said Botolph, "so what's that?"

CHAPTER 21
An Alternative Plan

Luka looked behind him again. It would still be a little while before the travellers caught up. He stopped, turned towards his two companions, took a deep breath and then said, in a rush, "He wants me to go to the court of King Oswiu in Northumbria and beg his help."

"Northumbria?" said Ash.

"King Oswiu?" said Botolph.

"Let's go back," said Luka quietly and turned south again inclining his head towards the two travellers as they passed them. Once they were out of earshot, Luka spoke again.

"This is a matter of the utmost importance to King Anna. We need to keep it totally secret. There are ears everywhere. We mustn't even talk about it amongst ourselves. That was why I brought you out onto the marshes. Even a whisper could be overhead and put both us and the king's court in extreme danger. Penda must get no hint of the fact that Anna's planning a return. It wouldn't be beyond Penda to break into Wessex and finish the job by massacring them all."

They stayed silent for some time, absorbing the magnitude of the news. Luka looked behind him again and waited as a horseman thundered past. Once he had gone Luka said:

"As you can now see, I am committed to what I must do - but the same doesn't apply to you two. It'd probably be best if you both remained here in Skirbeck where you'll be safe, but tomorrow *I* shall have to start my journey north. You'll have to decide between yourselves what you are going to do while I'm away and I'll need to know your decision in the morning. I'm sorry Father to put you in this position, but I'm afraid I can't delay any longer. Don't forget though both of you - from now on, no mention of what's involved."

--o--

Although the news had stunned Botolph, he comforted himself with the thought that the sooner the king returned, the sooner he would be able to start his work at Ycan - so he had a vested interest in the result. He could see the logic of Luka's suggestion that he and Ash should stay at Skirbeck, but going with Luka would give him the opportunity to spread the word of Christianity in the north.

He thought about Ash and wondered what he would want to do. The youngster seemed to like Skirbeck and he might well favour staying there - although against that, he loved to be with his father too. If Ash decided to stay then there was no doubt that Botolph would also have to remain, so his decision depended to a great extent upon what Ash wanted to do.

He prayed long about it that night until he fell into a deep sleep during which he dreamt that they were all being chased by Penda.

He woke with a start to find Ash gently shaking his shoulder.

"You were dreaming Father and it sounded as if you had the Devil after you."

"Hah," said Botolph. "Maybe I did."

"I'm going with Pa," said Ash. "What're you doing?"

"Out of the mouths of babes," said Botolph.

"What?"

"That's magic for: 'I'm coming too.'"

"Is it?"

"No ... but I *am*."

"You're beginning to talk in as many riddles as Pa does."

"Yes, it must be catching. Where *is* your Pa?"

The door suddenly opened and Luka burst in.

"Ah you two are awake at last."

"You were up with the lark Luka."

"I was up earlier than that. I've been down to the wharf talking to the locals."

Ash opened his mouth and was about to say something about 'spying' but remembered in time the warning his father had given them, so he closed his mouth again and remained silent. This action was not lost on Luka, who guessed the rudiments of his son's thoughts and blessed him for his young wisdom.

"Well then," he said. "Shall I get you some food and then be on my way?"

"We're coming with you Pa."

"What? Both of you?"

"Both of us," said Botolph.

"Ah ... " he said, obviously pleased but determined not to show it, "It'll be three lots of food then."

--o--

It was 19th August when they took a boat up to Lindum. They stayed the night there and the next day they had a ten-hour walk up the Roman road to Winteringe where they stayed a second night. The following morning they crossed the wide Humbre River in a tiny boat and stepped ashore at Petuaria early on the morning of the 21st

August. They stood to one side as the other passengers disembarked.

"Where now then Pa?"

Fig. 18. Eoforwic and northwards.

"Still further north. Although we're now in King Oswiu's territory our next problem is going to be finding him. I've discovered that he has a great hall at Yeavering and another closer to the coast - but he's rarely at either place for long. I think we'd better head for Yeavering and hope for the best. We'll need some horses though."

"Horses? How are we going to get horses?" said

Botolph. "We haven't anything to trade with."

Luka tapped the side of his nose. "Leave it to me Father. You two stay here - I won't be long."

Sure enough, he returned a short while later riding one nag and leading two others. He was clutching some newly-baked bread and a bladder of beer, which they took their time to devour before mounting the horses and taking the old road north. When they reached the burh of Eoforwic Luka decided it was time to look for accommodation.

To the north of the burh they found a dilapidated stone church which, they were told, had been built fifteen years earlier by King Oswald. It was on the site of a previous wooden church constructed specifically for the baptism of King Edwin in 627.

Their informant was a wizened old crone who told them that she was the church's caretaker.

"She's not doing a very good job then," Luka observed privately.

Nevertheless she directed them to a place where there were some stables and lodging and they were able to enjoy a good supper.

The following day they set off again but after a couple of hours, just after they had passed through the village of Sudtun, they heard in the distance the boom of a drum which was followed soon after by the sound of a bell. As it drew closer they saw that this was being rung by a man at the front of a long procession.

As they approached he called "Make way ... make way ... make way for the body of King Oswin."

Shocked at the thought that the king they were seeking was dead, they pulled their horses to the side of the path and numbly slid off as a mark of respect. Botolph crossed himself as the bier passed by, drawn by a single handsome horse. On the bier lay the body of a finely-dressed man with his arms crossed atop his sword. Behind the bier processed about thirty followers - men at the front and women and children behind.

Luka approached one of the men and walked with the group as he gleaned the news. Some minutes later he came back to Botolph and Ash.

"It's not *Oswiu*," he said, "it's his second cousin, *Oswin*. Apparently Oswin's been ruling Deira for the past ten years but Oswiu, as senior king, decided it was time for him to take over himself but Oswin would neither stand aside nor fight - he simply fled and hid. Two of Oswiu's men found him in the village of Gilling where they put him to death and now they're taking him to Eoforwic, where he'll be buried the day after tomorrow. The good news is that, as a mark of respect, King Oswiu's coming to the service."

They remounted and turned their horses back down the road, spurring them into a trot until they caught up with the procession which they followed back into Eoforwic. Here they returned the horses to the stables they had used the previous night and made arrangements to use the same lodgings for a couple of days.

The next day King Oswiu and his retinue arrived. Amongst them, to Botolph's joy, was Queen Eanfled, who recognised him immediately.

"Father Botolph, how wonderful to see you after all these years," she said after dismounting.

"Sire - can I introduce you to Father Botolph? He was Abbess Fara's chaplain when I was at Evoriacum in Francia."

"It's a pleasure to meet you Father," said King Oswiu "but who are these other people?"

"This is my dear friend Luka who has been my

constant companion for many years and this is his son Ash."

"A pleasure - but what are you doing here?"

"Actually sire, we were looking for you with little hope of finding you - but thankfully God seems to have brought us together."

"To what purpose?"

The king was half-surrounded by his men at arms and many other people including his secretary.

"I bring you a message sire but I need to speak to you in private," said Luka.

"Do you indeed? Well give the captain of my contubernium time to get the tents erected and then come and see me sometime before dinner. In fact, why don't you join us for dinner as my special guests?"

They took their leave of the royal family and walked down to the river.

"Why didn't you tell me you were close friends of the queen?" asked Luka."

"I'm sorry, but I'd forgotten," said Botolph.

"Forgotten? How can you forget that you're friends with a queen?"

"Well she wasn't a queen when I met her. She was just a young girl who'd been sent from Cantium to be professed as a nun at Evoriacum. You actually met her mother yourself."

"Did I?" said Luka, losing some of his indignation.

"Yes, she was Queen Ethelburga of Liminge."

"Ah - the aunt of Princess Eanswythe who brought me back to life."

"Brought you back to life Pa?" said Ash. "Oh yes - I remember - that was the story old Eric mentioned when we were in Folcanstane. You promised to tell me the rest of it but you never did."

They were standing at the river's edge leaning on a staging rail and watching the water flow past them.

"I'll tell you in greater detail one day but the short story is that we arrived off Folcanstane in a storm and the boat was forced ashore by some ferocious waves and in the process I was knocked unconscious. The Father here saved me, took me on land and cared for me for many days as my life slowly ebbed away and it looked as if I was going to die. Then Princess Eanswythe came to see me from her nunnery on the hill and suddenly I started to get better, didn't I Father?"

He looked up at Botolph and grinned. Botolph grinned back.

"Yes, but what he didn't say Ash, was that the only reason that he was knocked unconscious was because he came back to save *me*. I was trapped under the boat by a rope and would've drowned if your Pa hadn't come back and cut me free."

Ash's eyes were wide open. He was clearly unable to speak. He just looked from one to the other and back again. Botolph saw his eyes fill with tears. His father looked down fondly, put a strong arm around his shoulders and laughed.

"Don't 'e worry lad - we're with ye now 'n' that was all just part of our education. Right Father?"

"Right Luka. Come on, let's walk along the river bank."

--o--

Later that afternoon they found their way to the king's tent and, while Botolph and Ash waited outside, Luka was able to give Anna's message in private. Besides the king, the only other person in attendance was his secretary.

The king said nothing.

Luka waited.

The king looked up at the top of the tent and rubbed his chin.

Luka waited.

The king kicked his feet forwards, slid back in his chair and continued to rub his chin.

Luka continued to wait.

"You say King Anna is at Wintanceastre?"

"Yes my lord."

"That's a long way away."

Luka said nothing.

"And King Penda has said he'll kill him if he returns to Engla?"

"Yes my lord."

"Hmm. Well Luka," he said with a sigh, " I'll do what I can - when I can - but I can't promise that anything will be done quickly. As you've discovered, I've just taken over the rule of Deira and that will occupy me for some time. I have to ride and see my subjects - and let *them* see me. I have to look at the manors and the fyrds. It will take many months, so you must tell King Anna to be patient."

"Yes my lord."

"All we can hope for is that Penda's influence becomes less. That he gets weakened. Mercia covers a wide area now and Engla will be an extra burden. I wonder that he has sufficient loyal men to spread through such a large kingdom. When he weakens, I shall be able to help your King Anna. Tell him that."

"Yes my lord. Thank you for your audience."

"You're looking unhappy Luka - is there another problem?"

" . . . Well yes sire. My problem now is how to let

King Anna know that I've made contact with you. We can't go back the way we've come because Engla is thick with Penda's men, and we can't go straight back from here because there is a great swathe of Penda's Mercia in our path."

"That is the least of worries," said Oswiu. "Write your message - but keep it brief - and let me have it and I will ensure that it gets to Wintanceastre. I have trusted spies and messengers who are passing through Mercia every day."

"Now," he said, rising to his feet, "go and find your friends and tell them to come to dinner."

--o--

Dinner was a great success and, as honoured guests, Botolph and Ash spent a long while talking to Oswiu and his queen. Luka, on the other hand, spent most of his time at the far end of the table, drinking with the soldiers and, as the minstrels played their pieces, cavorting with the wenches.

"So," said the king as Botolph handed him the parchment that he and Luka had spent the previous hour writing, "now that Luka has done his duty, what are you going to do?"

"I'm not sure sire. We can't go back to Engla for the moment because we're too well known there. My calling is to spread the word of God so it seems that He has perhaps brought me here to carry out His wishes."

"Well stay then," said the king. "We've plenty of pagans here for you to work on, haven't we Lady Eanfled?"

"Certainly we do my lord. I know that the Father is a good persuader and by serving God he will also be serving you."

"He will indeed."

"When were you brought to Christ sire?"

"Ah - many years ago. I've known Christ all my life. My brothers and I went into exile in Dalriada when I was only four and we were educated by the monks of Iona."

"In Dalriada - with King Eochaid?"

"Yes, the very same. Do you know the kingdom?"

A daydream flitted through Botolph's mind. A daydream of camp fires on a Scottish hillside. A daydream of men and horses. He tried to clutch at it before it went but he was not quick enough.

"Do you know the kingdom?" Oswiu repeated.

"Sorry sire. Yes I've heard of it but no more than that."

"Oh," said the king, not altogether believing him. "Well if you stay with us for a while you might even be able to go and make your acquaintance with it now. King Eochaid's long since dead of course."

"Who were your brothers sire?"

"Eanfrith and Oswald, both of whom became kings of Northumbria. Eanfrith was more than twenty years older than me and he only lasted a year or so before he was killed by Penda and Cadwallan. Oswald was only eight years older than me. He was king for nine years before he was also killed by Penda in '42."

"Did they have sons?"

"Eanfrith didn't but Oswald married one of Cenwealh's sisters."

"What - Cenwealh of the Gewisse - where King Anna is staying now?"

"Yes, the very same. They had a son called Oethelwald whom I might yet ask to run Deira for me - but don't breathe a word of that - I'm still thinking about it."

Luka arrived back at the king's table very much the

worse for wear and flopped down on a bench. Botolph stood up and Ash, taking the hint, did likewise.

"I think, sire it is time for us to withdraw if you will permit?"

"Certainly," said the king with a knowing grin. "I will see you at the burial tomorrow."

As they had done many times before, Botolph put one strong hand under Luka's left arm and Ash pulled Luka's right arm over his shoulder and held his wrist and they marched him out of the tent and back to their lodgings.

--o--

The following day they were awoken by the booming beat of a drum as the funeral squad marched in and out of Eoforwic's streets, calling its people to the funeral.

"Do we need to go straight away Pa - before we break our fast?"

"Nay lad. Don't fret yourself. The funeral's not 'til noon. The squad will pass twice more before then."

As the sun approached its maximum height they joined others walking up the rise. They did not have long to wait before the sound of the drum started again and the bier was drawn up the hill onto the flat where an empty grave awaited. Close behind the bier came the royal retinue preceded by a group of white-robed priests.

The rites were intoned; the plainchant was sung; the body was lowered and the soil was cast over. It was not long before the graveside was deserted and the former king was left to his own decomposition.

At the bottom of the hill Oswiu's troops were preparing for departure.

"Are you coming with us?" called Eanfled.

"Where are you going?"

"I'm bound north to Yeavering but my lord is travelling south and taking a tour of our estates. You are welcome to join either of us."

Botolph and Luka looked at each other questioningly.

"Well, we've seen the south so perhaps we could join you and get to know the north a bit more? How's that Luka?"

"S'all right by me."

"We'll get the horses."

--o--

They followed the royal train up the Roman road for several miles until hill-country began to appear on their right.

"It's pretty desolate here," said Botolph - but all he got from Luka was a nod and a grunt.

"I'd rather go up into the hills. What do you think?"

Luka brightened a little: "The men at arms were saying it'll take us another couple of days to get to Yeavering. But then what do we do? Once we get used to the court it'll probably be as boring as it was in Wintanceastre."

"From what King Oswiu said it'll probably be months before he does anything to help King Anna. We can't go back to Engla until Penda's men have thinned out. As far as I can see we're stuck where we are."

"I'm sorry Father."

"What?"

"I'm sorry - it's my fault for dragging you all the way up here."

"You didn't drag us up here. If you remember you

told us to stay in Skirbeck but we insisted on coming with you.   None of this is your fault."

"We could go back to Skirbeck - Ash liked it there, didn't you lad?"

"Yes it was alright Pa."

"How about that then Father?"

He shook his head: "I don't know.   We could be in Skirbeck for many moons.   I'd feel I was wasting God's time buried there.   I want to get out into the countryside."

"We're *in* the countryside *now* and, from what Ash told me, the king and queen looked favourably on the prospect of your evangelising here."

"They said there'd be plenty for me to do."

"Well then?"

"Well then what?"

Luka sighed.   "Why don't we break away from this stupid train and ride up into those hills and get you started on your work?"

Botolph looked at Luka in surprise and silently blessed him once again.

--o--

Time passed easily between August 651 and March 653.   Each day slipped pleasantly into the next and winter had soon come and gone and before they knew it the next one was rapidly approaching.   The tireless Father Botolph travelled up and down between the great Roman wall of Emperor Hadrian and the River Humber founding dozens of new field chapels.   It was whilst they were celebrating the finishing of one of these that they heard that King Penda was threatening to take over Northumbria.   Botolph saw two aspects to this rumour if it turned out to be true: firstly, that Northumbria would no longer represent a place of safety for them and secondly, that it was likely that

Penda would need the services of those of his troops who had been idling in Engla.

On reflection he felt that his time in the north had been well spent and, other than over-seeing his new foundations, there was now little else for him to do here. So, by the time the spring flowers had started blossoming, he was ready to get back to his calling at Ycan. It seemed to be time to go.

Luka sold the horses in Petuaria to the very same ostler from whom they had originally been bought, and they took the little ferry back over the great river to Winteringe, which they found much as they had left it, and started down the Roman road that ran alongside the River Ancholme to Lindum.

A short while later they came to a crossing and, on a whim, Botolph suggested they should ford the river to Glanford and take the longer route to Skirbeck. The March water was cold causing Luka to express a few comments of disappreciation as they splashed their way through the ford. There was some compensation however, for the little villages tucked away in the wolds proved to be most agreeable. Botolph was inclined to tarry a while to add their inhabitants to his Christian collection until Luka reminded him of their urgent business in Skirbeck. He found no need to press his point too firmly because just the mention of Ycan was enough to spur Botolph on his way. He made a mental note however, that he would come back to Lindesege as soon as he was able.

It was close to noon on 15th March when they crossed the causeway on the marshy lands that led to Skirbeck and when they arrived they were tired and hungry, so their first target was the riverside tavern.

On their way south, they had been constantly asking travellers they met for information regarding the occupation of Engla. The results of their enquiries had been inconclusive. Botolph had hoped that he would find the latest up-to-date news at Skirbeck and that this would confirm that they could travel further south. To his disappointment the opposite was the case. Everyone they talked to said that the strictures in Engla were the same or even harsher than ever.

"How can that be?" said Botolph to Luka. "Is Penda planning to attack Oswiu with only half an army?"

"Well if he does," said Luka, "there'd be a good chance that he'd lose the battle and be killed, so there's a blessing."

"Hmm - true. I suppose we'll just have to wait then."

That proved to be the only solution - but 'sitting and waiting' had never been a welcome pastime for any of the trio and after many prayers Botolph decided that God might be calling him to Lindum. There were many more prospects there than out on the marsh at Skirbeck, and they would still be close enough to receive news quickly about changes in Engla's circumstances. Botolph put his idea to Luka and Ash who, as usual, were very supportive.

"There's one thing though," said Luka.

"What's that?"

"Bearing in mind your desire to get back to Ycan as soon as possible, there's one person - if he's still alive - who could keep an eye on the situation and let us know quickly as soon as there's any change."

"Who's that?"

"Prince Tonberht."

"Who's Prince Tonberht?"

"You remember Father," said Ash. "He's the Prince of the Fens who married King Anna's daughter just before the first time we arrived in Engla."

"Ah yes. Of course he married *Etheldreda* didn't he? I'd forgotten all about her. Would she have been safe in the fens after her father left? Surely we should have taken her with us to Wintanceastre?"

"I've no idea," said Luka, "but she certainly was not in our party, so King Anna must have been confident that Prince Tonberht would be able to look after her alright. She's probably got a brood of fen-babies by now," he chuckled.

"Her father said she'd sworn to remain a virgin and he wondered how Tonberht was going to deal with that. In fact she didn't want to marry at all but the prince persuaded her by giving her an island didn't he? What was its name Luka - can you remember?"

"Aye. They called it 'Elig.' 'Twas just across the water from the great hall at Exning - 'n' that's the place that's in my mind to visit."

"How d'you mean?"

"Well we can ask around in Skirbeck to find out if they're still alive 'n' if so, where we're likely to find them. The fens aren't that large 'n' my guess is that they'll still be on the island. If that proves to be the case then I think we should go and make their acquaintance and ask for Tonberht's help. Since this is all for his father-in-law's benefit, I can't see how he can refuse."

"Is it essential that we go and see him? Can't we just send a message?"

"You know how it is Father - information can get distorted. We might find that the prince is under the control of Penda's men and that our message gets into the wrong hands which will warn Penda of Anna's intended return. When the king *does* return he's going to need as much time as possible to collect his fyrds together. The worst thing that could happen would be that Penda would

attack before the king was ready."
"A trip into the fens it is then."

CHAPTER 22
The Fens

It was not as easy a journey as Botolph had expected. The weather was pleasant and warm and there was a gentle breeze from the southwest, but it was not strong enough to move the boat as fast as the boatman would have liked. The passengers consequently had to bend their arms to the oars for many of the eight hours that it took them to get to a destination which proved to be only half way.

They moored alongside a rickety wooden jetty which formed the first part of an old Roman causeway that stretched out to the east. The boatman told them that it crossed the great mere using foundations much in the same way that stepping stones would be used to cross a pond. Sometimes the road ran across long dry islands, but there were frequent gaps where the road passed over wooden bridges. He told them that in the latter case the current ripped past the wooden support piers quite spectacularly, and in storms it was not unusual for some of the bridges to be washed away.

They stayed the night at a small roadside hut that accommodated other travellers and the boatman. They were under the impression that he was going to take them to Elig the next day but he took them down to where a small vessel was moored on the inner side of the bridge and told them they could take that and make their own way to Elig.

"How far is it?" asked Luka

"'Tis about seven leagues - it'll take ye all day," he said cheerfully.

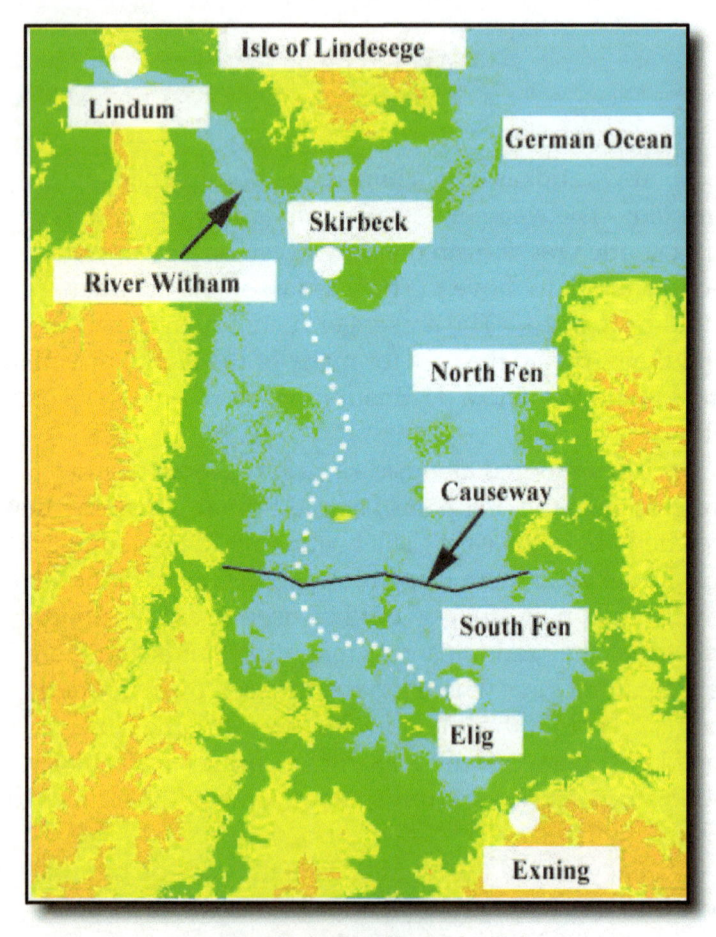

Fig. 19. Skirbeck, Elig and Lindum.

"How will we know which way to go?"

"It's straight over that way t' the south east," he said. "Ye can't get lost - there'll be plenty o' people out on the fens on a nice day like t'day. Just ask," and with that, he turned his back on them and vanished.

"Well there's a fine thing," said Luka indignantly.

"Come on Pa," said Ash jumping into the boat. "We can do it."

Sure enough, as the boatman had said, they regularly came across little cockleshells - usually containing a lone fisherman tending his nets and traps. It was mid-afternoon when the largest of the fen islands loomed up ahead of them and they felt their way through the shallow water into a natural harbour.

Ash was the first over the side after the boat grounded and he held the painter while the others clambered out. They hauled the boat halfway out of the water and tied the line around a solid-looking clump of sedge before making their way towards some buildings on higher ground.

It was not long before they were taken to meet Tonberht and his queen. None of them had met Etheldreda before but she knew all about Botolph who had apparently, in years past, been the subject of much family discussion.

"So ye're keen to get on with building yer abbey?" said Tonberht.

"Yes more than keen," said Botolph, "but I'm told it wouldn't be welcomed by Penda."

"I don't know about that," said Tonberht. "He's a funny chap and quite tolerant of Christianity in many ways but . . . ye never can tell. Ye're probably right to bide yer time."

"We'd heard he'd withdrawn his troops and gone to fight in the north, but once we arrived here we received the unwelcome news that they were as thickly spread as ever."

"Aye - that's true - so what are yer plans now?"

"We're going up to Lindum but it occurs to me that you're probably going to be the first to know if Penda pulls out and I wondered if you'd be able to get a message to us when that happens?"

"Oh aye - I could do that. I've had a message from King Anna asking me to do the same thing, so we're constantly watching what's going on over there. Where can I reach you in Lindum?"

"Ah . . . I've no idea at the moment."

"I'll tell you what, - I'll get a message to the bootmaker there. You'll find his shop in the centre of the lower city. Call in to see him from time to time - that should work alright."

After a couple of meals, a good night's sleep and another sail across the fens they found themselves back at the causeway. The next morning they boarded a vessel that took them all the way up to Lindum. Here, after mooring alongside a pier, they disembarked and entered the city through the postern gate in the south wall.

"Pax brother," said Botolph to a passing trader, "Where might we find the bootmaker?"

"Just ye pass along 'ere until ye get to the bridge street and turn right towards the upper town. Ye'll soon find his shop on the right."

"It's good to be back in civilisation again," said Luka as they threaded their way through the colourful noisy mass of people and market stalls that thronged each side of the road.

The smells of herbs and spices filled their noses and the hubbub of voices assaulted their ears as they moved up the gentle incline of the high street.

"The river won't flood this far then," said Luka, raising his sights to where the upper city rose above them.

"I've heard tell there's little to see up there but

Roman ruins," said Botolph, following his gaze."

"Well there must be *something* up there 'cos the main road passes right through it ... Whoa ... " he said, as a horse-drawn wagon suddenly thundered out of a side-street to their right and veered round them towards the bridge.

"That must be the cart-way up to the top town Pa," said Ash. "You can see how this road turns into steps further up."

It was at the beginning of the steps that they found the white-bearded cobbler sitting at his bench, tapping away with his hammer at the sole of a boot while he drove tiny iron tacks into the leather. As they entered his shop through the open doorway he looked up and removed some spare tacks that he was holding between his teeth.

"Good morrow," he said cheerily, "and what might I do for you fine creatures today? A nice pair of new sandals ready for the summer perhaps? Sit ye down," and he pulled three stools from under the bench and, dusting them off, waved his visitors onto them.

He seemed happy to chat all day but a queue of *proper* customers started to build up at the door so, after delivering their message, they pushed the stools back into their hiding places and took their leave - but not before they had received some advice on what good lodgings were available in the town.

Spring turned to summer and summer slipped into autumn and Botolph was beginning to wonder whether God was ever going to listen to his prayers or if they would have to stay in Lindum for evermore. He preached regularly in Lower Lindum and always collected a good crowd around him as he expounded philosophies about the trials of everyday life and their connection with the Lord Jesus Christ.

Merchants would frequently ask if he would take their children and educate them and as a result he set up a small school within the city walls. Every day would start and finish with prayers, and at lunchtime an over-generous amount of food was provided by the parents. The surplus food was given to beggars and wayfarers.

One day a group of six young men approached him.

"Father," one said, "we love God and wish to devote ourselves to Him. Would you teach us to pray and show us how to order our lives?"

The noisy bustling streets inside the walls of Lower Lindum were no place for contemplation and worship, so Botolph set Luka and Ash the task of finding somewhere more appropriate. As a result of their diligence it was not long before the young men were installed in a thatched hut down by the water's edge just less than a mile due east of the bridge.

Here the novices found peace and tranquillity with only the call of the birds and the rippling of the water to disturb them. They immediately took to wearing undyed habits secured with rope girdles and had their heads tonsured in the Roman fashion, and Botolph started to instruct them according to the Rule of the Holy Father Saint Benedict; the same rule that he had first applied at Norflot.

Word of the new foundation quickly spread amongst the townsfolk who fondly named it 'Monks' Abbey.'

A few weeks later a traveller who was on his way from the monastery of Lindisfarena to that of Cantwarebury, sought overnight shelter there and was so impressed with the location and ethos of the community that he asked if he could stay.

Botolph regarded this as manna from Heaven since the man was experienced both in the Holy Rites and in the tutoring of novices and, although Botolph enjoyed training the young men at Monks' Abbey and teaching the children at the burh school, he felt he was becoming inundated by these responsibilities.

"I feel I've dropped anchor in the Witham," said Botolph to Luka one day. "I can't get the anchor up and the burh walls are closing round me."

"You're certainly keeping busy," his friend replied, "but you can alwez weigh anchor again when you're ready."

"Well that's the problem. I'm not sure that I can. Not only that but I'm wondering if Penda will ever take his troops out of Engla - we could be stuck here for another ten years."

"Would that be so bad? We get on well with the people and the old bootmaker provides us with a constant source of entertainment one way or another."

Botolph laughed. "Yes he's a good soul and has turned into the fount of all knowledge as far as Lindum is concerned. He seems to be able to fix anything. I'm grateful to Tonberht for introducing us."

"Well then?"

"The fact is that I feel wasted here. I am not moving *forward*. I have been praying about it for weeks. I am enjoying life too much. I've plenty to keep me occupied but there are not enough challenges." He looked up into the sky as if he were talking directly to the Great Father Himself: "I need to devote all my energies to God and I want the joy of seeing His word spread like wildfire across the countryside."

"Maybe ... ?"

"Yes?"

"Maybe God's resting you and helping you to build up your energies ready for your next great project."

Botolph turned his head and looked sharply at his friend. He opened his mouth to speak but no sound came out. He closed his mouth again and contemplated Luka.

The corners of Luka's lips began to twitch. Normally they would both have burst out laughing at this point - but not this time - it was a serious matter and the instant passed.

Botolph put his arm around Luka's shoulders and said thoughtfully: "Perhaps you're right."

It was another month before the bootmaker appeared at the door of the schoolroom with a triumphant smile cracking his ruddy wizened features.

"They've gone."

"Who's gone?" said Botolph looking up from a manuscript that one of his pupils was slowly and falteringly reading out loud.

"*They've* gone - Penda's men - they've left Engla. He's taken them to fight a new battle in the north. Word's been sent to King Anna so he's on his way back from Wintanceastre and, sad as I shall be to see you go, it's time for you to move on too young Father."

--o--

With the bootmaker's help another tutor was found to look after the school and the new arrival at Monks' Abbey willingly agreed to act as prior and continue with the novices' training.

A week later, to a great send-off, Botolph, Luka and Ash boarded a boat that was bound for Hethburh on Lotha's River although it took them four days to get there. The first night they spent at Skirbeck and the second at Guella - a small inlet on the north coast of Engla.

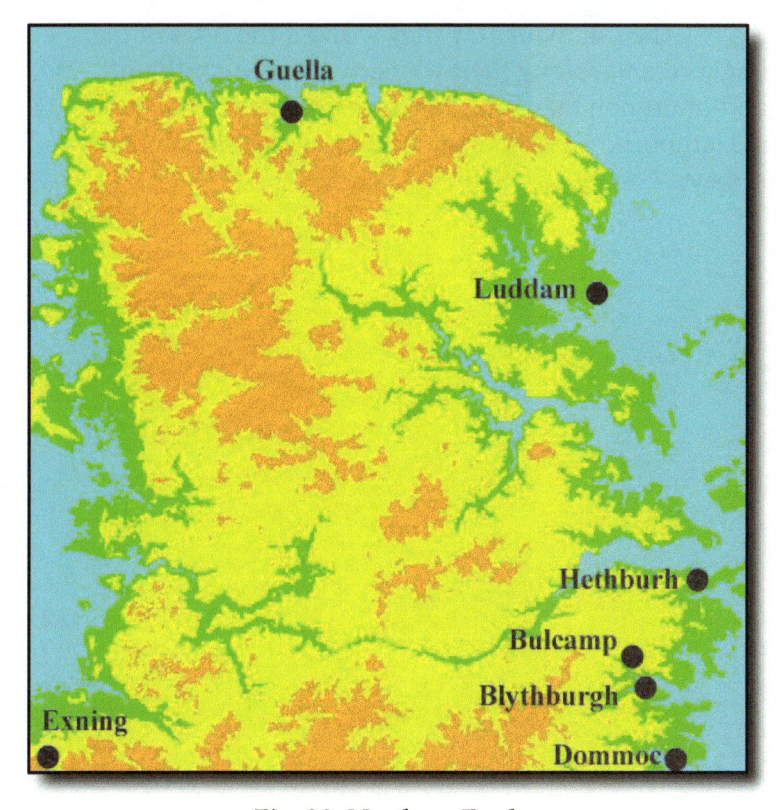

Fig. 20. Northern Engla.

Then they were blessed by a brisk southwesterly wind which gave them a lively sail on flat seas down to the Thurne Estuary where the skipper had some cargo to unload. The favourable wind turned against them here and they had to labour hard, short tacking through the shallows in order to work their way up the river. They dropped anchor in the lee of a little village called Pottam and waited for the wind to ease which it did as night fell. The fittest passengers were then called upon to take to the oars and row the last league into the port of Luddam.

The following day they worked the tides of the Engla rivers making their way towards the south until, in mid-afternoon they found themselves back at the little port of Hethburh.   Five hours later they arrived at Dommoc Abbey.

CHAPTER 23
Dommoc

There was a different atmosphere to the place compared to when they had left it. Even at Hethburh they found everyone smiling and helpful, whereas on their departure the whole countryside oozed apprehension. At Dommoc, in spite of the lateness of the hour, they received a great and happy welcome.

"Have you heard about our new abbot?" asked the ostler.

"New abbot?" said Botolph, "Did Abbot Thomas die then?"

"Aye he did, not six moons since."

"Of what?"

"We never knew. He just took to his bed and slowly faded away."

"Oh dear, I'm sorry to hear that. So who's abbot now?"

"Berhtgisl they call him. We had the archbishop up for the consecration - just like we did for Abbot Thomas."

"My word you've had some changes since we've been away. Did Penda not cause any problems about the archbishop's attendance?"

"Nay. None at all - although we expected him to."

The next day they went to pay their respects to the new abbot. He had received glowing reports from Archbishop Honorius about Botolph's work in Cantium and he had also heard about his proposals for Ycan.

"My Lord Abbot," said Botolph, "Have you heard if King Anna has returned yet?"

"We've heard nothing so I guess he hasn't."

"When is he expected?"

"We've no idea?"

"Who can I ask?"

"*Father*," said the abbot a little indignantly, "you know as much about King Anna as we do. The occupying troops have only just left - I am surprised you've arrived back so promptly. You seem to have come in through the back door as they left through the front. How did you find out so quickly?"

"Ah, well we had privileged information from the fens."

"But how could the fenmen be sure that the troops had left for good? Indeed how can we be certain even now?"

"Well my Lord Abbot, I am not sure about any of it. All I know is that we received the intelligence and it sounded and felt right. Perhaps we were a little foolhardy to act so quickly but the action was not taken in the absence of prayers - and here we are - and it *still* feels right."

The abbot was not a man given to mirth but he raised his eyebrows, rolled his eyes and shook his head a little and said, "So I guess you're wanting to get off to your Ycan as soon as possible?"

"Yes my Lord."

"You *do* know what you're taking on there I suppose? You've heard the stories about the place? You've heard of the lacerated bodies that have washed up in the river? You've heard of the evil that lurks there - an evil which *nobody* has been able to eradicate?"

"Yes my Lord, I've heard all these stories, and I believe that God's chosen me to do His will and drive the evil out and put Ycan's Hoe to good use." He added disarmingly, "Might I borrow some horses - and a cart - together with some other materials so that I can get started?"

"Borrow? Well I suppose so but you're not really borrowing from me. They're the king's horses and materials. We're only storing them for him. I expect he will want them back when he returns - so make sure you husband them well."

--o--

The next day they collected food, water, bedding and a selection of tools including five sickles, a sharpening stone and three rakes, and headed back towards Ycan.

Botolph was driving the cart which was leading a spare working nag, and Luka and Ash were following on horseback. As he drove, Botolph began to realise that something was wrong. He could not make out what it was. His excitement had suddenly vapourised. He had, over the years, learned to listen to and trust his instincts. What were his instincts telling him now? Were they heading into a trap? Were Penda's men still lurking somewhere? He looked ahead and then all around him. Everything seemed to be peaceful. He had the feeling that he should not go on - and yet at the same time it did not feel that he should abandon the plans and return to Dommoc. They passed through the hamlet of Snape and started down the incline that led to the ford. The water was low and they splashed through easily enough and, after rising on the other side, turned left towards the Hoe which they could see jutting out into the river.

Botolph pulled on the reins so that he could stop and admire it and the other two passed and stood ahead of him. Botolph's feeling of excitement returned. Luka, on the other hand, shivered violently as he suddenly had a flashback about the creepy feelings he had experienced when they were last here. The abbot's comments the previous evening had done nothing to improve his resolve. He observed the Hoe with the same sort of foreboding that a chicken might regard a fox that was getting ready to pounce. With a tremendous effort he pulled himself together and pointed and said as cheerily as he was able:

"There are the byres that King Anna said we could use for sleeping in while we are working on the Hoe."

Luka's shiver had not been lost on Botolph, who at last realised what it was that was wrong about their present situation and plans. In a flash his feeling of excitement gave way to despair as he realised what he had to do. He offered up an emergency prayer for help - there was no time for a properly-organised plea to God. He took a deep breath.

"Luka"

"Yes?"

"I don't quite know how to say this."

"What?"

Botolph paused and the tension built up as Luka tried to work out what was coming next. Ash gazed at them both.

"I ... I ... "

"What is it Father? What's the problem?"

"Oh Luka, my dear friend ... I don't want to offend you."

"Offend me? You're never likely to do that - now come on Father, spit it out, what are you trying to say."

Botolph was looking as miserable as Luka had ever seen him. He slouched on the driving seat and looked sadly at his friend.

"I ... I feel I'd like to do this on my own."

"On your own?"

"Yes."

"*What* would you like to do on your own?"

"I'd like to get to know and make peace with Ycan alone."

"Alone?"

An initial feeling of panic had built up in Ash's mind as this conversation had started but now he began to see the funny side of it and he was struggling to keep the smile from his face as his father and the priest exchanged confusing single word conversations with each other.

"Yes, alone."

"Oh."

"There, I knew it would offend you."

"Offend?"

"Yes, I'm sorry."

Ash was beginning to quake with suppressed mirth. Luka looked across at him.

"What's up with you?"

"Err - nothing Pa," he said with a broad grin.

Luka turned back to Botolph.

"You mean you don't want me to help you do the preparations for the new monastery?" said Luka as a great wave of relief spread over him.

"Yes I'm afraid so. I'm sorry Luka - it's just something that I feel is right . . . that at first I make my peace here and make my own personal mark on the place. Once it's all settled then *of course* I shall want you both to come back and share it with me. Can you understand?"

"Oh . . . oh yes Father . . . " he wagged his head sagely from side to side trying to keep the smile off his face . . . "Of course it'll be hard not being here . . . but . . . but I . . . I shall be brave about it . . . " - he shot a glance of venom at Ash who was still having difficulty containing his mirth. "If . . . if that's what you *really* want . . . then we will get you all settled into one of those byres and ... and then leave you in peace ... and perhaps pop down and see you every couple of days. Now how will that suit Father?"

"Luka you're wonderful - thank you *so* much for understanding."

"Right now, let's not mope about it, - we'll find somewhere to make you comfortable and then we'll get off as quick as we can ... won't we Ash? Let's first of all get your horse out of its shafts."

As bright as a daisy, now that the strain of the thought of having to do battle with the supernatural had been lifted from his shoulders, Luka busied himself with clearing out the best of the three byres. He and Ash raked out the droppings and covered the floor with fresh hay that had been stored ready to feed the animals. Once everything was in place and a sleeping pallet had been prepared, and wood and kindling had been made ready for a fire, Luka put his hands on his hips and stretched his back.

"Right Father, that's about all we can do for you for now, so we'll get off and let you get on with your work."

They hugged each other and Botolph then hugged Ash.

"Shall we leave the extra horse with you - or take it with us?"

"Yes - take him with you - I can't see that I am going to need him at all."

The horses were grazing contentedly nearby and Luka went over to them with a view to getting hold of the animal's leading rein, but it was not having any of it. Every time he approached it tossed its head and ran off.

"Never mind then," said Botolph, "Leave him here if he wants to stay."

"*Vale* Father," they chorused.

"*Vale et pax*," he replied raising his hand in blessing as they turned their horses away.

"*Vale*," he thought "- *be strong* . . . I know that the task I have before me is not an easy one, and it may be that the next few days of my life are going to demand greater strength than I have ever needed before. The question is 'Will I be strong enough - or will the powers of evil overcome me?' Will *mine* be the next body to end up floating down the river with terrible claw marks on it?"

--o--

Luka and Ash did not talk until they were through the ford and trotting side by side up the hill towards Snape.

"Well then Pa," said Ash.

"Well then what?" said Luka scowling at him.

"Well then, that worked out alright didn't it?"

"I don't know what you mean?"

"Not half you don't Pa - you never wanted to work on that site did you?"

"Well . . . ," Luka squirmed uncomfortably. If he had not been on horseback he would have twisted himself into the contorted position that had always made Mistress Meg laugh so much at Bradbryc.

"Well Pa?" - Ash was not going to let him off the hook lightly.

Luka gave up and looked his son straight in the eye.

"You're getting to be a knowing little devil aren't you?"

"Ha-ha, I know my Pa," he retorted and with that he dug his heels into his horse's flanks and cantered through Snape village with his father in hot pursuit. A couple of villagers scattered to one side of the street and looked at each other as if to say "Now what was all that about?"

CHAPTER 24
Botolph's Challenge

Botolph stood at the doorway of the byre and gazed across to where the Hoe stretched out into the middle of the Ald River. It was approaching the time of high tide. The water swirled wickedly around the peninsula, creating a number of whirlpools further upstream where a dead body would be spun cruelly round before being sucked into the depths. He wondered what animals lurked beneath the surface. He remembered that when they were at the king's court there had been talk of a great monster-like serpent that dwelt in the lower reaches and came up-river twice a day to feed. The coils of its body had been seen - and its mouth but rarely - although it was said to be large enough to take a cow in a single gulp. Indeed there had been many stories of cattle going missing from this bank and it was thought that all had gone to feed the monster's insatiable appetite.

Botolph shivered.

He turned his attention to the gorse-covered Hoe which even now was covered with tiny yellow flowers. No sensible human would be venturing into that tightly-packed prickly maze. It was going to take him a long while to clear it and he imagined the cuts that he would receive to his hands as the gorse fell sideways after each chop of his sickle.

He sighed and a vision came into his mind of Jesus with His crown of thorns and he realised that this was *his* cross which he had chosen to bear.

That gave him an idea. He went into the byre and rooted around until he found two pieces of wood of a suitable size. These he lashed together to form a crude but sizeable cross. He took this to the northeast side of the byre and, using a smaller piece of strong straight wood as a hole spike, he plunged it time and time again into the earth until the hole was wide enough and deep enough for what he had in mind. Grasping the cross, he plunged its base into the hole and forced it downwards until it was tight.

The sun was still clear of the horizon behind him as he knelt on the damp soil and sent his prayers to the east. He imagined them hitting the cross and ricocheting vertically upwards towards his Father in heaven as he prayed for strength, protection and guidance in the 'once in a lifetime' phenomenal task that he knew he would face the next day. By the time he had finished the night had closed around him and all was as black as scriptorium ink.

--o--

The following morning he rose before dawn and broke his fast on some weak beer and bread that had been supplied by the kitchens of Dommoc Abbey. As he went through the doorway of the byre, the horses, which he had not tethered, whinnied and came over to him. He patted their noses fondly and they followed him as he strolled across the hill towards the rising sun.

When he reached the second byre, unseen by him, the horses tossed their heads and spooked a little leaving him to carry on alone. They watched with panicky eyes wider than natural as he took the last few steps down the hill towards the isthmus. They tensed, the muscles on their forelegs rippling with anticipation as they waited for what was sure to happen. As he reached the edge of the gorse a low rumbling began. The horses spun round, fidgeting - wanting to go closer to support their master but terrified to do so.

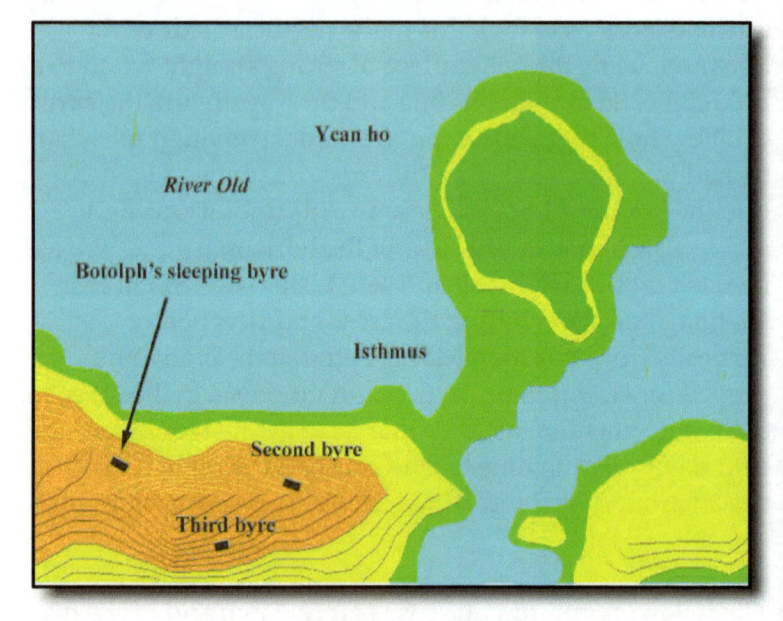

Fig. 21. Ycan Ho

Their eyes widened even further with fear.
Saliva foamed at their mouths and liquid dripped from their flaring nostrils.
The rumbling increased in volume.
Acrid smoke started to billow from the far side of the isthmus.
Botolph's eyes mirrored those of the horses - but not because of fear.
His were the wide eyes of determination.
They were the eyes of anger.
They were the eyes of righteousness fighting evil.

He walked up to the edge of the gorse, took the leather thong from around his neck, held his cross up in front of him and shouted with all his might:

"In the name of Christ, be gone!"

The rumbling was in crescendo and as he pronounced the last word it reached an ear-splitting climax and a great explosion sent a pall of black evil-smelling smoke skywards blotting out the morning sun. The smoke curled round and aggressively cocooned the priest as if it would bear him into the firmament, but he stood his ground and although he felt the smoke searing into his lungs he was able to generate his own great volume as he continued to hold his cross before him and shout:

"Again I say - In the name of Christ be gone!"

The rumbling stopped and there was silence, but the black cloud still swirled angrily around him and he thought he could see a shape. As he watched, the shape started to move towards him, although he saw that its base remained fixed somewhere close to the Hoe itself. The top of the shape expanded and grew larger and larger as it moved threateningly towards him. The smoke swirled and twisted - black in the centre but green-edged in the swirls. Twin areas reared above him like monstrous black eyes and he held his cross up towards them saying quietly through gritted teeth, his own eyes black with anger, "Help me Father I beseech Thee. Grant Thy servant Botolph protection from this evil. Give me the strength to overcome it. This I ask in the name of THY SON JESUS CHRIST."

He shouted this last as a massive talon ten times the size of an eagle's foot shot down from the cloud above him and he felt pain sear across his chest from left to right as it ripped towards his heart and cut through his shoulder.

He felt no fear - just inordinate anger at the devil

daring to inhabit God's own land of Engla. He, Botolph, had been called by his Maker to spread Christianity to all who would listen and he felt aggrieved that this evil, this blot on the landscape, this scum should have the brazenness to interfere with his calling.

The cloud was still swirling but now it seemed more grey than black. Botolph's right arm was hanging uselessly by his side but his left hand still held the cross, and this time he saw the second talon the moment it started to emerge from the cloud. He thrust the cross at it and once again shouted:

"NO! In the name of Jesus Christ be gone!"

The talon magnified massively as it approached him - but at his words it hovered as if uncertain - and then slowly retracted again and was lost behind the mass as its presence was replaced by a deep, gurgling, moaning voice which came echoing out of the maelstrom and slowly and hesitantly intoned:

"Botolph, Botolph - why do you treat us thus? Why would you drive us from our home? We've never done anything to harm you."

He would have replied and pointed out that his now useless right arm, his torn habit and the blood pouring down his chest bore witness to the falsity of the words, but although he opened his mouth no sound came out. The voice slowly continued:

"You are a great man. You have no need of us. Leave us here in peace we implore you."

Botolph's resolve had not weakened. His eyes still blazed. His heart still grieved at the impudence of the evil being which was obstructing his work. He thrust his cross forwards again and shouted:

"Enough! In the name of Christ begone!"

There came a wail, the like of which no man had

heard before. It assaulted his ears, was over and behind his head and under his body. It totally enveloped him as did the smoke so that he could no longer see the cross that his left hand held. The darkness seemed to last for ever, although in truth it was probably only a short while before the black fog lifted and then swirled and swirled again and then thinned and thinned further until, like a flock of starlings it swooped away, the Hoe reappearing as it did so.

There was complete silence. No birds were singing. There was no sound of water lapping. Even the clouds seemed to have stopped moving. The wind was not blowing. Botolph stood there unmoving like the rest of his little world. He still held his cross before him.

He tried to pray. He tried to give thanks. He tried to return to existence - but for the moment he could not. He was, like a statue, pale and immobile in the morning light.

And then ... he saw wisps of smoke coming from the Hoe and he wondered if the evil was regenerating for a second attack - but through the smoke he could see flame. The gorse was on fire, and with the fire there came from the north a wicked squall that fanned the flames towards him. Within minutes he heard the gorse beginning to crackle as the flames approached, and at last he was able to move. He placed his cross back round his neck, ran out of the smoke and back up the bank to where the horses were standing - side by side - gazing with blank shocked eyes which finally focussed on his approach. He greeted and comforted them both - placing a hand on each of their muzzles - and then realised what he had done.

He looked down at his right shoulder. It was working normally. There was no rent in his habit nor blood on his chest.

The time had come. He turned to the east and sank

to his knees and thanked the Holy Father for his safe
delivery from the forces of evil. He spent a long time with
his eyes closed beseeching the Lord to guide him during the
next few months and to help him to build both a monastery
and a ministry that would be a potent force for good
against evil for many years to come.

The smell of stale smoke brought him to the end of
his prayers and he opened his eyes. The wind had veered
to the northeast. The fire on the Hoe had burnt itself out.
A black crow hopped cheekily in front of him, cocking its
head on one side as if to say, "Are you alright Father?
Come on, - there's work to be done."

Botolph sank back on his haunches and laughed at
the little fellow. The birds were singing. The water was
lapping. Little puffballs of clouds were floating across the
sky. The two horses were still standing just behind him -
at once his companions, protectors and servants. He
sighed. Life was good - but, young Crow, you are right -
there's work to be done.

He rose to his feet and ran down the hill. When he
reached the charred remains of the gorse he gingerly placed
a sandalled foot upon it. The heat began to pervade and
singe the leather. He tried another step but the ground
was too hot. Was this the heat of a natural fire ... or was
it the exothermia of expurgated evil? Whatever it was he
decided to leave further explorations until the following
day.

--o--

At Dommoc Abbey Luka was doing his best to find
out what changes there had been in the country since King
Anna had been exiled.

From the abbey's point of view things had stayed
much the same. They had received no visits from King

Penda or his men. Visitors had told them that little had changed in the countryside either, except for the fact that Penda's soldiers were everywhere. Much of the time the soldiers occupied themselves collecting tithes from farmers and landowners. There were rumours that not all the payments found their way into the king's coffers.

Luka asked about Exning and what had happened to the soldiers of the fyrds who had survived the battle. It seemed that they had been allowed to go back to their farms and carry on their work as normal.

There had been no reports of atrocities on any religious foundations other than at Cnobersburg. It seemed that, in spite of his refusal to accept the Christian cross, Penda had left most of the Christian churches and communities in peace. Luka wondered what he had against Cnobersburg. He came to the conclusion that it was because the monastery was well-known as King Anna's favourite that Penda habitually attacked it as a means of drawing Anna into battle. Luka was tempted to go to Exning to find out what was happening there, but they had promised to go and visit Botolph every two days so tomorrow they would do that.

But the following day was not one for travel anywhere as a foul storm swept the countryside with strong winds and heavy rain. Trees were uprooted, fences blown down and streams overflowed. The next day was no better and Luka and Ash joined forces with others at Dommoc as they did their best to maintain the integrity of the settlement which was threatened by the sea on one side and the storm from above. The streets were awash. Mud was being trampled everywhere. Thatch was being ripped from the roofs and everybody was miserable and apprehensive.

"I've heard tell," said one forlorn soul to Luka, "that

one day this place will get itself washed away by the sea." The man reminded Luka of Martha's husband Eric at Folcanstane. Like Eric, this man was always doom and gloom and never had a cheery word to say about anything.

"Well," replied Luka, "Let's hope it doesn't happen today."

The next day was sunny and dry and they collected some fresh bread and newly-brewed beer and other vittles and set out for Ycan. When they arrived they found no sign of Botolph in the byre although Luka was pleased to find that it was still standing in spite of the storm.

They rode across to the Hoe and sure enough there was Botolph, stripped to the waist, raking burnt vegetation into the water.

"My word but you've made good progress," called Luka as they arrived.

Botolph stopped and leant on the rake.

"Yes, we've done quite well really."

"That was a great move" said Luka, "burning the whin instead of cutting it."

"Well it wasn't my idea," admitted Botolph, "God lent a hand and did it for me."

"Hmm," Luka thought to himself, "I could believe in a god like that. Perhaps Botolph's got a point after all."

He turned his head away but then suddenly turned it back in shock. "Good God! Where d'yer get that from?" he said, pointing to Botolph's chest. "I've never seen that scar before."

Botolph looked down at the jagged white line that crossed his chest from under his left nipple to his right shoulder.

"Oh, it's nothing," he said as he wiped the sweat away from it, the soot-black on his hand painting a dark shadow across his torso.

"That's much better," said Luka "you look like one of Boudicca's warriors now."

"That's enough comment about my manly body," said Botolph. "Have you come to help or are you just here for the view?"

It was only then that Luka realised how peaceful the place was.

"What happened to the demons then?" he asked.

"Who?"

"The demons, - the noises, - the foul smells."

"Oh them," said Botolph. "They left."

"What do you mean 'they left?' They wouldn't just have gone."

"Well they did. Can you see them now?"

"Er ... no. But then I didn't actually *see* them before."

"Well then."

"Well then what?"

"Well then get yourselves down off those horses and find some rakes and help me clear this char."

This was a new Botolph that Luka hadn't seen before. A Botolph who not only had cleared the furze from the isthmus in the blink of an eye, but a Botolph who seemed to have cleared the scrub from the road of his future.

"Right then."

"Right."

"Come on Ash."

CHAPTER 25
Another Miracle

They had raked three-quarters of the ground clear and had, meanwhile, been living in the byre and working hard. The fourth day had been particularly strenuous and, as the sun settled down towards the western horizon, the tired trio hauled themselves up the hill, looking forward to resting their aching limbs and having a meal. Luka, as usual, was particularly ravenous. They went into the byre, hauled open the shutters to let in the last of the daylight and Luka pulled out the piece of wood they used as a table.

"Is this all the bread we have left?" he said, looking in the food sack.

"I'm afraid so," said Botolph.

"There's hardly enough here for me - let alone for you two."

Botolph and Ash laughed but when they looked, they had to agree.

"What about tomorrow?" asked Luka. "Are we going back to Dommoc to re-stock?"

"That wasn't in my mind," said Botolph.

"Well what *was* in your mind?" said Luka. "I can't work without food."

"I really don't want to break off now," said Botolph, "we are so nearly finished, and I want to get everything done before the weather turns against us."

At this point there was a knock on the door.

"What's that?" said Luka.

"It sounds as if we've got visitors."

"Visitors surely don't come here - we've not seen a soul since we started - the locals will still all be scared of the demons."

The knock came again.

"Well we've definitely got a visitor now Pa," said Ash getting up and going to the door and pulling it open.

Outside stood a man who must have once looked young but who now looked as wrinkled and worn as Noah after the flood. His face was framed by a thick white scraggy beard from which emanated unruly wisps of hair, reminding Botolph of the Ycan gorse when he first found it. His eyes, topped by wild white eyebrows, seemed unnaturally large, the skin around them laying like dank leather against the underlying bones without having the luxury of body fat to provide support. His back was bent, his tunic torn and his shoeless feet were cut and calloused. He supported himself with a wooden staff which was as gnarled and scrawny as he was. It seemed that it was with difficulty that he managed to lift a shrivelled hand towards the two men who were sitting at a makeshift table with half a loaf in front of them.

"Alms," he croaked. "I beg for alms."

"Come," said Botolph, rising and hastening to the door. "Come and join us."

Under Botolph's guiding care the old man limped across to the table and sat down. Ash took his staff and poured him a horn of water, which he sipped.

"Luka," said Botolph, "cut that bread into four and give a piece to our guest."

"Four?" said Luka in despair, "that'll only leave us with a few crumbs each."

"Don't worry about it Luka. Do as I say, for God can restore all to us."

Luka took his seax from his belt and held it threateningly as he looked into the old man's eyes - but then his expression softened and he cut the bread and offered it gently to him saying, "Here my friend, eat this and may it give you strength."

By the time Botolph and Ash had sat back at the table most of the man's bread had gone. Botolph offered him his piece too but the man refused, giving his thanks and saying that his stomach was too small to take more. They offered him a bed for the night but the man insisted on moving on. He staggered to his feet and Ash returned his staff to him and helped him to the door. They stood watching him as he slowly and, it seemed, painfully made his way in the direction of the ford. As they turned to re-enter the hut, Luka felt his stomach give a growl of hunger.

"What's that?" said Ash.

"That's my stomach wondering what it's going to do with itself for the next three days of work without food," grumbled Luka.

"No, not that - *that*," he said, pointing down the river.

They followed the line of his arm towards a small black dot that had just rounded the river's curve.

"It's a boat," said Ash.

"Boats don't come up here," said Luka.

"No, we don't get visitors either Pa, but this day seems to be different. *Come on.*"

"The three of them ran down to the water's edge which they reached at the same time as the boat grounded on the muddy bank.

"What's this?" called Botolph "and where are you from?"

"We're from Abbot Berhtgisl at Dommoc," said one of them. "He thought that we needed exercise and that you might need vittals."

"How right he was," said Luka. "Welcome - you're the answer to a starving man's prayer."[1]

"But the starving man's gone," said Ash.

"Not him you fool - *me*. Now men, come ashore and let's see what you've brought us."

It had taken the sailors all day to get to Ycan and they too were ready for food. After a wholesome meal they bedded down in the other byre.

The following day they left early and, refuelled by the gifts from Dommoc, the three land workers set to with a will and managed to rake the rest of the ground clear in the one day. They then started putting in place wooden pegs to mark the outlines of the chapel, the dorter, the scriptorium, the guest house, the refectory, the kitchen, the infirmary, the storehouses, the latrines, the kitchen garden and the animal yard. Botolph decided that that was enough for the first phase of the construction - other buildings could be added as they became necessary. He was aware that, if the abbey grew as he expected, he might need two or even three dorters. Alternatively, by that time, if there were a quantity of more experienced monks in residence, they would probably merit their own cells.

Luka wanted to start laying out the kitchen garden and planting it up but, with some difficulty, Botolph was able to deter him from this on the basis that once the building work started people would be tramping all over the place, and it was likely that any such work done now would be ruined later.

"Where do we go from here then?" asked Luka.

"We're going to need wood, thatch and men," said

---

[1] This incident is recorded as a miracle in the *Acta Sanctorum* in the Life Story of Saint Botolph.

Botolph, "and that means we need King Anna too."

"Can't we go and cut the wood ourselves?"

"Well I suppose we *could,* but I suggest we go back to Dommoc and see if Abbot Berhtgisl can lend us some hands."

They were only a short way towards Dommoc before they met eight horsemen hastening in the opposite direction.

"Where're you off to in such a hurry then?" called Luka in his usual blunt way.

"Rendelsham," came the brief answer. "We're joining King Anna's court."

"He's back then?" said Luka.

"Aye, he apparently arrived a few days ago and is busy collecting his old faithfuls around him. So spread the word," and with that they trotted briskly away.

Botolph gazed after them. "What do you think?" he said.

"Well there's no point in going all the way to Dommoc is there? Surely we'd be best following them to Rendelsham."

So they turned their horses and headed back the way they had come. Within two hours they were greeting the king and Lady Saewara and all the many others they recognised. It was a joyous occasion and throughout the day more folk arrived and the camp became larger and larger.

Botolph told King Anna that they had prepared the land at Ycan.

"You have?" he said with raised eyebrows - looking truly astonished.

"Aye sire - it's all ready and stands pegged out and waiting for wood, thatch and workers."

"What about the demons and devils that lived

there?"

"All gone sire."

"What? Truly? Did you see them?"

"I saw smoke sire and I heard evil sounds, but the most I saw of the devils themselves was two huge eagle talons."

"And what did you do with those?"

"I did nothing but raise my cross at them sire and demand in the name of Christ that they be gone . . . and in time . . . they went."

"Weren't you injured in any way?"

"I was at one point but when the devils left God healed my wounds."

"Heaven be praised. Well, after such a triumph we must get on with finishing God's work there. My men are already engaged in cutting down trees in order to rebuild the great hall that Penda burnt here, so it will be easy enough to cut some more. I'll send both the wood and a quantity of men to you within the next few days."

And thus it was that Botolph began to timber his monastery of Icanho.

--o--

It took only six weeks to get the buildings up and thatched and, as word got around of the new monastery, and of its inspired leader Botolph, more and more travellers broke their journeys and came to see the work.

Many of them joined in with the labour and many of these, when they heard the Father's preaching as they ate their midday meals, decided they would travel no further but join this exciting new foundation. At the inaugural ceremony attended by King Anna's court on the sixth day of June in the year 654, the new Father Abbot was supported by eighteen founder novices.

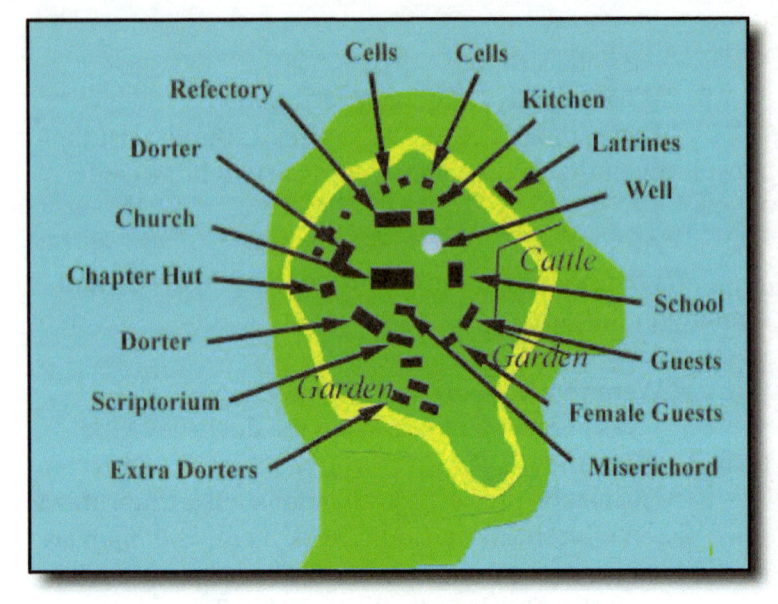

Fig. 22. Icanho Abbey buildings.

And, as Botolph said in his inaugural sermon, "This is the beginning of a great new era when I hereby pledge myself to do all in my power to spread the word of Christ throughout this kingdom. The abbey of Icanho will be like the trunk of a tree and the branches will spread throughout Engla and thence I hope throughout the country and the world. The rule we will follow will be the Rule of the Blessed Benedict, which I have found to be a kind and loving way of monastic life that is generally enjoyed by all and . . . " he looked round and beamed, "I hope you will come to agree."

This brought a few titters closely followed by a round of enthusiastic applause. Such levity was not usual on these occasions, and without the king's support, the titterers would have been embarrassed at their lapses and might have expected to start their life at Icanho with punishment duty. This was clearly not to be the case however, and the ceremony ended on a high note with smiles all round.

CHAPTER 26
Disaster

For the next few weeks the abbey went from strength to strength until disaster suddenly struck.

King Anna had been gradually re-building his former army and he and his brothers were north of Dommoc at Bulcamp village on the banks of the river Blythe when Penda and a substantial force of men burst through the nearby trees. There was a brief but vicious skirmish during which most of Anna's men were killed and he was summarily executed.

The first that they knew of it at Icanho was when a group of horsemen, on their way to Rendelsham to break the news to Lady Saewara, sent one of their number to Icanho Abbey to tell Botolph.

The monks were immediately summoned to a long series of prayers to petition for the safe delivery to Heaven of King Anna's soul.

As soon as this duty had been completed Botolph, Luka and Ash rode to Rendelsham to give what comfort they could to the new widow and her court. They listened horror-struck to the survivors' stories of the savage surprise attack. When asked what had happened to King Anna's body the men replied that, at the request of the captain of his guard, Penda had allowed them to take the body to Exning for burial.

"What about the king's brothers, Aethelhere and

Aethelwold,[1] were they killed too?"

"No - Penda spared them on the condition that they both pledged loyalty to him and that Aethelhere agreed to rule Engla as sub-king."

"Ha - a clever move. That'll give Penda the freedom to take his men to fight the Northumbrians. So we're annexed to Mercia now?"

"That seems to be the case."

"And what of Prince Jurmin - where's he?"

"Dead too, I am afraid Father."

"Lord have mercy on his soul."

"We must all be away to Exning then."

Botolph wondered if, as senior abbot, Berhtgisl of Dommoc would expect to conduct the funeral service, and he sent him a message to this effect. A reply soon arrived thanking him for his kindness, but saying that he was too sad to attend and asking Botolph to perform the honours in his stead.

As a courtesy and acknowledgement that it was to King Anna that the foundation owed its existence, not one of the inhabitants of Icanho stayed away from the funeral. Their procession made an impressive sight as it progressed to the pretty village of Exning at the edge of the fens. The crucifer proudly bore the cross at the head of the line and the following monks sang lustily. This was no downtrodden group. They might have lost their king but these men were the disciples of Christ and, inspired by their leader Abbot Botolph, they carried the message of Christianity proudly.

This was not wasted on the crowds who saw them

---

[1] The names *Aethelwald* (king of West Kent c.616-c.657) and *Aethelwold* (king of Engla c.655-c.664) are very similar but these factual characters are two distinct people.

and when they returned to Icanho a few days later their numbers had already swelled. Within a few more months the monastery would be feeding fifty.

Hundreds attended the burial including many members of the Gyrwa tribe together with their leader Prince Tonberht. His wife, the 22-year-old Lady Etheldreda, was fully occupied comforting her newly-widowed mother. The youngest sibling, the toddler Withburh, deprived of the attention she was used to receiving, started to add her own wilful wailing whereupon she was quickly whisked away by their foster sister Wendreda.

During his address Abbot Botolph pledged the monastery of Icanho as a memorial to the good and Christian works that the king had performed during his lifetime, and promised that through these works his memory would never die. In response the new monarch, King Aethelhere, promised to do all he could to support the abbey of Icanho.

Botolph's final duty was to pen a letter to his friends Ethelburg and Saethryth (King Anna's daughter and step-daughter) who were still at the monastery in Francia where Botolph had been professed. He found it difficult to choose the right words to break the news of their father's death.

There was one daughter who had not been present at the funeral and that was Seaxburh - the wife of King Eorcenberht of Kent. At the time she was in labour with what the couple were hoping would be their fifth child, but sadly the infant was stillborn. Her father's death came as a double blow.

Prince Tonberht's attendance at the funeral was one of his last duties, since he himself died only a short while later and his young widow Etheldreda retired in seclusion to the island of Elig.

And then, on 15th November, word arrived that Penda himself had been killed by King Oswiu of Northumbria on the banks of the River Winwaed. As might be expected, Botolph viewed any unnecessary death as regrettable - but Luka was overjoyed.

"That's God's justice if ever I saw it," he said. "Serves him right. If he'd only left others to live in peace he'd have his life still. Pity Oswiu didn't do it quicker."

"Well he warned us nothing would happen quickly and you couldn't expect him to drop everything just for King Anna."

"Perhaps not," said Luka, "but he's dead now and that can't be anything but good."

But then came the news that their new king Aethelhere had also been killed in the battle.

Anna's younger brother Aethelwold took over as the new king of Engla, and Mercia's new king was Peada - Penda's son.

--o--

As is so often the case, it was spring when Ash fell in love and the year was 656. She was a girl from the king's court at Rendelsham. Her name was Lislia and, as Luka pointed out quite unnecessarily to Ash, she was as pretty as a spring chick. After the death of his brother, the new king had decided that it was time to make some changes and one of the first matters that he addressed was the state of his forests. It was clear to him that they were being consumed at an alarming rate and, in order to regenerate more stock, he began to look for men who were knowledgeable in the ways of Nature and of her woods.

As Luka rested on the handle of his hoe in the abbey's kitchen garden, the sixteen-year-old Ash, who had raced from one of the guest huts where he had been talking to a traveller, breathlessly told his father the news.

"Can I Pa?"

"What, go all the way to Rendelsham everyday? What's wrong with us here. Don't you need us anymore?"

Ash suddenly realised the hidden implications of his proposed new venture and the smile dropped from his face. Luka put a hand on his arm: "There now. I'm only teasing you."

Retrieving his hand he stood back and said: "Look at you - you're nearly *twice* my height now. Of *course* it's time for you to put a frame like that to good use - you'll be tall enough to prune most of the trees without a ladder."

They both laughed.

"Really Pa?"

"Of course. I've been *waiting* for you to ask me something like this.   I was beginning to think it would never happen," he lied.

His tall but still gangly son threw his arms around him and hugged him tightly. When the time came for Luka to take a breath but found he could not, he struggled free and said: "But . . . "

"What?"

"You'll need to talk to the Father Abbot and get his permission."

"Do you think he'll give it?"

"I don't know - he values the work you do here with the animals - you'll be sorely missed."

"Yes, I'll miss the animals too."

"Well you'd better go and see him then."

"Will you come with me?"

Luka's immediate instinct was to say that of course he would but he stopped himself just in time.

"Y . . . No!"

Ash looked shocked.

"You're a man now my son. This seems to mark the first day of the rest of your life. Off you go - you're quite capable ... but come back and tell me how you get on."

Luka felt the butterflies fighting in his stomach as he watched him go - walking with an easy stride in spite of his gangliness. Seeing him every day he had not noticed him changing from a boy into a man. Soon he would see him every day no longer. The butterflies fought harder and his eyes started to sting. 'There must be a fire burning somewhere,' he thought, dabbing at his eye with the top of his sleeve and then bending down again and savagely jabbing the hoe harder than necessary into the unyielding soil.

Ash was soon back.

"What'd he say?"

"He said 'No'."

"What?" Luka jerked upright with surprise. "No?"

"No - not until I've prayed about it - and you - and the Father himself."

"Ah," said Luka.

"I told him that you said that I had to ask him because he is in charge but he said he wasn't. I didn't understand what he meant at first. He said I had to go and ask who really *was* in charge. I said 'Who's that then Father?' He said nothing but just looked at me with a slight smile. I suddenly realised who he meant so I asked him what I should do. He said that two days of prayer from the three of us should be enough to make sure that I'm making the right decision."

"How do you feel about *that* son? I thought you were keen to apply to the king straight away."

"I was - but I can see he's right. I can also see that

it's another lesson to add to the many others he's taught me.   I shall try to remember to follow the same lesson in the future - to pray before making any important decisions. I thought I'd tell you first - I'm off to the chapel right now."

Luka watched him a second time until he was lost to sight. He took the hoe across to the hut, wiped his hands and shook the dust from his clothes before strolling as nonchalantly as he could after Ash. He sauntered into the nave in an exaggeratedly slow way which said that he was doing this because he *wanted* to - not because he *had* to - before he knelt next to his mature and beloved son ... on the dry earthen floor ... in front of the altar.

--o--

Ash became a King's Forester in December 656 and the Master Forester to whom he was apprenticed was Lislia's father. Ash loved the work. It reminded him of his childhood in Gaul and the forest where Bonitius had been master of all. His romance with Lislia blossomed throughout the summer and was consummated on the top of a haystack on the Sunday after harvest. The Master Forester was pleased with the prospect of gaining Ash as his son-in-law and there was an autumn wedding which was sponsored by the king himself. The couple set up home in what had been a ramshackle hut on the forestry estate. Willing hands, including those of Luka, Botolph and several monks, had put the place to rights during the week before the wedding, and Luka was glad to see his son and his bride comfortably settled in.

Lislia was no slouch. When Ash and her father were away in the depths of the forest she would often walk the two leagues to Icanho where she would pray in the chapel before joining the brethren in the Refectory for lunch and then perhaps help Luka in the kitchen garden. Abbot

Botolph had known the nunnery of Princess Eanswythe and the mixed monastery of Abbess Fara but he had decided to keep Icanho strictly male, although he had no objection to the presence of women in the foundation from time to time. He reasoned that there were, after all, women in the world and that the men in his care should not be closeted from them but should learn the discipline of treating them with respect. He remembered the tragedy at Evoriacum - the terrible death of Sister Margaret and the anguish of Brother Sweyn.[1] Botolph's view was that the inevitable attraction between the sexes could not be contained but only managed and his way of managing it was to run a single-sex monastery.

On Lislia's visit in April of the following year it seemed that she was not alone. Luka was not sure. He kept surreptitiously turning his head to have a closer look. At one point he failed to avert his eyes quickly enough and she caught him staring.

"Ah," said Luka.

She held his gaze and smiled.

"Are you . . . ?"

She nodded, beaming at him.

"Aw," he said, enfolding her in his arms. She cuddled him back.

"When?" he said.

"Soon after mid-summer I think."

"Why didn't you tell me earlier."

"Ash said we should keep it a surprise until you noticed."

"It's a *wonderful* surprise," he said. "How's the father-to-be taken it?"

"He's *really* excited," chortled Lislia delightfully.

---

[1] Volume II of this trilogy: Brother Botolph and the Abbess p.198.

CHAPTER 27
Family Ash

On 24th July 657 Lislia gave birth to a beautiful baby boy whom Abbot Botolph baptised and christened Eldred. Two years later on 13th July 659 he was joined by a brother, whom they named Bron.

Another miracle was witnessed by Luka a short while later while he was looking after the chickens, whose care he had taken over from Ash after he moved to Rendelsham.

"There are only twenty-nine now," he complained to Botolph. "It's not easy to count them, they move about so much, but I am sure that we had thirty-five not long ago."

"Perhaps it's a fox?" suggested Botolph.

"Hmm - maybe but he must carry them off whole because there are never any feathers or remains left anywhere."

"Let's go and see."

It was approaching noon as they walked over to the chicken coops. The birds were out and strutting bravely as they pecked at nutritious morsels from the ground. One of the three handsome white cockerels flew onto the top of one of the coops and made his call as they approached. His 'cock-a-doodle' never reached its 'doo' however as a great shadow suddenly swooped out of the sun behind him and a powerful talon gripped his long white neck and lifted him high into the air. Both Luka and Botolph ducked as the great eagle swept across them, but as the Father Abbot straightened up he thrust out a long arm and pointed a finger at the retreating villain shouting:

"A curse upon you, wretched bird - bring that back at once."

To Luka's amazement the eagle wheeled towards the sun and flew back to them, dropping the startled cockerel on the ground as he arrived.   The eagle itself continued its glide towards Botolph and Luka was still working out which way to run when it fell dead at Botolph's feet.   Luka was uncharacteristically lost for words.   He stood there gaping at Botolph and pointing at the dead bird.

"He ... Ah ... What? ... "His mouth kept opening and closing but nothing coherent was coming out. He walked gingerly across to the eagle and prodded it with his foot but there was no doubt, it was definitely dead.   He looked up at the sky, to see if another of the creatures might be lurking above.   But nothing was there and by the time he looked down again he found he was looking at Botolph's back as he returned to the abbey walls.   Luka raised an arm as if to call after him but thought better of it and looked back at the dead eagle.[1]

"Well," he said, scratching his head, "I don't know if you meant to do that Father - but it would certainly seem to have solved the problem."

--o--

The next few years passed quickly as Abbot Botolph sought to establish his monastery as the best in the land. This was not done with any sense of false pride but on the basis of serving God and his monks to the best of his ability.

---

[1] This miracle of St Botolph is recorded in the *Acta Sanctorum* of 1701.

He himself was not aware of the fact that the marvels of his monastery at Icanho were becoming the talk of the country. Indeed it was not until a steady flow of admiring ecclesiastics started knocking at the abbey door asking if they could learn the secrets of his success that he realised that anybody other than vagrants and potential monks might want to visit him.

"Secrets?" he exclaimed to Luka one day.

"Secrets? I *have* no secrets apart from those I hear in the confessional. I'm happy to tell anyone and everyone how we conduct our days here. If there *is* any particular ingredient that might be called secret it is the ingredient of love. I love my monks, my slaves, my administrative workers, my horses, pigs, cows and sheep - I love the island and the river and the surrounding land and the bees and the birds - I even love you Luka."

"Oh, thanks very much," said Luka. "I notice I come after the pigs, cows, bees and birds."

--o--

In the late summer of 660, Abbot Botolph received a command to attend King Aethelwold at Rendelsham, together with Luka and Ash. On their arrival they were surprised to find another large royal party encamped in the vicinity. It transpired that the retinue had come from the south and that they attended King Merewalh of the Magonsaete tribe and his new bride Domne Eafe.

King Aethelwold had arranged a week of feasting to celebrate the couple's marriage and to cement an alliance between Engla, Cantium and the Magonsaete.

The Magonsaete were settlers from the west of Britain who had taken over some land by the River Severn some years previously and the young king had come east to find a bride.

Domne Eafe's father, King Eormenred of West Cantium, had insisted that before he would give his daughter's hand in marriage, King Merewalh and his attendants must be baptised as Christians.   Merewalh had accepted the condition gladly, and both the baptisms and the wedding had been performed at Norflot Abbey by Prior Selwyn who, as Merewalh said, "Had exhorted them to travel north to visit Abbot Botolph at Icanho where the poor instruction that he had been able to give them would be reinforced and consolidated by the Holy Father, whose abbey has a reputation second to none."

"Prior Selwyn - God bless him," said Botolph, "and did you find him well?"

"Aye," said Merewalh stretching back on his stool and casting a glance at his bride.   "He was in fine spirits wasn't he?"

She nodded and as she said her words of confirmation Botolph noted that, although her reply was demure, it was by no means shy.   Her blue eyes were rarely shaded and whenever she was asked a question she looked directly into those of her inquisitor.   Here was a lady who truly merited her title of Domne.

"So tell me a little of you and your family's history," said Botolph.

She gave a dazzling smile.

"Well . . . ," she started slowly, "my father's King Eormenred now sub-king of West Cantium.   He was the eldest son of King Eadbald and had been expected to take over from his father when he died, but he fell in love with my mother and they ran away together."

"So what's your mother's name and where's she from?"

"Her name's Oslafa - she was originally from Northumbria."

"Northumbria?" said Luka in surprise. "That's a long way from Cantium - how old was your father when he fell in love?"

She laughed. "He was only fifteen and my mother was a year younger. She was a member of the royal Northumbrian household. When King Edwin died, his queen, Ethelburga, took her children down to Cantium to the protection of her brother King Eadbald. My mother, Oslafa, was one of the queen's handmaidens."

"And that's how she and your father met?"

"Yes."

"So why did they run away?"

"Ah," she said, dropping her eyes, "It seems that my mother was with child and that King Eadbald wouldn't allow them to marry."

"So your father decided to leave?"

"Yes. They stowed away in a Folcanstane boat and had a disastrous trip to Northumbria."

"Why disastrous - was it stormy?"

"My mother was very ill and she lost the baby."

"Oh dear - I'm sorry."

"When they arrived they went to my grandparents' house and my mother hovered close to death for several weeks - but she recovered and they were married. It seemed that she was not going to be able to have children but after a few years I came along. Shortly afterwards a terrible plague swept the country killing my grandfather King Eadbald and my aunt the saintly Abbess Eanswythe. As the eldest son my father should have become king, but after my birth my mother was too weak for us to travel. She blamed herself for many years saying that it was because of her that my father never had the crown that was rightfully his. He wasn't bothered about it though, but always told her that he was pleased for his brother to be king and that he was happy with his life in Northumbria."

"So do you have other siblings?"

"Yes - I am blessed with a sister and three brothers."

"Are they all in Cantium now?"

"My sister and two of my brothers are, but we left my ten-year-old brother Oswine in Northumbria with his grandparents because he was happy there and they were very attached to him."

"So what made you leave?"

"When I was seventeen a messenger arrived asking father to return home urgently because his Uncle Aethelwald,[1] who had been king of West Cantium for years and years, had died. The kingdom was too large for father's brother King Eorcenberht to manage himself, so he asked my father to come back to rule the western half. Our home was at Uncle Aethelwald's court at Egensford."

"Ah yes - we know it well," said Botolph thinking nostalgically. "Did you worship at St Martin's?"

"We did," she smiled. "It's a lovely church and I know that you helped to build it."

"I can't say that we helped with the building - your Uncle Aethelwald had definite ideas about how it should be done, so in truth he built it himself and then suddenly presented it to us asking for it to be consecrated."

She laughed. "Yes, I'm told I'm like him for stubbornness."

"So what happened after that?"

"Nothing really," she said. "We all lived a happy life ... although as my mother's health deteriorated it was down to me to take over the running of the household."

---

[1] The names *Aethelwald* (king of West Kent c.616-c.657) and *Aethelwold* (king of Engla c.655-c.664) are very similar but these factual characters are two distinct people.

"Was that hard?"

"No, not really - I thoroughly enjoyed it - it was just a matter of being organised. They changed my name though."

"How was that?"

"Well the name I was given at birth was Eormenburga but once I started running the household my father said I was getting very bossy and sounded like a *domina* so, as a joke, he started calling me 'Domne' and shortened my given name to 'Eafe.' It seems that the rest of the court saw it as a mark of respect however so they took to calling me by the same name and 'Eormenburga' has now been thrown to the winds."

"And then your new husband arrived?"

"Yes - praise be to God." She blushed and looked across at King Merewalh, who gazed back fondly.

"I must confess," he said, "that I'd heard of Princess Eafe's virtues long before I arrived. I became a Christian last year and my mentor and spiritual guide, the blessed Abbot Eadfrid, urged that it was time for me to marry. I've twenty- two summers now and for the past four years I've been busy establishing my kingdom and far to busy to look for a bride. But now the time's come when I need heirs and the southeast has a good reputation for beautiful women - so I set off a-hunting and I've been lucky enough to trap the prize of them all."

Their eyes locked and he offered his hand which she grasped.

"I was reluctant to leave my parents," she said. "But my sister Ermengythe has twenty summers now and she's already taken over many of my previous duties - and my mother insisted that her own strength has now returned and that my presence was no longer necessary. I was a little hurt by that at first, but I prayed about it and the Good

Lord showed me that my task at home had been completed and it was time to move on to whatever else He has in mind for me."

"Wise words from both mother and daughter," replied Botolph sagely. "But *we've* met before," he said looking at Merewalh.

"Indeed we have," replied the Magonsaete king looking in his turn at Ash. "Nine years ago in the court of King Cenwaller at Wintanceaster. Ash and I were like brothers for a while until King Anna sent you all back to Engla. It's good to see you again Ash."

The day after the end of the feasting, Icanho Abbey opened its doors to Merewalh and his bride and their principal courtiers who joined in fully with monastery life. They were offered no favours and given no quarter, rising in the middle of the night for the office of Matins, eating and drinking simple fare, and wearing monasterial habit. Every day they received two hours of instruction from Botolph himself as well as from other members of the order, and they listened with rapt attention to the readings of the scripture as they supped their broth and ate the coarse brown bread.

Their favourite time of course was the Chanted Eucharist where each day they received the body and blood of Christ and they felt the warmth of the abbey's love enfold them as they offered themselves as members of Christ's family.

Exercise was not lacking. They toiled with Luka in the kitchen garden and helped with the milking of the cows and goats and the mucking out of the swine-sties. In all things the abbot impressed upon them that they should become as little children as it is, he said, 'only by lowering oneself to the most humble that one can start to grow in the stature of God.'

They bathed in the Old River, having been advised by Luka to use the opposite side of the island to the one where the latrines emptied.

Two weeks later they changed into their normal clothing and set off on the long journey to the west.

--o--

Two years later Abbot Botolph received the sad news that both Domne Eafe's father and mother had died. The king, apparently, had died first, but Oslafa was so consumed by grief that within a week she too was dead.

CHAPTER 28
The Synod of Streoneshalh

Ten years after its foundation Icanho's occupants numbered one hundred and eighty-three.

"We started off with eighteen," mused Botolph, "and now in ten years we have ten times that number."

"But we hardly have room for any guests now," grumbled Luka. "We'd be hard-pressed to take any more."

"No, you're right. God will guide us but I think we'll either have to consider building another dorter or some more cells."

God's guidance came in a strange way - for that year another plague swept the land. Icanho was remarkably unaffected by it, although several monks who left for the wider world with the intention of returning were never seen again.

Further to the north, King Oswiu called a Great Synod at the monastery town of Streoneshalh. Ostensibly this was to decide whether the *Roman* practice of calculating the date of Easter should be followed or whether the old *Celtic* practice was to be used.

"I've heard tell," laughed Luka, "that King Oswiu gets upset because *he* follows the Celtic pattern which has always been used in Northumbria, whereas his wife Eanfled, who comes from Cantium, follows the Roman one. So when he's celebrating the feast of the Easter resurrection, she's still suffering the deprivations of Lent ... and it's upsetting their marital life."

"Ah well, Eanfled was trained at Evoriacum like me," said Botolph, "and of course we followed the Roman pattern there and that's why I've continued to use it in all my monasteries and churches. That's also why I'm not going to the Synod of Streoneshalh - I don't feel that there's the need. Whatever's decided I'll continue to follow the Roman system."

"What, even if the Synod decides for the Celtic one?"

"Aye."

"But you told me that Abbess Fara was trained by a Celtic missionary from Ireland."

"Aye, she was - and his name was Columbanus."

"So why didn't you follow the *Celtic* pattern then?"

"We did during the early years, but then there came a change."

"Oh? How was that?"

"Abbess Fara became unhappy with the Columbanian Rule. It was rather severe and regularly involved corporal punishment for even *minor* misdemeanours. The abbess came to feel that it was wrong to beat her monks and nuns into submission - she believed in ruling by love - and so she turned to the rules of the blessed Father Benedict."

"Was he at Evoriacum too?"

Botolph laughed, "Bless you, no. He died a hundred years earlier. He came from a place called Nursia in Italy."

"So what's his story then?"

"Well apparently when he was young he fell in love with a beautiful woman, but for some reason or another he couldn't marry her."

"I know - she was already married."

"Luka!"

"Well - that happens."

"How do *you* know?"

Luka looked uncomfortable and did one of his 'embarrassed contortions" at which the Father Abbot could not help but smile.

"Anyway," continued Botolph, "instead of continuing his studies in Nursia and becoming a nobleman, he decided he had to get away - so he went south - closer to Rome."

"Women have that effect on you," nodded Luka sagely. Botolph ignored him.

"One day, Benedict, whose heart was still torn by love, was walking alone through a narrow gloomy valley towards the village of Subiaco when he met a monk called Romanus. Romanus could see that he was troubled and Benedict told him about his broken heart.

Romanus's prescription was that he should become a hermit and live for three years in a nearby cave, which was high in the mountains and overlooked a beautiful lake.

Benedict took his advice and Romanus kept him in food and drink. Gradually, as Romanus had predicted, Benedict matured in heart and spirit and the woman ceased to be important to him. His presence became known to the locals who regularly called on him for his wise words of comfort and advice.

When the abbot of a local monastery died Benedict was asked to take over but he was reluctant to do so. Eventually he was prevailed upon to give it a try on the proviso that if things did not turn out right he'd be allowed to go back to his cave.

Well, the whole thing was a disaster. The first thing the monks did was to poison his wine but when he blessed the goblet it shattered. Then they poisoned his bread - but just as he was about to eat it a raven flew in and carried it away."

"Ha-ha, that'll teach them thieving ravens."

"Luka - do you want to hear this story?"

"Yes I do Father, - sorry - it's very interesting - please go on."

"Well, as the people had promised he could, Benedict returned to his cave at Subiaco. This turned out to be more suitable from everyone's point of view because miracle after miracle happened there and disciple after disciple received guidance and teaching to the extent that, without even leaving his cave, Benedict managed to found twelve monasteries. Now how about that? Think of all the time and trouble it's taken me to found two. Benedict's greatest monastery was called Monte Cassino which is where he was eventually buried."

"So that's it then?"

Botolph nodded.

"Well why's he so famous then? He's hardly done any more than you Father, and you've a long time to go yet."

"Thank you Luka. I hope you're right about my having a long time to go. The reason he's so famous is because while he was in his cave he spent much of his time writing what's now known as his 'Rule,' which lists a series of requirements for the efficient running of a monastery and advice on how to live a Christian life."

"What do these rules say then?"

"Luka!"

"Yes?"

"There are *seventy-three chapters* of them and even if I *could* remember them all, which I can't, there wouldn't be time to run through them now. Just accept my word that most people who have read them agree that they are rules which make sense."

"So ... ? "

"Yes?"

"Why did that make your Abbess Fara decide to follow the Roman system?"

"Ah yes, - well done Luka, you've been paying attention after all. Well it seems she just decided that while she was changing from the Columbanian to the Benedictine Rule she'd change from Celtic to Roman practices at the same time. Actually it was a muddle for several years. Half of us were wearing a Roman tonsure and half the Celtic one."

"How do you mean?"

"Well you know how you tidy my tonsure by shaving hair from the middle of my head?"

"Aye."

"Well, as you know, the remaining hair represents the crown of thorns worn by Christ at his crucifixion."

"Ye . . . s."

"You'll also have seen other monks where just the *fronts* of their heads have been shaved."

"Oh ... yeah."

"Well that's the difference - *they're* the old Celtic style. The word is, that if young Bishop Wilfrid gets his way at the Synod of Streoneshalh, they'll be the last Celtic tonsures you'll see in this part of the world."

--o--

It was during the time of the Synod that a phenomenon occurred that shook the nerves of the whole country including Icanho. On the first day of May the sun blacked out. At first nobody noticed that it was getting darker, but suddenly you could not help but notice. Those who looked up at the sun were horrified to see that a great bite had been taken out of it, and the bite got larger and larger until the sun vanished completely.

People fell to their knees in the dark and prayed for salvation from what looked like the end of the world. And then their prayers seemed to be answered as the sun fought back and began to repair itself. First a little sunlight appeared and then more and more as the sun gradually overcame the great monster that was devouring it. Quaking people began to rejoice and thank God for their salvation. But what did it mean? What did it presage?

--o--

They soon began to find out as people started to fall sick and die. It was not only poor peasants who suffered losses but the hierarchy too felt the pain of the Black Sun Plague, as Bishop Cedd, the Archbishop of Canterbury, King Eorcenberht of Cantium and Ethelwald, King of Engla, all became victims.

And the Synod of Streoneshalh? Bishop Wilfrid *did* get his way and ecclesiastical practices in Britain started to follow those of Rome, with the result that much of the monastery world was turned upside down for a while with some notable clerics returning to Celtic Dalriada as a mark of protest so that they could follow their ancient customs in peace.

--o--

"The King is Dead. Long Live the King," was the greeting that was shared between wayfarers for the next few days.

"So young Eadwulf's king of Engla now then?" said Luka. "How old do you reckon he is?"

"Well," said Botolph, "he must have been about eighteen when we first met him at King Anna's court - and he came with us to the Gewisse - and Anna was there for three years - so I guess he must be about twenty-one."

"What do you give for his chances of lasting any longer than the others?"

"He seems a pleasant fellow," said Botolph, "I think he'll make a good king. He's had plenty of time to study where his uncles have gone wrong."

"It's yet another generation though," said Luka. "We must be getting old."

--o--

One May day in 669 there was a commotion at the gates of Icanho and the abbot was summoned to find that Domne Eafe, Queen of the Magonsaete, had arrived in some distress.

Leaving her entourage to fend for themselves, she and the father went into the church.

"I have much to tell you Father," she said. "But before I do so I'd like to give thanks to God for my safe journey and to ask His guidance in the things I am about to say to you."

"Take your time child," said Botolph. "I will leave you in peace. When you are ready, come to the Chapter Hut and we'll talk while you restore yourself."

As he left the church he found Luka outside - unsure whether to enter or not.

"Very tactful of you," he smiled.

"Well Father, I gathered it was something urgent and I wasn't sure if you might need me or whether I was best making myself scarce."

"She's fine at the moment," said Botolph. "She needs some time to recover her composure and then she's coming over to the Chapter Hut to talk, but I think I'll see her alone. It looks as if she has some confidences to share."

"That's alright Father. I'll go and look after her guards and their horses and get them fed and watered."

--o--

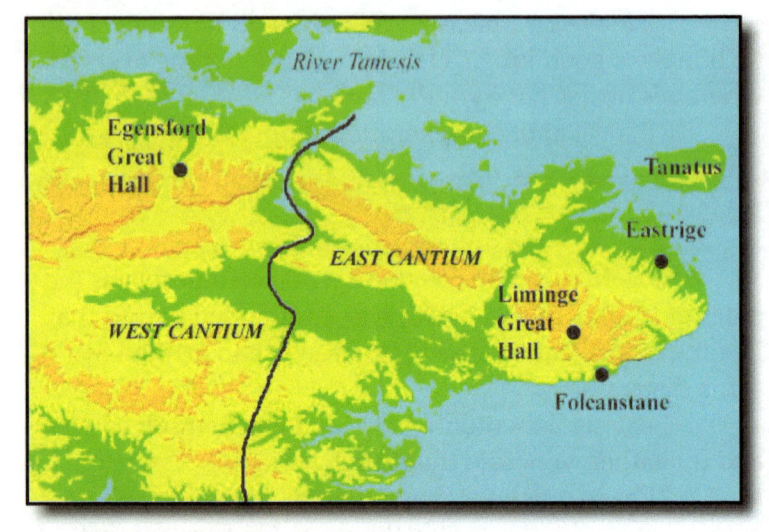

Fig. 23. Eastrige and the sub-kingdoms of Cantium.

They sat on opposite sides of a long table.

"Father - I hardly know where to start."

"You've had a long journey."

"It's not that ... it's ... " her face crumpled. There was nothing he could do except let her sob and wait until she pulled herself together.

"I'm sorry," she sniffed.

"Is it your husband King Merewalh? I see he's not with you."

"That's partly the reason for my sadness Father. I'm afraid it seems we're incompatible and so we've decided to end our marriage."

"Oh Eafe - I'm so sorry."

"I'm sure much of it's my fault. Merewalh's a good man but ever since a child I've been told that I'm selfish and domineering. I've tried to improve and I pray about it daily but ... I sin again almost as soon as the confession is out of my mouth. I'm afraid it's just my nature ... but there's more that I must tell you."

Botolph braced himself mentally, assuming that confessions of adultery would be forthcoming.

"Go ahead my child."

"It's my brothers."

"Ethelberht and Ethelred?"

She nodded.

"What about them?"

"They've been murdered."

"Murdered?"

"Mmm. Slaughtered by King Ecgberht."

"King Ecgberht?" He suddenly felt stupid repeating her words but they had come as such a surprise.

"Mmm. The boys were at the Royal Manor at Eastrige and he killed them there."

"How do you know this? Are you sure?"

She nodded. "Messages have been going backwards and forwards between us and Cantium for the past two moons. There's no doubt about it."

"Well ... why? Did Ecgberht kill the princes himself or get somebody else to do it?"

"No - he says it was done by Thunor, the royal secretary."

"But why?"

"Thunor says he misunderstood the king's wishes. They'd been arguing about the accession and it seems that Thunor told his master that he had no right to the crown."

"How do you mean? Ecgberht was the son of King Eorcenberht, wasn't he?"

"Yes but, if you recall, Eorcenberht was King Eadbald's *younger* son. It was *our* father Eormenred who was the *elder* son and so *our* family should have taken precedence."

"Ah ... I see ... so you think that the princes were killed to strengthen Ecgberht's claim?"

"Yes."

"But you told me that you've another brother who's still in Northumbria."

"Aye, Oswine - but I think the less said about him the better or his life'll be in jeopardy too."

"Do you *want* the crown of Cantium for your family?"

"No and I don't think Oswine wants it either. I think it's better just to let things be."

"So why are you here?"

"King Ecgberht has offered me land on the island of Tanatus as wergild for my brothers. He's said I can choose the amount of land I want when I get there. I've decided to ask for as much land as my pet hind can run around ... so I have been training the animal for the past moon," she giggled.

"At last a smile."

"I'm sorry I'm such bad company Father and have brought even more concerns upon you - but I've not finished yet ... I'm afraid I have a big favour to ask of you."

"Go ahead my child."

"Ever since my new husband and I had such a wonderful time here with you at Icanho I have dreamt of building my own monastery so that I can do for others what you did for us ... but ...." She sighed.

"What is it?"

"I've been working hard at this for over two years

now. It took me a long time to find some suitable land. I travelled the length and breadth of our kingdom looking for an ideal place - which I eventually found in the north of our realm. I then had to wait for my Lord Merewalh to come and see it and have it measured, and then there was the charter which had to be drawn up but ... praise the Lord ... everything was in place by the September before last and the building work started last spring. It's in a village called Wininicas. There was already an old ruined Roman church there and we knocked that down and started to build a new church on the old foundations. We thought we were doing really well at first. We'd achieved quite a height to the walls but suddenly the lower part started to collapse. It turned out that we'd not allowed enough time for the mortar to set before we added further weight; so we had to knock the walls down and start again. This wasted a lot of time, but when we re-started we could only build a cubit or so in height at any one time before stopping until the mortar hardened. So you see the work was slow."

"My word - such things to take into account - and what luxury to have a stone church. We've always had to manage with wood and thatch and the constant repairs that involves. So where's the problem?"

"The problem Father, is that now, having put all my efforts into building a wonderful monastery that only wants some shingles before it is ready to take in its monks and nuns, I find myself obliged, because of the actions of my cousin Ecgberht, to divert my attentions to Cantium where I feel duty-bound to build a foundation as a memorial to the souls of my poor dead brothers."

"You want to build a monastery on Tanatus?"

"Yes. I *have* to. I can't leave the land barren. I need to build a place to the glory of God and to the glory of my brothers for whose souls we shall constantly pray."

The abbot was silent, deep in thought while nodding slowly as the full implications of Domne Eafe's predicament sank in. She waited.

"And the favour?" he said.

Her voice sank to a whisper. "The favour that I have come to ask Father, is that you take over at Wininicas where I have left off. I would so like to see it completed and I know that King Merewalh would like that too. It would be a sort of memorial of the happier days of our marriage."

"So is that going to be it's name? Wininicas Abbey?"

She nodded. "It means 'White Place' in the Celtic language."

"Hmm. White Place eh? Wininicas."

Once again he sat with his head bowed. To all intents and purposes he was deep in thought. She began to wonder if he had died of shock. But, as was his habit in such circumstances he was deep, not in thought, but in prayer - racing through a communication with God - but God was not coming back with any quick answers. He suddenly opened his eyes, leant forwards, placed his hands together under his nose as if in prayer, and gazed deeply into the troubled blue eyes of the tragic lady he saw before him.

"Eafe ... my dear Eafe ... "

"Yes Father?"

"I would *like* to do all I can to help you - but you must understand that my first responsibility *must* be to Icanho."

She nodded.

He continued: "I cannot jeopardise *this* foundation for the sake of another."

"Yes," she said sadly, "I understand that Father."

"Good. Then I must pray about it and ask you to stay for a few days until I can give you my answer."

"Of course Father. I have no problem with keeping King Ecgberht waiting."

"Would you like to stay here in our guest quarters or will you be the guest of King Eadwulf at Rendelsham?"

"I think it would be politic to stay at the Royal Palace."

He nodded.

"Come and see me again in two days then and I'll give you my answer."

"Thank you Father." They both rose and he escorted her to the door.

CHAPTER 29
A.D. 670
Wininicas

Two days later she returned and they once again found themselves sitting opposite each other in the Chapter Hut.

"Eafe - I have prayed for many hours about this during the past two days and, guided by God, I have reached my conclusion. I am afraid that I *cannot* countenance travelling all the way to Wininicas and deserting Icanho."

Her face fell and he was afraid that she was going to burst into tears again so he went on rapidly, "But ... But ... there *are* ways in which I think I can help you."

Her face brightened.

"I will certainly visit your monastery. For a long while I've wanted to get back to travelling more and preaching on the road as I used to in my younger days. I shall be able to take different routes on my journeys to Wininicas and back and in that way spread the word of God."

She nodded. "Thank you Father."

"Now," he went on hurriedly, "we need somebody to oversee the monastery between the times that I am able to be there."

Her face began to shine a little more and she looked into his eyes attentively, wondering what was coming.

"In short we need an abbess and I believe that I

have just the person."

"You do?"

He nodded. "Her name is Liobsynde and she at present resides in Francia in the monastery at Chelles. We have been in regular touch over the years."

"Liobsynde? Liobsynde ... might that be my *Aunt Liobsynde*?"

"The very same."

"Oh she's *lovely*. She visited us ten years or so ago at Egensford and we got on *very* well. Although she's my aunt she's actually only about five years older than me."

"You think she'd be appropriate then?"

"Oh my - yes - but do you think she'll come?"

"Leave it with me - I'll write to her - we can only ask."

"Thank you Father, thank you from the bottom of my heart ... but there are formalities to complete. And this must be done before I can devote myself to Tanatus."

"What formalities do you have in mind?"

"The charter to Wininicas is in my name and I would like it to be transferred to you."

"My child, - I cannot accept such a gift myself - even as abbot. Underneath my abbatial title I am only a humble monk who has foresworn all possessions."

"Well to Icanho then."

"To the abbey of Icanho? That would make Wininicas a daughter monastery."

She nodded, looking pleadingly into his eyes.

"I think that would be acceptable. Who knows when the Lord will take me into his heavenly kingdom? Should it be soon, then my successor abbot will be able to carry out your wishes in my place."

"Is that settled then Father?"

He nodded and smiled.

"Hmm. You certainly *do* have a strong will don't you, *Domne* Eafe," he said kindly. "But I must say that I find your ideas sensible and benevolent."

"Thank you Father," she grinned triumphantly.

--o--

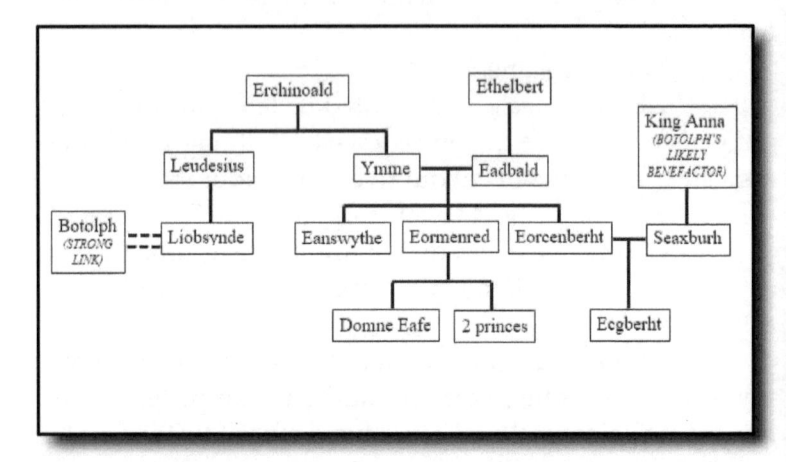

Fig. 24. Domne Eafe's family tree.

Two months and several letters later a tired but happy Sister Liobsynde arrived at Icanho after a long hard journey from Francia.

"Welcome Sister."

"Thank you Father. What a journey. But I do love to travel so, although it was tiring, it was far from tedious."

"Well we have another long journey ahead of us shortly but we'll let you rest first."

"When do you think we'll set off?"

"In a week or so I should think."

"Oh good. That will give me the chance to explore."

--o--

They left at the beginning of August and headed west. There were nearly forty of them. Most were walking although there were six horses, two of which were pulling the wains that carried the tents and food. Two other packhorses were being towed by the wains and two were being ridden by outriders.

Botolph was walking, as he loved to do, and so also was Sister Liobsynde. Luka was driving one of the wains and a brother monk was driving the other. They took the well-worn cart tracks across the heath and turned onto the Rendelsham road for a while before they picked up a wider trackway and tramped along it with the rising sun at their backs.

"This part's easy," thought Botolph as he wondered how they would manage when they reached parts further west through which they had not previously travelled. He was not unduly worried. They had plenty of time and there would be travellers whom they could ask. They might never have heard of Wininicas but, once they were closer, most would recognise the old Roman name Viroconium and once they were there, Wininicas was but a hop further.

The journey facing them was somewhere about seventy leagues and he doubted that they would average much more than five leagues a day - probably less - so they must reckon on it taking them three weeks ... and three weeks to come back as well ... and perhaps three weeks there ... It would be the end of September before they were home - God willing.

And as Heraclitus had pointed out many centuries ago - they would not be the same people when they returned as when they left. Indeed Abbot Botolph had plans in that respect.

During the week before their departure he had

selected thirty-seven brethren who were educated, stable and articulate. He smiled to himself as he thought about it. Of the two hundred and seventeen brethren now under his care there were many who would have been totally unsuitable for the mission he had in mind. He could imagine some of the antics they would have got up to. But those he had selected were all wonderful men and he knew that he could trust them implicitly. He had selected thirty-seven - an arbitrary number - but had offered all of them the chance of staying at Icanho. He was sure it was not because of any lack of love of Icanho that they had, to a man, chosen the venture he offered them. Each of the hopeful thirty-seven knew that they were candidates in a lottery to become leaders of a community and that, if successful, they would not see Icanho again for many moons.

And those for whom Botolph could find no flock? What would happen to them?

Who could tell on an ambitious mission like this? He hoped that all would return safely, but some might fall ill, some might succumb to injury, some might choose to stay either at Wininicas or at one of the other locations along their route. They had all taken their vows of obedience to their abbot but, true to the teachings of the Blessed Father Benedict, he wanted them to follow him out of love rather than compulsion.

At the head of the procession was the crucifer. Travellers coming in the opposite direction were alerted well in advance to the fact that they were about to encounter an extraordinary sight. At first all they saw was a great mass of people but as they came closer they identified the fact that all were be-habited and that they were following a cross. When the sun reached an appropriate place in the sky, in line with their normal practice at Icanho, they would recite their chants. This too made unusual entertainment for passing wayfarers.

Some - particularly when they saw the Father Abbot striding along aided by his light travelling crozier - would want to stop and ask his blessing. Even when he was tired and footsore, he was never averse to giving it - in spite of the fact that it sometimes meant his having to break into a run afterwards in order to catch up with the others.

There were times when a quick blessing was not enough and by the time the Father was on his way again, the procession would be out of sight. He was never alone however. There were always half a dozen who would stay with him and as soon as Luka spotted the fact that he had lost a large section of his party, he would reign his horse to a standstill and they would all enjoy a short rest while the Father caught up.

Luka wished that Ash had been able to come with them but he had a family to look after now and that would have kept him there - even if King Eadwulf had allowed him time away from his forestry duties . . . which he probably would not have done. My word, how time flies, thought Luka. Ash's eldest, Eldred had seen twelve summers now. It would not be long before Luka became a *great*-grandfather. He chuckled to himself, which made the horse flick back his hairy ears, wondering if there was something in it for him. Disappointed, he flicked them forwards again.

"The sun's on his way down, Father," said Luka. "Where d'ye want to stop?"

"Well we're up on the ridge here Luka,and there's no water for the horses. I thought we might turn off down the Burgh Valley and camp somewhere near the stream."

"Ah yes, I know where you mean. I'll send the outriders down there now and they can get a fire going and prepare for us."

That evening was one of many nights to remember. Word soon went round and the local villagers turned up in good numbers. Some of them just came out of curiosity. Some wanted to enjoy the picnic. Some brought food and drink. Some did not. Some just wanted a blessing. All was freely given. Botolph preached a wonderfully inspiring sermon while the food was being prepared, and then prayers and grace were said. As the food was being eaten, one of the brothers read mellifluously from the Bible. Prayers of thanksgiving came next, even though some were still eating and drinking. But it did not seem to matter.

And then as dusk fell - from out of the shadows there came the sound of a strange form of music - and the village people started to dance.

The village headman was deep in conversation with Botolph in the glow of one of the fires and inevitably, from a mixture of a will to give and a will to receive, the talk turned to a village chapel. A nearby site was decided upon and the headman went back to his hut a happy man.

The abbot was left sitting by the fire on his own - staring into the embers.

"My word this is easy," he said. "All you need is the right combination of love, goodwill and inspiration ... and the greatest of these is love."

"Are we building tomorrow then Father?" said Luka as he came and sat beside him.

"Yes, we certainly are."

"Thought so," said Luka with a mischievous grin that Botolph ignored.

"We need to press on though so we'll just stay long enough to make sure that the two chosen brothers and the villagers are happy with each other and then we'll be on our way."

They slept comfortably and Luka was up well before dawn preparing for their departure. Botolph had made his choice of brethren and they were eagerly awaiting the arrival of the headman. As the sun appeared over the horizon so the headman and a group of villagers appeared around the corner. The villagers were carrying axes and hammers and all sorts of other implements, and were determined to start without delay. Botolph introduced the two brother monks and explained how they were going to guide the building and running of the chapel. He explained that he himself would be back in a few weeks to consecrate the building.

The tents were stowed and the travellers and horses were ready. The new congregation knelt on the spot where the new chapel would be built. They faced the rising sun as the Father Abbot led them in prayer and then raised his hand in blessing ... and the travellers went on their way.

--o--

Four hours later saw them crossing a ford over the Gipping river. They took a wide valley to the west and followed it over a hill into another valley at the bottom of which was a shallow stream. After fording this they climbed a low hill, pitching camp on its summit. Again the villagers came out to greet them. Botolph preached a good sermon but the listeners showed no enthusiasm for anything further so, after blessing the elder and his people, he retired to his tent ready for an early start the following morning.

--o--

The next day they arrived at the abbey of Beodricsworth and were afforded a great welcome by the monks. The monastery, as the abbot lost no time in telling Botolph, was one of the earliest, having been founded in

633 - some twenty years before Icanho. Luka bristled at this and retorted that the nunnery in *his* village of Folcanstane (as if he had lived there all his life) was founded in 630. Botolph saw it as tactful to steer the conversation onto other subjects.

--o--

The following night found them at the king's court in Exning and thence onwards towards Grantabryc.

Botolph was sitting next to Luka as he drove the cart around the border of the fens.

"There's Elig in the distance," said Botolph.

"Aye, I thought it was. Seems funny looking at it from this side and thinking of the game we had getting our message to Tonberht."

"Do you know, - that's thirteen summers ago now."

"Is it really as long as that? I wonder what King Tonberht and Lady Etheldreda are doing now?"

Botolph looked at him quizzically. "Tonberht died several years ago," he said gently.

"Did he?"

"Only two years after we saw him. His lady lived on Elig for some time but then she married Ecgfrid - the prince of Northumbria - and went to live up there."

"Did she though?"

"I heard Ecgfrid was made king earlier this year so she's a queen again now - and queen of a rather bigger place than the fens.

"Aye," said Luka sounding impressed.

Botolph was worried. This was the third time over the years that he had told him Etheldreda's story. He had noticed other facts that Luka seemed to forget easily. He sighed. Old age was approaching fast.

They spent that night on land to the west of

Grantabryc and moved at first light the following morning.

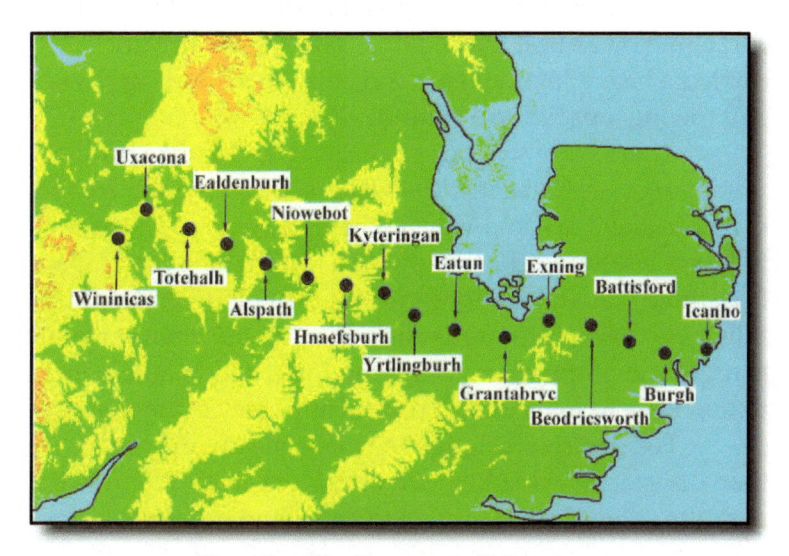

Fig. 25. The Journey to Wininicas

--o--

Travelling ever westwards they arrived in mid afternoon at the banks of a great river that flowed north to the fens.

"What shall we do Luka?"

"How d'you mean?"

"Shall we cross now and give everyone wet feet or shall we camp now and cross on the morrow?"

"It's a big river," said Luka, considering the options. "It looks as if it might be quite deep in which case they'll get more'n their feet wet."

"Ah - there's a boat putting out. It seems we might be in luck. Why don't you get as many as you can on the wains and the rest of us take the little ferry?"

The tide was low, which was good for Luka but bad for the boatman and his lad, because they kept running aground and this made for slow journeys.

Six brother monks climbed onto each of the wains and clung on as best they could. The wagon already carried a heavy load of tents and equipment and each was still towing a packhorse behind.

There were signs of a causeway and Luka was the first to urge his horse into the water after telling the second driver to stay back and watch where he went and then to follow the same track. Despite the fact that the water was low, there was still a strong current coming down from the hills. As they left the bank the wheels of the wain sank into soft ground at the river's edge and Luka had to take a stick to the horse to make it pull harder until they came free.

For the first furlong they made steady progress but then disaster struck when two of the wheels suddenly went over the edge of what proved to be an underwater causeway, and the wain lurched sideways throwing three of the monks into the water. As it was happening Luka had a flashback to his early sailing days at Cnobersburg when they would duck under the sail and quickly leap onto the opposite side of the boat to stop it capsizing. It had become a reflex reaction and Luka nimbly scrambled up the driver's seat onto the top of the wain as it rolled over.

The poor horse was struggling as the shafts of the wagon threatened to crush its rump. Fortunately the packhorse that was being towed behind was on a long rein and was therefore unaffected by the calamity.

"Off," he said to the other three monks who had scrambled up close to him. "Off with you all - your weight's making it worse. Get you round the other side and push the wagon upright."

It went against their instincts to get wet but they had no choice, and it took a great deal of pushing and shoving before the six muddy monks eventually managed to get the vehicle back onto an even keel. Luka had been afraid that a wheel or the axle might have broken - or the horse been seriously injured - but they seemed to have been lucky. To be certain, Luka snapped the reins and, with the monks still supporting the side they moved forwards a little until all the wheels were firmly back on the causeway.

Luka pulled the horse to a halt and, from his exposed position in the middle of the stream, stood up on the seat and called across to the driver of the second wain, which was waiting on the bank.

"Your monks'll have to wade across," he shouted whilst at the same time gesticulating with his arm. Neither the driver nor the monks reacted. They just stared back stupidly.

"Get . . . .Off . . . .Get . . . Off," he shouted, waving again. "Off . . . Off." At last they understood and jumped down. He waved for the other cart to move forwards and it slowly responded, the monks realising that they were going to have a soggy passage since, even after rolling up their habits, they were hardly able to keep their clothing dry.

"You two stay here," Luka said, "until the other wain passes. Just mark the spot to make sure the same thing doesn't happen to him. "You four - two on each side and if the same thing happens again, try and stop the thing falling right over."

He knew as he said this that the tents were now wet and the whole thing was so heavy that there was no chance of two men being able to hold it.

"Change of plan," he said. "Dig a couple of tent poles from out of the back . . . have you got them? Now the four of you go up to the horses head - two on each side. The monks with the poles will be on the outside and the other two will be on the inside holding the horse's bridle.

Well go on - get hold of it . . . that's right. Now you outer two - take the pole in your outer hand and use your other hand to hold onto your brother . . . yes that's it - I think you can see now what I've got in mind.

He looked behind him - the other wain had almost arrived. He stood on the seat again and shouted, "Follow me closely." The driver nodded and waved. Luka cracked the reins . . . and slowly and gingerly they eased both wains across to the opposite bank where the abbot and the rest of the group had now collected.

"Are you alright Luka?" said Sister Liobsynde with a concerned look on her face.

"Yes thanks Sister, I stayed dry - it's the brothers who came off worst. I'm not sure if any were hurt when they were pitched into the water - but they're certainly all very wet."

"We need to get them dried off," said Botolph.

"Fortunately the spare clothing and blankets are on the packhorses," said Luka.

One of the monks came over:

"Father it's alright - we're not too cold and there's still some sun left. We've rung out what we can of the water."

"Nevertheless," said the abbot, "you're too precious to be lost to illness. We'll cross to yonder slope, pitch our tents straight away and get a fire going. You twelve will be relieved of domestic duties tonight - just concentrate on getting yourselves warm and dry."

--o--

The following morning the event was put behind them as just one more experience that they could benefit from in the future - although they thanked God that no bones had been broken. Luka checked the wagon thoroughly and did his best to squeeze some duck fat between the axles and the wheels of both wains, and then they were on their way again.

At mid-day they stopped at a settlement by the name of Stow where Botolph found the villagers eager to listen to his sermon on the good news of Christ, and they followed what had become a regular routine. The Father Abbot's two nominated brother monks were readily accepted by the villagers and the rest of the party moved on, camping that night on the banks of the River Nyn which they crossed the following morning. The first village they passed through next day was   Yrtlingaburh but Botolph sensed no interest there - perhaps it was too early in the morning - so they turned to the northwest and headed towards Kyteringan.

Botolph decided it was time to rest his legs and enjoy Luka's company, so he hopped up onto the wain.

"Don't you feel a little bit like a travelling merchant Father?" said Luka.

"Well that's exactly what I am," laughed Botolph. "I travel from place to place marketing my wares.   In my case I sell the Word of God.   It's the same as those travellers who come knocking at our door wanting to sell us swan feathers, inks and paints.   I see my trade as searching the countryside looking for customers.   I have to use what skills the Good Lord gives me.   I can't force all and sundry to accept His Word whether they want it or not. I have to use all my senses - to look and listen and feel the mood of the people - and then, where I feel they are receptive, *that*'s when I have to stop and give them all my love and concentration.   If they're not receptive, then, not wishing to insult them, I move on.   Tomorrow is another day.   Perhaps by the time we visit them next - either on our return journey or in another year - they'll have come to know the Lord from their neighbours and be pleased to receive baptism."

"Baptism? We've not been baptising."

"Ah, no indeed - not yet - but once the chapels are established and the good brother monks have taught them the ways of Christ *then*, when we return, will be the time to welcome them into the family of the Church properly."

His eyes were sparkling and Luka suddenly understood the joy his friend was getting from this journey. He might be walking many miles every day but there was a spring in his step as, like a bee, he went from flower to flower searching for, what was for him, the nectar of his purpose in life. Luka rather liked this poetic concept he had just conceived and was about to share it with the father when there was a shout from behind and the procession came to a sudden halt. Botolph grasped his crozier, jumped down from the wain, and walked back to where there was a cluster of monks huddling round a sitting figure.

"What's the trouble here?"

The crowd parted to reveal Sister Liobsynde holding her foot.

"I fear I've twisted my ankle," she said. "I caught my foot on the edge of a stone and over I went."

He noticed, for the first time, the mud on her shoulder.

"I feel stupid - I'm so sorry."

"Don't give it a second thought," he said. "These things are bound to happen. Come, take my place on the cart beside Luka - he'll be pleased of your conversation - he must be bored with mine."

With willing support the sister hobbled up to the cart and the procession moved on.

CHAPTER 30
Field Chapels

Following their established routine, on the next day at noon, Botolph preached at Harringdun where two more monks were left. During the afternoon they made their way further westwards along a plateau and camped for the night at Hnaefsburh where, late as it was, the villagers were keen to hear Botolph's sermon . . . and he was pleased to oblige. Two more monks left the procession here and Botolph began to wonder if he had brought enough with him. He had not expected his harvest to be so fruitful. There were now twenty-seven brother monks left. He anticipated that some might want to stay at Wininicas and he would still need a good number for the return journey. He sighed and decided not to worry about it, but to leave it all in God's capable hands.

--o--

Botolph's next sermon was at Yelver where once again he received a good reception with the result that only twenty-five monks were with him when they crossed Waceling Street and stopped just a league further on at Niowebot for the night. A sermon, a sleep, breakfast and the release of two more monks, saw them heading towards Cofatre, which they reached after fording the River Sowe. Unusually, that day, there were no travellers or villagers who seemed inclined to listen to a sermon, and so they pressed on to Alspath - which again was fruitless. From being worried about being too successful, Father Botolph was now beginning to feel that he was perhaps losing his touch. He guessed Christ's fishermen must have had the same problem - all feast or famine and nothing in between.

--o--

The next day was in the same vein. They stopped to eat at a small place called Beormingan and camped for the night at Ealdenburh.

--o--

They had only been on the road for an hour the next day when the gubernator monk, whose responsibility it was to plan the route, called the procession to a stop and came back to Botolph looking very agitated. He brought with him some travellers - a man woman and child - who had been travelling in the opposite direction.

"What's the matter Brother Gubernato?" asked Botolph.

"Father - I was leading us to the Sabbina Crossing but these good people tell me it'll be impossible for us to pass there."

"Why's that?"

"Apparently the river's quite narrow, fast-flowing and deep, and although there's a ferry which could take the walkers across, it would be impassible for the wains."

"Oh dear," said Botolph. "So what do you suggest?"

"Well if we carry on as planned it will only be another day and a half before we reach Wininicas, but the alternative route is much further north through Viroconium."

"I thought that's where we were going anyway."

"I had hoped to by-pass it by taking the shorter

way."

"Will it take much longer via Viroconium?"

The monk nodded, looking miserable. "Two extra days at least father. I'm so sorry."

"Hah - it's not your fault brother - don't give it a second thought."

"But it was my responsibility to get you here Father."

"And very well you've done it too. You couldn't have been expected to know all the details of the route. No, a couple more days won't matter."

Luka had been listening to this conversation and interjected with, "Father?"

"Yes Luka."

"We could split up here. You could take the short route and I and the other wain could take the Viroconium road."

Botolph considered a moment but then turned to the family, thanked them for their help and gave them a blessing for the rest of their journey. Just before they left he asked, "What's the name of this next village?"

"That's Dudelei Father."

"Dudelei?"

They nodded and went on their way.

"Your idea's a good one Luka," he continued, "but I think it's best we stay together. "In the absence of any tents, we'd have to rely on the charity of villagers for the night and . . . . No - I think it's best we stay together - and in any case, it gives me more chance of finding a community I can preach to. It's been a bit quiet in that direction lately."

So on they went and stopped for the first night at Totehalh. On the next they found themselves on another section of their old friend Waceling Street and camped close to the old Roman fort of Uxacona. It was while they were having their evening meal that Brother Gubernato told Botolph that he reckoned they could make it to Wininicas by sunset the next day.

"But," he said, "I'm told we have a long shallow ford to cross - so that might slow us down - besides which Wininicas is probably six or seven leagues distant and we've only been doing about five leagues each day up until now."

"We must be away promptly then," said the abbot. "Perhaps you'd be kind enough to pass that on to the others."

The gubernator monk nodded.

"It would be a shame to have to camp within striking distance of our target, but if we have to - then that'll be the Lord's wish. Thank you brother - we'll see you at first light then."

--o--

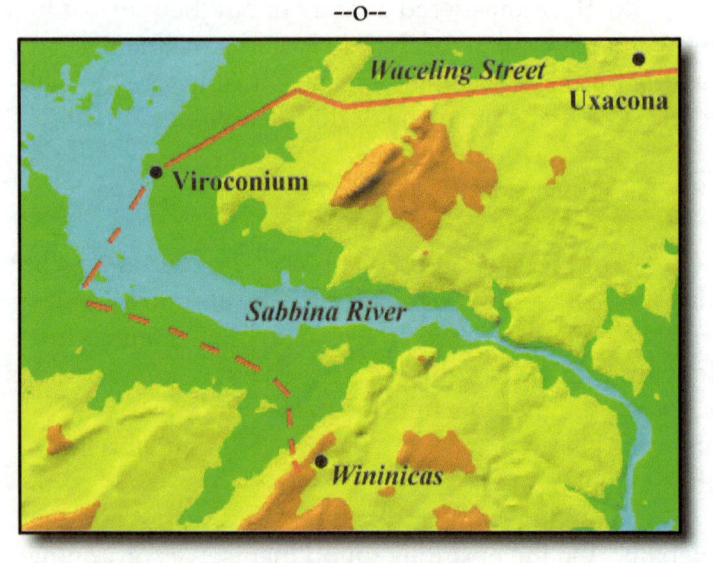

Fig. 26. Viroconium, Wininicas and the Sabbina.

Everybody was up bright and early ready for the final push. The Roman road ran due west and was flat for the first couple of leagues but then it turned to the southwest and became a gentle downhill slope. Because the road was in good condition, travelling was easy and Sister Liobsynde took to walking again, since her sprained ankle was slowly mending.

They saw the wide shallow River Sabbina stretching away before them with the ruined Roman city of Viroconium in the foreground. There was no causeway as such, but some kind soul had planted withies to mark the crossing. It looked to be about two miles in width. As it was already mid-morning they could not afford to waste any time.

Luka had learnt his lesson though and, following his earlier successful technique, two brother monks walked ahead of him prodding at the edge of his track with tent poles to test the depths.

It was noon by the time they reached the other side.

"How far now Brother Gubernato?"

"Not far sire. We are making better time than I expected. Probably another two leagues but we'll have a steep climb at the end of it, so it's likely to take another three or four hours."

"Well there's plenty of sun left and the weather's being kind to us - and we might not have to pitch our tents tonight, so I think we can afford to stop for a rest and build our strength up with food and drink for that final stretch."

And then turning to the others: "We're nearly there but we'll stop for a rest and some vittals to give us heart for the last bit. Don't forget the horses. Whereabouts *is* Wininicas, Guberno?"

"It's in the distance over there Father - just t'other side of yonder hill."

All ate and drank and some slept a little, but it was not long before everyone started moving about as if they were eager to complete the journey, so Botolph called a slightly premature end to their rest and they set off again.

They followed a flat track running southeast along the shore of the Sabbina until after a couple of hours the track turned more to the south and the going became harder. An hour later the road became *very* steep and the horses started to falter on the slopes. Luka rallied the monks and they leant a hand and pushed the wains from the rear. The horses battled on gamely and after a long struggle they won the ridge.

Before them lay a wonderful sight. Nestling in a basin at the bottom of the hill was a pretty little village facing to the northeast. They could make out the newly-rebuilt stone church that Domne Eafe had mentioned to Botolph, and they could also see some wooden huts set apart from the village itself. Their journey was nearly over. Now a different sort of work would begin.

"Come on now brothers - let's line up in good order and sing our hearts out to the praise of God as we go and greet our brethren."

Botolph had decided that this final entry into Wininicas should be done in style. Behind the crucifer came the thurifer swinging his censer. Then came the abbot himself proceeding slowly, purposefully and serenely - using his crozier as a walking aid and with his right hand raised in blessing. Behind him came Sister Liobsynde holding her head held high and walking as if she were being delivered by the Almighty himself with the protection of her colleague abbot ahead and a choir of heavenly chanters behind. At the rear of the procession came the two wains, the packhorses and the outriders.

The singing drew the villagers out of their huts and

an early crowd formed along the route. Liobsynde smiled at each attentive face and inclined her head in acknowledgement. They, in their turn, after the dramatic symbolism of the cross, the mystical smell of the incense and the awe-inspiring sight of the be-mitred abbot with his crozier, saw this tall lady with her shining face and bright eyes who seemed to exude love and friendship and to recognise each of them in spite of the fact that they had never met before. Who could she be?

Botolph had already discussed their destination with the crucifer before they had started their descent of the hill. He had worked out that they would need to walk through the village centre and then round to the left. Now that he was in the midst of the habitations and could not see the way ahead he hoped that he had been correct. It would be embarrassing if they had to turn about and retrace their footsteps. He need not have worried as the church soon loomed up in front of them. The procession came to a standstill whilst the abbot and the thurifer walked around the building. The abbot intoned a blessing on each of the four walls and finally, on the entrance doorway.

The blessing had given the curious villagers both the time and the courage to catch up, and they now stood around wondering what was going to happen next.

Botolph did not disappoint them. He had noticed, near the church, a slightly raised rock formation that made a natural pulpit and, handing his crozier to the thurifer, he walked up the little slope and then turned towards the people and began to preach using, as his text, the story of Elijah and Elisha.

He told them the story of the prophet's journey - not unlike the journey *they* had had, - and of the parting of the River Jordan - which *they* had not needed, the waters of the

Sabbina being, by God's grace, shallow enough to cross. There was some laughter at this. Nor, he said, did he have any plans of dying at the moment (there was more laughter).

"But . . . " and here he paused wagging his finger.

"But . . . " (another pause).

"But . . . I *have* brought you a new Elisha in the form of Abbess Liobsynde here and it is in her hands that your spiritual care will rest."

He motioned Liobsynde to join him, which she did.

"This is a new time in the life of Wininicas. We are here to complete the building of your minster. We shall be welcoming both monks and nuns into the service of God. They will live their lives according to the rule of the blessed Benedict - and Abbess Liobsynde will not only be their mother under God but also a mother to you all."

There was a lot of excited chatter at this point because the news was exactly what the village needed to hear. They had been disappointed when Domne Eafe had stopped work on their monastery and they were envious of their near neighbours seven or eight leagues down the road who had enjoyed the patronage of Leminster Abbey for the previous ten years.

"So we shall now pitch our tents for the night - and tomorrow we shall start work. We anticipate the arrival of King Merewalh sometime within the next few days and, on that matter, I would be grateful if the first of you to see him coming could run and tell us. And now I ask you to kneel or bow your heads in prayer as we ask for God's blessing on our new minster and on all who work on it or serve in it . . . "

He finished by raising his hand and offering God's blessing to all the village people.

--o--

They worked hard during the following days but it was a pattern that Botolph, Luka and many of the other brethren knew well. The villagers were enthusiastic and gave all the help they could. Although by the time that King Merewalh arrived they had only been in Wininicas for four days, Luka had been applying his management skills to good effect and much had already been achieved. In spite of this the king's party was a welcome source of more labour.

The days were getting shorter as winter approached and Botolph was aware of the need to start their journey home, but he kept delaying their departure until he could delay no longer.

After Vesper prayers with the sixteen monks who were going to stay - and admonishments to them to serve the abbess and the Lord to the best of their ability - Botolph blessed them all and they turned to their pallets in the hope of a good night's sleep. At first light on the morrow they would set off on the journey home.

--o--

Botolph had wanted to travel by a different route in the hope of achieving more conversions on the way back but time, days and monks were short in number so, for speed, they followed the same route as their inward journey.

King Merewalh had agreed to provide them with six armed escorts for the first couple of days - so as well as the two horse-drawn wains and four horses they had brought with them, there was another cart carrying tents for the escorts.

The reduction in their numbers meant that nobody needed to walk, and so at first they often managed to cover nine or ten leagues every day. But soon after the escorts took their leave they started to re-encounter the villages where they had left monks to organise the building of the new field chapels and Botolph insisted on spending a full day at each of these villages, during which time he preached to the people, consecrated their newly-built churches and baptised the newly converted. Without exception the trusted monks had fulfilled their functions admirably and all were looking forward to spending the winter with their new flock.

There was a pleasant surprise after they left Beodricsworth. As they passed through a small settlement on their way to the crossing of the River Gipping there came a cry from behind and a man, who later proved to be the village elder, came running to catch them up. He begged them to stop. Botolph recognised him as the man who had welcomed them into his village when they had camped nearby on their journey westwards. Botolph had preached but it had seemed that his sermon had fallen on deaf ears.

"Father," said the man breathlessly.

"Yes my son. Pax vobiscum. What can I do for you?"

"Pax Father. I come with a message from my people who wonder if you would be good enough to come and preach to them again."

"Was my first sermon not good enough?" said Botolph with a teasing smile.

The elder was pleased to see the smile. He had been somewhat fearful of approaching the holy man with such a request - bearing in mind that, on his last visit, his people had, to all intents and purposes, rejected the priest.

He smiled in return. "My people glory in their slowness," he said apologetically. "They watch - they listen - they think - they sleep - and two days later the seed suddenly sprouts. Mind you - once their decision's been made they never change their minds ... so you'll be pleased to hear that, late or not, they've decided to become Christians."

"Well that's well worth turning back for," said Botolph.

The lane was narrow and the carts were heavy. After much heaving and pulling they managed to swing them round and start their sweating climb back up the hill, where they found their reward in a joyous welcome of sunny faces.

After a hastily-prepared meal Botolph was prevailed upon to preach.

He started slowly and quietly, turning his body as he locked eyes with each of the villagers in turn. Some tried to avoid his gaze but it hovered over each head like a sparrowhawk over a mouse until the villager involuntarily raised his eyes and knew that he too was the one to whom the great preacher spoke. Once their attention had thus been captured, Botolph raised his voice a pitch and told them story after story of the great things that Jesus had done. And then came the climax as he raised his voice once again revealing to each the relevance of Jesus in their lives. He finished suddenly - and stood motionless, his right hand raised and pointing to heaven. There was utter silence and awe as each member of his audience - even Luka - focussed upon that finger - wondering what was coming next.

He held the moment ... and he held their hearts - and then the finger descended making, as it did so, the sign of the cross - as he finished softly:

"In the name of the Father ... and of the Son ... and of the Holy Ghost. Amen."

--o--

Later, since it was clear they would not be leaving before dawn, the headman asked if Botolph would baptise the believers. A line of adults, with children skipping by their sides, made their way down the hill to the stream and it was here that Botolph carried out the humblest and greatest of all ceremonies, where each believing villager was accepted into the family of the Christian faith.

As dusk fell a fire was lit and then began dancing and singing that lasted far into the night. At Botolph's request the headman had had some small wooden crosses quickly made and Botolph presented one of these to each of the newly baptised. Simple presents that they would hold dear for the rest of their lives.

"Well," said Luka as they made their way to the tents, "I can't believe the difference. When we were last here they seemed a dreary lot - and yet now, they've given us one of the best party's we've ever had."

"God works in a mysterious way," said Botolph happily.

--o--

It was mid afternoon in late September before the brothers who had stayed behind at Icanho joyously received the Holy Father and their colleagues back into their midst. They were eager to hear the tales of their adventures.

--o--

Over the next few years, visits to Wininicas became a popular part of the Icanho programme. They were always undertaken in the summer and Botolph consulted closely with Brother Gubernato to ensure that the routes were varied north and south in such a way that, as Botolph put it, "Being fishers of men we can cast our nets both far and wide."

Luka was amazed at how much planning these journeys involved. Parchments were constantly being sent from and received by the monastery, and many of these were to or from the field chapels on 'the Sea of Galilee' as Botolph used to call it.

Many of the epistles sent by Botolph were letters of encouragement and most that he received told stories of success - sometimes with requests for the abbot to visit on his next journey so that more converts could be baptised. Some letters were less welcome - and brought tales of brothers who had died - either as a result of accidents or of ill health - or they brought tales of sickness - or, even more sadly, they occasionally brought tales of brothers who had sinned or absconded. Botolph always blamed himself for these - feeling that he must have chosen unwisely. He grieved for the sin and he grieved for the brother. In these circumstances substitutes had to be found, together with a means of getting them to their churches.

Much of Icanho's administration had been taken over some years previously by a talented young monk called Aethelheah, whom Botolph appointed prior a short while later. This left the abbot with more time to administer his ever-growing 'diocese' of chapels and to oversee the training of monks who would eventually be sent out into the field. He sometimes reflected how much easier it would have been to follow Abbot Felix's example at Dommoc and travel and preach *without* setting up new churches. But he fervently believed that he was being called by God to work in this way. That conviction was enough for him to know that the extra work was worthwhile.

And then there was Botolph's constant need for solitary prayer. In Icanho's early days, although he took joy in living within the abbey confines, instinct had told him to retain use of the old byre. He was not sure at first why he had done this, but God's will soon became clear and he started to use the byre as a retreat. It was a humble place where he could go and spend time with God and make sure that he was hearing His messages correctly without interruption or undue outside influence. At these times his food was laid at the doorway and two of the younger brethren would busy themselves in a cultivated area nearby - ostensibly gardening but in fact ensuring their abbot's privacy. The gardening was Luka's idea as he hated to see idleness, and the vegetables grown by the 'guards' added to his produce from the kitchen garden.

As he became older he found it more and more difficult to pick up the reins after his visits to Wininicas, but the abilities of Prior Aethelheah meant that the abbey was always running sweetly on his return. He therefore took to the custom of retreating to the byre for a few days in order to gain strength from solitary prayer so that he could return - enthusiastic and refreshed - to the challenges that God and the abbey still offered.

Playing host to visitors was a time-consuming feature of Botolph's life but he recognised its value. People still came from far and wide, not only from abbeys and priories, but also from great halls and royal families. Although Icanho was a monastery of monks it was also always pleased to welcome female visitors - for whom a separate dorter had been specifically built.

One day in 671 as Botolph was doing some administrative work in the Chapter Hut, Prior Aethelheah popped his head around the door and announced the arrival of a certain Brother Ceolfrid.[1]

---

[1] This visit of Ceolfrid (or Ceolfrith - they are one and the same person)

"I'm sure you would like to meet him Father," said the Prior. "He's in the refectory at the moment. I offered him his own cell, but he said he'd be quite happy in the dorter."

"Where's he from?"

"From Inhrypum in Northumbria."

"Ah, Father Wilfrid's place."

"Yes Father," replied the prior - disappointed that he had not been able to impart that news himself - but, he reflected, he should have guessed - there seemed to be little with which the abbot was unfamiliar.

"I'll be happy to meet him but I must finish this first. Would you be kind enough to find Brother Luka and ask him to join us. It's he who will have to look after our visitor, so it would be a good idea for them to meet now. We'll then go and welcome our guest together. In any case I expect he's tired after his long journey and will enjoy having half an hour to himself."

A short while later the three of them strode through the refectory doorway. The visitor stood as they entered and was perhaps somewhat astounded by the number in the reception party. He was aged about thirty, of medium height with a pleasant complexion and demeanour.

"Abbot Botolph - what a pleasure it is to meet you at last. I've heard so much of you and your abbey."

"Brother Ceolfrid - I hope you've been *well* informed. How can we help you - are you just passing through or might you tarry with us for a while?"

The refectory was empty except for the kitchener and cellarer, who were fussing about at the far end of the building.

---

to Icanho Abbey is recorded in *The Anonymous History of Abbot Ceolfrith* written in about 715.

The visitor had just finished a bowl of soup. The remains of a small loaf were lying at the side of the empty vessel. Botolph motioned him to continue.

"Thank you Father but no - I've had quite sufficient."

"In that case perhaps we can join you here while you tell us your story?"

The visitor waved a hand in agreement and the four of them sat cosily at the refectory table, Luka gazing eagerly into the stranger's eyes.

"The prior here tells me you've come from Inhrypum - is Father Wilfrid well?"

"Yes indeed Father Abbot. I've had the pleasure of his tutelage for the past six years. Last year he ordained me priest and earlier this year he advised that I should travel around the monasteries of our beautiful land and learn as much as I could about how the best ones are run. He sent me first to Cantwarebury."

"Ah - a wise choice. You must tell us shortly whom you met there and what you learned but first, pray tell us your origins and what you did before you joined Bishop Wilfrid."

"My monastic life started when I was about 18 summers. My brother Cynefrith was abbot of Ingetlingham and he invited me to join him there - but I'd no sooner arrived than he left for Ireland and he'd hardly roosted there before sadly he caught the plague died."

"Oh, I'm sorry," said Botolph, crossing himself whilst silently invoking a quick blessing upon the departed brother.

"My cousin Trumberht took over as abbot and we had a very happy time for several years."

"Ah, Trumberht," said Botolph, "he became Bishop of Hexham did he not?"

"Indeed he did father. He'd studied for many years at the abbey of Lastingham under the saintly brothers Cedd and Chad and he came to us from there."

"You say you had a happy time for several years - what happened to disturb that?"

"Once again it was the plague I'm afraid. It took most of our brethren and reduced our numbers drastically. Soon after that Bishop Wilfrid returned from his consecration in Gaul."

"Oh yes - he had an exciting arrival as I recall," said Botolph with a smile.

"Ha-ha . . . yes. He was shipwrecked on the coast of the South Saxons. They did their best to kill him but he had God's protection and, after a fight during which one of the Saxons was killed, they managed to get away."

"Ah well - we know all about the South Saxons, don't we Luka?"

Luka nodded thoughtfully. "Yes, that was, let's see - thirty-four years ago now. They tried hard to kill us too."

Botolph did not want to go over that story again so he quickly interjected: "What's the good bishop doing now?"

"As I expect you know, when he returned to Eoforwic he found the whole ecclesiastical scene changed, so instead of being consecrated archbishop as he'd expected, he had to content himself with returning to his foundation at Ripon . . . but then the new Archbishop arrived from Rome and settled into Cantwarebury and everything changed again."

"Archbishop Theodore - yes - I hear he's a hard task-master and that one of the first things he did was to eject Bishop Chad from Eoforwic on the grounds that he'd not been properly consecrated."

"That's true but there was no malice in it and Chad

had no argument with the archbishop's decision. Bishop Chad knew, when he allowed the corrupt bishop, Wine, to consecrate him, that he was taking a risk. He maintained he had no choice - it was either Bishop Wine or no consecration at all, as there were no other bishops to choose from. King Oswiu was pushing him hard to get the matter finished so he gave in and let Wine do the officiation. I think the archbishop was secretly sympathetic to Chad but had no choice but to move him on. He did however as compensation give him the see of Lichfield."

"And now the stylish Wilfrid is Bishop of all Northumbria with a diocese larger than King Oswiu's kingdom itself?"

"That's right. There's a lot of criticism about the bishop's lifestyle - he does like to do things grandly and has innumerable followers, many of whom he dresses in royal regalia. It's not really the 'British' way - but it seems to work - he's certainly a force to be reckoned with."

"So where do you fit into this scene?"

"Oh I'm only a humble priest. Bishop Wilfrid was kind enough to ordain me two years ago and said that he felt sure that God had important work for me to do. For many moons I prayed and prayed for guidance but I couldn't see my way forwards. My ears must have been deaf and my eyes blind and it was through my Lord Bishop that God eventually spoke to me. After my ordination he told me that it was time to prepare myself. I should travel the length and breadth of the land studying both the way that the best priests lived their lives and how the best monasteries were administered. As I said, I started by travelling to Cantium where I stayed at the Cantwarebury monastery for eighteen moons studying the finer points of the priesthood. During this time I learnt the skills of the miller-baker and," he smiled, "became renowned for the quality of my bread."

Luka pricked up his ears at this. "I tried that at Cantwarebury," he said, somewhat indignantly. "I made the most delicious bread but all *I* received was criticism. My brother monks seemed to enjoy it but Prior Peter said that it was so tasty that eating it was a sin."

Ceolfrid laughed. "I know what you mean," he said, "there's a fine line between good eating bread and sinful bread."

"So how is it that we find you here?" said Botolph.

"Irresistible pressure. Both at Cantwarebury itself and further towards the coast I heard word of your Abbey of Icanho at every turn and was told that I must not fail to visit you on my way home. And during the journey, time and time again, the same recommendations came . . . so here I am."

"Well it's wonderful to see you," said Botolph to the nods of the others. "I think that's enough for one night - you must be tired now and ready for bed. You'll be excused the offices tomorrow but the day after that we'll expect your full participation in our monastery life. Prior Aethelheah will issue you with a duty roster."

--o--

The flow of visitors continued unabated and it was in the following year that there came another who was both unexpected and very special.

It was the middle of September 672 when Luka burst into the scriptorium where the abbot was writing a letter. Botolph expected comments or questions about the garden or the byre, but the expression on Luka's face suggested it was less mundane.

"What is it?"

"We have a special visitor."

"Oh? - and who might that be?"

Luka was trying to control the grin that was threatening to spoil the surprise. He kept his head down and slowly wiped his grubby hands on his apron until his mind had steadied.

"Come and see."

Botolph sighed and laid down his quill. There always seemed to be something to interrupt his work, but he knew that Luka would not have bothered him unless it was important . . . and . . . he reflected as he followed Luka out of the hall . . . guests are always important, no matter how humble.

Luka turned to the right as he left the scriptorium and they headed for the guest hut, which was only a few steps away. When he reached it he pulled open the door and stood back while Botolph entered. It took a moment for Botolph's eyes to adjust after the bright sunshine in the yard, but through the gloom he perceived a shadowy figure sitting on a bench at the back of the hut.

The figure rose and, picking up a long walking staff, made his way slowly and, apparently painfully, across the straw-covered floor towards him. He had once been a tall man but was now stooped and shrunken. He might once have born a Roman tonsure but in truth there was little hair left on his head - most of it was around his chin, for he had a white bushy beard that would have extended halfway down his chest had he been sitting. As it was, due to his stoop, gravity pulled the beard towards the floor.

Botolph blinked to clear his eyes and, as his vision settled, he moved towards his visitor.

"Pax brother and welcome," he said.

"Pax frater in veritate."

CHAPTER 31
A.D. 672
Adulph

Botolph frowned with curiosity at the somewhat unusual reply and re-focussed his eyes. He caught his breath.

"Adulph?"

"The same."

His newly focussed eyes blurred with tears while he, lost for words, clasped his brother's arms. Luka stood helplessly by - he too becoming infected with the emotion of the moment as the brothers stood locked in an ungainly geriatric embrace that would have been comical had it not been so poignant.

Adulph was the first to regain his composure.

"Sho, bruzzher," he said, "I she you hav' been busy while I've been away?"

Botolph laughed. "Yes I have - but no more than you I guess dear brother - what a lot we'll have to tell each other. Have you come home to roost? I pray so. Or am I soon to have the sadness of losing you again?"

"No bruzzher - I'm here to roost - if you'll have me. I'm old and frail and not a lot of ushe to anyone any more, but you'll not lose me until God's ready for me to do hish work in heaven."

"May that be a long while hence. You must be tired and hungry. I've a million questions to ask but we'll save those until later. You remember Luka of course from our days at Cnobersburg."

"Ah yesh of coursh - the man who helped ush get our boat away when we were shtuck in the mud."

They laughed - partly because of the memory and partly, in Botolph and Luka's case, because of Adulph's strange accent. Luka wondered how such an accent could be acquired. He was not even sure if it *was* an accent or due, perhaps, to Adulph's lack of teeth.

It was a fortnight later before they found time for Adulph to tell his story and by then, Luka noted, the odd accent had almost vanished.

They sat huddled around the central hearth as the glowing logs defied the rain that was hammering on the thatch. Adulph was furthest from the door with Botolph on his right, and next to him sat Luka. They had made as much speed as they could from the church to the misericord, bearing in mind Adulph's age and infirmity. When Luka finally wrenched the door open they found the building already occupied by six brothers who had been scheduled to work in the kitchen garden, had the drenching rain not given them respite. The brothers rose to leave but Adulph said "No - stay - I have a story to tell and I am sure that God would be pleased for you to hear it too."

They shook their habits free of surplus water while the brothers pulled a couple of benches and some stools around the hearth, so that all could enjoy Adulph's story in some comfort.

"So where shall I start brother?" said Adulph.

"Well the last I saw of you," said Botolph, "was as a hazy shape on the *Manigfual* when we finally managed to get you afloat at Cnobersburg."

Adulph chuckled.

"Yes, we didn't even have time to say goodbye did we? One moment we were stuck aground in the creek with Penda's army getting ever closer and the next we hurtling towards the open sea."

"I hear you landed at Gesoriacum."

"Hah! Bless you no. I believe *Manigfual* made landfall there eventually and that was certainly our first intention but we had a southwesterly wind which was having none of that. We *tried* to point south, and indeed the tide was pushing us that way, but we soon found that it made life more comfortable if we came off the wind and headed towards the rising sun. We would go where the Good Lord sent us."

"So you stayed in the German Ocean?"

Adulph nodded.

"And how many sunrises did you see before you found land?"

"Ah, - well only one actually."

"My word that was quick - it took us a lot longer than that to reach the other side and we nearly drowned in the process didn't we Luka?"

Luka had been gazing at the floor but he looked up and nodded happily.

"I say we headed *towards* the rising sun but once risen it was to one side or behind us for most of the time. We had a good voyage - taking it in turns to steer - and getting shouted at by Torrel for our misdemeanours. The wind was constant and the sea was flat. What more could we have asked? We sailed through the night and when the sun finally poked his head above the horizon we headed straight at him."

The old man was an animated speaker. As he spoke he turned his head and held each of them with his glinting eyes which sparkled as they reflected lights from the now flaming logs. He pointed across the hearth to an imaginary scene in a black shadow that flickered on the other side of the room.

"The sun raised 'imself up leaving a line of clouds. Below these were some little black dots which, as we came closer, proved to be a cluster of small fishing boats. We chased 'em for quite a while before they eventually let us catch 'em," he laughed.

"They gave us some fish which, they said, were good enough to eat raw. They were right too. They pointed out a gap in the clouds and told us to head that way. Once the sun had risen enough to stop dazzling us, we could make out a line of surf from

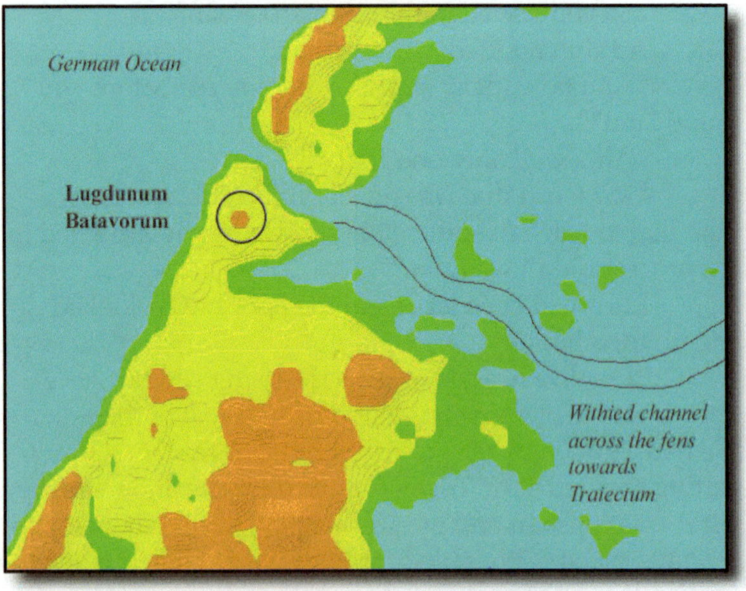

Fig. 27. Lugdunum in the Frisian Islands.

which gradually emerged land so flat and so low that it just looked like a different colour sea. I was at the helm and Torrel bade me steer towards a cluster of sails, which turned out to be gathered around a gap between two desolate-looking mud banks."

He lowered his voice creating a sense of drama and mystique and added slowly, "It was no ordinary gap. It was the secret entrance to a different world."

They stayed silent, spell-bound by his tale. Luka was the first to speak.

"So where were you? What was the country's name?"

"The place was *Friesland* - a group of low islands surrounding a wide area of mud, capriciously covered and uncovered by the tides and known as the *Wads*."

All eyes were focussed on Adulph's extended hands as he used them to good effect raising them to show the rising water and lowering them so that they almost expected mud to appear between his fingers.

"We slid through the gap wondering what we would find but suddenly . . . there on our right . . . just around the corner, the bustling harbour of *Lugdunum* came into view. It was crammed with trading boats of all shapes and sizes from north, south, east and west."

He paused while they contemplated the sight.

"Did you stay there?"

"For a while, yes, but in truth, having arrived, we weren't sure what to do next. We had the codices and scrolls from Cnobersburg with us together with wraps of vellum, quills and all sorts of other odds and ends. Torrel was quite concerned that they'd get damaged or stolen. We'd discussed this several times during the voyage. Torrel's first priority was to get back to Britain, but the wind was blowing in the wrong direction, so he concluded that we should sit it out until the wind changed and then take the scrolls to Cantwarebury. Two weeks later that's exactly what happened and
the last I saw of them was early one morning when a

sailor's wind pushed *Manigfual* out of the harbour on her way home."

"It was Father Fursey who told me you'd landed at Gesoriacum."

"Father Fursey?   You've seen him then?"

"Aye he visited us at Evoriacum.   He said you went to the Low Countries but overland."

"Oh - well you know Father Fursey - he was a great character but his head was always a bit in the clouds.   He was old when we first met him so it's not surprising if he got things wrong.   The story I heard was that *Manigfual* called into Gesoriacum on her way home so perhaps he thought I was still on board then."

"Anyway - you weren't - you decided to stay." interrupted Luka, keen to get on with the story.

"Well I'd seen nineteen summers and made lots of friends in Lugdunum so I felt comfortable there.   I found a job as a fisherman, did whatever work came my way and got married."

"Married?"

Everyone suddenly came to life - the comment was so unexpected.   A wicked half smile appeared on Luka's now *very-interested* face.

Botolph cleared his throat . . . "So, err - how did that happen then?"

"Well I'm not sure really - it just did.   As I say, I was nineteen and very green behind the ears.   It only lasted a couple of months afore she ran off with a Frankish sailor."

"Ah - so no children then?"

"Not as far as I know."

"Not as far as you . . . ?   Oh yes - I see.   So what did you do then?"

"I lived a miserable life, feeling I would die, and

then being afraid I wouldn't. It was a very low time and I drank a lot more strong mead than was good for me."

Luka's smile had vanished and he looked sympathetically at Adulph, remembering his own low time after the death of Clarisse.

"Eventually I pulled myself together and decided that life had to go on, but felt I couldn't stay in Lugdunum. The memories were too painful and, to be honest, I felt embarrassed. I felt a fool. I felt I had to run away."

"Was that the right thing to do?" asked Botolph.

"I think it *turned out* to be the right thing to do ... but probably for the wrong reason."

"So where did you run to?" asked Luka.

Adulph laughed. "Well actually there's nowhere you *can* run from Lugdunum. It's either surrounded by water or filthy brown mud. One day some folks came in on a boat which was too big to cross the *Wads* and they asked me how they could get to the east. One of my fishermen friends had a suitable vessel, so he agreed to take them. On a whim I decided to go too. On the way we stopped off at an island called Traiectum. I decided to stay there while the others carried on down the *River Rhenus*."

"Didn't you have a problem with the language?" asked Botolph.

"I hardly understood any of the locals from the time I arrived in Lugdunum. Even the British words were unintelligible - but somehow one gets by. In Traiectum I met some Christians. There weren't many in the town but those there were spoke Latin and it was thanks to Latin that a group of us started to meet regularly. The king of Traiectum heard of us and persuaded us to set up a school."

"Did they all want to speak Latin then?" asked

Luka.

"Bless you no. The king just thought that because we could all speak Latin we'd make good teachers. Ha-ha ... how wrong he was."

"Didn't it work out then?"

"Oh yes - eventually it worked very well - although at the beginning we were all stumbling about in the dark and some of the group soon proved to be totally unsuited to the task. Thankfully most of those left quite quickly. Because of its position on the River Rhenus the town had a constant flow of visitors and this made our school grow rapidly. We all had a thirst for knowledge and actively sought out travellers of note and encouraged them to come and talk to us. One day a holy man came to visit and turned the tables by starting to teach *us*.

"When I first arrived at Lugdunum I thought I was going to be a fisherman for the rest of my life and that my connection with monasteries was going to remain a thing of the past. Indeed I even wondered about the strength of my connection with God. But God obviously still had plans for me, because from our forum a group developed consisting of people with an interest in spreading the word of God. As a result of this several of us were professed as monks by which time we'd set up a church and a scriptorium as well as the school."

"So where did the money and support come from?" asked Botolph.

"The local people kept us well-provisioned with food - and the church constantly received gifts. Later we started offering accommodation to travellers and this brought in a regular income. The local kings were very supportive too."

"Kings?" said Luka, "how many did you have then?"

"Well only one at a time but they were always changing. There were constant battles - both actual and political. It wasn't a stable community - in fact *we* were probably the most stable part of it."

"How long were you there for?"

"Thirty-two summers all told."

"And what made you come home?"

"Things changed. We were a very close-knit bunch - doing our best to help all and sundry, but then the Franks started to take control of my priests."

"*Your* priests?"

"Yes, by then I had priests out on many of the islands as well as those that were in Traiectum itself."

"So you were in charge then?"

"For the last few years -yes. The father who *had* been leading us had died a while previously and the monks and priests of our community elected me as their leader. They called me 'bishop' - but that was a new term for the Frisians who'd never had a bishop before. It all came about as a result of Frankish travellers remarking that in other countries there was always a bishop to lead the holy men so, when I was elected, the community decided that that was what I should be. They also gave me a new name."

"Oh - and what was that?"

"They called me Bishop *Germanus* after their territory because they wanted to make it clear to the Franks, who, even then, were always trying to interfere, that I was the holy leader of Germania. The Germanic tribes are a proud people and they wanted there to be no doubt that they were their own men and not slaves to the Franks."

"So what were the tribes called?"

"Well in the western islands we had the *Canninefates* and to the east there were the *Batavii*."

"Did they fight?"

"From time to time, but they were generally peaceable - if they fought anyone it was usually the Franks."

"But you said the kings changed often - were they killed?"

"Sometimes - but other times they just died. The *Wad* wasn't a healthy place - particularly in the summer when the midges and flies could bite you half to death ... and kings came and went like the rest of us."

"But you survived."

"Yes, I don't know why. I was either just lucky or God had work for me to do ... but we lost a lot of good young monks to disease."

"So the Franks pushed you out?"

"Well I was getting old and felt I'd done all I could for the community. It was time for a younger man to take over. He just happened to be a Frank."

"Did the community elect him?"

"Eventually. He'd been professed at the abbey of the Blessed Arnulf at Mettis and to everyone's surprise he quickly became a very useful member of our community. To be honest I was pleased to hand the reins over to him - he was a competent young man even if he was a Frank."

"But you were a foreigner too."

"Aye. Funnily enough the Frisians didn't seem to mind that - it was only the Franks they had an aversion to - although I gained the impression that they were even getting over that."

"How did you get back to Britain?"

"The same way that I arrived really. A waddenboat carried me from Traiectum to Lugdunum and then a trading vessel took me to Cnobersburg."

"Oh my word - you went back there?"

"Well I didn't know where else to go. I guessed that after thirty years the fighting would surely be over - and I must say . . . " he said with a smile, "I found it peaceful but deserted. I started to make some enquiries and, as soon as the word got around that I was the brother of the famous Abbot Botolph a boatman came up and begged me to allow him to transport me to the abbey of Icanho. He gained my permission and here I am," he concluded abruptly, making them all laugh.

CHAPTER 32
The Final Chapter

The annual summer visits to Wininicas continued, although to his sadness, Brother Germanus was unable to join them because of the painful state of his bent back, which every rut would have jarred had he travelled by wagon. Even Botolph was beginning to find the journey a struggle and he took to insisting that young Prior Aethelheah came along on each of the journeys to the west, so that he could take over when the abbot himself became too old to travel. During their time away it was Brother Germanus who took over the running of Icanho.

Two years after Germanus' arrival, Icanho celebrated a joyous occasion when Ash's son Eldred married a girl from Rendelsham called Maria. There was a similar celebration in the March of the following year when the middle son married Nelda. A month later Luka's first great-grandson was born and they called him Lufan.

The great-grandchildren came thick and fast after that but they were all boys and, love them all as he did, Luka longed for a girl . . . but it seemed that it was not to be.

In 678 Botolph, Luka, Aethelheah and their retinue of monks and retainers set off on what proved to be Botolph's last visit to Wininicas. On the return journey while camping near Grantabryc he was bitten on the leg by a snake.[1]   Luka was with him at the time and, in spite of Botolph's protests, the snake was quickly dispatched.   A tourniquet was placed around the leg and every effort made to suck the poison out but, as he lapsed into a coma, there seemed every likelihood that the abbot would die. They dared not move him and he remained close to death for over a week with Luka constantly at his side praying for his recovery.   At length, to Luka's great joy, Botolph opened his eyes and soon after that began his long slow journey back to Icanho.

The wound itself never did heal.   It had to be redressed daily and the abbot's mobility was ever thereafter severely hampered.

Botolph was pleased that he had made adequate preparations for any potential infirmity, and when Prior Aethelheah set off on his journey the following year he left not only with the abbot's blessing but also with his confidence that Wininicas Abbey and Liobsynde were in safe hands.

It was in mid-summer while they were away that Brother Germanus went to meet his Maker.   In accordance with Botolph's instructions his brother was buried in the southeast corner of the church.

"Bury him deep," he said, "so that when my time comes there's room for me also."

There was great sadness at the monastery - for Brother Germanus had become loved by all during the seven years that he had lived at Icanho.

The sadness was not only due to Germanus' passing: it was clear that Abbot Botolph's health was also continuing to fail.   Towards the end he was nursed night

---

[1] Recorded in *Vita Botulfi* in the 1701 *Acta Sanctorum* which was composed from a compendium of 23 ancient manuscripts.

and day by his faithful companion Luka, but on the seventeenth of June of the following year the great traveller left on his final journey to pass into the joy of his Lord.

As he had instructed, they opened his brother's grave and he was gently laid on top of Germanus' shroud-covered corpse and the earth was replaced.

Luka could not keep still. He stomped around as much as his old bones would let him, moving from one part of the abbey to the next. As soon as he had arrived he would be up again and moving back - perhaps to whence he had come or to some other location. As soon as a door shut behind him he wanted to get outside again. As soon as he was outside he wanted to get back in.

He would spend hours every day sitting or kneeling by the grave. Nobody knew whether he was praying to God or talking to his old friend, but the general consensus of opinion was the latter.

Others came to the grave too - but they came to ask for the saintly Botolph's intercession with God rather than for his company. There were just a few petitioners at first and they were mainly from the monastery but then, as the word of Botolph's death spread, there came a steady stream of villagers too.

King Eadwulf was an early visitor who came to pay his respects and to bring his condolences to the monastery.

The stream of pilgrims became larger as reports started to circulate of miraculous cures that had been achieved as a result of prayers at the shrine, but Luka turned his back on all of this and resorted to spending his time with Botolph at night when the pilgrims were all abed.

As autumn turned to winter Luka's night-time vigils became less comfortable although he maintained that he did not feel the cold in spite of his ancient bones.

The arrival of Christmas did nothing to cheer him

up although the family had done their best for him. He had been living at Ash's house a league or so south of Icanho. They had all hoped that having the boys around him might take his mind off his loss but, try as he might, he could not summon up any great-grandfatherly enthusiasm. Both Eldred's wife and Bron's were heavily pregnant and it seemed to Luka that they were breeding their own army.

After dinner on the day after the first day of the new year he decided that he could bear it no more and, taking his walking staff, he slipped out when nobody was watching and made his way sadly through freshly-fallen snow down to the edge of the fast-flowing river that bordered the settlement.

He stood on the bank and stared despairingly at the turbulent water that was fuelled into spate from melting snow on higher ground, and he wondered how cold the water would feel. Would he even notice? Did he care if he did? Should he do it now?

There was no hurry.

There was no hurry now in anything to do with this life. He was spent. His usefulness had died with his dear friend and companion.

His eyes were focussed on the swirling water that was beckoning him forwards.

He took the weight off his left leg ready to move it forwards - his eyes still riveted on the eddying confusion.

There came a sound.

A new sound.

Something told him to pay no heed.

Keep looking at the water.

Move on.

The sound came again.

Rustling.

Concentrate.

It came from the bushes to his right.

Ignore it.

Walk.

A new sound was added.

His gaze faltered and he turned his head . . .

. . . to look into brown eyes.

The dappled muzzle of the young fawn was making a sucking sound.

He put out his hand.

The little creature moved forwards and licked it. He felt its warm breath on his calloused palm and the rasp of a pink tongue. Its eyes were locked with his but, perhaps disappointed at finding no food, it skittled away. The bushes curtained behind it . . . and he felt another sense of loss.

His eyes blurred and he remembered the horrors of that day. Then too he had been by a river bank . . . waiting . . . waiting.

He had heard the cry: "Luka . . . Luka . . . come quickly . . . the baby."

His head fell forward as he relived the torment and, born from an emotion deep within his throat, a sob burst forth.

It came again: "Luka . . . Luka . . . come quickly . . . the baby."

He would have welcomed his own death after the loss of his dear Clarisse but at that time he had to live for Ash's sake. But he is not needed now and he is free to make his own choice. He looks back at the turbulent water and this time his leg obeys his command and he moves forwards and feels the icy water grasp his foot. He starts to move the other leg and the teasing torture starts again, driving him onwards to a watery peace: "Luka . . . Luka . . . come quickly . . . the baby."

A hand grabs his arm.

"No-o-o-o-o ... " he pulls away from her and steps forwards again.

"No-o-o-o-o ... "

"A girl."

The word spins into his befuddled brain.

"A girl ... a girl?"

He turns. It is the old woman from the village.

She sees the glazed expression pass from his eyes.

"A girl," she says gently. "Come - Maria has had a girl."

She takes his hand and together they stumble back up the slope.

In the hut Maria is peacefully resting on her pallet, her long dark hair dangling down the right side of her neck, while suckling at her left breast is a tiny newborn female child with a shock of red hair.

The all-smiling family are gathered inside and as Luka enters they pull back, leaving him space ... but nobody speaks. The child stops suckling.

Maria lifts her towards Luka.

He takes the child and holds her up in front of him while he gazes into her pretty face.

"Clarisse" he says and cuddles her to his chest as the tears pour down his cheeks.

End

The South English Legendary

There are various sources of the story of Saint Botolph's life but appended below is the author's translation (borrowing heavily from work done in 2006 by Jasmiijn de Huis at the University of Utrecht) of a version of the South English Legendary. It is believed that the legendary was written in about 1300 by two monks in Gloucester and it is perhaps significant that this potential source lies so close to Wininicas.

Saint Botolph was a holy monk and Adulph was his brother
They both were born in England, - as was many another.
They both became attracted and to godliness drawn
And counselled each other to love God's holy law.

So for that reason, to cross the sea they went
To learn such of Holy Orders as our Lord's grace would send.
Beyond the sea they travelled and long they livéd there
In a house of Holy Learning, among the monks they were.

They learned their scriptures right, so that no default was near
Their good reputation spread from year to year.
The king of that country praised their holy fast
And for their great saintliness his heart on them he cast.

The elder brother he became Bishop Saint Adulph
And the same the king had in mind to make St Botolph
But Botolph he decided there time not long to spend
As he wanted to practise his faith at home in England.

Though his brother, the bishop, he was loath to leave but went
Home to his own country to live life to its end.
In the House of Learning, two sisters there were -
Both born in England, though long had livéd there.

The sisters of Athelwold (as I understand)
King - though of the south end of England.
The sisters bade Saint Botolph that he to their brother went
And to Dame Sare the queen, letters to whom they sent
Asking that the king should grant this holy man a place
Where he might begin to minister, through our Lord's good grace.

The saintly monk St.Botolph, off to England went
And took home the letters that they by him sent.
But the king him rejected and would not grant him ought
Though the queen, who was good, worked hard to turn his thoughts.
- For women to each and others so much goodness bring
And she cried both night and day unto her lord the king
That if her request were granted she would seek no other grace
So St. Botolph won at last and was given there a place.

Somewhere in some wilderness of which nobody knew
Where neither tree nor fruit nor any good thing grew
'T'was here the king granted him a place at such an end
Though he promised to see that no harm to him went.

There was in this wilderness a place that men called Eiye
That was full of evil things, - both around it and beside.
For devils and evil ghosts lived undisturbed there
And had dwelt so for many years because no men came near.
Though when Saint Botolph was granted the estate
He boldly went thither and nothing him stop would make.

He went to search for a fair site wherein he might be
The devils though saw him come and they began to flee
And cried out with ghastly yell and howled with grizzly grue
"Botolph, Botolph, - what you doing here?   What are we now to do?
Thither we run but who can know where our path will lead.
For now we have no place to live but in sorrow and wretcheed.
This is our rightful home and we here for years have dwelt
All on our own till doomsday but now the end you have spelt.
Thou art to us an evil guest and also far too strong.
Why do you want to drive us out? We've never done you wrong?
You have often been so merry – full of joy and light
A dark and dismal place this is – do you think you have the right?

Why would you want our wretched state when you might better be?
But we won't dare to abide here long - we'd rather elsewhere flee!"

He *was* to them an evil guest, but not harmed by them at all.
He was, you might say, as is said in jest - "A new king in the hall."
Saint Botolph, in our Lord's name, he went with easy tread.
He went boldly on his own and the fiends straight away fled.
Now a devil well might he flee - from north and from south
"Amen" all *now* say ye.   Why not open then your mouth?

Saint Botolph made holy that awful place of ills.
An abbey of monks he founded and that was where they built.
And the monks a great convent they made anew
And he himself the abbot was, and others to them he drew.
And of this dwelling from where the fiends had been outcast
He made a holy sanctum and long there did it last.

There in our Lord's name he lived life to its end
And to be blessed in heaven his soul it then went.
Now for our Saint Botolph's love, God such grace does us send
That we have all been blessed with joy and the devil has been damned.

Amen.